COELASH

"Little Red!" Cinn——————————————t James would connec————————————. What are you three doing? W——y are you shaped like coelasharks?"

Little Red stopped in mid-roar to answer. ☆James told us how coelasharks talk! *Great* way to talk!☆

◊If we take shape of coelasharks, then we think more like coelasharks, so we can talk more like coelasharks,◊ Little White explained.

"The method-acting school of language lessons," interjected Richard sarcastically.

"What's the language like?" Cinnamon asked.

⬜We will speak as coelasharks do, and James will translate our words for you,⬜ said Little Purple.

◊Some meaning may be lost in translation,◊ warned Little White.

☆Especially threats!☆ added Little Red. ☆They loudest and most FUN!☆

The three flouwen returned to their corners and resumed their coelashark shapes. Soon they were rushing at each other and emitting shouts and roars that could be easily heard through the thick tank walls.

☆Come any closer and I'll *bite* your leg off!☆ yelled Little Red.

⬜Listen to the weakling threaten me!⬜ bellowed Little Purple in response.

◊You're both so timid, you'd belly-up at the sight of blood!◊ roared Little White.

Aghast, Cinnamon said, "*That* is the language of an intelligent life-form?"

BOOKS IN THIS SERIES

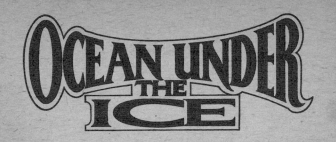

OCEAN UNDER THE ICE

ROBERT L. FORWARD
&
MARTHA DODSON FORWARD

BAEN

OCEAN UNDER THE ICE

Copyright © 1994 by Robert L. Forward & Martha Dodson Forward

A Baen Books Original

Baen Publishing Enterprises
P.O. Box 1403
Riverdale, N.Y. 10471

ISBN: 0-671-87600-7

Cover art by David Mattingly

First printing, June 1994

Distributed by
Paramount
1230 Avenue of the Americas
New York, N.Y. 10020

Typeset by Windhaven Press, Auburn, N.H.
Printed in the United States of America

ACKNOWLEDGMENTS

The authors wish to thank the following people, who helped us in several technical areas: Julie Forward Fuller, Eve Forward, Brian Kirk, Vonda McIntyre, Gerald David Nordley, and Vernor Vinge.

The "Christmas Bush" motile was jointly conceived by Hans P. Moravec and Robert L. Forward, and drawn by Jef Poskanzer using a CAD system.

All final art was expertly prepared by that terrific team in Marina Del Rey, California—MultiGraphics.

Contents

PROLOGUE

The wind was not blowing as hard now, but it still had enough force to whistle as it widened the grotesque tunnels it had carved in the icy promontory. The bulging mound of compacted snow loomed above the dark waters below, themselves nearly frozen and greasy-looking with irregular sheets of ice. The wind had created the huge lump it was now destroying; shaping and scraping the surface with hard-frozen dust as abrasive as diamonds, undercutting the exposed surfaces at the vulnerable base of the bulge. Finally the critical point was passed. With a horrendous crack, the snowy mound separated along a nearly vertical fissure and splashed into the cold ocean waters.

In the city, Silver-Rim heard the splash. The icerug had never seen an iceberg form, but it was aware of what had caused the explosive sound. The red-colored sunlight flooding down from the rising Sun-God onto Silver-Rim's acre-sized carpet warmed and invigorated the icerug as its velvet textured cyan-colored body absorbed the weak red sunlight and turned the energy into food.

1

On the opposite side of the sky from the Sun-God was the strange new moon that had arrived from outer space many seasons ago. Almost as big as the other moons, it was not a sphere but a flat circle. And instead of orbiting the Night-God like all the other moons, it wandered as it willed. Right now, it seemed to be moving closer to Ice.

With its attention now directed outward, Silver-Rim noticed that it was easy to move, this morning. Silver-Rim had been composing a new song, so intently that it had paid no attention to the weather. Now it realized that the wind was not blowing ice-dust into its eye and it was able to stand upright on its pedestal without having to lean into the wind. An unusually substantial meal of country-raised flesh added to the icerug's sensation of comfort, and Silver-Rim noted that it was indeed a good day. Silver-Rim glided across its carpet toward the massive stone Grand Portal that led to the Great Meeting Hall; in the distance it could see Clear-Eye making for the same entrance. Clear-Eye's carpet, a brilliant blue, was easy enough to distinguish even at a great distance and Silver-Rim's large orb was unusually keen, even for an icerug. The two met at the entrance, glided side by side down the glittering hall upon their parallel travel strands, and entered the music room chatting companionably.

"Hear this, now, Clear-Eye, I've been working on this melody all night." Silver-Rim flipped open its dressy cloak, and two of its four tentacles reached for a long, narrow harp with thick strings. The tentacles stretched and shortened themselves as they plucked the strings, and the deeply rumbling notes of the new melody sounded sweet to both of them.

SAILING

Six light-years distant from the Sun, a spacecraft sailed through the sparse "wind" of photons emanating from the red dwarf star Barnard. The most visible portion of the spacecraft was its gigantic circular lightsail, a vast expanse of highly reflective aluminum foil, three hundred kilometers across. As the dim red photons from Barnard bounced off the reflective surface of the sail, they each gave the sail a tiny push. Together, the pushes added up to a significant light pressure force that was able to increase or decrease the orbital speed of the lightsail around the red sun, allowing the spacecraft to move either inward or outward through the Barnard planetary system, so that its human crew could visit the multitude of planets and moons that orbited around the star. The crew called the spacecraft *Prometheus*—the bringer of light—for it had arrived at Barnard traveling on a beam of blue-green laser light—transmitted across the vast interstellar distance between Sol and Barnard by a gigantic sun-pumped laser.

Almost lost in the vast expanse of the lightsail was the

habitat that held the exploration crew, a cylinder as big as an apartment building, connected by tension lines to the rigging. On the hydroponics deck of the habitat, Nels Larson—lounging comfortably in his regeneration tank—was giving instructions to his hydroponics deck crew, Cinnamon Byrd, Deirdre O'Connor, and Katrina Kauffmann. Cinnamon had just awakened from her sleep shift and was sipping quietly from her breakfast drink-ball squeezer full of hot pseudo-coffee. Around the circumference of her drink-ball was painted a scene of white snow-capped Alaskan mountain peaks interspersed by valleys filled with glowing blue-green glacier fields. Her personal robotic imp on her shoulder, its multicolored laser lights twinkling among its multibranched green-laser-illuminated metallic "twigs," was carefully plaiting a braid of her dark straight hair below her left ear. When the motile finished braiding, it curled up the two short braids around Cinnamon's ears and settled itself down in a band across the top of her head like a set of twinkling earphones. One tiny twig from the motile, tipped with a deep red laser, reached in behind her ear. From there it could monitor her pulse and vital signs, and, using laser reflection spectroscopy, even measure the chemical constituents of the blood flowing through the capillaries just under her light reddish-brown skin. Another twig curved down to one side of her mouth where its tip could pick up her slightest whisper.

Deirdre's imp was in its usual place, in a six-pointed star holding up a mass of dark curls sitting on top of her head. One of its secondary twigs was extended down near her mouth, while another touched her ear. Deirdre's shoulder, which was normally occupied by her pet, Foxx, was empty; but there was a large lump in Deirdre's right breast pocket. She leaned against a stanchion, a quiet, slender figure—unobtrusive in a soft brown coverall and gleaming brown pseudo-leather ankle boots. As she held her own hot coffee close to her nose, her sleeves revealed the glint of gold from the thin torques which encircled her wrists. These, along with the strange flat stone in one ear-lobe, Deirdre wore always, without thinking of them. She squeezed the drink-ball expertly, to inhale the aroma without actually dispensing any liquid.

Katrina stood nearer the regen tank, her dark-blue eyes warm with compassion and interest. It was seldom the petite biologist was able to look down into another person's face. Nels had been patiently sitting in the strange fluid for some weeks and planned to spend another eight or ten. It had been the alien flouwen who had taught him how to activate the leg growth genes in his DNA that had been blocked by a chemical accident to his pregnant mother, and had devised the chemical solution that would fool the cells in his leg stumps into thinking they were in a mother's womb. He hopefully expected that the result would be a serviceable pair of human legs, rather than the flippers he had been born with. He'd lived forty years with the result of that accident to his mother, and he regarded this experiment with scientific interest as well as personal desire. If the regeneration process worked on him, it would work on anyone, and the whole world would benefit for centuries to come from the knowledge that had been gained from the flouwen. Now he spoke to his hydroponics deck crew, enlisting their aid in making sure the small buds from the flouwen were well cared for.

"With the 'Littles' on board, we now have three more mouths to feed," he said. "And with me stuck in this regen tank, it's going to be up to you three to carry the full load."

A deep voice spoke from the laser-illuminated spider-shaped imp sitting on Nels' right shoulder. It was the distinctive voice persona of the ship's main computer, James. "I can assign a 'Christmas Branch' subset of the ship's motile to hydroponics shift duty."

"That won't be necessary, James," said Katrina. "The three of us can easily manage the lab. Besides, the Christmas Bush has a lot to do just now, taking care of both Nels and John."

Cinnamon agreed. "John is a long way from recovering from that lungful of ammonia-water he got on Rocheworld, and a sub-branch has to be inside his lungs at all times, keeping the air passages clear. You and your motiles are busy enough, James. We humans should do our part in keeping the ship running. We'll handle the hydroponics deck." Then, not really appreciating that she was about to add to James' workload, since she and the rest of the crew had been taking James and its ever-present imps for granted for decades, Cinnamon finished her coffee, and tossing her drink-ball lightly into the air, she whispered out of the side of her mouth to the imp on her ear, "Done."

A one-sixth-size segment of her personal imp detached itself from her hairband. Its three bottom "feet" blurred as they vibrated into motion, flying the butterfly-size motile through the air to the squeezer, where the fuzzy fingers of its three front "hands" caught the container in its leisurely low-gee trajectory and pushed it off through the air toward the central shaft. The imp hadn't gone far before it was met by a larger imp that had flown up from the galley. The galley imp took the drink-ball back down to the kitchen, where it would be cleaned and stored until Cinnamon asked for another cup of coffee.

"I'm mostly concerned about the food supply for the

three flouwen," insisted Nels. "I'd like you to check and see how all the flora and fauna are doing in the flouwen habitat tank. Now that we have left Rocheworld and can no longer get flouwen food supplies from its surface, it's important that they not only survive, but thrive, in order to give the flouwen adequate variety in their diet. I want the three Littles happy with their meals."

"We'll check that first," reassured Cinnamon, reaching over to adjust the collar on Nels' coverall. "Anything else before the Christmas Bush gets you ready for your sleep shift?"

"I keep worrying about potential problems, but when I check them out on my control console, I find that one of you has anticipated me and taken care of them."

"We intend to keep it that way," replied Deirdre. She heard a rustling sound in the corridor and looked around.

The Christmas Bush had arrived, walking along the carpeted corridor using two of its six main appendages as legs, the fine fibers at the tips of its hexfurcated feet gripping the carpet securely. Two of its "hands" were carrying objects. It stopped near Nels' tank and rearranged appendages until it was implanted firmly into the carpet on just one "leg," leaving four "arms" and a bushed-out "head." In this configuration, with its multicolored laser lights glittering from the green-illuminated branches, the meter-tall robotic motile looked very much like a small artificial Christmas tree. This Christmas tree, however, was bearing some most unusual gifts in its branches: a bar of soap, a squeezer full of hot water, some washcloths and towels, and a custom-fabricated bedpan. Although Nels weighed almost nothing in the low acceleration environment of the lightsail-propelled spacecraft, he still had a significant mass, and it took a full-sized Christmas Bush to hold his body in the proper positions while it assisted Nels in taking care of the necessities of bodily hygiene.

Cinnamon spoke up. "Although I mostly trained as an EMT, I've learned to give a good sponge bath. If James could use the Christmas Bush elsewhere, I'd be glad to take over."

Nels' pale skin suddenly flushed all over, the blond hairs on his arms standing out in sharp contrast to the reddening skin underneath. The blush extended up his forehead and under his long blond swept-back hair.

"Ah-ah . . ." he stammered in panic.

The smaller "twigs" on the bushed-out top portion of the Christmas Bush vibrated into invisibility, moving the air around it and causing the voice of James to emanate from the "head" region of the motile.

"Thank you for the offer. But I think it best that I handle it," replied James. One of the "hand" branches of the motile elongated by a factor of three and reached up to pull a curtain around Nels' tank. As the curtain drew closed, Deirdre turned and grinned wickedly at Cinnamon, who winked but said nothing. The constant presence of their personal imps tended to make all the humans just a little watchful of their speech, and these two were more reserved than most.

Katrina, Deirdre, and Cinnamon now left Nels and bounced off down a long corridor on the hydroponics deck in low gravity leaps, their feet occasionally pushing against the looped carpet that lined the floors, walls, ceilings, and shafts throughout *Prometheus*. After using the central shaft stanchion to swing themselves around a corner into another corridor, they brought themselves to a halt by planting their feet firmly on the carpet and bending their knees in a controlled flexing motion that absorbed their energy and momentum. They were now standing before the thick clear window of the large habitat tank that held the three flouwen. The wedge-shaped tank reached from floor to ceiling along one wall of the corridor. It was two meters high, six meters long, and varied from two meters wide near the central shaft to six meters wide near the outer walls.

Placed in the middle of the corridor facing the tank window was an out-of-place sofa, dragged up from the lounge area. There was a couple relaxing on the thick pile sofa, held in place in the low gravity by Velcro "sticky-patches" on the back belt-line of their coveralls. The small black woman with the trim razor-creased uniform was Space Marine Major General Virginia Jones, Commander of the Barnard Star Expedition, while the large older white man was her second in command, Colonel George Gudunov.

When Deirdre saw the two mission commanders there, she moved around behind Cinnamon and remained quiet, letting Cinnamon greet them. Wakened by the bounding trip down the corridor, Deirdre's familiar was back on her shoulder, its bushy reddish-brown tail nearly indistinguishable from Deirdre's locks. Foxx belonged to a once rare, but now prospering, squirrel-like marsupial species Deirdre had discovered in the forests of South America and saved from extinction. Katrina and Deirdre moved close to the tank, looking intently at the small, flat, light brown creatures visible on the plants in the rear.

"Look you, Katrina, that gingersnap species is doing almost too well. It's the balance that's tricky, to keep the water clean, and with exactly the right proportion of nutrients."

"Right," murmured Katrina. "I'll do a thorough analysis." She bounded off to the lab, and Deirdre bent closer to watch the little plants undulating in the stream of hot "smoky water" loaded with hydrogen sulfide and minerals. The artificial volcanic vents were modeled after the ones occurring naturally on Rocheworld and were carefully designed to sustain the plant life, which in turn nourished small animals much enjoyed as food by the flouwen. The hot-water vent field was blocked off from the cold water in the larger part of the tank by a maze of clear floor-to-ceiling baffles, backed up by circulation pumps operating through holes in the tank sides. Deirdre automatically checked the thermometers: the liquid, ten percent ammonia by weight, was well below freezing in the habitat and boiling hot near the vents. All was well within the little world; they would not yet need the supply of dried and frozen flouwen food they had brought with them from Rocheworld.

George was eating his evening-shift dinner from his flip-lidded free-fall tray, while General Jones was on her morning-shift coffee break, enjoying a drink-ball squeezer of coffee and a croissant. Her drink-ball had two stars and the words "THE BOSS" painted on it. The two commanders were conversing quietly about crew rosters and science schedules, while keeping a relaxed eye on the contents of the tank. Inside the tank, the brightly colored flouwen swam around and around in hypnotic swirling motions.

"That smells heavenly, Jinjur," said Cinnamon, inhaling the delicious aroma of the freshly baked algae-flour croissant. "The galley imp must have let Arielle into the kitchen again."

"She was putting another tray into the oven when I left," replied Jinjur. "If you hurry, there may still be some left."

"Order one for me, too," added George, flipping up

one of the lids on his tray to take a peek inside. "I've got a little algae-butter left in my condiments compartment."

After whispering a command to her imp, Cinnamon moved across the carpet to the tank window. She crooned a melodic greeting as her light brown fingers touched the cold glass.

"Good morning! Good morning! Isn't it a lovely morning! Good morning! Good morning to you! . . ." Cinnamon's imp picked up her song and passed it by digitally-coded laser beams to the central computer James, who translated the words into flouwenese, shifted the tune down in pitch to the flouwen's middle range, then passed it along as a sonar signal to the alien creatures in the tank.

The flouwen swimming in the habitat tank were shaped like amorphous blobs of living jelly, each as big as a very large human. Their bodies were brightly colored and shimmered internally like liquid opals. Each of the flouwen in the tank had been budded off from a "primary" body, a gigantic multiton creature many meters across, which was still back on Rocheworld. A normal-sized flouwen was too large and heavy to be accommodated on human vehicles, but three of the flouwen had each budded off a portion of themselves in order to go exploring with the humans. The buds still retained the personality and memory of the primary body, although they were slightly diminished in mental ability because of their smaller size. On their return to Rocheworld, the buds would rejoin the primary bodies and pass on the knowledge they had gained.

One of the buds, called Little Red by the humans, was a bright flame-red color. His primary back on Rocheworld, Roaring☆Hot☆Vermilion, was called Loud Red by the humans. The second was Little White, with a partially transparent opalescent milky white color. He had budded from the flouwen Clear◊White◊Whistle, given the name White Whistler by the humans because of his white color and high pitched whistling tones when he spoke. The third was Little Purple, with a deep grape-colored purple hue. The oldest of the three, he was many thousands of years old. He had budded from Strong⊓Lavender⊓Crackle, called Deep Purple by the humans.

Upon hearing Cinnamon's greeting song, Little Red undulated over to the window and spread himself against the inside of the window. Through the thick glass Cinnamon could hear a modulated roar that ended in a whistling chirp. A sonar pickup inside the tank sensed the sounds and sent them to James, who translated them from flouwenese into English and passed them on to Cinnamon's imp via coded laser beams transmitted from laser diodes hidden in the corners of the corridor ceiling.

☆Are we there yet!?!☆ came Little Red's query out of the "earphones" of the small imp on Cinnamon's head. The tone, although not the volume, was James' attempt at a reasonable imitation of what Little Red probably sounded like to the two older flouwen. ☆I'm bored! I want to go explore!☆

"We've only just started," replied Cinnamon. "Although Rocheworld is close to Gargantua in this part of its elliptical orbit, it's going to take weeks to transfer to an orbit around Gargantua, and a few more weeks before we are ready to land on one of Gargantua's moons."

☆Too long!☆ complained Little Red.

Just then, one of the galley imps rose up in the lift shaft at the end of the corridor, levitated by the rapidly beating twigs on three of its "feet." In one "hand" it was carrying Cinnamon's drink-ball, while the other "hand" held four still-steaming croissants. As the imp passed the croissants out, Deirdre quietly accepted one, broke off one end, and passed it up to Foxx, who took it in tiny paws.

The squeaks and chirps coming from the tank increased in frequency and intensity as Little Red used his sonar to scan the corridor outside the tank. Although the bodies of the flouwen were sensitive to light, they had no eyes, and so normally they did not use light as a method of looking at things. Instead they used sound pulses. In the liquid environment of their home ocean, this was a superior method of observation. It didn't depend upon light from the dim and often absent Barnard, so the flouwen could "see" in the dark depths as well as they could near the surface.

With sonar, the flouwen didn't just look at the surface of an object, for the sonar penetrated inside the object and gave the flouwen a three-dimensional image of what they were seeing. Sonar travels best in water, and a portion of Little Red's penetrating sound pulses bounced off the thick glass. Of the part that penetrated into the glass, a large portion was reflected by the glass-air interface, and only a small portion reached the air in the corridor. In the air, the sound waves traveled five times slower than they did in the water, and by the time they reflected from the soft, absorbent clothing of the humans and back through the air and glass, and into the water, there was little left. It was enough, however, for Little Red to "see" that Cinnamon was eating something.

☆You eat!☆ Little Red announced. ☆I eat too!☆ The red flouwen peeled himself off the window and, forming himself into an efficient swimming shape, undulated away to the maze of baffles in the far corner of the habitat tank. The infinitely flexible body of Little Red had little difficulty in penetrating the maze, so it wasn't long before he had jumped an animal that looked like an orange-red blob—as structureless as a flouwen. The animal screamed as it attempted to elude the red pseudopods that Little Red formed to trap it.

"I think I'll go now," said George, getting up as Little Red caught the small creature. He handed his tray to the galley imp, peeled himself off the sofa, and pushed down the corridor to the central shaft.

"Me, too," said Jinjur, following him while still carrying her squeezer of coffee.

Cinnamon averted her eyes and left, too, as Little Red started to tear apart his living and still screaming prey into little pieces. Each part continued to scream until its sounds were finally muffled by being absorbed into Little Red's body. As Cinnamon made her way down the corridor, she raised a hand and made a twisting motion next to one of the "earphones" on her imp headband, as if turning up the volume on an audio set. In response to the motion, James obliged her by playing a loud Sousa march.

Deirdre, however, trying to learn as much as she could about the little-observed process, looked dispassionately into the tank and watched carefully as Little Red devoured his meal. The orange-red "rogue" that Little Red was eating was one of a dozen that she and Cinnamon had budded from a larger rogue in their Rocheworld fauna breeding tanks and placed into the flouwen tank vent field. The bud had originally been the size of a small sausage, and now it was as big as her forearm. The vent field must be operating well if the rogue grew that much in the few weeks since they set up the flouwen habitat tank.

It wasn't pleasant watching Little Red eat, but Deirdre

knew that Little Red was doing what he must to survive. Deirdre had once raised snakes, including large pythons that required rabbits for their meals. It was unfortunate that the food animals that the flouwen ate could not be humanely killed before being eaten, but that was the way life was built on Rocheworld. Like the flouwen, the rogues and most of the other Rocheworld fauna could not be killed. Trying to kill a flouwen or a rogue was like trying to kill a slime mold or an ant colony. One could tear any of them apart into smaller and smaller pieces, but each piece would be just as alive as the larger piece, until finally only individual cells were left.

Little Red had torn the rogue into bits which were small enough to digest easily, and they were now dispersed as separate orange-red blobs inside the large flame-red blob that formed Little Red's body. Deirdre watched carefully as the orange-red blobs grew smaller and smaller until there was only flame-red where orange-red had once been. Deirdre had watched the process of assimilation under a microscope and knew what was happening as Little Red digested the rogue.

On Earth, where humans, animals, and plants have distinctive proteins, humans must digest the animal and plant proteins down to simple compounds like sugars and starches and amino acids, then build them back up into human proteins. On Rocheworld, where all the animal life-forms used the same basic cell, the process of digestion didn't go as far as it did on Earth. The basic Rocheworld cell was quite large compared to a human cell and had a dumbbell-shaped body of clear jelly that varied from glassy to almost liquid depending upon the water content. When enlarged with water, it was the size of the body of a very small ant. The cells replicated by growing larger, splitting in two, then forming a necked down portion. A group of these cells would spontaneously collect together into a cross-linked blob, with necked down portions interlocking with end knob portions. On the surface of each cell was a complex pseudo-random pattern of grooves and indentations that operated as a "template" for the genetic code of the organism. In the higher animals, such as the flouwen, portions of these patterns were changeable and served as the repository for the long term memory.

Once a blob of cells had collected together, a liquid crystal layer would form between the cells, with the large complex organic chemicals in the liquid crystal layer being determined and ordered by the grooves and indentations on the surface of the cells. The optical properties of the thin layer of liquid crystal gave the flouwen and other fauna their distinctive bright colors. The liquid crystal layer acted as the coordinating nervous system or "brain" of the collection of cells. Because all of their body cells were involved in their thinking and memory processes, the flouwen were, in essence, all brain. The genetic code information in the surface of the cells was used to organize the liquid crystal "brain," while the liquid crystal layer in turn could impress grooves and patterns onto the cells to store memories. When Little Red was "digesting" the rogue, all his body was doing was dissolving the orange-red liquid crystal layer of the rogue, using its own flame-red liquid crystal to change the genetic pattern on the surface of the cells, which then became Little Red cells.

Now that the screams had stopped, Cinnamon returned. With her was the ship's chief engineer, Shirley Everett, and one of the expedition's geoscientists, Richard Redwing. Both were well over six feet tall and well muscled, like professional basketball players. Shirley's long, blond braid was held in place behind her left ear by her imp, shaped into a crescent-shaped hairclip, while Richard bore his imp on his shoulder, like all the men on the ship. They came up behind Deirdre, close to the window.

Deirdre had been so absorbed in watching Little Red eat that she hadn't been paying attention to the other flouwen in the tank. Now, she noticed Little White plastered up against the tank window—and her left ear was ringing as if it were being subjected to intense noise. She turned to look at the arrival of the other humans, and the pressures in her ears changed. At the same time, she also finally noticed that Foxx was emitting a continual complaining chitter and was fussing with her ears. Deirdre then realized that while she had been staring into the habitat tank at Little Red, Little White had been staring out of the tank at her—scanning her body with high frequency sonar pulses.

◊There is something moving on your shoulder,◊ said Little White. ◊It is not the Talking⊗Sticks that some humans have on their shoulders. It has stiff sticks inside, but it is covered with soft flesh and a thick fuzzy surface—like hair—but it covers the whole body, not just the top of the head. I have never seen such a thing before. What is it?◊

"It's my pet, Foxx," replied Deirdre. "The fuzzy surface on it is called fur—it is dark red in color."

◊Interesting,◊ said Little White. ◊I must 'look' it using light as well as see it using sound.◊

☆Pet with red color?!?☆ exclaimed Little Red. ☆I must look it too!☆

The two flouwen each formed a pseudopod with a large spheroid at the end and held the spheroid between their body and the window. After a few moments concentration, the color of the red and white spheroids slowly began to fade, while the intensity of the color in the arm of the pseudopod grew. The flouwen were withdrawing the strongly colored liquid crystal layer from between the transparent cells that made up the spheroid. Finally, all the liquid crystal was gone, leaving only a transparent sphere. Initially, the sphere was nearly invisible, since the jelly in the cells was nearly saturated with water molecules, but as the flouwen squeezed the water from the cells, it became denser and more visible, changing shape as it did so.

Finally, it transformed into a large thick "magnifying glass" held on the end of the colored pseudopod of each flouwen, like a monocle on a stick. The light from the corridor passed through the curved lens of transparent flouwen flesh, which focused it onto the surface of the flouwen body behind. There, the light-sensitive flesh of the flouwen could detect the hue and intensity patterns of the light. It was the primary of Little White—White Whistler—which had discovered the concept of a light-focusing lens some decades ago, before the arrival of the humans, and had taught the other flouwen the technique of making an eye that could focus light images.

Deirdre took Foxx down off her shoulder and brought the animal up near the tank window so the flouwen could look at it more clearly. While the flouwen watched, she had Foxx go through a few actions; racing up one arm and back down another, hanging from a finger with one hind foot, and jumping from one hand to another. All the while, Foxx chittered away excitedly.

☆What does it say?☆ asked Little Red. ☆I do not understand its talk!☆

"It can't talk," replied Deirdre. "It just makes noises."

☆It can't talk!?! Then it must be good to eat!☆ pronounced Little Red.

"We don't eat pets!" said Deirdre firmly.

With that revelation, Little Red was disgusted. ☆Pet not good for talking! Pet not good for food! Pet not good for anything! Pet DUMB!☆ The red flouwen absorbed its transparent "eye" back into its body and undulated away. Little White, however, was still interested.

◊I would like to know more about this Foxx creature.◊

"James has a large file on Foxx and the many other animals on Earth," Deirdre replied. "You can look at it on your taste-screen console."

The white flouwen kept one portion of his body near the window holding the imaging lens so he could continue to look at Deirdre and her pet, while the rest flowed across the habitat tank to one wall that contained what looked like the screen of a computer console. It was specially built by the ship's computer James for use by the flouwen. In addition to the usual touch-screen and optical display, it had a "taste-screen" overlay embedded with electrochemical sensors and transmitters that allowed the flouwen to interact with the central computer using the chemical senses that they normally used for transmitting information. Soon, one part of Little White was tasting the information on Foxx coming from James through the taste-screen on the wall, while another part of Little White was looking at the surface of Foxx using light focused through the lens onto its surface, and still another part of Little White was seeing the entire volume of Foxx using sonar pulses.

◊Very interesting creature,◊ Little White said finally. ◊Especially the tail. Do humans have tails?◊

"No!" replied Deirdre.

◊Why not?◊ asked Little White in the typical blunt flouwen fashion. Deirdre was saved from having to answer by an announcement from James. "There is a call coming up from the laser link communicator that was set up in Agua Dulce bay on Rocheworld. Deep Purple wishes to converse with Little Purple."

Little Purple went over to the wall console, and Little White pulled away from the screen to let Little Purple take his place. The conversation didn't take long and Little Purple soon returned.

⊓My primary called to say he is leaving Agua Dulce for a while. He is going to return to the beaches on the Isles of Thought, there to rock up and continue his thinking on . . ⊓ There was a pause as James tried to translate the thought. ⊓ . . . advanced mathematics⊓, the translation ended lamely.

"I am sorry," James apologized to the humans through their imps. "There is no referent known in human mathematics to the phraseology which the two flouwen used in discussing the topic. I am quite appalled at my inability to translate."

"If you think *you're* dumb, James, how do you think that makes *us* feel?" said Richard with feeling.

Little Purple continued to talk. ⊓When I was talking to my primary, there was a delay between my question and answer, as if my primary were far away in the water. Why is that?⊓

"That's because the laser light used to send messages back and forth to Rocheworld takes time to travel," replied Shirley.

⊓Is that true?⊓ replied Little Purple. ⊓If so, light must move very fast. When lightning strikes ocean, light always comes before sound.⊓

"The speed of sound in water is about fifteen hundred meters per second, while the speed of light is three hundred million meters per second—two hundred thousand times faster." Shirley waited while James and Little

Purple carried on a side conversation to make sure that Little Purple had understood what the metric units meant in terms of distances and time intervals which the flouwen used.

⧍That is very fast indeed,⧍ Little Purple finally agreed.

"But the distance between planets is so large that even light takes a long time to travel from one planet to another, or in this case between Rocheworld and *Prometheus*. Which is why you noticed a time delay. Incidentally," she added, "I don't really understand it, but I am told that the speed of light is always the same to every observer, no matter how fast they are moving."

◊That is not logical,◊ interjected Little White. ◊When I calculated mathematical logic for motion of Barnard and Gargantua and other lights in sky, that system of logic says that if one object is moving at one velocity and another object is moving toward it at another velocity, the relative velocity is sum of velocities.◊

"I would agree with you," replied Shirley. "But I am told that the logic which applies to massive bodies does not apply to light or objects moving close to the speed of light. If you are traveling at the speed of light, and a light beam is sent at you traveling at the speed of light, you do not see the light beam coming at you at nearly two times the speed of light—just one times the speed of light. For things that move very rapidly, you need to use a different system of logic. It's called relativity theory . . . and don't ask me to explain it."

⧍A different logic for things that move very rapidly . . ⧍ murmured Little Purple in thought. Soon the dark purple body was visibly growing smaller as it expelled water and became more dense in order to increase its rate of thinking. ⧍ . . . the speed of light is always the same to every observer . . ⧍ The thinking purple blob moved slowly off to one corner, thickening and becoming more and more purple as it shrank in size. Finally it settled to the floor of the habitat tank as a deep purple rock—a thinking rock.

Little Red spotted his good friend Richard. ☆Hey! Richard! This tank is too small! Get me out of here!☆

"Sure, little buddy!" Richard replied. "Let me check out your drysuit and we'll go for a walk so you can stretch your legs."

There was a short pause while Little Red listened to the translation coming through James. Suddenly, the flouwen emitted a high pitched scream of laughter that continued on and on as the red cloud literally turned itself inside out. The portion of Little Red nearest them pushed deep into the center of the body and burst out the back end, dragging the rest of the body around with it. It split into an opening flower and continued back around, shaping the convoluting body into a ring of rotating red jelly twirling like a smoke ring. Little White, joining in the merriment, also gave a scream of laughter and, forming himself into a snake-like shape, sinuously wove his way through the opening in Little Red's body. After a number of rotations, the red smoke ring collapsed and the screaming subsided as the alien took his normal shape.

☆Stretch my legs! Little Red *have* no legs! Richard FUNNY!☆

Richard gave a broad grin in response, then looked up at the corridor ceiling to find the two-meter diameter airlock door set in the ceiling between some air-conditioning vents. Standing on tiptoe in his Velcro-bottomed slippers, he added his long reach to his 195-centimeter-long frame, grabbed the airlock latch and pulled the door open. This airlock had once been used for access upward from the hydroponics deck into the first of their landing rockets, the Surface Lander and Ascent Module, SLAM I. Now, on the other side of the outer airlock door was attached all that was left of the original lander, the Ascent Propulsion Stage for SLAM I, that had returned the exploration crew safely back from their first visit to Rocheworld, after the nearly disastrous crash of their exploration airplane, *Dragonfly I*.

Shirley, with the aid of James and the Christmas Bush, had made modifications to the airlock to accommodate the flouwen. Inside the airlock were three strange-looking garments—"drysuits"—custom made for the flouwen by the Christmas Bush. James had modified a standard space rescue bag made with tough glassy-foil fabric by adding a spare spacesuit neckring that held a custom-molded plastic helmet. The drysuits were wrinkled, as if they had been sucked empty, and were connected by a pair of hoses to electronically controlled valves in the airlock wall.

"Everything looks okay," Richard said to Shirley, closing the airlock door and lifting himself up by the hatchway handholds so he could peer into the airlock window.

Shirley turned to the flouwen in the tank. "Are you ready to transfer?"

Little Red undulated over to a short hose sticking out of the back wall of the habitat tank. It too was connected to an electronically controlled valve. Little Red impaled his fluid body on the end of the hose and said, ☆Ready!☆

"Pump away, James," Shirley muttered to her imp. Valves clicked open and the vibrations of a powerful pump started. Little Red was sucked into the tube in the habitat tank wall, with the electronic valve closing behind as the last little bit of red jelly passed through the wall.

"The drysuit is filling up nicely," Richard reported as he watched through the porthole in the airlock door. "Very little water transferred—helmet filling up nicely with red jelly."

There was a muffled mutter coming through their imps. It was Little Red, talking through the imp assigned to his drysuit.

☆Too tight! All of me not fit in suit!☆

"Squeeze some water out of yourself!" answered Richard. "Remember, you have to make like a gummie if you are going to move like a gummie."

☆Little Red not a gummie! Gummie's DUMB!☆ Nevertheless, Little Red knew what he had to do and shed water from his cells until all of his body had condensed enough to fit inside the suit. James aided by pumping the ammonia water out of the suit and back into the habitat tank as Little Red squeezed the liquid out. The airlock imp disconnected the hoses, but since a little ammonia water always seemed to escape that point, it temporarily opened the airlock to outside vacuum to sweep out the ammonia fumes, then brought the lock back to ship pressure.

Shirley double-checked the airlock indicators and finally allowed Richard to open the inner door. Down from the hole in the ceiling, slowly falling in the low acceleration, came a shiny rotund ball with a helmeted head and three octopuslike arms extending from holes in the helmet neckring. At the end of each of the glassy-foil covered arms was a three-fingered glove. The flesh inside the arms·and fingers was highly condensed and had a strong rubbery consistency instead of the fluid consistency of normal flouwen body tissue.

"Phew, you stink!" yelled Richard. Despite the vacuum airing the airlock imp had given Little Red's drysuit, the pungent smell of ammonia wafted from the airlock.

Little Red reached a pseudopod down to the rescue bag zipper that allowed access to the interior of the suit.

☆I can stink worse!☆ warned Little Red, his helmet looking in the direction of Richard. Molded into the front of Little Red's helmet were two plastic lenses in about the same position as the eyes of a human. The plastic lenses focused the light into two stereo images that appeared upside down on the red flesh filling the inside of the helmet. The flouwen had practiced with the suits and helmets during their exploration of the land of the gummies on the Roche lobe of Rocheworld, and they were now proficient in using sight instead of sonar to navigate their way around in their drysuits when they were out of the water.

"Let's go," answered Richard, heading off down the corridor, his long legs in their Velcro-bottomed slippers pushing off the looped carpet.

Little Red, looking like a child's punch-toy in its legless drysuit, was not as clumsy as might have been expected. The suit had been provided with a number of Velcro "sticky patches" at strategic points on the bottom, side, and arms. Crouching down on the bottom sticky patch and tilting forward, Little Red pushed off the carpet in a jumping motion and launched himself down the corridor after Richard in a series of long hops, guided by an occasional brush at a wall. As they came to the central shaft, Little Red launched himself over the railing with obvious enjoyment and started to fall down the shaft.

☆FREE-FALL!☆

"Richard!" screamed Shirley after them. "Don't let him do that!"

"Stop worrying," Richard called back to her. "He won't build up too much speed in this low acceleration. Besides, he has no bones to break, and the glassy-foil can take it."

"I don't trust that zipper!" yelled Shirley. "Although our atmosphere doesn't bother him, we are sure bothered by his. It'll take James and me a week to air out the ship if that zipper springs a leak."

Richard swung himself over the railing and dove down the central shaft to catch Little Red before he crash-landed on the bottom deck.

"There we go, little buddy," said Richard, as he lowered Little Red down onto the top of the science console. The two looked down and out through the three-meter diameter dome set in the floor of the deck. Off in the distance was a double-planet. Its two lobes were so close to each other that instead of being spheres or ellipsoids, their inner points were pulled into egg shapes, as had been predicted by the French mathematician Edouard Roche in the 1800s, who never dreamed that a dual-lobed planet-world would some day be named after him. To Richard, Rocheworld looked like an infinity symbol spinning through space. The inner points of the two lobes were separated by less than one hundred kilometers, and although the surfaces of the two lobes were not touching, they shared a common atmosphere, which could be seen by the clouds occasionally passing over the gap from one lobe to the other. When the humans had visited Roche-world, they had been able to fly their exploration airplane from one lobe to another, passing through the zero-gravity point midway between the two massive planetoids.

One lobe of the double-planet, named the Roche lobe by the humans, since "roche" is French for "rock," was a dry rusty-brown and had a few sparse clouds hanging over it. The pointed end of the Roche lobe was heavily fissured and contained a number of active volcanos. Their calderas could be seen glowing up out of the darkness of the shadow cast by the other lobe lying between it and

Barnard. The other lobe, named the Eau lobe by the humans, since "eau" is French for "water," was in sunlight. It was completely covered with an ocean of water that had a multitude of cyclonic cloud patterns moving over it. The ocean was unique in that a mountain of water grew up out of it at the shadowed inner point, pulled upward by the gravitational attraction of the nearby Roche lobe. The water mountain was 150 kilometers high with a rounded top, while its sides were sloped at an impossible-looking sixty degrees. Although the strength of the gravity force varied from near zero at the peak of the mountain to eleven percent Earth gravity at the base, the water did not flow to higher levels of gravity, since the gravity force also varied in direction along the sides of the mountain and pushed the water into its mountain shape.

With the light from Barnard heating up the atmosphere of Eau, the winds were now blowing up the water mountain, driving the water ahead of them. The wind-driven swells moved upward toward the top of the mountain, where the surface area was smaller and the gravity was weaker. As a result, the energy in the waves was concentrated into a smaller area. At the same time there was less gravity to keep the wave amplitude down. The swells grew into ring waves that reached hundreds of meters in height and finally met in a ring-geyser that fountained up a spray of foamy water toward the zero-gravity point that lay halfway between the two planets. The bottom of the geyser fell back on Eau, while the top drifted across the zero-gravity point to spawn tornadoes and thunderheads over Roche, which dropped salty rain onto the volcanoes below.

"There's your home—Rocheworld," said Richard, pointing.

☆Pretty!☆ replied Little Red. Richard could only

agree. After watching the two co-orbiting gumdrops move slowly around each other for a while, Richard turned to look at Little Red.

"Those are the worlds that we are leaving. Now let me show you the worlds that we are heading toward," he said. He turned and whispered to the imp on his shoulder. "We'll need the elevator, James." He looked up the sixty-meter-high shaft and saw a doughnut-shaped platform start down from the top deck. As the elevator lowered, James controlled the pace of the descent so that the hole in the center of the platform passed safely over the humans moving up and down the shaft, propelled by occasional kicks or pushes against the handholds in the shaft wall.

Richard and Little Red rode the elevator to the top of the shaft. Richard lifted them both up into the starside science dome in the ceiling of the top deck and swung out the floor support that kept them from falling down the shaft. Looming large in the black star-studded sky that filled the dome, was the nearly fully illuminated orb of a large planet surrounded by its retinue of orbiting moons. The reddish gas giant was mottled with gigantic white cyclonic storms and weather fronts. Richard turned to look at Little Red. The custom-made helmet on the makeshift drysuit of the alien was filled with featureless red jelly, and on the surface of the jelly, easily seen in the darkness of the dome, were two upside-down images of Gargantua and its moons. Richard suddenly felt strange, for by being able to look into Little Red's eyes to see what his friend was looking at, he felt he was intruding into the alien's mind. Slightly shaken, he turned back to look out the dome again.

"That is Gargantua," said Richard. "You call it Warm. It is too big for us to land on, so we are going to visit some of its moons. You can easily see the four largest ones from here. The white one closest to Gargantua is the ice-covered moon Zulu. The blue-white one next closest is the water-covered moon Zuni, while the reddish one is the smog-covered moon Zouave." He looked over to one side of the dome, then lifted Little Red a little higher so he could see too. "The furthest one out is the dry world Zapotec. It is something like the Roche lobe on your Rocheworld and something like the planet Mars in our solar system. There are five other moons, but they are much smaller and hard to see."

☆The Zapotec moon not round like the others, but only half-round! Why?☆ asked Little Red.

"Since we are coming from the direction of Barnard, Gargantua and the three inner moons are ahead of us and fully illuminated by the light from Barnard. We are about to cross the orbit of Zapotec, however, so we are seeing it from the side. The front half is illuminated by Barnard, while the back side is in shadow."

There was a brief moment while Little Red digested the idea.

☆Of course! Now I see reason for shadows. Also, I see other moons are not truly round, but show shadow on one side.☆ There was another pause. ☆Cone of shadow made by Zulu will soon intersect sphere of Gargantua.☆

"Little Red is correct," James whispered through Richard's imp. "The transit of Zulu's shadow across Gargantua's face will start in thirty-two seconds."

"Let's watch it," said Richard, impressed that the immature and impetuous alien was also an intuitive mathematical genius with an IQ many times that of the smartest human. Little Red had reasoned out the complex mechanics and optics of the multimoon system after just a few seconds of thought. A dark streak soon appeared on the side of Gargantua near its equator and quickly turned into a black dot traveling rapidly across the vast expanse of brightly illuminated surface. It didn't take long, however, before Little Red got bored.

☆Spot take forever to get to other side! Show me something new!☆

"Well, let me show you something you don't see every day," said Richard, pointing to a bright object in the forward starfield. It was the size of a star, but it flickered in a strange way. "Its getting pretty far away now, so we'll need a telescope to see it clearly. James?"

James responded by swinging a telescope out into the dome above them. Instead of trying to teach the eyeless alien how to use an eyepiece, Richard merely displayed on a convenient video monitor the image as seen in the telescope. It looked like a planet with a hole in it.

"That's the ring sail that brought us here," said Richard. "It's made of the same material that the sail of *Prometheus* is made of. The hole in the ring sail is where *Prometheus*'s sail used to be."

☆Sail on *Prometheus* very big!☆ said Little Red, impressed for once. ☆That sail much bigger!☆

"It's a thousand kilometers across—nearly one-third the size of one of the lobes of Rocheworld. When we left the solar system, that ring sail and the *Prometheus* sail were attached together. The laser around the Sun pushed both sails up to speed—twenty percent of the speed of light. After forty years of travel, we finally arrived at *your* star system. As we approached Barnard, the *Prometheus* sail was detached from the ring sail and turned around so the reflective surface faced the ring sail. The laser beam from the solar system bounced off the ring sail, pushing it even faster through the Barnard system and out the other side, where you see it now. But the laser light reflecting off the ring sail was focused back onto the *Prometheus* sail, pushing it in the opposite direction to its travel and slowing it down. Because of that ring sail we were able to stop here at Barnard and come to visit you."

☆And teach me new things,☆ said Little Red, sober with thought for once. ☆The word 'visit' means a short stay. When do you go back to Earth?☆

There was a long silence as Richard tried to swallow the lump that had suddenly risen into his throat.

"Our expedition was designed to be a one-way mission that would keep us busy exploring for our entire lifetime," he answered. "We will never return to Earth."

☆Good!☆ said Little Red. ☆You stay and be my friend forever!☆

"Sure," said Richard, putting a massive muscled arm around the large alien and giving the squashy body a hug. "Friends forever. . . ." Although Little Red knew the facts about their comparative lifetimes, the red flouwen didn't really appreciate yet what those differences meant. To the nearly indestructible young alien, who was already hundreds of years old—and could expect to live many thousands of years—"forever" was just a very long time. To Richard, however, who was nearly fifty years old, "forever" was another forty years of life at best—probably a lot less. . . .

☆Why is there water in your eyes?!☆

"Never mind. Let's go pump you back into your tank."

As Richard was watching Little Red being squirted out of the hose back into the habitat tank, he noticed that Little Purple was stirring from his rock-like form in the corner.

⊡I have calculated mathematical logic of relative motion,⊡ Little Purple announced. ⊡It results in very interesting mathematics. Not intuitive at all. If speed of light is same for all observers as the humans say is true, then things must shrink in their direction of motion, moving masses are heavier than stationary masses, and time moves more slowly for moving observers.◻

◊I agree. Not intuitive at all,◊ said Little White. ◊Yet, if you say it is logical, it must be. I must taste that.◊

☆I taste too!☆ demanded Little Red, extending a flame-red pseudopod.

Little Purple concentrated some memory juices into the end of a pseudopod and passed the knowledge on to his two compatriots. The memory juices contained complex chemicals that coded the logical arguments and mathematical equations that Little Purple had recently developed during his latest session of serious thinking.

◊Very interesting taste—very logical—definitely not intuitive . . .◊ mused Little White, mulling over the multitude of ideas derivable from the mathematical formulas contained in the succinct chemical patterns that had been passed from purple brain to white brain.

☆Wow!☆ exclaimed Little Red. ☆Terrific taste!☆ Amazingly enough, the very active, very vocal alien was suddenly silent and still—obviously thinking at great speed. Suddenly Little Red burst into a series of shrieks and turned himself inside out in exultation at his discovery.

☆$E=mc^2$!!!☆

There was a short silence on the flouwen side of the window as Little White and Little Purple thought through what Little Red had uttered.

◊Of course!◊ said Little White.

◻Yes!◻ exclaimed Little Purple. ◻I missed that consequence of the equations. I must be getting too old. My memory is so full of facts I don't have any brain left to think with.◻

☆You two are too old! You have to be young and big and smart to think fast like me!☆ bragged Little Red.

There was a shocked silence on the human side of the window.

"James! Did he really say Eee equals em cee squared?" exclaimed Richard.

The calm deep voice of James spoke confidentially through their individual imps. "The phrase actually spoken in flouwenese, when literally translated, would have been roughly, 'A quantity of mass can logically be converted to a quantity of energy with the conversion factor being two multiplies of the speed of light, and vice versa.' I think that, on the whole, I translated the technical content quite accurately and succinctly." There was a trace of a superior tone in James' voice pattern.

It was time for a shift change. Soon the corridor outside the habitat tank was empty and the three flouwen were left alone for a while. With no humans around needing a translation, James bypassed the translation program and just kept a record of the flouwen's conversation in flouwenese.

☆I have something to show you, Subset of Clear◊White◊Whistle. Come over to the Talking⊗Plate and I will have James⊗Server show you the Look⊗View the Stiff⊗Mover Richard showed to me.☆ The red blob swam to the taste-screen on the habitat wall and, forming a red pseudopod, expertly manipulated the icons until a picture of Gargantua and its moons appeared on the screen.

☆After you have tasted the Talking⊗Plate, Subset of Clear◊White◊Whistle, look it too, to see the different colors of the different moons.☆ The white creature spread itself against the screen to taste, see, and look at the enlarged image there.

◊In my many years of observing Warm and its Pets from the oceans of Water, I have never observed such detail!◊

☆You will soon observe even more detail, for Big⊗Circle will soon arrive at Warm! Then we can all leave this small tank and explore!☆

SURVEYING

Jinjur showed up early for her shift on the control deck, carrying her drink-ball. She looked around at the quiet but busy scene. George was at the command console having a muttered discussion with the lightsail pilot Tony Roma seated a few consoles away. George, reaching the end of his shift, was looking gray and tired. The crew had all used No-Die, a life-extending drug, on their outward flight from Earth, which had slipped them through forty years of calendar time while their bodies only aged ten years. George, the oldest person on the mission, was nearly a century old by the calendar, while biologically, his age was only sixty-six years. Jinjur whispered something to her imp, which was formed into an illuminated comb stuck into her military regulation afro just above her left ear, while continuing to watch the two men.

Tony, in contrast to George, hadn't seemed to age a bit, and looked just as Jinjur remembered him when he had been the best lightsail pilot in her Space Marines Interceptor Fleet—small, dark, and handsome, with a neat mustache and wavy dark hair that now produced a curl on his forehead. His uniform was as crisp as when he began this shift, and his cheerful enthusiasm for the mission never slackened. From long experience, Jinjur could tell the two men were talking together, since their consoles each contained the same image, and as Tony touched his screen, a green dot would show up on George's.

Although the men were not more than two meters apart, they didn't raise their voices to speak directly to each other but used their imp link through James. It was partially to keep the noise level on the control deck down, but mostly it was force of habit.

Linda Regan was at the space science console, zeroing in one of the many telescopes on *Prometheus* on a large facula which she and James were monitoring on the surface of Barnard. Jinjur could feel a "clunk" through the deck floor as a port opened under the circular science rack in the center of the deck, and a deep-ultraviolet spectrometer was thrust out into the vacuum to collect data.

Next to Linda, at the planetary science console, the tall, gray, lanky figure of Sam Houston hunched over the screen, looking at one image after another which James wanted him to check. The robotic explorers on each of the many moons of Gargantua sent back many images a second. Most of those James took care of automatically, numbering, cataloging, and storing the image as sent, and then using a processed and rectified version of the image to update and perfect its global image map of that moon. Occasionally, however, the image would contain some object that was not easy to categorize. The image would be sent to a human, in this case Sam, with the unknown object circled. Most of these were false alarms, especially on the more barren planets. But there were enough interesting discoveries found on some of the moons, such as earthlike Zuni which had a multitude of plants and a few small animals, and especially Ganymedelike Zulu, which had some really strange life-forms, that the job of working the planetary science console was usually interesting. Right now, however, the results of the survey seemed to be boring. Jinjur could hear Sam muttering, "Nope. Nope. Nope." Jinjur suspected that the images were coming from Marslike Zapotec, which seemed to be barren, not only of life, but even of fossils.

On the other side of the deck, Caroline Tanaka was monitoring the display on the communications console. The task was almost automatic, since James had charge of keeping the laser communicators pointed back in the right direction to the solar system, and keeping the multitude of outgoing channels full of the scientific data which was pouring into the ship from the exploration robots scattered all over the Barnard system. Occasionally, however, one of the robots exploring the many moons of Gargantua required a decision—such as what to explore next— the answer to which was not immediately obvious to James. On those occasions, the whims of a human, driven by inquisitiveness and intuition rather than pure logical extrapolation, were required.

Gargantua kept nine moons in their steady orbits; Caroline had mapped them before leaving Earth, using an orbiting laser-controlled phase-locked interferometer array which she had designed and operated. She had also assisted in the naming of the moons, with names the Astronomical Nomenclature Board had decided should all begin with the letter Z. Before they started, they knew that they would find the large moons, Zapotec, Zouave, Zuni, and Zulu, and the five asteroid-sized rocks, Zeus, Zen, Zion, and the Zwingli-Zoroaster pair that shared the same orbit. Upon arrival at the Barnard star system, neither she nor the others were too surprised to discover many smaller moonlets in existence. These were supposed to be given Z-numbers in order of discovery, but the more creative among the crew were not content with that, and one particularly tiny close-in moonlet continued to orbit rapidly onward, uncaring that its name was now Zipcode.

George finally noticed that Jinjur had arrived. He rose, Velcro patches on his back and bottom making a ripping sound as he pulled himself free from his seat. Kicking off from his console, he floated off across the control deck in an arc that brought him to a halt near her, arriving just after the galley imp had delivered a second drink-ball. Jinjur was looking out one of the four portholes at the stars slowly rotating by. A good portion of the upper part of the view out the porthole was blocked by the vast expanse of lightsail overhead. Just below the sail, however, was a large half-moon. Jinjur handed George the second drink-ball. As George took the squeezer, he noticed that it was cold on the outside and clanked on the inside.

"You looked frazzled, so I had James make you a refreshing martini to help you relax at the end of your shift." She held up her own drink-ball.

"Coffee," she said, unnecessarily.

George took a welcome sip of his squeezer. "We've crossed the orbit of Zapotec at sixteen hundred and fifty megameters," he reported. "I have been assuming that we weren't going to spend one of our last two landers there, so I didn't have Tony plot a course to match orbits with it. I guess it's about time we made a decision as to which moons we are going to use our last two landers on—and which one we do first."

"Offhand, I'd agree with your assessment of Zapotec, but first, let's go through the data summaries to date on all the moons to make sure we make the right choices," Jinjur replied. "Remember, we don't need to land on a moon to learn about it. We can collect almost as much data from orbit using our imagers and sensors and a few well-chosen robot explorers."

She headed for the command console with George following behind. The other members of the upcoming shift were drifting in and discussing the shift changeovers with their counterparts. Carmen Cortez took over the communications console from Caroline, Reiki LeRoux took over space science from Linda, and Elizabeth Vengeance took over the planetary science console from Sam.

"Boring as hell, Red," Sam muttered to Elizabeth as the tall woman came to stand beside him while he finished examining the latest set of images. Her intensely red hair contrasted nicely with her well-fitting bright green jumpsuit. "Looking for signs of life on Zapotec is like trying to find placer gold in the Empty Quarter of Arabia."

"Or looking for nickel-iron nodules in a carbonaceous chondrite," replied the former asteroid prospector as she took over control of the console. One of her nickel-iron finds—an asteroid containing one hundred million tons of nearly pure metal—had made her a multibillionaire, but she had given it all up to come on this mission to the stars. All she had left of her fortune was a single gold coin, kept in her shirt pocket as a souvenir.

Jinjur whispered to her imp, "Hook George and me up with Sam and Red, and bring up the planetary science console screen." James alerted Sam and Red of the linkup, and soon the four were in conversation.

"Now, Sam," asked Jinjur. "Which exploration robots

did we send to Zapotec and what have they reported so far?" Sam bent his lanky form in its trim-fitting denim over the science console, and his fingers played over the touch-screen to bring up the data.

"During our fly-through tour of the Gargantua system before we decided to visit Rocheworld, we dropped off four exploration robots at Zapotec," reported Sam. "Seeing as how the place is a lot like Mars—even has a little atmosphere—we chose a couple of different robotic vehicles. One was the orbiter *Carl*; it has cameras for global imagery, both high and low resolution. It's also got a laser altimeter for topography profiles, a gravity gradiometer for subsurface mass distribution, and a whole bunch of spectrometers—visible, infrared, gamma ray, microwave, ultraviolet—specially directed at finding water and life-associated chemicals like free oxygen. *Carl* also fetched along a couple of aeroshells, which it turned loose after looking the place over. One had *Wilbur* in it, a robotic plane modeled after the ones we used on Mars, with great big wings for the thin air. The other aeroshell had *Pushmi-Pullyu* aboard—that's a pair of crawlers fastened together with a cable on reels, so they can haul each other up and down steep parts, if need be." Sam's voice changed slightly as he shifted from reporting to commanding.

"James?" said Sam. "How about giving Jinjur a summary report of what the exploration robots have found so far?"

James swiftly produced the desired report for Jinjur. They were close enough to Zapotec that the communications time delay was negligible, so James let the vehicles themselves give the summary.

"Orbiter *Carl* here," came a sibilant tenor voice. On their console screens appeared the image of a rocky, barren planet. "After a brief initial survey of Zapotec from a near equatorial orbit, I dropped the aeroshells containing *Wilbur* and *Pushmi-Pullyu* near the large equatorial rift valley." The picture enlarged and continued to rotate, taking them on a simulated flyover of the chasm, which not only exceeded in length and depth the Grand Canyon but also the Valles Marineris. "I then switched to a polar orbit with an altitude so that successive ground tracks would ultimately provide complete coverage of the planet under various lighting conditions." The image changed to that of one of the polar regions. It showed a dirty ice cap pocked around the edges with rounded mounds of lava with broad calderas in their centers.

"Special attention was paid to obtaining high resolution images of the volcanic chain ringing the south pole ice cap. During my nearly two years of observation, a number of the volcanoes have showed activity." The picture of the polar region switched from a high-resolution cleaned-up view to an obviously stop-motion view—where the beginning of an eruption on one of volcanoes would be caught in one orbital passover by *Carl*, and successive orbits would track the resulting dust and ash cloud as it moved down wind.

"Richard's been having fun analyzing those," remarked Sam over their imp links. "The ashes and gas released have a real effect on the climate, especially when the ashes cover some of the ice."

"Preliminary evaluation of the imagery and sensor data produced no indications of life nor anything else of significant interest," *Carl* finally concluded.

"This is *Wilbur*," came a deep, matter-of-fact voice. "As a high-altitude robotic plane with VTOL landing capacity, my task was to supply ground-truth data for the images and sensor data taken from orbit, and to collect a few samples of anything important that could not be reached by the crawlers. The atmosphere of Zapotec is thin, but I had no problem flying or hovering in it. I first surveyed the floor of the rift valley and identified important points along the rift wall for the crawlers to investigate in more detail." The screens in front of Jinjur and Sam showed close-up images of a cliff wall, which contained layer after layer of what looked like sandstone interspersed with black ash. "After finishing the rift valley, I started on a programmed spot survey of the planet." The image switched to a close-up of a volcanic caldera shooting up red-hot ashes, lightning flashing continuously from the glowing ash cloud to points on the rim of the crater. "I am now in my second tour, with landing spots chosen to be intermediate between those of the first survey. Preliminary evaluation of the surface samples and the airborne imagery produced no indications of life nor anything else of significant interest," *Wilbur* concluded.

"This is *Pushmi* reporting," came a squeaky voice. "I and *Pullyu* landed on the plains outside the rift valley and we began exploring at the locations indicated to us by *Wilbur*. I lowered *Pullyu* down the walls while it took selected samples of the various exposed layers." Close-up pictures of the layered side of a cliff showed up on their screen. "The light-colored layers are sandstone from ancient dune field buildups, alternating with thin layers of ash and occasional thick layers of volcanic lava. There are no indications that Zapotec had any significant surface water at any time in its history. After sampling all around the perimeter of the rift valley, we traveled south to explore and sample the polar volcano field." There were pictures from *Pushmi* of *Pullyu* being lowered into a caldera, taking samples off the steep slope as it descended. In the image, the humans could see a large bubble forming in the lake of lava far below. The bubble burst, sending streamers of glowing lava up along the sides of the caldera, one of which engulfed *Pullyu*. As the lava fell back, it left only the melted tip of the high-strength polymer cable behind.

"*Pullyu* was lost in crater seventy-nine south one hundred twenty east," reported *Pushmi*. "No samples were lost except those of that particular volcano, since we divided up samples after every survey mission so that each of us had a duplicate set. I have now limited my surveys to safe regions. Within one year, my sample hold will be full and I will need to transfer the samples to the return stage waiting back at the aeroshell. My preliminary evaluation of the samples has produced no indications of life nor anything else of significant interest," *Pushmi* concluded.

There was a brief silence.

"Hunh," said Jinjur. "No indications of life nor anything else of significant interest—cubed."

"That about sums it up," agreed George. "Doesn't sound like a really exciting place to visit in person, does it?"

"Nope," agreed Jinjur. "James, tell the Zapotec exploration team to keep up the good work. We'll be back to collect their samples later. Now, how about the next moon in—Zouave?"

Just then, Arielle Trudeau came sailing down the shaft to take over the navigation console from Tony Roma. She had obviously stopped by the galley on the way for some provisions to last her between breakfast and lunch.

Tony stood and stretched to his full five feet six. "After all the fun of Rocheworld, that report on Zapotec was something of a letdown. Well, Arielle, Jinjur says we aren't going to Zapotec, so we'll just maintain our present course to the inner moons. I don't think you'll need to do anything for a while except monitor James."

Arielle didn't reply, because her mouth was full, but she slid willingly into the seat for the navigation control console. Her imp, sparkling with color, moved over her ears to form headphones, while one long tendril moved swiftly and delicately out to remove an errant crumb from her cheek and tuck it neatly between her lips. Her slender hands firmly secured the food and drink she carried into convenient receptacles on either side of the console screen, and then lay relaxed in her lap. However, the huge brown eyes were intent and watchful on the screens. Since she had little to do except monitor James—who almost never made a mistake—she switched most of her screen to the planetary science images and arranged for her imp to listen in on the discussion about Zouave.

"Well, now. Zouave's all covered with smog, kinda like Titan," explained Sam. "Plenty of air, we knew that—three atmospheres full. And radar said there was thick ice over the rocky core, but we knew it was too warm for liquid nitrogen rain like Titan's. There might have been snowdrifts on top of the ice, or maybe lakes of methane, or ethane, or some stuff that might wreck a crawler's sensors. So we sent down *Punch* and *Poke*, a couple of penetrator probes to get right down to bedrock and find out chemical composition, temperatures, and seismic data. They also took along a couple of high-pressure balloons, *Tweedledee* and *Tweedledum*. They've been hangin' around, drifting between surface and clouds, blown from one place to the other by winds and collecting samples as they go."

"What have they found so far?" asked Jinjur.

"*Punch* and *Poke* aren't really intelligent enough to carry on a conversation," interjected James. "But the balloons are. I'll let them tell you themselves."

"Ice!" came a high-pitched piercing computer voice through their imps.

"Snow!" came a slightly lower computer voice with a harsher tone.

"More ice than snow!"

"More snow than ice!"

There was a spluttering from the space science console. The normally reserved Reiki was trying to keep from laughing and was not succeeding. "I tried to program a little personality into the voice personas to match their names. Perhaps I overdid it." The piercing voice dropped slightly in tone as the semi-intelligent central computer of the balloon became more controlled. "This is balloon explorer *Tweedledee* assigned to obtain surface samples of the northern hemisphere of Zouave. The amount of ice cover I have surveyed is 51.5 percent compared to snow cover of 47.3 percent. Only 1.2 percent of the surface area is bare rock, most of it sheer cliff faces in the mountainous regions of the far north. My sample return rocket will be full in 1.3 years."

"This is balloon explorer *Tweedledum*. It is obvious that *Tweedledee* has been exploring the wrong hemisphere to obtain the correct ice to snow ratio. The amount of ice cover I have surveyed is 46.3 percent compared to snow cover of 52.9 percent. Only 0.8 percent of the surface area is bare rock, most of it in the calderas of volcanoes just south of the equator. My sample return rocket will be full in 1.2 years."

"Doesn't sound very promising—nothing but a frozen landscape," said George.

"Any signs of life?" asked Jinjur. There was a slight time lag before the reply.

"None," came the simultaneous answer from the two balloons on the opposite hemispheres of the planet.

"Why are you echoing me?"

"Echoing you? You were echoing me!"

"I said 'none' first!"

"No, I did!"

"I did!"

Jinjur made a motion near her imp like turning off a volume control knob and James stopped transmitting. "Tell them to keep up the good work and we'll be back in a year or two to pick up their samples."

"Well," said George. "As we expected, that leaves Zuni and Zulu. And they are both worth spending landers on, since they both have life-forms which we'll want to examine firsthand. You can't really learn much about a living organism by examining a few samples that were punched out of it by a robotic corer."

"Well," mused Jinjur, "since our exploration robots on Zulu have come across life-forms that use artifacts and seem to be intelligent, then it's obvious we should go there first."

A soft but insistent voice spoke out from across the room. It was Reiki, who, instead of using her imp to talk through James to Jinjur, was speaking directly at her. "If I may make a suggestion. . . ."

When Jinjur heard that phrase from Reiki, she knew that whatever Reiki had to say might be important.

"Certainly, Reiki," said Jinjur. "Suggest on. . . ."

"Because of our involvement with the flouwen and the starfish creatures on Rocheworld . . ." she began (Reiki had always disliked the name "gummies" and refused to use it) " . . . and the minutes-long communications time delay between Rocheworld and Zulu, we have not had much opportunity to develop a working dialogue with the dominant life-forms on Zulu. Although it might seem obvious that we should go there first, it *may* be better to visit the other moon first. While the exploration crew on the ground are collecting samples of the vegetation and the animals on Zuni, the crew on *Prometheus* could be interacting with the Zulu aliens through the crawlers and improving James' translation programs so that our ultimate visit there would be much more profitable."

"She has a point there," said George. "We'll have to think carefully about which moon should be visited first."

"To really determine whether our translation programs are adequate for a visit, we ought to try them out in real time," said Jinjur. "And that means getting close enough to Zulu that the communications time-lag is negligible. James? Get me Arielle—"

"I listening," replied Arielle.

"What course did Tony leave us on?"

"A trajectory inward to match up with Zouave."

"Change the target to Zulu." She then looked across the deck to where Arielle was perched on her chair. Arielle now had one hand expertly flickering over the touch-screen, setting up the new trajectory for the light-sail, while the other held the remains of a sandwich of cucumbers and pickled 'ponics-fish in soured pseudo-cream on pumpernickel bread. Jinjur then looked down at her console. James had automatically changed the display on Jinjur's screen to the display on Arielle's navigation console screen. The light blue line that indicated their trajectory passed close to the surface of the giant planet Gargantua.

"Zulu is closest in," said Arielle through her imp. "If we to match orbits with it in minimum time, we must go inside Zulu orbit and catch it on other side. I can choose another approach, but that means slowing *Prometheus* down and it take eight days longer."

Jinjur turned to George, who had studied the atmosphere of Gargantua in some detail during their initial flyby of the gas giant. "Any problems with getting that close?"

"I don't think so," said George. "James?"

"We will be well above the atmosphere. Since we will be going in low near the equatorial plane, there will be no radiation belts to worry about. I have calculated that the gravity gradients will not cause torques on the sail that the sail controller cannot cope with, but the strong magnetic field of Gargantua will cause some eddy current drag in the sail material. That is easily compensated for by an adjustment in the incoming trajectory."

"Forgot about those little side effects," said George, thankful that the nearly omniscient computer was always looking out for their welfare.

"In a few days, we be passing close to Zuni on way in," added Arielle.

"Good!" said Jinjur. "We'll be able to check them both out at close range before we make a decision."

"In that case, I'm going to have an early dinner and hit the sack," said George back through his imp, as he swung himself off the control deck and up the central shaft to the living area deck above.

After a few days, their sunlight-powered infall toward Gargantua brought them close enough to Zuni that they could communicate with the robotic explorers they had left there without incurring a significant time delay. Jinjur and George were again together on the control deck, and Richard was at the planetary science console. Outside one of the portholes on the control deck, George could see the moon itself, a blue marble with a multitude of brownish-green dots overlaid with a swirling pattern of white clouds—looking like a miniature Earth as seen from above the island-dotted oceanic "hemisphere" between the Americas and Asia-Australia. Zuni was in three-quarter phase, with a sharp weather front that extended over the terminator onto the dark side, where its centerline could be traced by the multitude of lightning flashes lighting up the clouds.

Richard started the report. "The exploration robots that were left at Zuni during our first flythrough of the Gargantuan moon system were the orbiter spacecraft *Bruce*, to obtain synoptic imagery and global sensor data; a VTOL flyer, *Orville*, to provide high-resolution imagery from the air and to obtain samples from areas not easily accessible by the crawlers; and two amphibious crawlers, *Bubble* and *Burble*, to explore and obtain samples from the islands and the shallower waters. One of the crawlers, *Burble*, was lost."

George now remembered the laconic voice of the orbiter spacecraft *Bruce* as it reported the loss of one of the amphibious crawlers that had been exploring the oceans and islands of Zuni.

"*Burble* is experiencing technical difficulties. *Burble* is submerging rapidly off the southern tip of island 105 east, 35 north. *Burble* has ceased communication." There was a pause. "All indications are that *Burble* is no longer operational."

George recalled that he had been too busy coping with the activities on Rocheworld to respond with much feeling.

"Right, *Bruce*. You, *Orville*, and *Bubble* carry on," was about it, as he remembered.

"For the global summary of Zuni, I'll let *Bruce* give the report," said Richard. On their screens was now a high-resolution computer-generated picture that had been built up from a combination of images taken by both *Prometheus* and *Bruce*.

A calmly resonant computer voice spoke. "This is *Bruce*. I am presently in polar orbit about Zuni continuing my global survey of imagery, gravity, topography, and remote sensing. Zuni is a water-covered planetoid 3800 kilometers in diameter, a little larger than the Earth's Moon. It has no large continents, but has a multitude of islands—ninety-five major ones. The atmospheric pressure is half an Earth atmosphere, and the surface gravity is 28% of Earth's gravity. Zuni's surface temperature is typically thirty to forty degrees centigrade, equivalent to the tropics on Earth. Since the orbit of the moon lies between Zulu and Zouave, both of which are ice-covered, this temperature is anomalous. The full explanation awaits further analysis, but part of the reason is that Zuni is tidally locked to Gargantua, and when either Zulu or Zouave passes by, their gravity tides cause it to rock about its tidally locked position, creating heat by internal friction. Since it is rocked by two neighbors, it experiences twice as much heating. Another suspected cause is chemical. All three of the moons are too small to prevent their volatiles from escaping into space. Zulu looses water from its geysers, Zouave looses smog from its atmosphere, and Zuni looses air and water from its atmosphere. The escaped volatiles cannot escape from Gargantua's gravity well and remain as gas toroids centered about the moon's orbital track. Most of the gasses are eventually recaptured by the moons that emitted them, but some of the smog from Zouave and some of the water from Zulu are collected by Zuni. The water and smog react chemically to give additional heating to Zuni. The reaction products obviously provide nourishment to the life-forms on the surface. These definitely include plant life, since my remote sensors detect the presence of complex organic compounds with absorption bands peaked at the Barnard spectrum, and free oxygen. This has been confirmed by the surface explorers, *Orville* and *Bubble*."

"Those ninety-five islands are all tops of volcanos," added Richard. "Which really keeps the planet churned up. There isn't going to be much 'geo' down there to do geology on, but what there *is* is going to be interesting."

"What did the surface exploration robots find?" asked Jinjur.

"I could have *Orville* and *Bubble* make their own reports," interjected James, "but there is so much detailed information to cover, that I shall condense their findings for you. In summary, the planet Zuni is full of life, both plant and animal, on land and in the water. Certainly, with only one flyer and one crawler working, not all of it has been found, much less examined and understood in detail. As expected, plant forms dominate, with some of them reaching very large sizes, some in height and some in breadth." As James spoke, single-shot pictures flashed up on the screen, most of them obviously taken by *Bubble* in its traverses of the various islands it had briefly visited. There was a group of tall trees like coconut palms, except that their canopies were quite large and overlapped. Around one of the smaller trees coiled a vine. There was a shot of a very dense thicket, behind which could be seen some stout trees about four meters tall, with some color in their foliage.

"This thicket was so thick that *Bubble* could not penetrate it to obtain images of the trees inside."

There was another tree, like a banyan tree with vertical supports growing down from the spreading horizontal branches.

"There are also many plants in the water," added

James, "some of them rooted in the shallows, usually near volcanic vent fields, and some of them floating like seaweed. In the plants live many kinds of small animals that crawl, swim, and fly. Many of them seem to have symbiotic relationships with the plants. None of the small creatures are large enough to have a significant brain."

There was a picture of a small six-legged green-furred animal peering out from the foliage, a blurred shot of a small owllike bird with green feathers, and a picture of six fish with strainerlike mouths floating near a large underwater plant.

When James had finished, Jinjur turned to George. "Well, there is definitely lots of animal life, but it seems very unintelligent," she said. "The land creatures are extremely small and simple, and the ones in the ocean don't look promising, either."

"Yes," said George. "It may not be intelligent life, but it *is* life, and definitely worth expending a lander on. For one thing, such a wide variety of living things would be interesting to study. And for another, the climate and terrain don't seem to be as extreme as on the other moons. Let's go take a look at Zulu, see if we have prepared ourselves enough to land there, and then reassess the situation."

"I agree," said Jinjur. "James. Hook me up to Thomas."

At the navigation console, Captain Thomas St. Thomas tilted his head to listen to his imp.

"Please set our course for Zulu, Thomas," ordered Jinjur.

"Aye, aye, ma'am," replied Thomas in his best military manner, then his voice brightened up with anticipation. "We're going to get a real close look at 'Garg' this time! I ought to get some swell pictures." He took a look at the timing marks on the new trajectory for *Prometheus* that

James had just calculated for him. "Shucks!" he muttered to himself. "I'll be on navigation duty shift at the time of closest approach."

George immediately replied back through his imp. "I'll be glad to take over your shift duty, since I was going to be here as a bystander anyway. That is, if Jinjur doesn't need me for anything else?"

"Aren't you going to be doing some studies of the Gargantuan atmosphere along with Arielle?" reminded Jinjur.

"Yes, but since navigation console duty at that time will involve nothing but watching James control the lightsail flutter, I could use the navigation console to do both at the same time."

"Sounds fine with me," replied Jinjur.

"Great!" replied Thomas. "I should be able to get some *great* pictures!" He munched happily on one of his special crisps, enjoying the crunchy feel under his teeth as much as the super-hot Jamaican spice flavors on his tongue. With any luck, these photos might be sensational enough to transmit in his monthly electronic letter to the family on Earth. Although most of them barely remembered their most famous relative, since he had left Earth forty-five years ago, they were still intensely proud of him, and the letters were read and discussed for weeks, while the reply, full of all the gossip from Kingston, was being composed—without regard to the fact that it would be six years before Thomas received it.

"I'll get my equipment laid out now, ready to go. Thanks a lot, George! I can hardly wait!"

George couldn't, either. It was surprising how interstellar exploration was a lot like fighting a war. Months and years of doing nothing, then suddenly there was more to do than you could cope with. And, like a war, it occasionally got dangerous. . . . His mind went back to that still horrifying moment back on their first visit to Rocheworld, when he found himself ten kilometers up in the sky—falling headfirst toward the surface without a parachute. The only thing that had saved his life that time was Thomas' expert piloting of the Ascent Propulsion Stage. Thomas had swooped the rocket around and down, and scooped George right out of the sky, as if George was the ball in the childhood cup-and-ball game. For that, George owed Thomas *much* more than a mere duty shift switch.

A few days later, they started their flyby of the gas giant Gargantua. Four times more massive than Jupiter, it emitted more thermal radiation generated by its internal gravitational contraction and chemical phase changes than it received in heat and light from its small primary, Barnard—which, because of its greater density, was actually smaller in diameter than its major planet. If Gargantua had been slightly larger, it too would have been a star like Barnard—but even smaller and denser.

The surface temperature of Gargantua was near the freezing point of water, which was much warmer than the three degree temperature of the empty sky, so the warmth from the large globe provided a major contribution to the heat input of the climatic cycles of its moons. Gargantua had a strong magnetic field, driven by the convection currents in its metallic hydrogen core, but its radiation belt was weaker than that of Jupiter because Barnard didn't emit much solar wind.

Gargantua rotated once every 162 hours, compared to the ten-hour rotation periods of Jupiter, Saturn, and Uranus. As a result, the weather patterns in its upper atmosphere were not the multitude of belts and zones found on the solar system gas giants, but instead consisted of a series of gigantic cyclones, spawned near the equator, and moving into the high latitudes, where they dissipated into storm fronts. Except for the scale, they looked similar to the weather patterns of Earth. Gargantua had a larger rock core than Jupiter, and its liquid metallic hydrogen "ocean" and its gaseous atmosphere were proportionately thinner. As a result, the ocean and atmosphere were affected by the solid surface below. These showed up as permanent spots in the weather pattern. There were hot spots near the equator which were the seed spots for hurricanes, and colder areas which depleted the strength of any cyclone pattern that wandered near them. The larger hot spots were also identified with atmospheric "volcanoes," gigantic upwellings of gaseous hydrogen driven by a hot spot under the metallic hydrogen ocean.

In the lounge on the commons deck, David Greystoke and Deirdre gazed outward at the alien surface rolling, endlessly, before them. The massive planet filled the three-by-four meter viewport as the slow rotation of the sailcraft moved it ponderously by the window, its surface swirling with gigantic endless storms and pocked with violent atmospheric volcanoes.

"Needs theme music," said David, more loudly than he had meant. "Sorry," he said more softly. "All that turbulence and activity, it seems impossible for it to be soundless. My mind keeps hearing chords, mostly loud and dissonant—" He broke off at Deirdre's murmur of understanding.

It was off-duty time for both of them. Deirdre slouched further into the sofa, her long legs stretched comfortably, wide shoulders relaxed. Her narrow, high-arched feet in sleek boots were propped on the ledge in front of her. Foxx, awakened, also stretched and yawned, and settled down again on the back of the woman's neck.

The imp holding Deirdre's hair shifted slightly to avoid the animal's furry tail, and one of its six "hands" settled down again on the side of Deirdre's neck to continue its constant monitoring. David was sitting upright, intent and still. His slight frame was taut with creation. The music forming in patterns in his mind absorbed him utterly. The computers he tended with such skill and care would help him, later, to bring to all the crew a new vision of the gigantic storm he was watching, as he translated it into a sono-video concert.

Deirdre remained silent and relaxed. She rarely had much to say, and the landscape passing ponderously by was absorbing all her attention. *Another cyclone, starting up from what must be a hot spot.* The comment was unvoiced. Deirdre's usual tasks, in the hydroponics lab, precluded her spending much time in the communal lounge, but she found the unfolding panorama fascinating.

Down in the control room, curiosity and excitement were increasing as *Prometheus* drew closer to the surface of the giant planet. The crew, specially augmented for the encounter, continued to monitor the data being collected. Off on one side of the deck, Shirley took Thomas through the checkout of his spacesuit.

"Every trip outside involves *some* risk," complained Shirley, as she roughly punched button after button on Thomas' chestpack, the rocket pilot rocking slightly with each punch. "We've got plenty of big cameras in the science bays. Why do you have to go out in the vacuum with your piddling little seventy millimeter?"

"You're just a worrywart," replied Thomas, secretly glad that it was Shirley checking him out. She was indeed extremely safety conscious. She never skipped over checklists, no matter how many times she had been through them before. "The others need the big cameras for the scientific work and they can't afford time to compose a shot like I can. And I don't want those thick portholes distorting my pictures." Once more he was grateful that George had taken his shift so that he could go out. Excitement surged through him—as it had so often in his lucky life. New discoveries, new experiences—they had always thrilled him, and he had plunged without a second thought into wherever they would lead him. Now, however, he tried to reassure Shirley. "I promise I'll stay on the walkway and keep two safety lines on at all times."

"Be sure you do," said Shirley. "Don't forget that *Prometheus* is *not* in free-fall—it's under constant acceleration. If you let go of the safety line, she'll fly away from you. If you let that happen, I'll never speak to you again—literally."

With that sobering thought, Thomas let Shirley cycle him through the airlock. He stepped out the door onto the roughened portion of the outer hull that was made of magnetizable metal with tiny loops built into the surface. It was a gray path around the circumference of the ship, normally used for inspection of the outside seals of the portholes on the control deck. A similar path led upward to other areas needing inspection. Both magnetic grippers and Velcro footpads stuck equally well to the gray surface, and Thomas had both on the bottom of his spacesuit boots. He switched one of his safety lines to a metal stringer on one side of the path, and the other safety line to the stringer on the other side, then followed the path around until Gargantua came into view over the curved hull.

"Wow . . ." he whispered softly to himself, his heart pounding in awe at the sight of the colossal globe nearly filling the sky. "It sure looks bigger out here than it does when it's framed in a porthole." He got his electrocam out of its pouch and started taking pictures. Through the sausage fingers of his spacesuit he could feel, rather than hear, the electronic whistle as the liquid crystal shutter activated to take the picture, followed by the chitter of the microprocessor as it compressed the digital data representing the picture and loaded it into the memory chip. The piezoelectric acoustic generator that Electropix had added to the camera to reassure their customers that the picture was *really* taken and stored was not really of much help in vacuum. Down in the dark region of the south pole, which was in shadow during this "season" in Gargantua's 120-day "year," Thomas noticed some lightning flashes. He zoomed his lens in on them, but decided they were not artistic enough to photograph. He was sure George or Arielle were using the large spacecraft cameras to take the shots they needed for scientific purposes.

"Goddam strange!" Arielle, busy at a science console, sped slender fingers over the screen in front of her. "George! Jinjur! I keep watch on these clouds on south side as we approach and take pictures. Now I speed 'em all up, and look!" George and Jinjur switched their screen displays to match hers.

On the video display, Arielle revealed a massive weather pattern, spawned about mid-planet and drifting southward, but only briefly. Just as it was on the point of disappearing into the darkness of the south polar cap, it rebounded, went west against the prevailing winds, bounced off something else hidden in the southern polar region, and headed northward again.

"Bumped into something? Hidden in the dark, there?" asked Jinjur.

George manipulated the icons on the side of his screen, and soon, superimposed on the image, was a computer-generated map that showed the slightly oblate sphere of the gargantuan planet with latitude and longitude marks indicated by fine blue lines. The shadowed region of the planet was lightly hatched with gray lines. Near the south pole, inside the shadowed region, was a large feature in white, with dimensions indicated on it. It was a mound in the atmosphere, reaching up five thousand kilometers above the normal Gargantuan surface and spreading out thirty-five thousand kilometers—half as big as Jupiter. On top of the mound was a central peak as big around as the Earth, rising up another thousand kilometers. George pointed to the feature, and where his finger touched the screen a green blob appeared on their screens.

"That's where I noticed an atmospheric volcano during our first flythrough. . . ."

"George always quick to spot tits," teased Arielle. Indeed, the computer-generated image of the mound looked very much like a woman's breast.

George continued, ". . . so it's not surprising the storm bounced off that region—there's a constant outflow of air off that mound." They all watched as James ran the stop-motion sequence again. Sure enough, the storm ran into the computer generated drawing of the volcano at the point where it gave the first bounce. "But what is causing the second bounce? There was nothing at that point last time."

"There is now," said Arielle. "Lots of lightning. Wonder what it is?"

"Use our searchlight, like we did before," said Jinjur.

"Right!" replied George. He quickly reconfigured the screen on his navigation console display screen to show the relative positions in three-dimensional space of Gargantua, its moons, and *Prometheus*—along with the shadow cones that they cast and, most importantly for now, the expanding reflected light beam from the sail of *Prometheus*. It turned out that it didn't take much of a tilt of the sail to make the reflected light illuminate the southern polar region. George had James curve the light-sail slightly to concentrate the beam in the region around the volcano. The newly illuminated portion of Gargantua brought a gasp from the watchers, some of whom were watching screens, while others looked out the porthole on that side of the ship.

"Two tits!" exclaimed George over the comments. Sure enough, where there had once been one atmospheric volcano, there were now two, one slightly larger than the other. From hot spots deep in the core came geysers of liquid metallic hydrogen that spurted upward at high pressure to climb for twenty thousand kilometers through the thick atmosphere until they erupted into outer space. As the geysers rose, the metallic hydrogen, released from the internal pressure that kept it in its relatively dense metallic form, converted back into buoyant hydrogen molecules, then atoms, then ionized plasma as the kinetic energy in the stream was converted into heat. The "tits" of the atmospheric volcanos gave off continuous lightning flashes as the flowing hydrogen atoms rose into space, recombined back into hydrogen molecules, then fell in the strong gravitational field of the planet back onto the upper cloud layers. Now a very light gas instead of a heavy metal, the falling hydrogen built up into a permanent "high-pressure" area that slowly spread out in an atmospheric version of a lava shield and eventually flowed back into the surrounding atmosphere.

"Arielle!" commanded George. "You take the new one

and I'll resurvey the old one." The hands of the two atmospheric scientists quickly moved into rapid activity on their console screens, as they directed James in gathering as much scientific information as possible during their brief flyby.

"High-res UV photos of interior of caldera."

"Doppler radar map of flow velocities along flanks. . . ." The mechanical noises from the circular bank of science instruments in the center of the room increased as one sensor after another was brought into play.

Outside in the vacuum, Thomas was walking slowly along the gray path, keeping Gargantua in sight as *Prometheus* slowly rotated, his seventy-millimeter electrocam clicking and buzzing. They were moving so rapidly by Gargantua that the planet was changing phase with each passing minute. When he had first come outside, Gargantua was three-quarters lit. Now the terminator between the light and dark side cut the planet in half. The zoom lens moved in and out as he switched from taking an overall shot with different wavelength settings on his liquid crystal electrofilter to close-up shots of a particularly interesting looking curlicue at the tip of a weather front. When the searchlight beam from the sail swept onto the previously dark southern polar regions and exposed the twin volcanos, he reached into his lens pouch for his super-zoom lens.

"*Got* to get this!" he exclaimed, changing lenses, and the electrocam was soon back in action, cramming image after image into its large memory chip.

In the lounge, David and Deirdre sat up, amazed. They gazed in wonder at the two enormous, seething mountains, with their central jets giving off vivid flashes of lightning.

The watchers aboard *Prometheus*, as they took in the

awesome sight, reacted in their own ways. In the lounge, the symphony in David's mind swelled with organ tones; while outside, the camera in Thomas' hands took on a life of its own, focussing, shifting, closing in. Jinjur, knowing that all the possible forms of technical data were being efficiently gathered in by James and the team of scientists, concentrated on absorbing as much as she could of the magnificent, total sweep of the sight. Katrina, for once incapable of reducing to words the unfolding sight before her, was silent, enraptured by the weird beauty. Arielle's hands occasionally paused and quivered over a close-up image, as with only her eyes she soared and sailed through that turbulent atmosphere in an imaginary airplane. Carmen's scalp crawled and tingled; the violence out there awoke horrifying memories of the earthquake that had once ravaged her home. Among the many humans, two, on separate decks, shared a common emotion: in the minds of Reiki and Deirdre there was only room for joy, and gratitude for the privilege of seeing this wonder. The promise of scenes such as this was what had lured them, when the mission itself seemed a dream; and what had sustained them through the long dreary years of childishness, and illness, before their arrival at Rocheworld.

Then, quite suddenly, the searchlight beam faded and went out. All of Gargantua was now dark.

"What happened? I wasn't finished!" complained George.

"We have passed into Gargantua's shadow cone," James reminded him.

"I got good data on new tit," Arielle said contentedly, as she looked over the new information James had added to its computer map of the two features. "They need names," she finally decided, and after a brief period of thought, she added names beside the drawings on James' map—"Big Ma'am" on the newer, smaller volcano, and "Great Big Ma'am" on the older, larger one—while the whole southern polar region now had the name—"Gudunov Heaven."

There was a warning gong from the airlock, and an elated Thomas cycled thorough, his brown eyes sparkling. The minute Shirley got his helmet off, he started talking.

"Such great purples and pinks! You should've seen the sunset I got over a hurricane bigger than Jupiter! I can't wait to get these pictures in my image processor!" Impatiently he shucked off his suit, shoving the various parts at Shirley and the Christmas Bush, then, grabbing his camera, he headed up the central shaft to his apartment.

Slowly *Prometheus* continued on its way, carrying minds whose memories would never lose the incredible vastness of what they had seen. The tired encounter science crew, their senses overloaded almost to the point of physical shock, closed down their consoles and returned to their own confines, while the next shift came on to monitor the flight back out from behind Gargantua to catch up with the speeding Zulu in its close orbit around the giant planet.

Jinjur trotted down the carpeted aisle of the control deck and bounced easily up the central shaft of *Prometheus*, the low gravity provided by the modest acceleration of the sail always a satisfaction to her. She had been intrigued with the thought of what Thomas might have captured with his camera, so after a quick stop at the galley to get something to tide her over until dinner, she headed up the shaft to the living quarters decks.

Thomas' suite was on the same level as hers, two doors around. The room between theirs had once belonged to Dr. Wang, the ship's doctor. It was now sealed off.

William had died on the long trip out from an infectious cancer that had attacked nearly the entire crew. He had sacrificed his life by delaying the debilitating chemotherapy treatment on himself in order to insure the best treatment for the rest of the crew.

Reaching the second crew quarters floor, she swung around the railing, perched herself on her Velcro-bottomed slippers in front of Thomas' door, and pushed the doorbell button above the palm plate. As was her custom, while on the way up the shaft, she had signaled James to give advance notice of her approach to a crew member's quarters.

The door responded promptly to her ring by sliding sideways into its slot, and Jinjur entered Thomas' room, wedge-shaped like all the rest. To the left was the standard bathroom, with both the bathroom door and shower door open. Jinjur noticed that the shower head was up near the top of the shower; Jinjur kept hers lower down so she could reach it to adjust the spray head. To the right was the "personal office" area, but instead of a standard touch-screen console, bookcase, and writing desk, plus a few "shelves" for storing knickknacks, holoportraits, and other personal items, Thomas' whole wall was covered with a complex set of specialized instruments for carrying out intricate image processing of pictures. There were a few small monitor screens, but nothing like the standard console touch-screen.

Thomas was standing at the back of the apartment in the "living room," which had a large sofa on the right wall that butted up to the office equipment and faced the floor-to-ceiling double-sided viewwall that separated the living room area from the bedroom area. The back wall of the living room area was a smaller viewwall, set into a fake picture-window frame, usually set by most of the crew to some favorite "living picture" scene back on Earth, while the larger viewwall was used for entertainment videos. Thomas was by the larger viewwall, examining it closely, while behind him the small viewwall displayed a large image of Gargantua in crescent moon phase, obviously taken late in the recent encounter.

Before Jinjur could speak, Thomas was exulting.

"They're going to be wonderful! Sure it was dim, but as soon as I process them, we're going to see—" Suddenly, he remembered who she was, and years of training brought Thomas to taut attention in the presence of his commanding officer. "Excuse me, ma'am." Even the laxness of discipline brought about by their isolation and friendship couldn't erase the basic training some of the crew had undergone in their pasts.

He relaxed, however, as Jinjur waved him at ease and began to examine his photographs of Gargantua. Soon the two were silent, and the pictures were studied, Thomas moving back and forth from the viewscreen to his equipment to carefully brighten pixels, stretch spectrums, rectify areas, and combine adjacent areas.

"Ummm," murmured Jinjur. "Look at this volcano, just forming. Just a baby, kind of cute."

"Some baby," said Thomas. "Considering it's bigger than the Earth, but it's doing quite nicely, looks like."

"Kind of a shame we don't dare go any closer, really," said Jinjur. "But I know the moons will be spectacular enough, and since they have life-forms on them, there will be plenty to do there to keep us busy for the rest of our lives."

CHOOSING

The giant spaceship, slowed by its lightsail, finally matched orbits with Zulu. Deirdre had been intrigued with the preliminary reports coming in from this planet concerning the life-forms and quietly determined to be watching on the control deck as they approached. She stationed herself at a spare console next to Sam, who was on shift duty at the planetary science console, and matched her screen with his. All the biologists on board *Prometheus* were, at the moment, connected with Sam's screen in one way or the other, Katrina from the sick bay, where she was watching over John, Nels from a console that swung out over his regen tank, and Cinnamon from a portascreen monitor sitting on her lap while she took a coffee break from her hydroponics lab duties. She was sitting in the favorite break spot of the crew: the sofa in front of the flouwen habitat tank. The flouwen were not just swimming around in colorful display, however; they too were watching their underwater console through "eyes" formed on the ends of pseudopods.

Sam, who had previously explored Ganymede back

in the solar system, was explaining the resemblances.

"'S real simple, how it's made. The central core is rock, and that's all covered with water. The water is mostly frozen—all the way down to the rock. There're some geysers which form lakes that have a thick ice shelf around the edges. Zulu is so close to Gargantua it's tidally locked, with the inner pole always facing the big planet. The tidal pull is so strong that Zulu gets kinda squeezed out o' shape."

Tony, at the navigation console, brought *Prometheus* into a position where it matched orbital motion with Zulu.

"Jinjur?" Tony murmured to his imp.

"Yes?" she replied from the command console.

"I've arranged *Prometheus'* trajectory so that we will arrive just after local sunrise over the inner pole of Zulu, where the two surface exploration robots, *Splish* and *Splash*, are in contact with the two different species of intelligent aliens. That way they'll have the ambient light they need to transmit up real-time imagery as we talk with them. The morning sunlight period will last just three hours. There will be an eclipse period of ninety minutes while Zulu passes through Gargantua's shadow, then another three hours of daylight before sunset."

"Should be enough time," said Jinjur. "When is local sunrise?"

"One hour," replied Tony.

George, who was standing behind Jinjur, remarked, "We don't need to wait until sunrise to talk to the orbiter."

"You're right," said Jinjur. "James, put the orbiter on all imps so everyone can hear the report."

There was a slight pause as James set up the connections.

"This is *Jacques*," came a nasal tone from their imps. "I

am presently in a near-polar orbit of Zulu. I summarize my findings. On my initial approach to Zulu, I confirmed that Zulu is losing air and water vapor at a high rate because of its low gravity and the large geysers that shoot up hot water into the upper atmosphere and out into space, where they form a toroid of air and water centered about Zulu's orbital path. Much of it is collected again by Zulu during subsequent orbits, but some of it drifts outward, where it is captured by the next moon out, Zuni."

"Zuni makes out best," interjected Sam. "It also collects smog from Zouave. Richard figured out it's increasing in mass, while both Zouave and Zulu are losing."

"After exploring water toroid," continued *Jacques*, "I dropped off aeroshells containing the amphibious surface exploration vehicles and went into a polar orbit, where I began with a global survey of imagery, topography, gravity, and remote sensing of the composition and characteristics of the atmosphere and surface. The temperature on Zulu is well below freezing everywhere except near the hot water geysers. The surface gravity is twenty-one percent of Earth gravity. The day is 14.8 hours long. The atmosphere has a pressure that is eighty-one percent of Earth pressure and is mostly nitrogen gas and water vapor, with small amounts of both oxygen and carbon dioxide present."

"You'd expect oxygen and carbon dioxide in the atmosphere if both animal and plant life exist on the planet," remarked Deirdre. "I wonder if the air is breathable?"

"Not for you, li'l lady," said Sam kindly. "Not enough oxygen in it, although it isn't poisonous like Rocheworld. But we'd need suits, anyway, with the temperature what it is. Still, with that pressure, lightweight exploration suits ought to be enough."

Jacques continued on with its report on the exact dimensions of the triaxial shape of the planetoid and the variations in the thickness of the ice cap over the ocean.

"There are eighteen active large geysers on Zulu. Most of the geysers are grouped in bands around the two tidal bulges on the inner and outer poles. These are places where the strains on the crust would be a maximum . . ."

Jacques finally finished with its report. "Since the surface exploration vehicles discovered potentially intelligent life-forms, I did not repeat my orbital survey to improve the data statistics. Instead, I switched to my present near-polar elliptical orbit where the high oblateness of the gravity field of Zulu precesses my orbit enough to keep my apogee over the inner pole of Zulu where the exploration vehicles are stationed. In this manner, I can supply them maximum communications relay support."

At the center of the control deck, Jinjur looked out one of the portholes on the control deck at the mottled white marble which nearly filled the glass. Some of the darker round patches, indicating large lakes of open water, were now in sunlight. "Is it sunrise there yet?" she asked her imp, expecting James to answer.

"Barnard is just rising," came a tiny voice in reply instead. "This is *Splish* reporting. I am near the lake containing the largest geyser. With me are some members of the alien species who live on the ice around the geyser."

"This is *Splash*," said another tiny voice. "I am floating in a lake some distance away from the largest geyser. Below me are members of another alien species which live in the ocean. Since I cannot maintain radio contact with you while I am submerged, it is not possible for me to put you in direct contact with the underwater species, so I will transmit some video sequences of the creatures taken previously."

Their screens now showed an underwater scene looking down at the bottom of a moderately shallow portion of the ocean with reddish sunlight streaming in from above. At various places along the bottom could be seen small peaks of grayish pumice stone with smoky plumes of water coming from them, and broad shallow craters with bubbling sand at the bottom, indicating there were a number of volcanic vents and hot springs operating. Close to those vents and springs grew grayish-white bulbs of something that looked like sponges or coral. Close to them were various seaweeds through which darted small swimming and crawling creatures.

"I figure that water's hotter than a hundred cee, right there," remarked Sam. "The only thing keeps it from boiling is the pressure."

"Some sponges and seaweed I've seen would like that fine," murmured Deirdre.

Swimming lazily around each major vent field was a large fishlike creature with brown knobby armored skin, gill vents, and a short tail. Instead of swimming fins, it had four stubby finned legs. The head had two bulbous eyes and a large mouth full of vicious looking sharklike teeth. Coming out of the chest area below the mouth, looking something like a goatee, were four short stubby tentacles. Most of the creatures carried one or more stones in their tentacles, many with sharp points.

As the creatures drew near one another in their patrols around their perimeter, they displayed their teeth and rushed forward to shake their sharp stones at each other, while at the same time emitting complexly modulated roars that sounded like two elephant seals swearing at each other. Nothing much happened at these encounters except threats, and the participants usually withdrew and resumed their marches around their own territories.

Occasionally, one of the creatures would look inward at the territory that it was defending and spot some small fish or crawling animal which had ventured out from the protection of the seaweed. Then, it would drop its stone and, relieved of its ballast, use its four feet as fins to swim inward at amazing speed to capture its prey. Sometimes the prey looked very much like miniature versions of the four-legged, shark-toothed fish that had caught it.

"These are most unusual-looking fish," said Cinnamon, staring at the picture on her monitor screen.

"They look a little like sharks and a little like those fish on earth that were thought to be extinct, don't they?" said Deirdre.

"Yes, like coelacanths, only sharkier," said Katrina.

"Coelasharks," suggested Richard, who was staring over Sam's shoulder at the picture.

"Not bad," came a grudging multivoiced murmur over the imp network, and the name was adopted.

"What can you tell us about the coelasharks, *Splash*?" asked Sam.

"They seem to be semi-intelligent," said *Splash*. "In a savage or perhaps presavage stage. They are obviously solitary and territorial, with the strongest coelasharks controlling a particular vent field and using it to feed themselves—and only themselves. I have not seen evidence of mating pairs, or of a coelashark taking care of children. In fact, there seems to be no compunction whatsoever against eating smaller individuals of their own species. Although they do not have a cooperative social structure, which would indicate a high level of intelligence, they do use tools. Those sharp stones that they carry in their tentacles are not only used for ballast, so they can use their powerful legs to move across the ocean bottom, but they are also used as weapons when a challenge display turns into a real battle. These occur when a volcanic vent dies out, or a coelashark gets too large to be supported by its vent and needs a larger one. The sharp stone can be used to stab at the throat and eyes of an opponent, or to pry open its mouth if it has obtained a grip. I have also seen coelasharks change the stone in their tentacles from one with a sharp point to one with a thin blade, which is then used to open up a clamshell to get at the meat inside."

"Using tools definitely shows signs of intelligence," remarked Katrina.

"In addition to tools," continued *Splash*, "they also seem to have a crude language."

"They do?" exclaimed Jinjur. "That's important. Have you learned to speak with them?"

"Yes," replied *Splash*. "Early in my explorations under the oceans of Zulu, I came near the territorial vent of a coelashark almost as large as I was. It was nearly two meters long, and thicker and more massive than a human. Other coelasharks had avoided confronting me because of my large size, but this one attempted to eat me. I pulled in my antenna, stowed my imager and other sensors, closed my sample hold door, and let it attack. After breaking a few teeth, it gave up. When I didn't attack it in return, it was puzzled. When I took one of the fish that I had collected from my sample hold and gave the fish to the coelashark to eat, it was astonished. After a while, it realized that I was no threat to its territory, so it started making sounds at me, obviously attempting to converse with me. Instead of continuing with my explorations, I stayed to talk with it and observe its interactions with its neighbors. Finally, after many months of observation and effort, I was able to converse with it. I have built up a translation program containing their vocabulary and grammar. The translation program is not a large one, as the vocabulary of the coelasharks is limited and their grammar is simple. I am presently sending my most recently updated version through the data channel to James."

"Very good, *Splash*," said Jinjur. "James, make sure that the coelashark translation program gets distributed to all the computers on the exploration vehicles and suits so we can talk to a coelashark if we happen to run into one."

"It will be the flouwen that would be most likely to encounter a coelashark," James reminded her. "I will make sure that the program is included in the computers in their drysuit backpacks, also. After examining the program, however, I find it is so simple that I suspect that the flouwen, with their large memory and high intelligence quotient, could easily memorize it in a very short time. I am now in the process of transmitting it to them in their tank."

Soon, some flouwen remarks came over the open imp network.

◊Interesting. All the words mean food, things, actions, or curses.◊

⊓Simple grammar. Very simple phrases. Mostly threats.⊓

☆EASY!☆

The human connections to the imp network were silent for a while as the humans realized their inadequacies in the face of the greatly superior intelligence and memory of the flouwen.

"I wonder what kind of an IQ that takes," mused Richard finally.

"Since the present flouwen buds are significantly smaller than their primaries, their intelligence quotient is proportionately lower," answered James. "I would estimate that the IQ of the buds is . . ."

"DON'T SAY IT!" yelled Katrina. "I don't want to know!"

"Very well, Katrina," replied James, with a programmed note of contriteness in its usually superior sounding tone.

"Don't vex yourself," Deirdre comforted Katrina. "It means naught to us; we've not the IQ to comprehend what a really high IQ means."

Cinnamon noticed a flicker of activity in the flouwen's habitat tank and looked up from her lap screen. The three flouwen had stopped looking at their underwater console and were now crouched in opposite corners of the wedge-shaped tank. They had assumed the shape of coelasharks and were making roaring noises at each other.

"James!" she said through her imp. "What's going on?"

"They are practicing speaking like coelasharks," said James. "Now that they have memorized the vocabulary and learned the grammar, they need to gain some experience so that they can converse fluently with the coelasharks when they encounter them."

"The rest ought to see this. I presume you have an imager that covers what goes on in the tank. Send it to the others." Almost instantly, a picture of the inside of the flouwen habitat tank, with its large red, white and purple versions of coelasharks appeared on her lap monitor.

"Little Red!" Cinnamon called out, knowing that James would connect the link through her imp properly. "What are you three doing? Why are you shaped like coelasharks?"

Little Red stopped in mid-roar to answer. ☆James told us how coelasharks talk! *Great* way to talk!☆

◊If we take shape of coelasharks, then we think more like coelasharks, so we can talk more like coelasharks,◊ Little White explained.

"The method-acting school of language lessons," interjected Richard sarcastically.

"What's the language like?" Cinnamon asked.

⊓We will speak as coelasharks do, and James will translate our words for you,⊓ said Little Purple.

◊Some meaning may be lost in translation,◊ warned Little White.

☆Especially threats!☆ added Little Red. ☆They loudest and most FUN!☆

The three flouwen returned to their corners and resumed their coelashark shapes. Soon they were rushing at each other and emitting shouts and roars that could be easily heard through the thick tank walls.

☆Come any closer and I'll *bite* your leg off!☆ yelled Little Red.

⊓Listen to the weakling threaten me!⊓ bellowed Little Purple in response.

◊You're both so timid, you'd belly-up at the sight of blood!◊ roared Little White.

Aghast, Cinnamon said, "*That* is the language of an intelligent life-form?"

"At least that answers one question," came Jinjur's voice over the imp network. "We certainly will be prepared to interact adequately with *one* of the alien species on Zulu. Three of us can even talk directly with them without having to have a computer act as an intermediary. Now let's see if we are similarly prepared for the other one."

With difficulty, the flouwen were made to calm down and stop playing coelasharks, for it was now time for the report by *Splish*, and the flouwen should hear that, too, although in all probability they would not be interacting with these land-dwelling creatures as much as the humans would be.

"This is *Splish*," came the tiny voice from the surface as their console screens showed a computer-generated image of Zulu with a green dot on it near the largest of the clear water lake regions of the icy white moon. "The green dot indicates my present position." The moon grew in size as the view zoomed rapidly in on the lake shore containing the green dot. As more details became clear, the round lake shore broke up into jagged edges, while in the lake were floating large icebergs which had calved off the shoreline.

"Looks just like an ice shelf region in Antarctica, icebergs and all," murmured Sam.

"Except there, you have a small cold ice-covered land region completely surrounded by a warm body of water, while here you have a small warm body of water completely surrounded by cold ice-covered land," pontificated Richard.

As the zoom proceeded, some structure and coloring began showing up in the region around the lake, which soon turned into a semiorganized pattern of differing shades of greenish-blue. The zoom came to an end, and the computer-generated image was replaced by a live picture of one of the aliens, taken by the video camera extending from the top of the amphibious exploration vehicle. All of the crew had seen still images of the aliens that *Splish* had sent back previously, but it was different seeing one of these bewildering creatures in motion.

Splish had learned early in its interactions with the aliens that they called themselves "coverers-of-the-ice," where "ice" was used in a generic sense, similar to the way that humans used the word "earth" as meaning "terra-firma" rather than "dirt."

At first, when the humans referred to the aliens among

themselves, they tried to use the correct name, "coverers-of-the-ice." That proved too long, and an abbreviation, "icecoverers," took its place. That still proved awkward and the name "icerugs" was finally coined. Despite the protests of Reiki and Deirdre, it stuck. James, however, assured them that the icerugs would never hear what the humans really called them, for the translation program would always change it to their correct name.

The strange being appearing on their screens seemed to be half-plant and half-animal. The camera was now panning over the large plant portion, which covered the ice like a carpet, a carpet with a purplish blue-green color like an unripe plum. Almost an acre in extent, the carpet was thin enough to reveal even slight contours and bumps in the ice underneath. The fine plum-colored threads that covered the carpet had a light-absorbing velvetlike texture.

"That is certainly an efficient surface for trapping the reddish photons from Barnard," remarked Katrina. "There must be photosynthesis going on in that portion of the body."

"The blue-green plum color is distinctly different from chlorophyll-green, however," said David, who possessed a color sense as discriminating as his tonal sense.

"Probably a similar molecule that works better with red light," responded Katrina. "I can't wait to get a sample to analyze."

Deirdre's eyes shot a green glare at her. "Aye, and would you be extending a finger of your own, in return?"

The video scan stopped on the "node," the animal part of the icerug. The "foot" of the node consisted of a thick plum-colored pedestal about a half-meter high, which rose smoothly and seamlessly out of the carpet which it was riding. On top of the thick pedestal was a spherical "head" the size of a large beach ball. In the middle of the head was a slit mouth with tiny sharp teeth that were occasionally visible. Between the head and the pedestal were four stubby tentacles, most of them in continuous motion, as if the creature were nervous. Two of the tentacles held artifacts and were quite different in length, indicating that they were alterable as well as flexible. Extending from the top of the head was a large single eye on a flexible stalk. The entire node, except for the lens of the eye, was covered with the same plum-colored velvet as the rest of the body. The bright owllike eye with a pink iris was staring fixedly at the camera. The eye blinked occasionally by closing a six-leaved nictating membrane over the pupil. The leaves of the membrane overlapped, somewhat like the six-leaved aperture stop in a camera.

"Except for its size, the eye looks just like a human eye," remarked Richard.

"Or a bird eye, or an alligator eye, or an octopus eye," said Cinnamon. "There seems to be only one good way for nature to make a video camera out of jelly."

"This individual is named Pink-Orb," continued *Splish*. "One of their chief scientists, with the specialty of astronomy. We spent many months together while I learned their language. I have built up a translation program that I believe is adequate to allow you to converse with them, although it is certainly not complete. Fortunately, many of the words and phrases that are used in ordinary conversation are honorific and polite rather than containing any real information, which makes translation easier."

"A sign of a civilized being," said Reiki.

"Can we talk with it, do you think, James?" asked Jinjur.

"The translation program that *Splish* has transferred up looks adequate," replied James. "The exploration robot has a small portable video display screen stored away in its sample hold just for this contingency. I have instructed it to take it out and display it to the alien. A picture of you and George is now on the screen."

The icerug came closer to the small screen. The motion brought a gasp from a number of mouths.

"It *glides*!"

"Look how the skin moves up the pedestal, over the head region, and down the other side, as if it were moving *under* the skin."

"Well," said George. "Since we have a translation program, let's give it a try."

Reiki, with her obsession for politeness, was concerned that George would say something that would offend the alien, getting them off to a bad start. However, George, to do him credit, treated the strange native with his usual ceremonial tact.

"Greetings, great and noble one!" he started. "I am known as Colonel George Gudunov and this is Major General Virginia Jones, leader of our expedition. We are humans from the planet Earth around a distant star. We are presently in the large circle-shaped machine that you see in your sky. We wish to visit your most magnificent world to learn more about its wonders. We wish to meet you. We have come in peace, and do not desire your land or your property. We will stay for a short while, and then must leave again. But we will leave machines like the one that is there now so that we can talk with you in the future, if you wish. Will our visit be welcomed?"

The sides of the spherical head of the icerug began to vibrate visibly and a deep booming reply rang in the ears of the humans. The translation program on *Splish* automatically converted the booming tones and simulcast the translation over their imps.

"Welcome, great and noble visitors from the most magnificent planet Earth. I am called Pink-Orb and my people are called coverers-of-the-ice."

In the sky behind Pink-Orb, clouds of water vapor began to rise up into the sky.

"The geyser is starting to erupt, James," said Richard. "Is it going to be a big one?"

"No," reported James. "It is only Zuni passing by, as it does every two Zulu days. The eruption should peak in about an hour and a half, then fade off."

"It will be interesting to watch it from the point of view of someone underneath it," remarked Katrina.

"The Munificent God of the Sea awakens," said Pink-Orb, rolling its eye around to gauge the height of the geyser. "Unfortunately, it will not be possible to communicate during the eruption because of the noise. The great Colonel George Gudunov and the Major General Leader Virginia Jones will please excuse me while I accept the bounty that falls to me." The node moved off to the center of its carpetlike body and lifted its eye to the sky to watch the rising jet of water.

The geyser rapidly built up in intensity, and shortly after that, a mixture of rain, slush, and snow began to fall. *Splish* was kept busy keeping the lens clean.

Richard looked down at his planetary science screen, which contained a high-resolution image showing the geyser from above. "Wow! Look at Big Bertha blow!"

"Big Bertha!" exclaimed Cinnamon. "That has to be the worst name for a geyser man could invent. Big Bertha was a gun—not a geyser!"

"All right," replied Richard agreeably. "What *should* we call it?"

Reiki added in a quiet but firm tone, "The proper choice for the name of something on some other species' planet, is the name that *they* choose for it, not one some human has chosen."

"The problem," said David, "is that the word is probably a proper noun, which may or may not have a meaning that can be translated, *and* we can't use the icerug word directly, since we can't imitate the icerug's pronunciation without using a synthesizer."

"Manannán," suggested Deirdre.

"What was that?" asked Jinjur.

Deirdre glanced up. "Pink-Orb called the geyser the Munificent God of the Sea. In Celtic myths, the god of the sea was called Manannán, and the fishermen asked him for fine rich harvests."

"Good enough," said Jinjur. "Let's change the name of the geyser to Manannán. Anything's better than using the name of a World War One cannon. I like the sound of it, and it'll be easy to spell in the report."

"There's an accent over the final 'a'," said Deirdre wickedly, "but I doubt anyone will notice if you leave it out."

"How did you hear of such a god?" whispered Katrina curiously. "I always liked mythology myself—it's fun to allude to those old gods in a poem—but I never heard of that one."

Deirdre's eyes did not look up as she answered briefly. "Curious about my name, I was, so I read all the books I could find about Celtic mythology. Most people are curious about their names, aren't they? You catch any mention of what means yourself, and like to follow up the stories and what they mean. I once spent some time on the Isle of Man, named after Manannán."

With a roar, the geyser shot even higher than before.

"Wow!" repeated Richard, trying to be as sincere as he could. "Look at Manannán blow!"

"Better," said Reiki approvingly, giving him a warm smile.

The spray of rain and slush turned into snow as the geyser rose higher and the water had longer to fall through the frigid air. Soon the plum-colored carpet was covered with a light blanket of snow that melted almost as fast as it fell. Suddenly, something fell to the ground between the camera and Pink-Orb.

"What was that?" exclaimed Katrina. "James, replay that in slow motion for me." She stared carefully at the screen on her monitor as James showed her an enlarged view of the falling object. "Looks like a piece of seaweed."

"It is," confirmed James. "The spectrum, adjusted for the different lighting conditions, of course, matches that of one of the many plants seen by *Splash* around the volcanic vents."

The geyser slowed, and Pink-Orb dropped its eye and arms, and started to return. As it did so, the strand of seaweed resting on the plum-colored carpet in the foreground seemed to come to life.

"The seaweed is moving!" exclaimed Richard.

"No!" replied Katrina. "The carpet underneath it is moving and carrying it along like a cork on a wave."

They watched as the seaweed stalk was transported by ripples in the icerug's body toward the approaching node, where it was picked up by a tentacle and carried to Pink-Orb's mouth.

"It's eating it!" exclaimed Katrina. "Pink-Orb was right to call the geyser the Munificent God of the Sea. In addition to getting nourishment from photosynthesis, it must get a portion of its food from the fallout of the geyser."

Pink-Orb returned to stare into the camera, the big

pink eye only occasionally blinking when a large snow-flake fell on it. Its mouth was busy chewing on the seaweed, but that didn't prevent it from conversing, since it talked by vibrating the surface of its "head."

"I apologize to the great and mighty visitors from the sky, Major General Leader Virginia Jones and Colonel George Gudunov, for the delay in returning to converse with you. We have no knowledge of who or what you are, but all the coverers-of-the-ice most urgently wish to meet you and learn more about your amazing machines, such as the Crawler-on-Ice-and-Water that talks with us, and the Circle-in-the-Sky that does not fall. If you come in peace to teach us about these things, you will be most welcome."

George looked at Jinjur. "I think, Jinjur, that the translation program is good enough," he said.

"You're right about that," said Jinjur. "*And*, Pink-Orb's invitation is a good enough excuse for me. Zulu will be the site for our next landing."

The duty shifts changed again, and those going off shift gathered in the lounge for dinner.

"If it's to be Zulu, I'll want to modify our exploration suits," said Shirley, as she finished her dessert of algae-ice cream cubes covered with hot chocolate from James' chemical synthesizers. "If I add an air concentrator to take the right amounts of oxygen and nitrogen out of the Zulu atmosphere, we won't have to carry anything but an emergency oxygen supply to be used in case the concentrator fails. But, with ambient temperatures low enough to be lethal, James and I will have to make sure the heaters are in top shape."

"Make sure they fit right, too," said Katrina. "Those gloves of mine are still too big, and it's hard to make precise cuts for samples, much less pick them up, with those bulky fingers."

"That's what tools are for," said Shirley patiently. "You don't need to use fingers at all."

"I know," said Katrina stubbornly, "but when you're working with live animals, it helps if you can give them a comforting pat occasionally."

Shirley sighed and Deirdre shared her feeling. "I doubt if any alien animal can interpret your 'comforting pat' as anything more than another alien touch. As a scientist, how can you give in so easily to anthropomorphism?"

"Oh, I don't, really," said Katrina hastily. "I appreciate how different they are. I just wish to be nice to them, as well." The small biochemist tucked herself more deeply into the cushions of the communal lounge and selected another colored strand for her needle. The little basket beside her overflowed with bright threads, destined to be part of the intricate pattern in the frame on her lap. "It's not just as scientists we're here, anyway. It's as people living lives—and caring about the creatures around us!"

Shirley sighed again. This was an old debate. It promised to continue indefinitely, although Jinjur's firm command kept any unscientific meddling with the aliens at a minimum. She herself maintained a brisk attitude of detachment even from the flouwen, likeable as they were.

Deirdre had regarded Katrina's attempts to treat Foxx as a cuddly pet with amusement; Foxx had handled that situation with cool disdain. Lately, however, Deirdre had been puzzling anew over their situation. Forever to be among these, and possibly other strange living creatures, was it not perhaps better to enter, albeit cautiously, into their existence as much as they could, rather than to remain aloof and disinterested observers? And yet, as she knew very well, even the slightest interaction between species might result in calamity, despite the best intentions of all concerned.

"The planned and stated purpose of our mission is to explore, to report, to learn—lots of other things," said Shirley firmly. "I don't recall a single mention of—doing good!"

The contempt in her tone aroused Carmen. "If there's a choice, wouldn't you do what's right, rather than what's wrong?" she asked with some heat.

"Who's to say what's right?" asked Thomas from the other side of the lounge. He chuckled. "Of course, if my old Gran were here, there'd be no problem. We'd just ask her. She never has any doubts!"

"Old people on Earth seldom do," said Carmen. "But then, they still have a faith."

Deirdre slid from the lounge as silently and swiftly as a breath. At any hint of the discussion turning in the direction of religion, she always vanished. She swung up the central shaft and headed toward her room. Warring within her were the passionate desire to see these strange creatures for herself and, almost as strong, the feeling they should be left alone. By the time she reached her quarters, however, the first had won out, and she flung Foxx to the sofa and dashed off after her in a glorious game of chase, as she exulted in hope that she would be given the chance to explore this frozen world.

Before the crew could plan their landing, they had to refine and update the global survey of Zulu which *Jacques* had begun. Ponderously, the lightship moved into a polar orbit around the planet, while the humans and James collated the data from the multitude of sensors focused on the icy surface below. The north and south poles proved to be like their namesakes on Earth—at the height of Earth's worst glacial period. They had permanent caps of ice, many kilometers deep, with the ocean frozen right down to the surface of the rocky core. At the leading pole, where the air and water vapor from the gas toroid fell inward on the moon, the ocean was also ice-bound and frozen clear to the bottom, but here the ice was thinner.

David's sharp eyes picked out an interesting pattern on the topological maps prepared by the laser altimeter. "Look. Here's a series of broad bands, coming from both the north and south poles," he indicated with a slender fingertip. "Then they become indistinct at about the equator. What causes that?"

"The ice is flowing," replied Sam. "It piles up at the north and south poles, and then flows thousands of kilometers to the four poles in the equatorial regions, where it slowly warms up and sublimates."

"If an average temp of twenty degrees below freezing at the equator can be called warm," mentioned David. "Let's see if that pattern shows up on the trailing pole." He flipped the picture skillfully. "No, all I see is snow."

"That's because all the storms end up there and dump most of their snow, hiding the ridge pattern. The glacier cap must be really thick there. The molecules of water on this planet really have an exciting life cycle," continued Sam dreamily. "Start out as vapor, falling in from that big ol' gas toroid orbiting out in space, change to storm cloud droplets that spread out over the planet, land as snow on the north, south, and trailing poles, freeze into ice, slide out to the inner and outer poles, then melt to form the geyser lakes. Geyser heats them till they're vapor again, and squirts them back out into space to form the gas toroid again."

Thomas, doing his regular stint of duty as lightsail pilot, usually had little to do at the navigation console, so he spent a good deal of his time engaged in astrodynamics studies. Using the powerful radar on *Prometheus*, he checked the exact position of a transponder that he had left on the surface of Rocheworld, and one that he had in an orbiter close to Gargantua, and plotted two more points on a graph which he had been building since they had arrived at Barnard. Each successive point was approaching closer and closer to an integer line on the graph. He grunted in satisfaction at the result. The ratio of the period of Gargantua's circular orbit around Barnard, to the period of Rocheworld's elliptical orbit around Barnard, to the corotation period of the two lobes of Rocheworld about their center of mass was exactly 480:160:1—now to better than *one* part in fifteen places. Every third orbit, Rocheworld came close to Gargantua, where the gravitational pull of the giant planet added just enough energy and angular momentum to compensate for the tidal losses, locking the three periods to each other.

He also checked the transponders on the penetrators which he had placed on the two small inner moons of Gargantua—Zwingli and Zoroaster. Zwingli, 32 kilometers in radius, was in an orbit that was 40 kilometers lower than Zoroaster, which was 30 kilometers in radius. Since the 40 kilometer difference in the orbits was less than the 62-kilometer sum of the moon radii, it would be expected that they would collide. But as Zwingli, traveling faster according to the laws of orbital dynamics, would overtake the slower Zoroaster, their joint gravitational interaction would slow Zoroaster even more, sending it outward, while Zwingli's speed was increased, sending it inward, just enough so the two avoided a collision. After they had passed, the gravitational attraction was reversed, restoring the two moons to their original orbits.

"Hmmm," mused Thomas, looking at the data. "Looks like they will be keeping up that do-si-do for another few hundred thousand years at least."

He then took a look at the dynamics of the whole Barnard system by bringing up a computer simulation and running the planets and moons back and forth in time at high-speed. Suddenly, he stopped the motion at a particular point.

"That's right!" he said to himself as he noticed a certain configuration of the moons around Gargantua. "Nearly forgot that event was coming up, because of all the excitement about meeting Pink-Orb." He set up his screen and asked James to connect him with George and Jinjur at the control console.

"Yes, Thomas?" replied Jinjur through their imp link.

"I almost forgot to mention it—although I'm sure James would have mentioned it soon if I hadn't—there is going to be a quadruple conjunction about twenty-six hours from now. That should produce an extremely high tidal stress on Zulu and activate all the geysers, especially Manannán at the inner pole."

"Quadruple conjunction?" queried Jinjur.

"Well," said Thomas. "Technically, from the viewpoint of someone on Gargantua, it's a triple conjunction and an opposition. Three moons will be lined up on one side of Gargantua, while Barnard will be on the other side of Gargantua. Copy my screen and I'll show you." James set up a copy of Thomas' display on Jinjur's command console, and Thomas ran the moons and planets through their motions.

"First," he said. "Zulu, in its 14.7-hour orbit, will be catching up with Zuni in its 29.9-hour orbit, as it does every 28.9 hours or about once every two Zulu days. This joint conjunction of the two moons causes most of the tidal action on Zulu, an eight-meter pulse tide that lasts for three and a half hours. At the same time, they both will be catching up with Zouave in its 48.3-hour orbit. This triple conjunction will add Zouave's two-meter high tide on top of the eight meter Zulu tide. In addition, all this will occur at high noon, so Barnard will be lined up with the three moons, but on the other side of Gargantua. In any case, its three-to-four meter tide will be added to all the others, for a total tide of some fourteen meters. On Earth, we only see tides like that at the Bay of Fundy. That pull outward on the inner and outer poles should produce a very large strain on the crust, activating all the geysers."

"Wait a minute," said Katrina, who had been listening in from her planetary science console. "Zuni and Zouave are orbiting further out than Zulu and are going over the outer pole. I can see their gravity pulling up the outer pole region— but shouldn't they pull *in* on the inner pole region, not outward?"

"You're right that gravity pulls, Katrina," explained Thomas. "But since the rocky core of Zulu is in free-fall, it *too* is pulled by the outer moons—pulled right out from under the water and ice on the inner pole—which, being further away from the outer moons, is not pulled as much as the core. From the viewpoint of someone on Zulu, the net effect is an outward pull on both the inner and outer poles, producing two bulges. That's why the tides come twice a day on Earth."

A day later, everyone was awake to watch the quadruple conjunction. Tony had put *Prometheus* into a powered elliptical orbit with its apogee within sight of the inner pole so they would stay in sight of the geysers during most of the eruption period, yet the sail stayed outside the shadow cone of Gargantua, so it could illuminate the geyser during the noonday eclipse period when Barnard went behind Gargantua. Tony remained at the navigation console past the normal end of his shift partially to make sure *Prometheus* kept its beam pointed at the right geyser, and partially to free up Thomas to take pictures from outside.

Everyone else, plus the flouwen in their tank, was watching the view from the big telescope in the science bay Linda was operating. She also arranged to capture the infrared version in the multispectral imager.

Shirley was at one of the porthole windows, keeping one eye on Thomas walking around the outer hull and one eye on Gargantua, whose immense presence nearly filled the window of the porthole. Zouave had long ago disappeared into the shadow cone of Gargantua, and Zuni had soon followed. Both were barely visible dark gray ghosts in the black sky, dimly illuminated by the light scattered from the cloud-tops around Gargantua's rim. Just then, the moon below them faded and went out as it entered Gargantua's shadow. Only one small spot on the surface was illuminated.

"Zulu is within forty minutes of conjunction," reported Shirley.

"There was already activity at each of the geysers before we entered shadow," responded Richard.

Shirley noticed that Thomas was hanging over the safety stringer, camera in action. She looked down with her modest human eye, trying to see what Thomas was seeing through his zoom lens. Through the shifting clouds of water vapor remaining from the preliminary activity, she could barely discern the round dark geyser lake area on the mottled gray-white surface. Looking curiously artificial, the black spot was in reality, she knew, a lake of water, kept melted by the furious heat coming up from the core of the planetoid. Frustrated by the inadequacy of her eyes, she left the porthole window and went to look at the telescope image of the Manannán geyser like everyone else.

They all watched, almost breathless, as the water vapor clouds over the lake thickened and increased as the geyser erupted. Rising toward them, clearly visible, and with an almost solid shape of its own, was a column of boiling water. Swiftly it ascended, becoming thicker as it rose, until the awed observers were able to see clearly that the water was now tens of kilometers above the surface. At the height of the eruption, huge quantities of water began to fall back toward the surface, blown by the eddying winds far from the parent pool, changing to cool water nearby, and farther out to sleet, and farthest away of all, to snow. For nearly thirty minutes the incredible flow boiled up, was transformed, and fell back to the ice. Finally, slowly, the jet of water began to lower, although still spewing forth vast volumes of hot water into the air, the water vapor rising into space and the liquid water falling on the surrounding countryside. Almost reluctantly, the giant geyser subsided, grumbling, and finally returned to the surface of the lake, bubbling violently in its final spasms of activity.

No one wanted to speak. From inside the flouwen habitat tank, Little Red broke the silence with a very small, soft, ☆Wow!☆

George and Jinjur chuckled. "That's the word, all right."

The quadruple conjunction maximum geyser eruption was over, not to occur again for 68 Earth days—or 111.5 Zulu days, for the next eruption would occur at local midnight, when Barnard would be behind Zulu, but illuminating Gargantua, so instead of having to use *Prometheus*, the geyser would be fully illuminated, although weakly, by planetlight from the giant planet.

One of the things which had to be decided was where the lander would set down. Since much of the area around Manannán geyser was covered with bodies of coverers-of-the-ice, this required some negotiation with the icerugs.

Those on the bridge listened, totally absorbed and bemused, to the conversation between James, the robot crawler *Splish*, and the icerug Pink-Orb.

"When the humans come down out of the sky to visit your world, they will be arriving in a machine that rides on a strong wind made of flame. It will be putting forth a very loud noise, great heat, and a strong hot wind," explained James. "You must tell us of an area near you where the noise and heat and strong hot wind will do no harm."

"Could have been more tactfully requested," grumbled George, and Reiki, listening, agreed silently.

"I understand," said the deep booming voice.

"When you have selected a suitable landing site, you will take the Crawler-on-Ice-and-Water to that place so it can direct the humans to it."

"I understand," came the alien response.

George swiveled in his chair, glanced at Reiki, and instantly understood her look of dismay. Firmly overriding James, George spoke in his slowest, most orotund bass: "We come to share knowledge of our world and knowledge of yours. We are glad to know that you exist, as we do, and we intend to do only good as we meet and converse. We are extremely grateful for the opportunity to visit your world, which is so different from anything we have ever seen before. Please show our machine a place where our lander will not hurt or annoy you or the others of your—" he thought desperately for a word "—kind," he concluded rather lamely. There was a brief delay.

"I understand," was the laconic response of the strange being.

"It understands," added *Splish*'s tiny computer voice.

"Oh, well, I felt better for it," muttered George, and grinned at Reiki's smile of approval.

Selecting the ten members of the exploring crew was Jinjur's job as Commander of the Barnard Star Expedition. Although she outranked George, she valued his judgment highly and had no hesitation in talking over the possibilities before each mission.

"Got to have good pilots for the rocket lander and the *Dragonfly* airplane, of course. I thought Arielle for this one." In fact, Arielle was usually selected, for the sound reason that she was simply the best pilot aboard. Her diminutive frame and elfin looks concealed a cool and calculating calm, which, with training and experience, had made her able to deal with any crisis in flight as easily as a bird shifts its wings.

"Several of the others are competent pilots, too, of course. Shirley, then, and Thomas, and Cinnamon. Shirley's good at coping with repairs, if needed, and Thomas is almost as good a lander pilot as Arielle."

"Besides, think of the pictures he'll get!" added George.

"Yeah, we'll have to limit him on the amount of camera stuff he can take along, or he'll have the lander full," agreed Jinjur. "Cinnamon's ichthyology training just might be a good thing to have along for understanding the coelasharks. I'm including Katrina for her biology background, as well as filling the primary medic slot for the ground crew."

"I suggest both Sam and Richard for this excursion, too, Jinjur," said George. "As geoscientists with experience on the ice-moons Ganymede and Callisto, they're the best people to get a real understanding of this place. All that ice, and all those boiling geysers! They'll have a great time."

"Sounds good," said Jinjur. "And David to coddle the computers, if they need it, and they might in those temperatures. And Deirdre—this will be her first chance at exploring. Her knowledge of biology and exotic zoology makes her a natural for trying to figure out the workings of the coelasharks and the icerugs. She also might be able to teach them some hydroponics."

Privately, George doubted that Deirdre would presume to try to teach anything foreign to the natives—she had always been such a cool observer of life around her, but he dismissed the thought for the much more interesting one of whether or not he, himself, might go.

"With Cinnamon, Katrina, and Deirdre on the landing party, Nels will have no one to run the hydroponics deck," George reminded her. "Should we really send all of them?"

"With Nels to direct me, I can handle the routine work on the hydroponics deck with the Christmas Bush motile," reminded James.

"Well, that fills up the slots on the exploration team—except for the commander slot," said Jinjur.

There was a long and pregnant pause.

"Well, George," said Jinjur, grinning warmly at the hopeful face. The two had shared a great deal over the years, and he didn't really need to look so blatantly wishful. "One of us has stay on *Prometheus* to mind the store, both of us would love to go down to visit Zulu, and each of us has had a chance to go on one of the two previous missions. So, for this one we'll choose scientifically as hell. . . ." George looked puzzled, but almost instantly grinned. He knew this woman very well indeed.

"We'll use statistical science," declared Jinjur, producing a gold coin from her tightest pocket. "I borrowed this from Red. It's the only one on board. Heads or tails?"

George left the control room, almost literally walking on air. Jinjur would have the fun of telling everyone the chosen roster, but he certainly didn't begrudge her that. He'd also succeeded in not being envious, when she commanded the return to Rocheworld, six months ago. But he was jubilant at his luck while busily running over in his mind all the necessary preparations that must be made for the landing.

Dropping down the central shaft, he nearly collided with Arielle and David, who were ascending. They looked at him searchingly, but were silent. Briefly, George considered waiting for Jinjur to notify them both officially of their selection, and then compromised by giving them a hugely meaningful grin and wink. The pair responded with equally silent leaps of joy, and their personal imps, monitoring all this physical activity without verbalization, made notations in the section of memory James had reserved for the task of trying to understand the logic of human behavior. So far, the giant computer was still baffled by many of the things that humans did. The three then went to the airlock in the ceiling of the hydroponics deck to check over the lander they were going to be using.

"And make sure everything is in good shape," George reminded them unnecessarily. "Nothing like an eyeball check, although, of course, James—" He stopped. They all knew James and the Christmas Bush had the lander, as well as all the rest of the equipment, under constant scrutiny and maintenance.

The others selected for the mission reacted according to character. As predicted, Thomas immediately began the arduous task of choosing which electrocameras and lenses were the most vital, most impervious to cold, and most dependable. Reluctantly, he abandoned the quick idea of bribing some of the others out of their allotted space on the lander. Suddenly excitement hit him. Of all things, he loved seeing something new, and what could be newer than this peculiar planet? He left his room and went down to the galley to get a snack. While practically dancing through the lounge, he met Katrina, bouncing along in her own glee.

"You, too?" she cried. With mutual whoops, they seized each other firmly and spun in a wild polka, around and around the large lounge until they were both breathless. With an enthusiastic hug they parted, Thomas heading for the galley while Katrina shot up the central shaft to the hydroponics deck. She found Cinnamon, joyfully congratulating herself with a song, but Deirdre was gone.

In her own comfortable quarters on the deck below, Reiki was listening to Deirdre in one of her rare moments of volubility. As always, when excited, the pure Irish of Deirdre surfaced, and she practically chanted as she revelled in the thought of an adventure. "I'll be out on the surface of a new world! I've been hoping and wishing for this chance so *hard*, Reiki! Even dreaming of it, I've been, in my dreams I'm wandering in castles of ice and snow—of course that's just fancies, as the dreaming mind would see, but what I'll be seeing will be real, and strange, and unearthly like nothing else I've ever seen! Dennis and I talked, hours sometimes, of what we'd see, and find out, when we finally got the chance we knew would come to travel to the stars, and explore strange worlds, and touch new creatures! And I wasn't selected for Rocheworld, but I knew the luck would come, and it has, it has! Fierce, I'm feeling, Reiki, fierce and tingly and proud—what shall I see, down there? What discoveries shall I make? Dennis would love this—he *does* love it! and shares it, as he is—he is part of my pride, and my joy, as he is still part of myself—this world is frozen and desolate, James says, but there is life there! Intelligent life! World of ice or no, *I* am burning, it's all I can do to keep from exploding!" Reiki was touched. Deirdre rarely mentioned Dennis, or the passionate love they had shared with wild intensity until his tragic death. Reiki knew only that it had been enough for Deirdre, so completely engulfing and satisfying that, after her mourning time, she had looked at herself and concluded that she needed no more. She enjoyed, as did Reiki, the work that she did and the life she lived; together they derived much entertainment from the behavior of the rest of the crew, but Deirdre's heart was forever, now, her own.

"Grand it'll be to step off our ladder onto this planet! What will it feel like, on that ice? How can it be that thinking beings can survive, could even have come to exist, in such hostile and harsh conditions? Will they be able to tell me how, and when, and what they have done. . . ."

Still bubbling quietly within herself with joy, Deirdre left Reiki's quarters and bounded down the central shaft to the galley. Here, the galley imp prepared most of the crew's meals on demand, utilizing the products of the hydroponics lab and occasionally putting together one of the "special" meals for a crew member; either one containing some rare spice or preserved food the humans had selected before leaving Earth, or one containing their "real meat" ration for the week, using fresh meat obtained from one of the fish tanks, or one of the tissue cultures carefully tended by Nels and his crew on the hydroponics deck, such as "Ferdinand," "Lamb Chop," and "Chicken Little."

There were, however, some supplies kept on hand for those who fancied doing a bit of cooking on their own; Nels, among them, was an excellent chef. Possibly the most frequent user of the galley, however, was Deirdre; it was her delight to perfume the entire ship with the wonderful aroma of baking bread, or gingerbread, or chocolate cookies. Of course, James soon eradicated every trace of scent, but by then most of the crew would have followed their own noses eagerly, to share in the freshly made goods. The algae, yeasts, and cultures of the hydroponics lab were transformed, in these bakings, and tasted marvelously of home and hearth. On this occasion, with Deirdre still wildly though privately celebratory, the result was a huge pan full of fat cinnamon rolls, steaming gently through their heavy cloak of melted sugar. By the time they were ready, there were people prowling about the door of the tiny galley, waiting; the last of the fragrant treats was blissfully consumed before it had cooled. Not much was said; Deirdre's ribs ached from the hugs, and her green eyes glowed.

Calmer now, she dove silently up the central shaft and slipped into the empty corridor leading to the flouwen habitat tank. Stretching long fingers over the surface of the glass, she sang softly, her voice trilling a long series of numbers in time and rhythm to a complex tune full of trills and grace notes.

"Three point one four one five nine, two six five three five eight nine, seven . . ."

One idle Sunday back at the university, she had

managed to put the first hundred digits of pi to a tune—
and with the tune to assist—had soon memorized it. In
this manner, Deirdre shared the ability of her druid an-
cestors, who had passed their history on from generation
to generation by rote memorization.

Upon hearing the song, the milky-white drifting shape
within the tank came closer and joined in for the remainder of the tune. When they finished, they switched to a
tune the two had recently created together. This song
recited the first sixty-four numbers that represented pi in
the octal system—the base eight numbering system that
the flouwen preferred.

"Th-r-ree point one one oh th-r-ee s-e-v-v-e-n-n, f-f-i-
v-e f-f-i-v-e t-two f-f-ou-r t-two . . ." the two sang
together, giving each word a trill with the number of
stops equal to the number that the word represented, as
was the flouwen custom. Little White's multitoned voice
also gave each number a set of overtones that were distinctive as violin, bell, and drum. The number seven
emanating from Little White's body sounded as if it were
a multiply-harmonic septuple-tongued trilling chord
emitted by a living pipe-organ—which it was. Little
White and Deirdre had shared their fondness for the
rigid preciseness yet apparent randomness of transcen-
dental numbers ever since the first tentative effort on
Deirdre's part had elicited an enthusiastic response from
the white flouwen, who was impressed that a mere
human could display such a memory feat, but Deirdre
had spoken of it to no one. After they had finished their
second duet, her delight soared again, and she whispered,
"I'll be going along with you to Zulu, Little White!"

◊Good! When do we leave?◊ said the flouwen.

Deirdre chuckled, and said, "I don't know, it's not been
decided, but we *will* go, and how can I keep from

singing?" The phrase hit her memory, and, still softly, her voice rose in the clear pure notes of an old song, gliding effortlessly through the Celtic grace notes and accents:

"It sounds an echo in my soul . . ."

Little White's voice blended with hers, in gentle chords, and David, silent just outside the doorway, felt the hairs rise along the back of his neck. He had known for years that Deirdre sang, but he also knew, somehow, that if he ever spoke of it, he'd never hear her sing again: so now, as always, he listened without daring to breathe, and slid silently out of sight when she stopped, quieted by her own music.

LANDING

Now that the destination had been decided, the entire crew of *Prometheus* moved smoothly into a routine that assured nothing was left unplanned. Reiki, David, and Arielle spent their working hours on Surface Lander and Ascent Module III. SLAM III had been named *Victoria* after the one ship in Magellan's initial fleet which had made it all the way around the globe and back to Spain again. This powerful chemical rocket was designed to take the crew down to explore the surface and back up again to *Prometheus* at the end of the mission. It was shaped like a tall cylinder, with four descent engines and two main cryogenic tanks, which now held liquid hydrogen and liquid oxygen, recently electrolyzed from water taken from the consumables tanks on the top decks of *Prometheus*. Until it was activated, *Victoria* had been waiting its turn, silent and empty, upside down on the top of the hydroponics deck. Although its condition had been monitored ceaselessly by James over the decades, and repairs made as necessary, it was nevertheless important that everything on board the lander was in top condition.

Assisted by the Christmas Bush, the three humans double-checked every command *Victoria's* computer could expect and every mechanical action which resulted from the commands.

In a long slender crease that ran down the SLAM's length, nestled the Surface Excursion Module, Arielle's beloved aerospace plane, *Dragonfly III*. Arielle checked out its flight controls, while David took the computer hardware and software through its selfcheck procedures, and Shirley exercised the life-support subsystems while monitoring the Christmas Branch as it checked the exterior of both the SLAM and the SEM.

Later, while replenishing her energies with a sandwich, Arielle encountered Deirdre, and smiled happily.

"Maybe geysers make updrafts, and we can have ride down there!"

"Like a hot-air balloon, would it feel?" asked Deirdre.

"More like roller coaster—swooooop!" Arielle's free hand described an impressive curve through the air. Deirdre's own smile was less enthusiastic.

Thoughtfully she returned down through the SLAM III airlock and went to the corridor where the flouwen were swirling in their tank. Caroline, with the assistance of James and the Christmas Bush, was modifying the flouwen drysuits, with much advice being given them by the flouwen themselves. She was adding the communications equipment which would be needed to ensure that, when the flouwen were deep under the ocean or ice, they could stay in contact with *Prometheus* and the exploration vehicles, as well as any humans outside on the ice. That meant installing an underwater sonar transmitter and multimode communications software, which would provide a high reliability link to a sonar-to-radio transponder floating on the surface of a nearby open body of water, which in turn would provide a radio link to one of the communications relay spacecraft above.

◊Make sure we can talk to everyone,◊ said Little White.

⊓Not just each other, but humans, too, when we go below surface.⊓

"The underwater relay system is built right into the backpack of your drysuits; you can speak as you usually do," Caroline promised.

◊And we can hear like we do here, too?◊ Little White had no desire to lose contact with his human friends.

"Even while you are swimming at the bottom of the ocean, you will be in close touch with James and all the humans, through sound if not sight," Caroline reassured them. "It will even work in the dark, so you can keep working away at collecting data day and night."

Little Red was not quite so pleased. ☆We not work *all* the time! We play some time! Geysers sound like fun place to play!☆

Deirdre admonished him in stern tones. "You'll be doing nothing of the sort! It would be terrible bad if you got caught in that thing—sucked up and tossed out like a wee toy—helpless and all. . . ."

Little Red was undismayed. ☆Surf back down!☆

Josephine, the computer persona of *Victoria*, was endlessly patient as the various members of the crew plied her with questions and requests. With precision, she used her Christmas Branch to shift and stow the oncoming bulk of supplies for the most efficient use of her capacity. Programmed by Reiki with the voice of a kindly British nanny, she made use of the indirect question when a dubious suggestion was made.

"But, Richard, if you bring along your own favorite trenching tool, and Sam brings his, you'll be duplicating one item unnecessarily, won't you? And that's what we're trying to avoid, isn't it?" The descending inflection was difficult to argue with.

Joe, the persona for the computer aboard the *Dragonfly* airplane, was, in contrast, optimistic and confident, with just a hint of Scots in his "voice." Designed by Reiki in an unaccustomed mood of mischief, his performance was as impeccable as his voice was unmistakable, and everyone had adjusted to being regarded as "bonny lasses and lads."

As they progressed through the routine check-out, each member of the designated landing crew had reason to speak with both computers. Sam and George listened, with delight, as Deirdre explained to Joe and Josephine the necessity for a restraining strap on Foxx's cage during flight.

"There's a suitable clamp, already installed in the tool cabinet, don't y'know. It could be utilized for this mission, couldn't it?" Josephine was determined to save mass.

"What I'm wantin' is a lighter, temporary sort of thing, which I can use to fasten Foxx in with me both in the lander and the plane, *not* some great flipping iron belt in a cabinet with the heavy tools!" Deirdre tried to remain cool. Being Irish, she resented, ever so slightly, the British tones with their trace of superiority.

"The mission is involving a great deal of my capacity."

Deirdre understood perfectly. Josephine's reply was said in the classic manner of "I've only got two hands," but she responded patiently.

"It's not a big thing I'm askin', is it? I'm sure you or Joe can rig up something perfectly lovely, with no trouble a'tall," she coaxed, the Irish lilt becoming positively honeyed.

"Aye, lass," spoke up Joe comfortably. "I think I can

fashion a wee strappie to hold down the cage in your bunk. Come and show my Christmas Branch just where you want it to go."

Within a few days, humans and computers agreed that full preparations had been made. Every cubic centimeter of the lander had been packed with carefully chosen supplies, and the crew members's private allocations were no less carefully decided. Thomas' agony over the choice between an extra-long zoom lens and clean shirts remained private, and he made the final decision only two minutes before the deadline. Foxx's needs had to be fitted into Deirdre's allotment, but she shrugged away any difficulty; her own austere tastes in dress made it easy for her to leave behind everything but essentials.

A few hours later, George and Jinjur received a report from *Splish*. "Some twenty kilometers away from the Manannán geyser lake, there is a mound of volcanic basaltic rock about four hundred meters in diameter," reported *Splish*. "It must have happened in recent geologic times, since the rock is still internally warm and any snow falling on it melts. A number of the aliens normally occupy this area in order to collect sunlight from Barnard. They have vacated it to make room for your landing. The basalt should be unaffected by your rockets."

"Hunh, basalt. Yes, that'll be unaffected, but will we? Stuff can be pretty lumpy." George called Sam, to get his opinion of this landing pad.

"Sounds fine by me," Sam assured him. "Basalt is real stable stuff—long as it's the same as earthly basalt!" James, consulted, compared the spectral data of the rock composition it had received from *Splish* and assented.

"*Victoria*'s landing legs have enough adjusting capacity to handle three meters of variation in terrain; my laser topography mapper has measured the variations of the ground in that area as less than one meter."

"Well," replied George with rising anticipation, "it looks like we've got a safe place to land."

"I have received word from Josephine and Joe that all equipment is installed and all supplies stowed," James announced.

Jinjur looked over to Elizabeth at the planetary science console.

"What's the status of the geysers and the prognosis, Red?" Jinjur was pretty sure of the answer, but as commander, she always collected all available advice before making a decision.

"Major eruptions are over, following that recent quadruple conjunction. Things are settling down rapidly now. No large eruptions are expected until the next Barnard-assisted Zuni conjunction, which will take place in sixteen Zulu days. Ten Earth days, that is." Red's normally neat red hair was tousled, as though she had gotten out of bed too late to leave time for her imp to comb it. She must have spent most of her sleep shift saying good-bye to someone.

George and Jinjur exchanged a long look between themselves. There was little need for further talk, and their own farewells had been said last night. George nodded, and Jinjur spoke decisively, through James, to the entire ship. "The landing party will assume their stations on *Victoria*!"

Immediately, the smooth routine began. Tony, at the navigation console, stabilized *Prometheus* into the proper orientation and acceleration level for SLAM separation, while Red, at the planetary science console, kept in contact with *Splish* at the landing site.

"You're in charge of the bridge, Mr. Roma," Jinjur said

through their imp link as she left the control deck with George. "I'm going up to the airlock to see the landing party off."

The others who were to remain on *Prometheus* slipped, with the ease of long practice, into their supporting roles; Reiki gave David a quick hug before she took control of the computer operations console; Carmen left the sick bay, where she'd been talking quietly with John, and went swiftly to the communications console; Caroline settled in at the little-used airlock control console to monitor the airlock between *Victoria* and *Prometheus*. Linda, technically off duty, went down to the docking airlock to assist in any way necessary. Her normally bouncy cheer was subdued, just a trifle, by the magnitude of this good-bye; she had time to hug everyone, most thoroughly, before they went through the airlock.

Back in one corner of the hydroponics deck, Cinnamon touched Nels's shoulder as he half-reclined in the fluid of the regeneration tank. His new legs were growing nicely, and he had only two months to go. He would be out of the tank and walking before Cinnamon returned from Zulu. He glanced briefly up from the console screen at her touch.

"Everything's going fine on the hydroponics deck," she reported. "While we are gone, James will run the lab as usual. Shall I bring you back a snowball?" The tone was joking, but Nels looked at her blankly.

"How? Why?"

"Never mind," said Cinnamon, and sighed. Impulsively, she stooped and lightly kissed the cheek of the big man, sitting so patiently in the tank. Then she was gone, in a swirl of black hair like the turn of a raven's wing. Nels stared, puzzled, and then shrugged.

Their last task was to transfer the three flouwen from

their tank on *Prometheus* to the smaller tank on *Victoria*.
It would take a number of days for *Victoria* to set up the
communications net around Zulu and do a last minute
low-altitude detailed survey of the landing site, so the
flouwen couldn't just travel in *Victoria* in their drysuits.
They needed a place with food and fresh ammonia-water.
Running down the center of *Victoria* was a central column which contained the tanks for the consumables—air
and water. To accommodate the flouwen, Shirley and the
Christmas Bush had shortened both, leaving room for a
habitat tank where the flouwen could relax and eat.
Inside the tank was a built-in underwater taste screen
similar to the one on *Prometheus*, and a small porthole in
place of what used to be an inspection plate, so they and
the humans could see each other as the humans climbed
the passway ladder. They didn't have the luxury of a volcanic vent, however, and had to make do with the
flouwen equivalent of backpacking food—a net containing storage bags of thick, partially dried chunks of their
various favorite foods. To get the flouwen on board, the
pumps and hoses which had previously been used to
transfer the flouwen from the habitat tank to their suits
had been rerouted to connect the tanks.

Shirley sent Richard on board *Victoria* to look through
the porthole to observe the flouwen's safe arrival, while
she monitored the larger tank on *Prometheus*.

"Are you ready to be 'piped aboard'?" she asked the
flouwen through her imp.

☆I go first!☆ roared Little Red, swimming to the end
of the input hose on the wall of the habitat tank and surrounding it with its fluid red flesh.

"Pump away, Josephine!" said Shirley through her imp,
and in less than a minute, the red flouwen had been
sucked into the hose and was gone.

"Everything okay, Red buddy?" came Richard's query over the imp link, followed by Little Red's complaining voice.

☆Dark! Small!☆

"It'll be only for a few days," reassured Richard. "Then you can have a whole ocean to explore."

It didn't take long to repeat the process for the other two flouwen. It was now time for the humans to board.

Minds filled with their wide variety of concerns and hopes, the ten members of the crew received a parting word from Jinjur. Those staying behind at the consoles on the control deck were too busy with the count-down procedures to give more than a wave over the cameras, as they rather wistfully watched the adventurers clamber aboard and settle into their stations, which, because of *Victoria*'s inverted stowage position above the hydroponics deck, were upside down in the low-acceleration field of *Prometheus*. Arielle and Thomas somersaulted into their stand-up harnesses and buckled themselves in, Arielle in the red copilot harness and Thomas in the blue pilot one. Hanging upside down, Arielle's mind instantly zeroed in on the flight ahead of her, to the exclusion of everything else, except, possibly, the sandwich she was finishing. Beside her, buckled upside down into her seat at the communications console, Cinnamon felt the old joy rising in her again—she loved to fly, even if she wasn't at the controls.

George, the last aboard, closed the airlock door and walked across the ceiling of the bridge to his console, being careful not to step on the glass docking window. Swinging himself upward until the sticky patches on his uniform grabbed the loop pile of the seat at the command console, he buckled himself in. Setting up the icons on the screen in front of him, he took the command program through its paces, checking and double-checking with the two pilots, Arielle and Thomas, and the two ship computers, James on *Prometheus* and Josephine on *Victoria*.

The six not directly concerned with flying the SLAM had already strapped themselves firmly into place in their bunks and adjusted their own view-screens in their Sound-Bar doors for the journey. Deirdre wriggled her booted toes on top of the sturdy padded cage strapped in at the bottom of her bunk, in which Foxx drowsed, tranquillized and content. All of them listened intently as the take-off procedure followed its orderly course.

"Airlocks emptying." Caroline's cool voice spoke into her imp, as she used the airlock imps to survey the seals around the small connecting area between *Victoria* and *Prometheus*. One by one, the indicating lights flicked on to complete the check.

"Docking port secure. Clearance for breakaway," reported Caroline.

"You are cleared for breakaway, *Victoria*," said Jinjur.

"You guys have a nice trip, y'hear?" came Linda's voice.

Cinnamon grinned and glanced at Arielle, motionless beside her. Arielle reached to a red switch cover, raised it, and both she and Thomas looked over at George at the command console.

"Take her away, Captain St. Thomas," said George.

Arielle flicked the mechanical switch inside the switch cover. There was a series of metallic clanks vibrating through the hull, indicating the opening of the clamps which had held the SLAM in place on *Prometheus*. The *Victoria* remained motionless, held in place only by the slight acceleration of the lightsail. Then Thomas gently eased forward the controls to the cold gas jets, and the ponderous cylinder tilted and started to move.

"Now at a half-meter a second," Arielle reported, watching the indicator on the copilot screen.

The hissing of the jet stopped. They were now in free-fall. Instantly, the four on the deck experienced a change in their point of view. They were no longer upside down in *Victoria*'s bridge, they were right side up, and *Prometheus* was upside down.

Thomas and Arielle looked up through the docking window as the edge of the hydroponics deck slid slowly past above them. As soon as they were clear, Thomas would activate more powerful jets and fly them out between the shrouds and away from the sail.

The next few days were spent installing a system of communication relay spacecraft so that any point on Zulu was always in sight of at least one. Three orbiters were set up at points 120 degrees apart in an equatorial orbit, while two statites were established over the north and south spin poles.

Shirley and Richard suited up and took the second of the statites into the airlock on the engineering deck. It looked like a large hockey puck made out of metal, two meters in diameter and a meter thick—designed to fit, just, through the airlock door. They pushed the statite through the open airlock door and watched as it drifted away from the lander, rotating slightly.

On the crew quarters deck above, a number of the rest of the crew were watching the deployment out of the viewport window in the small lounge, while having a lunch that had been prepared in the nearby compact galley. Most of them contented themselves with drink-ball squeezers filled with a nourishing "milkshake" of algae protein, essential minerals and vitamins, and various artificial flavors, but Arielle, unable to wait, was eating one of

her "specials"—a flip-top tray of crisp green beans, cauli-
flower buds, and strips of white meat from Chicken
Little, coated with James' secret seasoning and pressure
fried to a crisp, golden brown. The smells brought Arielle
a great deal of attention, and she sacrificed one strip of
real meat to those around her, one tiny bite at a time. Little Purple, who had been in the video lounge in his
drysuit, watching children's cartoons broadcast from
Earth, was drawn by the commotion and floated over to
ask questions about the food they were eating. Cinnamon
kindly took Little Purple aside in order to explain what a
chicken was.

After letting the statite drift for a while, Shirley gave it
a call.

"You look like you're far enough away, now, *Colin*," she
said. "You can start deployment of your lightsail."

"I have been programmed to orient my spin axis
toward you, so you can watch deployment," said *Colin*, as
its attitude jets fired, first turning the spacecraft so that its
upper face was toward the two humans standing in the
airlock in their exploration suits, and next setting the
spacecraft into a moderately fast rotation. "Deployment
commencing." Slowly, four collapsible booms extended
out from the main body, dragging with them a shiny gray
foil of finely perforated aluminum.

"Deployment looking good!" reported Richard encour-
agingly as he scanned the unfurling acres of lightsail.
Suddenly the deployment stopped.

"I sense an imbalance in tensions," reported *Colin*.

"I see the problem!" said Shirley. "There is a small tear
starting in the third quadrant, about ten meters from the
central body. It'll continue growing if you keep up the
deployment. You'd better send out your Christmas Twig."

At the center of the spacecraft body, a bundle of

greenly illuminated twigs, laser beams flashing from their tips, emerged from a small hole carrying some small round patches. Using its finest cilia to grasp the nominally smooth metal surfaces, it climbed like a fly across the spacecraft body and out along a mast. It split in two, each half carefully crawling across the thin sail foil until it reached the tear. They placed a patch over each side of one end of the tear and paused while their arms seemed to blur.

"What are they doing?" Richard asked Shirley.

"Sewing up the tear," replied Shirley. "First they sew a patch on the ends to prevent further ripping, then they lash the edges together." As she spoke, the actions of the statite imp replicated her words. The imp went back inside the spacecraft, and the deployment commenced again.

An hour later, the last of the sail was pulled forth from the flat metal cylinder. "Deployment completed," reported *Colin*. "No indication of any further malfunctions."

The statite, its sail now fully deployed, started to drift away from the lander as the light pressure forces from Barnard pushed it to higher and higher speeds. Like a giant gray moth, it flew off toward the nearby moon.

"Your assigned position is over the north pole," Shirley reminded it. "Report in to James and Josephine when you get on station."

"Will comply," radioed *Colin*, and the statite went off to hover over the north pole of Zulu, where the light pressure from Barnard would counterbalance the gravity pull from Zulu. Being situated over the north pole, instead of orbiting the moon, it was always in sunlight, except for the few hours when Barnard was behind Gargantua. Each Zulu day, a few hours before the eclipse,

Colin would use its excess sail area to lift itself higher, so that its drop during the darkness would return it to its nominal altitude.

Soon, the last of the relay spacecraft had been deployed, and they were ready to proceed with landing. George, Cinnamon, and Arielle joined Thomas on the bridge, while the rest closed down the galley, pumped Little Purple back into the flouwen tank, then went to their bunks and buckled themselves in. As soon as the first glimmer of sunrise appeared on the icy fields surrounding the gray-black basalt knob, George spoke.

"Take her down, Captain St. Thomas."

"All hands!" Thomas broadcast through his imp. "Stand by for deorbit burn! For those who haven't been through this before, this'll be the most gees you've felt since you left Earth, so make sure you are buckled in."

Deirdre reached down with her toes and pushed against Foxx's cage to make sure it was securely strapped.

Slowly Thomas moved the main engine throttles forward. Inwardly, he revelled in the feel of the controlled power in his hands. Precise and smooth, but immensely strong, the engines responded to his skill. He and Arielle sank in their stand-up harnesses, while uncomfortable groans were heard from the deck below.

"That was only half gee," Arielle announced over the imp link. "Two and half more gees to go."

The huge metal cylinder tilted and slowly began the backward descent, engines roaring full blast, then throttling down to a more controlled thrust as it passed through the thickening atmosphere, letting the friction of the cold thin air do its work in dissipating the energy of the falling eighty tons of machine, humans, and flouwen. Human eyes and flouwen bodies, watching eagerly on their various screens, looked out at a bleak and inhospitable land, stretching to the horizon with the rough contours of thick ice. Where there was no ice to see, the surface looked like irregular fields, differing from each other in their blue-green shade, but approximately equal in area.

"Like a patchwork quilt made out of triangles," murmured Katrina over the imp link. "Made by someone with not much choice in patches."

"Or interest in design," said David. "A crazy quilt, I think they called it."

The rocket's mighty jets lit up the black rock beneath them with more light than it had ever received before. Then the light dimmed, as the controlled thrust of the jets lowered the eighty tons of metal almost delicately, while frost formed, and vanished, on the silvery duralloy surface. Ponderously, but perfectly, the *Victoria*'s lowered landing struts accommodated themselves to the uneven surface and took the weight of the lander upon themselves. The engines cut, as Josephine recognized the support and shut the motors down. It was suddenly eerily silent on the bridge.

"*Victoria* has landed. All is well." George's quiet message to the waiting lightcraft above was unnecessary, as James and Josephine between them had established that fact, but the human report was equally vital for Jinjur and the others to hear.

Rapidly, George undid the restraining straps that held him to his console seat and stood, just a trifle stiffly. The flight had been brief, but no one had really relaxed during it, rather they had maintained a curious tension. Like Foxx, the others felt the need to stretch, and quickly did so, restoring their harnesses and bunks to neatness and preparing to move outside.

"We've only a few hours before Barnard sets today, so

let's get out there, meet this Pink-Orb fellow, hook up with *Splish*, and assess the situation." Sam and Richard looked at George, then each other, and grinned. Old habits of command were coming back to George—but it was good to see; both men knew the value of someone, even nominally, "in charge."

Carefully and methodically, the practiced routine of disembarking was completed. Suits were donned, with Foxx assuming her usual place on Deirdre's shoulder, inside her helmet.

"You don't want to leave her safe aboard?"

Deirdre smiled briefly at Katrina's quick concern. "With me, she'll be out of the way. It's better—I'm used to it," was the reply.

Arielle completed the securing of the landing rockets and took the preliminary steps to ready the Ascent Propulsion Stage as a precaution in case of the need for an emergency takeoff. Richard, ready first, cycled through into the airlock to assist the flouwen as Josephine pumped them into their suits. As usual, Shirley ran a sharp eye over everyone's suit telltales as they lined up by the sealed airlock door. All of this took time, and during it, the noontime eclipse began.

"With the three flouwen and Richard in the airlock, there is only room for three more on this first cycle," said Shirley. "George is one of them, of course. Who wants to help me and Richard hook the flouwen up to the winch?" From the volunteers, Shirley selected Thomas.

Once the three had joined Richard and the flouwen in the airlock, and the inner door had been cycled shut, Shirley firmly opened the outer airlock door and swung it inward, like an airliner door. It was pitch-black outside, alleviated only locally by the landing lights glaring down on the gray-black rock below, while above them was a black circle in the star-speckled sky that was Gargantua. As the airlock allowed the frigid Zulu atmosphere in, there was a momentary fog of frozen water vapor, and soon the lock was at the 820 millibars of Zulu pressure, instead of the 500 millibars used inside the lander. The life-support systems in their backpacks began humming and hissing, adjusting the suits to the outside atmosphere, while also extracting oxygen from it to lessen the load on the oxygen tanks. Shirley swiveled to reach for the winch on the ceiling of the airlock, and her suit, not quite at outside pressure yet, contracted noisily, allowing some of the glassy foil outer layer to press inward on her arms and legs.

"Migod, it's *cold*!"

Her involuntary comment brought a chuckle from the rest. Her suit-imp quickly equalized pressure and raised the suit's temperature in the affected regions. Comfortable again, Shirley disengaged the locked-down winch and pulled it toward the end of the overhead beam. They waited until the first bead of light from Barnard appeared from behind Gargantua, signaling that the eclipse was over.

"We've only got three hours of daylight left," said George. "Let's get a hustle on."

He and Shirley made their way down the rungs of the ladder and past the spot where the rungs became steps on one of the landing struts, while Thomas and Richard used the winch to lower the excited flouwen to the surface. There, George steadied them while Shirley undid the harness and sent it back up again. Just before George reached the bottom rung, he had thought briefly about saying something notable as he stepped off the landing pad onto this new world. But since the "people" who owned the world were watching them from a distance, he decided that it would be inappropriate.

The second group soon cycled through and made it down to the ground via either winch line or ladder rungs. The visitors were quiet a moment, trying to take in the entire scene before them. In the sky overhead, Gargantua hung, as huge as the palm of an upstretched hand, nearly dark except for a fingernail slice of light along the side towards Barnard. Coming out from behind it, Barnard shone dimly, half as big as the Sun appeared from Earth. Off on the other side, two of the other alien moons swung in their orbits. All around the gray-black basaltic knob they were standing on was ice. It looked so frozen that Arielle, watching out the lounge window forty meters above them, shivered and no longer regretted that duty required her to stay within the ship in case they needed to take off again in a hurry.

Deirdre stepped silently off to one side of the group, every nerve tingling with awareness of her position. Her mind was racing—she almost wished she had a recorder like Reiki's—as she strove to absorb the uniqueness of this world. Deliberately, she relaxed her muscles, the better to experience the wonders all around her. Barnard's distant light enabled her to see curious shapes in the mounded and tumbled ice—wind and spray had carved some of the taller drifts into fantastic tunnels and peaks, which glittered and threw strange shadows. The wind thrust exploratory gusts into every crevice, whirled flakes of snow about, and whistled little sounds, constantly changing. Stretching before her, the landscape was essentially flat, but scarred and littered with grotesquely beautiful shapes in ice and snow. She breathed a deep sigh of satisfaction.

Richard spoke so softly that only Cinnamon turned to him in concern. "Damn! How can those toes still hurt?"

His grin reassured her; the sight of this icy world had

triggered the strange sensation, common to amputees, in which the lost member seems to be aching. Both of Richard's little toes had succumbed to frostbite, years ago in the French Alps during a rescue, and they were now putting in their belated message.

Little Red was the first to pronounce judgment. ☆Hunh! Lumpy! Empty! Cold! *Nothing* to see!☆

At first glance, George was inclined to agree.

"Yes, there is," said David in quiet jubilation. "Look there!"

Coming toward them was the familiar shape of *Splish*. It looked like a miniature landing craft, about one meter wide, a half-meter high, and nearly two meters long, with a broad boatlike front, flippered treads along the side which allowed it to move equally well on the water, ice, or ocean bottom, and a large pressurized cargo hold which stored analysis equipment and samples. On the top were cameras that acted as its eyes, while its arms were two manipulators that could extend to reach any part of itself for repair work.

After a brief, confirmatory glance at the basalt knob they had landed on, Sam and Richard walked toward the approaching robot in order to look more closely at the surface of the ice surrounding the knob. Deirdre followed.

"Fresh snow from that last big burst of geyser activity." Sam's gloved hand picked up a portion of the top layer and squeezed it. When he opened his hand, the snow fell from his fingers.

"Gritty, and pretty dry," he said. "Ice dust."

Deirdre scuffed her boots in the snow, reaching crusted ice at a depth of a few inches. "Not a big snowfall," she commented, hoping Sam would say more. She knew of Sam's habit of keeping up a running commentary

when analyzing some portion of terrain—his every word
picked up by his suit imp, stored in memory in his suit
computer, and transferred back to James on *Prometheus*
at the first opportunity. Listening to Sam was a good way
to learn a great deal in a short time.

"No, but I reckon there's never a real big snowstorm.
The stuff just keeps coming, piling up, freezing, never
melting, an' slowly sublimating away—a little at a time,
over centuries." The calm words made even Deirdre
shiver. She looked around at the desolation. Apart from
the dark gray rock on which the lander stood, the terrain
seemed to be all ice.

Splish arrived at the boundary between the ice and
rock and was greeted by George.

"Status report."

Splish's reply was in the carefully formal tones it had
been programmed to use. "All is well. The landing
appeared normal in every respect. The aliens await to
greet you, at a safe distance. Here is the most recent
information I have collected on the alien's vocabulary and
grammar."

The small robot transferred the translation data to
Josephine, who made sure that the translation programs
in the exploration suit computers of the humans and flouwen contained the updated information, and they
prepared to walk to the distant fields. Stepping out with
long legs, Sam was immediately forced to shorten his
stride.

"Sastrugi 'dunes' under that new snow," he warned.
The unevenness of the wind-carved hard-packed snow
undersurface was concealed by the fresh snowfall, and
the crew found themselves slipping frequently. Shirley,
trying to look about her at the scenery, took a full-length
fall, much to her disgust. "Haven't done that in years,"

she grumbled, scrambling up and brushing the snow from her suit.

"Let me look at your chest," commanded George. Shirley was surprised, but then realized what he meant.

"Not too good for the suit material, is it, George? Rolling about in this gritty stuff."

"I doubt it," he answered, pushing check buttons on her chestpack. "But you look okay."

After this, the crew proceeded more slowly, watching where they put their feet, and for quite a while there was only the squeak of the ice beneath their boots and the clicking of *Splish*'s tread. The flouwen, plodding along in their baggy suits, looked like someone walking in a sack. Because of the low gravity, they had no trouble keeping up. They came to the top of the low ridge of ice around the basalt knob, where they could look down at the vast expanse of multicolored waiting icerugs.

"They really *do* look like rugs! Elegant, sculptured velvet carpets, fit for a castle's halls!" Katrina was entranced, as was David.

"Look at all the different colors!" exclaimed David, whose color sense had not been diminished by the dim reddish light of Barnard. "Not just blue-green. That one's pure peacock, and the one next to it's a deep plummy shade, over there is one like moss . . ."

Barnard was now getting lower in the sky, and as they drew closer to the creatures, their shadows stretched across the ice and onto the colorful bodies of the icerugs.

"Look there! Where the shadow of our helmets falls on their surface. . . ." Thomas, always alert for interesting lighting effects, pointed at his shadow. Around the shadow silhouette of each of their helmets was a halo, of deepest velvety black, dense in the extreme.

"What causes that?" asked Shirley, puzzled.

"It's sort of the opposite of the bright halo effect you get when you look at your shadow on dewy grass," said Thomas.

Deirdre looked at the effect thoughtfully. "If that is a growing plant, right enough, then there's photosynthesis going on, and they'll be wanting to capture all of this poor light that they can. They must turn the fine fibers that give their surface that velvety texture toward the sun to capture the maximum amount of light."

The flouwen, to whom sight was a secondary sense, were unable to appreciate the curious black halo effect. They had moved ahead of the slowly following humans and were now close behind *Splish*. Quickly catching up, the humans spread out to stand and observe what was awaiting them. From out of the backpacks of the humans and flouwen clambered their suit imps, each carrying a jury-rigged speaker cone made of a circular piece of glassy-foil, so the imps could generate the deep bass notes which the icerugs used for speech.

The attention of the humans was now riveted on the three beings behind the crawler. Taller even than Sam, each was topped by a large eye, nearly ten centimeters in diameter, resting on a flexible stalk, regarding them with apparent benignity.

"No nose on the head portion," remarked Cinnamon over their intersuit link. "Like plants on Earth, they must respire through their skin."

Deirdre was taking in every detail of the new creatures with passionate interest; their very peculiarity made them more fascinating than anything simpler would have been. Deliberately, she suppressed the tendency to view new life-forms in human terms; however, it certainly seemed as though the differences between the specimens before her were based on costume and preference, not actual form.

"It's a cape, that's what it is!" said Katrina breathlessly. "Look, Deirdre, how it's draped to fall along the back, not interfere with the arm-things!" The garment, if that is what it was, thought Deirdre carefully, looked as if it served no practical purpose; it hung, in shimmering folds, from an intricately woven band about the creature's eye stalk, and fell over the globular head portion nearly to the ground. It swirled gently in the wind, but offered no apparent protection to its wearer. The others of the strange creatures before them were similarly attired with capes, although not as ornately embroidered. The jade-colored one had a lower "neckband" fastened at the narrow junction below the spherical head and above the tentacle arms, from which hung a multitude of colored ribbons which fell in between the arms without constricting their motions. Hanging in back, under the cloak and partially hidden by the ribbons, was a large device of unknown purpose. The turquoise-colored one carried a large pouch attached to a wide band around the narrow junction where the pedestal connected to the four arms.

Sam muttered, "That pouch looks like a tool kit. See how the things inside are held by straps and pockets?"

"Careful," warned Shirley. "Not necessarily a tool kit; possibly weapons, possibly . . ."

". . . lunch." Katrina giggled nervously.

Cinnamon and Deirdre moved slowly closer, examining, as thoroughly as distance would permit them, the strange objects held in various tentacles.

"Looks like wood," said Deirdre, "or perhaps bone, but green—and look you how there is a bit of something, twisted around, to keep the disc in place. The disc looks like glass, doesn't it?"

They realized that *Splish* had been speaking. With its mechanical precision, the robot was introducing the three aliens with a flourish of one of its manipulators.

"I present Pink-Orb, Yellow-Star, and Gray-Mote, who have supplied me with most of my information." Turning its video camera eye toward the icerugs, *Splish* pointed to the explorers and completed the introduction.

"I present Expedition Leader Colonel George Gudunov, and his crew of humans and flouwen, from the lightship *Prometheus*." There was a silence. *Splish* was not much of an ambassador, thought George wryly, and for lack of a more carefully thought-out greeting, he straightened, brought his heels together sharply, and saluted. Then he dropped his arm immediately, at the sound of a smothered giggle behind him. He cleared his throat and spoke formally.

"How do you do . . . er . . . sirs," said George, his mind racing. "The names of my people, here, are . . ." He listed them, using first names only, and each stepped up in turn.

"Say something to give them the sound of you," urged David privately through their imps. "We all look alike in these suits!" When each of them had done so, the humans waited, silently, for more. The humans were, illogically, startled when a deep, rumbling bass voice replied, accompanied by a translation by their suit imps. Whenever the translation program in their suits was stumped, Josephine, with its much greater computational power, used context information to assist with the selection of the proper word.

"I am Pink-Orb, an Astronomer from the Center of Scientific Studies. Since you have come from the stars, I was assigned by the Presider of the Governing Council to converse with you. These others are from the local association. This is Yellow-Star, a master bard and interassociation communicator. This is Gray-Mote, a physician and the Leader of the local association."

All three carpets, it was clear in this light, were of different hues of blue-green; but now that they had had time to assimilate the features of the aliens, it was easy to discern differences in the creatures. Pink-Orb's body was a soft plum color, while the iris of its eye was a pale pink. Yellow-Star's body was a deep jade color, and streaks of yellow produced a starlike pattern in the light brown center of its eye, while Gray-Mote had a turquoise body, and had obviously been named because of a curious mote that distorted the normally round aperture in the center of its iris of silvery gray.

"Their names seem to be keyed to the differences in iris color and structure," David murmured. "Easy to distinguish, as long as there's not too many!" There was another pause, for which the humans were grateful, as they struggled to comprehend these strange-appearing, yet obviously civilized, creatures.

"And in the distance are others from the local association, who have come to see you out of curiosity." With a wave of a tentacle, which stretched double its previous length during the all-encompassing sweep, Pink-Orb indicated the carpets behind it, and the humans noticed crowds of similar stalked nodes, clustered in between the carpets of Pink-Orb and Yellow-Star on one side, and Yellow-Star and Gray-Mote on the other side, while others were off on the outskirts of Gray-Mote and Pink-Orb, as if they were trying to get as close as they could without treading on the territory of the three primary ambassadors.

George introduced the flouwen. "These are friends of ours, but not like us. We call them Little Red, Little Purple, and Little White. They wear our protective clothing, but they are native to this star system. They have come to visit you from Rocheworld. I do not know your name for Rocheworld. Have you a name for the object in the night sky made of two moons. . . ."

Josephine's, "They understand the word Rocheworld," and Pink-Orb's rumbled, "Yes," sounded almost simultaneously in George's ears. A deeper rumble started and their suit-imps passed on the translation. It was Yellow-Star speaking.

"Pink-Orb is the principal astronomer of our nation. All of the bodies in our skies are known to him, and his delight is to calculate their future behavior. He keeps us informed of the approaching conjunctions, when the tides increase and the Munificent God of the Sea awakens."

At these words, human and flouwen minds alike were both intrigued. These aliens were obviously highly intelligent and knowledgeable about the world around them and deserved respect, and the humans in particular resolved to pursue their quests as tactfully as possible; but also it was obvious that there was much to be learned.

"I hope our approach did not alarm your people?" asked Cinnamon.

"No. It was loud, and bright, but we have known for some time of your coming. We are not fearful of noise or light; they have no power to harm."

"I assume we appear very strange to you."

Yellow-Star answered this. "Through the songs passed down to me from the bards of the past, I know all the strange things that have ever been seen before. We have seen nothing like you or your machines, nor had we expected to receive such a visit. It is interesting—little happens outside the daily routine. You humans seem to travel both in large machines and by balancing on two of your four limbs, while the flouwen seem to travel in a manner partially like a human and partially as we do."

"Yes," said George succinctly, cutting off Shirley's attempt to explain more fully. "Exactly how do you travel?"

Deirdre and Cinnamon both looked askance at the direct question. But Sam muttered, "Yup. Got to get on with it. And it doesn't look—upset." The alien, Gray-Mote, answered and seemed interested in the opportunity to talk about his physiology.

"My node travels wherever it will, freely. Here, on my own body I move thus. . . ." And, demonstrating, the curious pedestal arrangement glided away, more swiftly than most humans could run, and then returned. It was a breathtaking sight. Moving rather like a cork on a wave, the node moved across its turquoise turflike base with a silent glide, smooth and effortless. On its return, it was equally fast and then simply stopped before the humans. There was no indication of effort or stress. It then moved off its carpeted area across the bare ice toward them, a wave of turquoise flesh preceding it, while leaving a trail of turquoise behind. "Going into a new area requires that I first put down a portion of myself first—this is not difficult, but it is much slower. Once I have laid down a trail, however, I can move as rapidly as I do on my own area." It quickly zoomed back onto its main carpet and slowly the turquoise trail it had left behind grew thinner as it drew back into the main body.

"Please, can you tell me the—can you tell me how your carpet is—made?" Katrina was trying to be polite, while every instinct in her wanted to touch, to probe, that strange velvety nap.

"It is not made, it grows, it is—my body," replied Gray-Mote.

Deirdre drew close to the end of the shrinking turquoise trail leading out from Gray-Mote. "If it would not give offense, it would be most enlightening for us to be taking a look, and perhaps the gentle touch, of your beautiful carpet." Deirdre's singing tones were dulcet, and she lingered over them. The alien looked at her directly: "It would not give offense."

Deirdre, Katrina, and Cinnamon dropped to their knees, together, reaching gloved hands gently to probe and stroke, and lift the edges of the thin, softly-textured ice-covering on which the pedestal stood.

"It's almost like moss," said Cinnamon, patting the surface.

Katrina poked the tip of her finger under the living creature and lifted its edge. "Look, there are roots, too. Fine, like the upper surface, and they go directly into the ice!" Deirdre was nearly flat on her stomach now, barely touching the fascinating life-form, but looking intently at the beautiful structure of each tiny fiber, endlessly duplicated in the carpet before her.

Meanwhile, David entered into discussion with Yellow-Star. "Among our people, a bard is someone who is both a musician and a historian. Is that true among your people?"

"Yes, I remember and retell the history of our people through music." The translation programs in their chest-pack translated the word "music" for the humans properly, but the word-sound coming from Yellow-Star sounded like a gong. "I will be composing a song to commemorate our meeting." Yellow-Star used its back tentacles to bring out the device that had been hanging under its cape. It looked like a cross between a harp and a drum, with a number of heavy strings stretched across an elliptical drumhead. Two of Yellow-Star's tentacles held the instrument, while a third plucked the strings, and a fourth punctuated the music with a complex rhythmical beat on the back of the drumhead using both ends of what looked like a bone. To all this Yellow-Star added its deep bass voice.

"From the stars they came, on a circular moon; in flames they land, in a tower of stone. . . ." The music stopped and Yellow-Star added. "That is only the beginning, of course. I will add more later."

"You play and sing very well," said David, whose fingers itched to try the harp-drum.

"We all enjoy music, especially singing. Gray-Mote, there, is extremely accomplished, and a great addition to our choruses. He is one of the few who can sing . . ." Josephine had a moment's difficulty with the newest word ". . . tenor, so he is frequently called upon."

Meanwhile, George, with Sam and Richard, was listening to Pink-Orb's elaborately worded invitation. "My normal rooting area is near the center of our city, Windward. After the site for your landing was chosen by our Governing Council, I uprooted myself and traveled here in order to greet you properly. Those that make up the Governing Council are anxious to meet you. They will welcome you as soon as you can get there." Questioning, aided with *Splish*'s prior knowledge of the icerug's measuring system, revealed that the center of their city, Windward, was twenty kilometers distant on the shores of Manannán Lake.

"Windward?" queried David, puzzled.

"I would guess that name comes from the fact that their geyser is the closest to the leading pole," said Richard. "There are always winds coming from that direction."

"Fortunately, twenty kilometers is not too great a distance," said George gravely. "We have a smaller machine with us, less large and noisy, with which to travel about your countryside. We shall use it to go to Windward in a few days."

Here Katrina interrupted with a carefully worded request for a small sample of the icerug's "body."

"How large is what you call small?" cautiously asked Gray-Mote. Katrina indicated the space between her thumb and forefinger, and the ice-rug assented. "That is very small, indeed; I shall not miss it. A large piece, of course, would be expensive." Deirdre and Cinnamon caught the odd use of the word.

"Expensive? Josephine, have you translated that correctly?" Josephine was definite. Shirley, whose tact was never her strong suit, asked, "Do you buy or sell your—body?"

"Of course. Out here, in the country, where the dwellers have the space to grow to a large area, their principal occupation is growing extra flesh which they use in trade with those of us in the city for manufactured goods and services."

This statement produced another silence, as the humans and flouwen tried to comprehend. Katrina knelt, biopsy punch in hand, but the icerug had already pinched off a small portion of its turquoise body. There was no indication that this caused any discomfort, or indeed, any feeling, to the icerug. Pink-Orb and Yellow-Star also cooperated by donating small samples of their velvety flesh. Unlike small budded-off portions of a flouwen body, which move about actively, these pieces of flesh were flaccid. All Katrina had to do was pick them up and put them into some sample bags. Before she did so, she took a quick look at the sample with her pocket microscope.

Her actions caught the attention of the scientist, Pink-Orb, who curved sinuously over the small human, to bring its large eye closer. "Is that a . . . microscope?" Once again, Josephine's incredible speed at translating from context produced the desired word with only a second's delay.

"Yes. Not a very good one, but portable." Katrina proffered the tool. Deirdre started to speak, but the icerug was already examining the microscope and talking.

"We have similar devices. Our lenses are made of fine ice, highly polished, but they are more fragile than this. We cannot carry ours about. This must contain very hard ice, indeed."

"It is not ice at all. It is another substance which is common with us. Please accept this one as a gift," said Katrina impulsively. Both Shirley and Deirdre protested immediately.

"This is interfering already! Way beyond our mission!" said Shirley.

Deirdre's voice was vibrant with disapproval. "You're thinking it's a scientist, a person, and you've no basis for that!"

Katrina's blue eyes were round with dismay. "But it said microscope . . ."

George interrupted. "The icerug used a word Josephine was able to interpret as one we know, and it's intelligence is obvious. I see no harm in giving the 'scope away—rather kindly meant, I'm sure." The blue eyes in their sooty lashes looked gratefully at George. Sometimes, thought Deirdre in resignation, it was difficult not to pat Katrina on the head. Barnard was about to set, and although Gargantua was now at half-moon stage and provided more illumination, it was far from bright.

"Well!" George shifted his feet and coughed. "This has been extraordinary, Pink-Orb, Yellow-Star, Gray-Mote: another limitation my people must deal with, which neither you nor the flouwen apparently share, is the need for sleep. As Barnard is about to set, and we are very tired, I should like us to return to *Victoria* for a time while we rest."

Little Purple attempted to explain to the icerugs: ⌷Humans get used up. Have to waste time doing nothing at all for a while.⌷

"You are welcome to remain in conversation, if that's mutually agreeable," said George somewhat stiffly.

"Sure!" said the flouwen, and the icerugs remained motionless. With murmured thanks, the weary humans returned across the rock to climb up the ladder and into the airlock on *Victoria*.

The first through the airlock door chanced to be Cinnamon; her mind full of the strange encounter, she stepped through the open hatch and instantly slid across it to slam into the opposite side. Her squeal of dismay stopped Sam, who was following, but then she rose, unhurt because of the low gravity. He laughed, and stepped in himself, only to grunt as he slipped and fell. The others, distracted by their own thoughts and ready for the comfort of the ship, paid little attention to the antics of those who preceded them, and most of them too lost their balance and fell to a greater or lesser degree. Richard, the last to arrive, saved himself with a quick grasp at the winch beam, and stared in astonishment at the last of his fellows, staggering upright. Arielle, who had been watching through the airlock porthole, was puzzled.

"Why everybody come crashing home?" she asked through the imp link.

"Ice," Richard replied, raising his boot to show its bottom. "The thick tread on these boots gets packed with ice, and when we step on the floor of the airlock, which is just a degree or so warmer than the freezing point, it instantly becomes slick as glass. We'll have to be careful of that first step inside—or else put down a doormat!"

Soon they were all inside and out of their suits. With a sigh, Sam plopped himself into the sofa in the lounge.

"After all those months in zero gee, just carrying myself around is work," he said.

Richard agreed, and headed purposefully for the hot shower, stepping neatly in front of Shirley. She glared, but sat down again.

"Guess we better get the reports going before we for-. get anything," she said.

"Those icerugs . . . I don't know what to say," said Katrina.

"A first," whispered Deirdre to Cinnamon.

"Well," said David, "they're very intelligent, they live somehow I just can't understand, and they've got some kind of sophisticated government, even! I'm just glad they're musicians!"

"Doesn't help the rest of us," grunted George.

"They're a very different life-form from anything we've ever met," concluded Cinnamon.

Deirdre concurred. "A combination, it is, of plant and animal—and intelligent. Still, it concerns me that you gave it the microscope, Katrina."

"It was nothing, such a little thing, and I meant it to be friendly!" protested Katrina.

"Isn't history full of such well-meaning gifts?" said Deirdre grimly. "Starlings, now, what could be the harm in them? And the lovely gray squirrels . . ."

"Oh, now, Deirdre," said Cinnamon. "This isn't the same. Pink-Orb said they already have microscopes, they use them as we do . . ."

"But they are not us, nor like us at all!" maintained

Deirdre fiercely. "And we cannot logically expect it. We must remain detached, and learn, but neither help nor hinder when we don't know which it is we're doing!"

The dispute had ended inconclusively, as always, and amity was restored swiftly over a relaxing meal of a hearty soup with real vegetables and chewy chunks of algae pseudo-beef, served with Arielle-baked croissants, prepared in the tiny galley and eaten together in the small lounge. Three people crowded into the soft sofa looking out the large viewport window at the distant gathering of icerugs and flouwen, with two more sitting on the floor, two perched on the sofa back, and two on the galley stools. Gratefully they slurped at the mugs, which were a nice change from free-fall squeezers, while making themselves comfortable again. The humans, so carefully chosen years ago for their cooperative natures, had long since discarded any tendency to quarrel.

"I don't know about you," interjected Thomas, nibbling the crusty bits at the ends of his croissant that he had saved for last, "but I'm heading for my bunk. Slavedriver Shirley will be needing my body tomorrow to lower the *Dragonfly*."

"Don't forget to do your debriefing reports," reminded George. "Our primary purpose here is to gather information and pass it back to Earth."

"Let's sort out our report together," suggested Katrina to Cinnamon and Deirdre. "We'll direct it to Nels, including everything we saw. Perhaps, with James' help, he can come up with some answers to how this icerug creature lives—and how it got that way!" Cinnamon agreed instantly.

Deirdre was less enthusiastic. "Send Nels all we know, that's fine, but we're the ones who can best study the creatures, being on the spot. Reports of icerugs—it'll read like reports of dragons—he'll not be quite able to believe it's the truth we're telling."

Shirley stood, as Richard emerged from the shower, refreshed and dressed in his night coverall. "My report can wait just a bit," she said. "My turn for the hot water."

George glanced up. "Let's not linger over these reports anyway," he advised. "Just dump all the facts and observations you picked up into James and let him sort through them. We need to get some sleep. We've got only seven hours to sunrise, and first thing tomorrow we have to put the *Dragonfly* together. I'd like to get the flouwen into the water as soon as possible after that, then we'll visit the big city."

LOWERING

During the first part of the seven-hour night, well-illuminated by Gargantua moving from half-moon through full-moon and back to half-moon again, the flouwen learned from Gray-Mote that the icerugs also spent some part of the day "doing nothing at all."

"During the dark period that occurs near the middle of the day, when the Sun-God goes behind the Night-God, so that the eye of the Night-God is completely closed, it becomes very dark indeed. Without the energy coming into our bodies from the light emitted by the Sun-God, we imitate the Night-God and close our eye and rest. During that time, we will not be able to converse with you."

☐We find something else to do then,☐ said Little Purple. ☐Maybe find something to eat.☐

☆Hungry now!☆ announced Little Red. Within the confines of his suit, Little Red manipulated one of the self-sealing bags that carried a supply of preserved food, removed a strand of dried flatweed, and proceeded to digest it. The top of the strand could be seen in his head behind his "eyes," where the images of the three icerug nodes were focused on the red flesh inside his lensed helmet.

"How extraordinary!" exclaimed Gray-Mote, putting a monocle up before its eye to look closer at the slowly disappearing strand of seaweed. "I can see you digesting your food! How did it get there? Where is your mouth?"

☆All of me is mouth,☆ replied Little Red nonchalantly.

"But I can see your eye portion looking at me, so that isn't mouth," objected Gray-Mote.

In reply, Little Red moved the piece of flatweed right to the surface of his body and continued to digest his snack right where the image coming through his left lens was focused. ☆All of me is mouth,☆ he repeated. He swirled his fluid body around inside his helmet, the piece of flatweed moving with it, until he had cleared his lenses and had two eyes back again. ☆All of me is eye, too.☆

"But you have arms," objected Yellow-Star, pointing with one of its four jade tentacles at the glassy-foil covered pseudopods extending from holes in the neckring of Little Red's suit. "Three of them."

In reply, Little Red collapsed all three sleeves and drew the flesh into his suit, then filled the sleeves again. ☆All of me is arm, too.☆

"But you are obviously intelligent beings, so you must have a brain," said Pink-Orb.

☆All of me is brain, too.☆ said Little Red smugly. ☆*Smart* brain!☆

"Then you have *no* specialized structures inside that protective clothing?" asked Gray-Mote, finally beginning to comprehend the true alienness of the colorful creatures standing before it.

◊All cells in our body are the same,◊ said Little White.

◊All of them work at all things. But the whole of us is more than just all cells added up. The bigger we grow, the smarter we grow. We three are buds from our primaries, which are much bigger. They much smarter too.◊

"Most extraordinary," echoed Pink-Orb. "My fellow researchers at the Center for Scientific Studies will be most interested in hearing about a creature that is all brain."

Gray-Mote added its agreement. "And I am certain that when my reports are received at the Center for Medical Studies, they will be most interested in hearing about a creature that is all mouth. Indeed, all everything." Gray-Mote looked close again at the fast-disappearing seaweed strand. "That looks like a piece of seaweed."

☆Flatweed,☆ said Little Red.

◊Flatweed is plant, grows near volcanic vents in ocean of Eau on Rocheworld,◊ explained Little White. ◊May be like plants you have in your oceans.◊

"We could compare," said Gray-Mote. "I have some seaweed stored in my food locker. I will bring it here, along with some samples of the other kinds of food we eat."

Little Red opened his food bag to get some pieces of food to share. He was about to open the zipper on his suit to put them outside when he paused.

☆If we touch air here, what will happen?☆

◊The human Shirley said air is not poisonous to humans, so it cannot be too dangerous.◊

Little Red unzipped a small opening in his suit and extended a cautious red probe of flesh. Reassured, he said, ☆Thick. But not poisonous.☆ It did indeed seem dense to the flouwen. On their native planet, Rocheworld, the pressure was twenty percent that of Earth. Here—as the humans had observed—it was four times higher in pressure and density.

Little Red brought out some of the food supplies Cinnamon had stuffed into his suit, some flatweed, a flitter wing, and a light brown flat creature that the humans called a "gingersnap."

☆Here, taste!☆ said Little Red, thrusting the food toward the icerugs in the direct manner of the flouwen. The three icerugs each took a tiny sample, put them into their sharp-toothed mouths and chewed thoughtfully.

"Peculiar, but not inedible," said Gray-Mote. Its eye turned away to look back on its carpet. "The samples of our food will be here shortly." With their limited eyesight, the flouwen were not aware of anything approaching, until all at once they spied some objects moving towards them across Gray-Mote's carpet, as though they were flotsam moving on top of a turquoise wave.

"Ah," said Pink-Orb, looking with satisfaction at the approaching food. "There is a tasty portion—a coelashark head. The cheek muscle meat is especially delicious. Do sample it."

"I also brought a smallfish and some boardweed, somewhat like your flatweed but thicker. When dried it makes a good building material."

"And when you are finished using it to make things, you can always eat it," added Yellow-Star. "If you are hungry enough."

Gray-Mote removed a small stone scalpellike knife from a scabbard in the pouch hanging from its belt, and with its amazingly sharp blade sliced off small portions of the various samples of food. Cutting a slice of meat off the coelashark head was the difficult part.

"You can't get at the cheek meat from the outside," said Gray-Mote, tapping the point of its knife on the armored jaw of the dead coelashark. "You have to go through on the inside." With deft motions, the icerug surgeon used two tentacles to hold open the mouth of the coelashark, exposing the soft white skin inside, and used the other two to slice open the skin and remove the cheek muscle.

"No vermicysts, I suppose," said Yellow-Star, bending its large eye down to look inside the coelashark mouth.

"No. I checked. Long ago," said Gray-Mote. "The cheeks are snowy white."

Gray-Mote held out samples of all the foods to the three flouwen.

Little Red was eager to try, and his approving remarks induced the other two to join him. Little White remembered to put a small portion of each different type of food into sample bags. "To take to Katrina," he said.

"The human Katrina collects samples of everything," said Gray-Mote with understanding. "Certainly you may take back samples. In fact, you may take back the remains of the whole coelashark head. There is much to learn from examining it."

⊓Very tasty indeed!⊓ said Little Purple after finishing his bit. Gray-Mote moved closer, trembling just a bit with interest.

"That is surely significant that you can not only eat, but enjoy our food!"

◊We must share a common ancestor,◊ started Little White, but for once the translation computer, which had been ably handling the conversation so far, stopped at the last word.

"I am sorry," apologized Josephine as it took over the translation task from the computer program in Little White's suit. "But there seems to be no icerug word for 'ancestor.'"

"Strange!" interjected Thomas, who was monitoring the conversation of the icerugs and the flouwen from the comm console on *Victoria*. "Not even father or mother? How about husband or wife, or brother or sister? How about just 'relative'?"

Josephine was firm. "No words indicating any personal relationships at all."

"Must be a strong taboo—possibly related to a taboo about sex," concluded Thomas. "Better steer away from that topic, Little White."

"For some reason, that last phrase was not completely translated," Gray-Mote finally said after a long wait.

"We must share a common *taste*," corrected Little White, conscious that he was telling his first lie in his extremely long life. Flouwen could not lie to each other. Their mental processes were literally too transparent to the three-dimensional view of their insides that sonar sight provided. The coming of the humans had now taught Little White how to do something else that had never been done before by flouwen—and Little White was not sure he liked it.

"Yet, how different we are," mused Gray-Mote for a moment, then suddenly the icerug physician had another idea. "Here! Taste you of my flesh!" The flouwen were silent, horrified at such a suggestion.

◊Although we share memories with other flouwen by giving them a small taste of memory chemicals, we don't eat each other's flesh. We only eat animals and plants.◊

"No, no, it's quite all right. We don't mind a bit," Gray-Mote replied in reassurance. "We routinely trade flesh with each other. It will be a most interesting scientific experiment to see if you like it! You don't need to reciprocate if it would bother you." The icerug budded off three small portions of its body and held out the turquoise chunks of its flesh with its tentacle. The pieces of flesh remained flaccid, unlike an equivalently small portion budded off from a flouwen—which would have been very active.

Not so eager now, Little Red waited until both Little Purple and Little White had brought their shares within the confines of their suits and tasted them.

⊐Strange!⊐ said Little Purple. ⊐First, almost a memory, but not quite—like sharing thoughts with someone far from your pod who uses different words for things. But then . . . it just tastes like food.⊐

◊I tasted that, too,◊ said Little White. ◊Strong memories with bright pictures, all strange to me.◊

☆Almost, I understood,☆ said Little Red with unaccustomed seriousness. ☆A bit, about water, almost clear, but then—crazy sounds and colors.☆

◊We can taste some of your memories,◊ concluded Little White. ◊But they are not clear.◊

"The fact that you could taste any memories at all is most interesting," said Gray-Mote. "This will certainly be of interest to those in the Center for Medical Studies—transferring knowledge by means of taste. Perhaps you could go there to help them conduct some experiments."

◊We have other work to do here,◊ said Little White firmly. ◊We must explore ocean under ice and meet the coelasharks.◊ Little White, however, being a flouwen astronomer, was anxious to talk further with Pink-Orb, the icerug astronomer, to test the icerug's level of understanding of planetary dynamics. He turned from Gray-Mote to Pink-Orb.

◊You told us the largest eruptions of the Geyser-God Manannán occur when Near-God and Far-God and Sun-God are all in a line behind Ice. How do you know the Gods are all in a line when you can't see them?◊

The translation program in Little White's suit converted the flouwen's question, and the suit imp on the outside of Little White's suit used its speaker cone to convert the question into deep sounding tones centered in the icerug's hearing range. There was a pause as the eyes of the icerugs rolled around on their bent stalks as they looked at each other. Obviously, something again had gone wrong in the translation.

"I will answer your question," finally replied Pink-Orb, after rolling its eye back to look at Little White. "But first, we need to remove a misunderstanding between us. Your statements, as we hear them from the glittering machine, refer to the objects in the skies with words that imply they are deities to be worshiped. It is true that our ancient astronomers gave those objects the names of gods, and sometimes, even today, we refer to their actions as if they were living beings—such as saying 'the Night-God closing its eye'—but we know those objects are not gods. They are just spherical bodies composed of various different materials that are orbiting around each other following the orbital laws."

Thomas interjected a comment. "Same thing back in the solar system—Mercury, Venus, Mars, Jupiter—nearly all the planets and moons are named after old-time gods."

Little White was relieved to hear what Pink-Orb had to say. ◊Good! I thought you use stories about gods instead of mathematics to predict conjunctions.◊

"Of *course* not!" said Pink-Orb loudly, and then went on. "I have excellent telescopes with which to observe the various objects in the sky. I have long observed the motions of the moons and recorded their positions with respect to the stars. I also use mathematics to calculate their orbits with great precision and my calculations agree with my observations. It is relatively simple to use the orbital equations to calculate when those objects which are out of sight must be lined up with those objects which we can see."

◊Tell me how you calculate orbits of moons,◊ said Little White.

"It is not easy." The astronomer Pink-Orb was slightly condescending. "It starts with a simple mathematical rule, based on the logic of gravity for a spherical mass: One massive object will attract a second massive object with a force that is directly proportional to the product of the masses of the two objects, and inversely proportional to the square of the distance between the centers of mass of the two objects. The rule is relatively simple to apply to two or three spherical masses, but after that it is simple no longer and must be solved by using approximations. With great patience, I and others at the Center for Scientific Studies have worked out the orbits and cycles for all of the objects in our sky, but it took a great deal of time. It is very complex mathematics, and only a few of us are capable of understanding it. I, however—"

Little White could not restrain himself longer. ◊It is simple! Rule for many spheres is simple!◊

⊓That's right,⊓ said Little Purple. ⊓Rule combines complex variable substitution with coordinate transformation into an nth root dimensional space, where n is number of spheres.⊓

The icerugs were silent for a long moment. "I do not understand," said Pink-Orb finally.

◊Maybe translation unclear . . .◊

☆Here, taste!☆ said Little Red impatiently, opening his suit and moving a fleshy red pseudopod to within reach of the alien astronomer's tentacles. Slowly, hesitantly, the velvet-furred plummy tentacle arose and met the glistening wet red pseudopod, and for an eerie instant, the two representatives of such different and alien species touched each other.

"There was a strong and very complex taste, but that's all," said Pink-Orb flatly, who, unlike the flouwen, was unable to pass on information by taste chemicals.

◊It is so beautiful,◊ pleaded Little White, frustrated. ◊Simple nth root dimensional space! It makes difficult equations easy.◊

"I do not understand." Pink-Orb's bass voice took on a deeper growl. Little Purple, remembering the injunction of the humans not to overstay their welcome, decided it was time to leave. Diplomatically returning to discussion of their shared interest in what might lie beneath the surface of the ocean, the flouwen chatted a few moments longer, promising to share further information later.

"I must say good-bye now," said Pink-Orb. "I have a very long way to travel. Please inform the humans that I will be returning to my assigned area in the city, from where I will inform the Presider and the Governing Council that they may expect a visit from the humans shortly."

Gray-Mote and Yellow-Star parted their carpets along their adjoining edges, leaving a narrow path of ice, and Pink-Orb's pedestal started down the path, a surging wave of plum-colored flesh preceding the node as it laid down a carpet for the pedestal to travel on. Long after the node had passed on, the stream of velvety flesh flowed out of the field that Pink-Orb had been inhabiting. After the last portion of Pink-Orb's body had disappeared, the gap between Gray-Mote and Yellow-Star closed, and the two icerugs glided silently away over their colored carpets into the Gargantuan-lit gloom of nighttime to return to their own affairs, while the flouwen plodded back to the lander, burdened with sample bags.

There, night-watchman Thomas, with the aid of the Christmas Branch, hauled them back up on the winch and sucked them back into their habitat, where they refreshed their bodies with crystal-clear ammonia-water.

At first light, Josephine awoke the crew with her accustomed gentleness. "Rise and shine, my dearies."

Deirdre, accustomed to rising quickly to attend to Foxx's few needs, was startled to find herself a trifle stiff in movement. A moment later, Richard groaned, and after climbing out of the hanging harness of his vertical bunk, designed more for free-fall than gravity, he bent double several times in the narrow aisle, twisting as he did so.

"Boy, you think you keep in shape, working out in the gym on *Prometheus*, but then you do real work, in real gravity, and find some surprised muscles."

The rest discovered their own sore spots quickly, but the small aches were soon dissipated in activity. Since there was hard work coming up, they settled down to Josephine's "cooked breakfast" of cereal, juice, scrambled algae-egg, pseudo-sausage or slices of real ham from Hamlet, toasted algae-flour bread, broiled mushrooms and cherry tomatoes from the hydroponics gardens on *Prometheus*, and a hot beverage.

As they ate, scattered here and there in the lounge and galley stools, George went over their plans, the flouwen in their tank being connected to the discussion through George's imp.

"According to Josephine, by the time we get suited up and down on the surface, we'll have about three hours of light, which we'll use to get the *Dragonfly* down and ready. Then it's going to get really dark for about an hour and a half, and we'd better not try to take off until that's over. Do you Littles want to suit up? While we work on lowering and assembling the *Dragonfly*, you could go visit the icerugs, with one of us along if you want."

Little Purple considered. ⌐Not worth it. Takes time to get there. Then, when deep dark comes, they do nothing, like when you sleep. They told us that.⌐

Here was a new fact for Deirdre, Cinnamon, and Katrina to mull over.

"Photosynthesis cuts off?"

"Sounds like it."

"No energy input, so they have to shut down."

Little Red was eager to get into the water and start exploring. ☆Don't want to talk to icerugs any more. Icerugs not *dumb*, but not as smart as flouwen, either.☆

◊I think,◊ said Little White mildly, ◊we wait here while you get *Dragonfly* ready.◊

Little Red was disappointed. ☆I come out and help!☆

"I know, ol' buddy, you want to do what you call helping," said Richard. "But it'll go a lot faster if you stay put this morning!"

After passing in their trays to the galley imp to clean, all the crew except Cinnamon climbed into their exploration suits. Cinnamon was scheduled for shift duty inside the *Victoria*, monitoring the activities outside, making sure all the communication links back to *Prometheus* and Earth were functional, and ready at any time to activate the Ascent Propulsion Stage of *Victoria* for quick takeoff, in case they had to leave in a hurry.

By the time Barnard rose in the east, eight suited figures were gathered on the ground at the base of the lander looking up at the task that lay before them. In a long crease that went up the side of the forty-six-meter high cylindrical lander was an airplane with clipped off wings, *Dragonfly III*. On the top and bottom of each of the wing stubs was a circular cover that protected the two-meter-diameter VTOL fans underneath. Shirley was now in her element, supervising the lowering and assembly of the *Dragonfly*.

"Thomas!" Shirley called through her imp. "Is the upper nose winch hook in place?"

"Yes," replied Josephine, echoed by Thomas.

"Okay, Josephine, release the hold-down lugs!" The strong claws of the holding clamps opened all along the side of the *Dragonfly* in a rippling clank, and the airplane tilted free of the elastomer seals and hung, swinging slightly, from its nose, with its tail still fastened firmly to the top of the landing strut.

"Let out the top winch!" Josephine started the nose winch rotating, paying out cable. Slowly the long vehicle, part airplane and part spacecraft, tilted away from the side of the lander, pivoting around its tail, still fixed at the base of the lander. As the nose of the *Dragonfly* came clear, the watchers on the ground could now see the triangular windows on the flight deck. Behind them were the bulbous hemispherical glass domes on each side of the airplane that together allowed the port and starboard science scan platforms a view in nearly every direction from the ship. It was partially the bulbous eyelike domes that gave *Dragonfly* its name, plus, when its wings were on and its engines were powered up, the airplane—like a dragonfly—could not only use its jets to fly at high speed, but use its VTOL fans to hover motionlessly.

"Now, Josephine, let out both winches at the same time!" Deep inside the *Victoria*, the two winches, one up near the nose and one down near the tail, rotated in synchronism, slowly letting out more cable. Then, tilted at a thirty degree angle, the *Dragonfly* slid on its tail down the lowering rail built into the landing strut. As the rear of the airplane came free from the crease in the lander, the watchers could see the tall tail rudder come into view. On either side of the rudder could now be seen the two sets of tapered hollow wing sections.

When the tail reached a point about two meters from the end of the lowering rail, Shirley called a halt. Then, after checking everything once more, she started the upper winch again. Slowly the winch, squeaking slightly in the frozen air, lowered the nose of the plane down, and the long fuselage rotated about the pivot point near the tail until it was horizontal. Thomas, high up on the engineering deck, held onto the handholds in the open airlock as the lander tilted noticeably under the load.

"Lower landing gear," said Shirley, peering beneath the belly of the plane. Three slots opened, releasing metal struts with skids on the bottom.

"Lower away!" commanded Shirley, and the winches, slowed even further by Josephine's sure touch, gently deposited the *Dragonfly* onto Zulu's surface, its smooth duralloy surface submitting unmoving to Arielle's tender pats. With the body of the aerospace vehicle on the ground, but still wingless, Arielle and David cycled through the airlock of the *Dragonfly*, woke up Joe, and started taking the computer and the vehicle through its self-check routine.

"That's got it!" shouted Shirley. George and Richard, who had been waiting at each end, undid the hooks at the ends of the lowering cables, and the winches began to retract the cables. Shirley used the hook retreating into the lower winch to hoist herself up into the base of the lander where the wing sections were nested.

"Right. Now everyone out to catch the wing pieces! Thomas, man the winch up there!"

Thomas pushed out, on its rollers, the beam in the

ceiling of the airlock, until the winch on the end of the beam hung over the side of the lander. Josephine sent the Christmas Branch down the hanging cable to the hook at the end, looking like a giant glittering spider climbing down its thread to get a fly. The Christmas Branch attached the hook to a lifting lug on the inner piece of the nested wing sections. The sections were hollow graphite-fiber composite structures designed without internal bracing, with their inner and outer contours shaped so they would nest together into a compact package. With Shirley shouting instructions and guiding the sections out of their storage position, Thomas and Josephine used the upper winch to slowly pull each section out one at a time and lower them down to teams of waiting crew members.

With uplifted arms the humans received them, minding Shirley's admonitions: "Slowly, now! Let the winch bear their weight. Guide them into their proper position on each side of the *Dragonfly*, slowly, slowly . . ."

"You'd think we hadn't done this before," grunted Richard, his arms outstretched to help Sam, George, and Katrina as the four of them swiveled the five-by-six-meter section of wing into position.

"She acts the same way every time, too," said George. "She sure likes playing crew chief."

"Boss lady, you mean," muttered Katrina under her breath, so softly even her imp missed it. Normally cheerful and eager to help, Katrina found her lack of height to be a real handicap in operations of this sort. She was happy to step away when the load was on the ground and reach for the descending packages of struts and telescoping poles.

Paying only moderate attention to Shirley's shouted directions, the crew moved into their well-practiced drill of assembling the wing sections on the airplane. Using the telescoping poles, they erected a tripod over the first wing section with a winch at the apex. With a boost from Richard, Shirley climbed up on top of the stub of wing on *Dragonfly*, and operated the winch control from there, lifting the wing section up by a central lug set over its center of mass, while Richard, George, Sam, and Deirdre guided the wing section until the edges of the larger of its open ends was matched up with the opening in the wing stub. Inside the hollow wing stub waited the Christmas Branch assigned to the *Dragonfly*, holding an internal strut Katrina had handed it. Once the new section of wing was nearly in place, the Christmas Branch jumped the narrow gap and installed the strut inside the new wing section. With the sparkling motile still inside, helping to guide the edges together, the tall humans swung the hollow wing section gently into its proper place. Just before the moment of contact, the imp removed the protective covering from the seals on either side of the joints. At this point, Shirley straddled the narrowing joint herself and used her own considerable strength to bring the two sections closer with the aid of a long, pointed pry-bar. As the sections clicked together and were fastened internally by the Christmas Bush rotating lag screws into place, Shirley slapped a gloved hand with her pry-bar and gave a satisfied snort.

"Her favorite tool," said Sam. "Did you ever move too slowly for Shirley?"

"No," replied Richard, slightly puzzled.

"I did," said Sam, reflectively rubbing a spot high up on his long thigh. "Once."

Deirdre, working beside him, said nothing, but glinted a bright glance up at Sam.

Shirley looked up at the sun. It was more than halfway between the horizon and Gargantua overhead. "Keep it moving!" she demanded. "We've only got a little daylight left!"

The work continued without interruption or flaw. Finally, the last two outer wingtip sections were installed. Joe, under Shirley's close scrutiny, pumped the air from the wing tanks and verified that there were no leaks. Then, while Cinnamon monitored Josephine's gauges, and Arielle monitored Joe's gauges, the wing tanks on *Dragonfly* were filled with the residual monopropellant fuel left in the oversized attitude control fuel tanks inside the *Victoria*.

As Barnard set behind Gargantua, and the noon-day eclipse darkness fell, the crew left the *Dragonfly* waiting on its skids on the snow-blown rock and clambered back up into the *Victoria* for one last meal together. In the afternoon, they would separate into two teams, one team of four people to stay with the lander and carry out exploration missions from that fixed base, and the other team of six people, who would go off in the airplane and explore more distant sites. As they came out of the airlock into the engineering deck and took off their helmets, they could smell fresh-baked rolls being cooked in the tiny galley in the crew deck above.

"Smells good," Richard hollered up the passway ladder. "What are they—cinnamon buns?"

"Just for that crack, you don't get any," came Cinnamon's retort back down the passway. "They're just plain hot dog rolls. We're having pseudo-wieners and carrot sticks for lunch. Even you should be able to eat those without spilling food inside your suit."

Since the crew assigned to the *Dragonfly* were going right back out after lunch, they didn't bother to take off their exploration suits, but sprawled out, tired, on the engineering deck. Cinnamon and the Christmas Branch brought the food down, and they had a picnic on the floor. Sometime during the meal, however, they each took turns using the special extractor on the engineering deck to empty out the urine collectors in their suits.

"Say," said Richard, after he finished using the extractor, "I was wondering how the flouwen manage in their suits. How often are we going to have to bring them back to the habitat tank?"

"They can last a long time, but if it becomes urgent, they just unzip their fly and let it fly," replied Shirley.

"You're kidding!" said Richard. "They don't have a . . ."

Cinnamon, who had made a detailed study of the flouwen needs, gave Richard a lecture on flouwen physiology. "The flouwen, because their bodies are made of undifferentiated cells, and because of the highly varied environment they evolved in, have a lot of ability to control their body chemistry. Although they require some ammonia, and prefer water with ten percent ammonia to ninety percent water, their ocean on Eau varies from extremely cold ammonia-rich water near the poles to extremely hot ammonia-free water near the vent fields. So, they've evolved an internal chemistry that is tolerant to large temperature variations and chemical concentrations."

"Including waste products?" asked Richard.

"Yes," she replied. "The metabolism of their individual cells produces waste, and since the lifetime of the cells is only a few weeks, when the cells die they become waste, too. Normally, in the ocean of Eau, the flouwen body just transports those wastes to the surface and dumps them. When they are in their suits, however, they just concentrate the unwanted compounds in a globule somewhere in their body. Since we have asked them to avoid polluting this planet, they will normally wait until they return to their habitat to void the contents of their waste globule. But, if necessary, as Shirley said, they can just unzip their suits, and bring the globule to the surface and expel it."

"I'm glad they're house-trained!" Richard said with relief. "I'd hate to smell what they are trying to get rid of. They smell bad enough fresh."

☆Hey!☆ came Little Red's voice over Richard's imp.

As the crew finished eating, George reminded them of their plans for the afternoon.

"As soon as you've finished eating, head back outside. Even though it's still dark, we can use the outside lights on the two vehicles while we transfer personal belongings, supplies, tools—everything Josephine has listed—into the airplane. Then, all we'll need to do at daylight is a walk-around inspection, then go aboard and take off. Our first and most important mission is to find a good spot to put the flouwen into the water."

☆Good!☆ interrupted Little Red's voice. ☆About time!☆

"May take us a while," warned Richard. "We need a hole in the ice, but not a boiling geyser, interesting though it might be to drop you into the pot, Little Red."

☆Hunh,☆ said Little Red, unworried.

"So, flouwen," George continued, "it's back into your suits, so you can fly with us in the *Dragonfly*." He turned to look at the assembled crew. "As planned, Thomas, Sam, Cinnamon, and Katrina will be staying here with the lander at the main base, taking shifts at the communications center."

"Good," said Katrina. "That'll give me and Cinnamon time to put some of those samples we collected under a good microscope."

"And I'll be wanting to explore the geology around the landing site," said Sam.

"Of course," replied George. "And all of you can take turns getting to know the local icerug community better. We need to know what life is like out here in the icerug equivalent of 'the sticks,' as well as what goes on in the big city. Make sure, however, that one of you is always at the communications console." He got up and reached for his helmet. "The remaining six of us assigned to the *Dragonfly* had better start packing."

"Good!" said Thomas. "The sooner you guys go, the sooner we can take apart your bunks and arrange them into something more comfortable to sleep in than a hanging harness."

"Amen to that," said Sam. "My feet are still sore from trying to sleep vertically last night."

"I'll start the flouwen transfer system, if someone will go into the airlock and watch to make sure they get pumped into their suits safely," said Cinnamon, climbing up the passway rungs to the flight deck at the top of the lander.

The rest of the midday eclipse seemed very brief to Deirdre, as, with the others, she quickly sorted through the few belongings she would take over to her storage area on the *Dragonfly*. Shirley glanced quizzically at the small bundle Deirdre had under one arm, the other arm swinging Foxx's travel cage, caps now screwed onto its portholelike windows to make it a hermetically sealed box.

"You *do* travel light, don't you, Deirdre? That parcel would barely hold my extra socks, let alone shampoos and lotions."

Deirdre didn't bother to answer. The efficient shower aboard the *Dragonfly* worked as well as the one in her apartment aboard *Prometheus*, and Deirdre was content with the daily scrubbing that kept her fair skin glowing and smelling faintly of soap. She was soon back in the airlock, helping Richard check out the drysuited flouwen.

Cinnamon's voice was warm and reassuring over the link from the communications console as she checked the quality of the communications channels to and from each of the flouwen's chestpacks. "We'll be able to keep in constant touch, I know. David's got a great software package rigged up to insure that—he'll tell you about it as you go."

☆Let's go!☆ said Little Red as soon as he had filled up his suit and pushed out the unwanted water. He surged towards the outer airlock door, heedless of Little White and Little Purple still going through their checkout.

"Now, when you meet up with the coelasharks, be sure to find out where they eat, as well as what sort of food it is," said Deirdre.

Katrina, who was now monitoring the airlock controls and watching the suiting up process through the airlock porthole, injected her own admonitions. "We need to know if they are entirely dependent on the volcanic vents for food. But be very careful. Even if they are intelligent, they sound like they are bad-tempered. We don't want you ending up as part of their menu!" Katrina laughed gaily, but Little Red stopped in his tracks.

☆Hunh, more like other way around,☆ he growled.

"Aye, it would be," agreed Deirdre softly. When she and Richard had the flouwen checked out, Katrina opened the outer airlock door. One after the other, the flouwen were lowered to the ground, where they plodded, slid, and rolled their way across the snow-blown rock, looking like penguins crossing hummocky ice, until they got to the airlock door of the *Dragonfly*. There, Richard boosted them up, while Deirdre cycled them through.

The airlock for the *Dragonfly* was under the left wing.

Inside, it opened into the back portion of the long fuse-lage that was used for utility functions—suit storage, air-conditioning, laundry, and the Christmas Branch's work wall—a labyrinth of narrow corridors lined from floor to ceiling with racks of compact analyzing and syn-thesizing machines. Aft of the work wall was the power conditioning section, and behind that was stored the spare air and water, and a large tank of monopropellant fuel that augmented the fuel tanks inside the the hollow wings. The equipment, consumables, and fuel, along with a heavy lead shadow shield, provided shielding for the crew from the radiation emitted by the small nuclear re-actor in the tail.

Forward of the utilities section, closed off by privacy curtains at each end, was the crew quarters section with six private bunks and a toilet and shower. Forward of the bunks was a small galley and food storage, and forward of that were the two science consoles and the computer console. At the nose of the plane was the cockpit for the pilot and copilot, while between the cockpit and the work consoles were the port and starboard science scan plat-forms, whose sensors looked out through the bubblelike domed windows. Because the imaging sensors on the scan platforms produced a better view of the outside than could be seen with the human eye, the only views out of the plane were from the cockpit windows, around the instruments in the scan platform domes, and through the porthole in the airlock door.

Arielle and George went forward to the cockpit, swiv-eling by the chairs at the science consoles occupied by Richard and Deirdre, Arielle stopping off at the galley first to grab an algae-shake to take with her. David fol-lowed along behind and settled himself in at the computer console, while Shirley stayed in the back, checking out and hanging up all their exploration suits. Then, she jury-rigged a harness inside the airlock to hold each of the three flouwen, ostensibly for their safety in case the flight became rough, but mostly to keep them from getting in the way. As the sun was peeking out again from behind Gargantua, Arielle, David, and Josephine put Joe through the final checkout of the *Dragonfly*.

"Self-check routine continuing—eighteen." Josephine's voice was precise, and so was Joe's.

"Right, luv. Eighteen." Arielle was amused by this, but recognized the phrase meant only the more traditional "Affirmative," as did Joe's occasional, "Oo, aye." Sitting in her favorite place, at the controls of the *Dragonfly*, Arielle felt the warm sense of anticipation she always did before a flight. As interested as she certainly was in the alien icerugs, and eager always to learn more, she still felt most at home in this seat, with her hands waiting in her lap, holding the remains of her algae-shake. She used her imp to call the galley imp forward, and after handing it the empty shake tumbler, she took firm hold of the controls.

Seated beside Arielle, George contented himself with admiring the skill with which she piloted the airplane. With exquisite care, she powered up the electrically driven VTOL fans on the wings, and the craft slowly and smoothly rose vertically from the rocky surface. Only at safe altitude did she increase reactor power and cut to the jet-bypass turbines, which sucked in air from the alien atmosphere, heated it up by passing it through heat exchangers connected to the nuclear reactor, and jetted the hot air out the exhaust nozzle in the tail to provide forward thrust.

Despite Shirley's company, Little Red was soon bored. ☆Doesn't feel like flying at all.☆

◊And nothing to see,◊ said Little White.

"Why not check the mail?" suggested David through his imp. "That's what I do when I'm stuck somewhere."

Deirdre chuckled. How often she'd seen Katrina, confronting a recalcitrant problem, nonchalantly stand and stretch and stroll away, murmuring something about seeing if there were any messages.

☆Mail?☆ Little Red was puzzled, but Little Purple was pleased with the idea of mail.

⊓We can use our suits to talk to our primary selves on Rocheworld.⊓

A query was put through Joe to Josephine, and then to James, who opened up a link between the flouwen drysuits and the underwater communications console in Agua Dulce Bay on the Eau lobe of Rocheworld. Although the transmission delay through the laser communicators was several minutes long, since Rocheworld was now moving closer to Barnard in its highly elliptical orbit, the massive flouwen back on Rocheworld could indeed communicate with their traveling small buds. Soon, messages were on their way back, and as the words of support and encouragement began to be received, all three flouwen settled more comfortably into their confining suits:

"Nothing like a letter from home," said David, just a little wistfully, as he monitored the communications link. Home was only minutes away for the flouwen, while for the humans it was six years—twelve years for a round-trip message.

"Look at all the icerugs down there!" exclaimed Richard as they rose higher into the air. "They cover the ice clear to the horizon."

"They *do* call themselves the 'coverers-of-the-ice,'" reminded Deirdre, who was monitoring the imaging instruments on the scan platform that looked in the other direction from the *Dragonfly*. "But, on the left there, out about a kilometer, there's none at all. It must be we're on the edge, here, of the colony."

"Look at all the different colors," said David appreciatively, switching his screen to Richard's. "Peacock-blue, cerulean-blue, malachite, there's a sort of lapis—no two of them exactly alike."

"It's a grand view, indeed," said Deirdre. "We can collect some statistics, with that number of samples. Josephine, what is the average area per icerug?"

"Discounting the regions near the boundary, which are bound to be atypical, the average area seems to be about four thousand square meters," Josephine replied. "That would be a square about sixty-five meters on a side, although they seem to favor triangular shapes that allow a number of them to come together at one point."

"What's that come to in acres?" asked Richard.

"About an acre, or four-tenths of a hectare," replied Deirdre, who had learned both systems in her youth. "And why so much, I wonder?" she continued. "So large as that, they cannot move easily, nor can they get together readily."

"Well," suggested Richard, "if they're plants, running on photosynthesis, maybe they need all that area to capture enough of Barnard's weak light to keep their node alive. Josephine, what is the total illumination falling on an icerug?"

"Since the visual luminosity of Barnard is only one two-thousandth that of the Sun, while Barnard is about four times closer to Zulu than the Sun is to Earth, the light here is one five-hundredth of that falling on Earth, or about three watts per square meter, so the total illumination on a four thousand square meter icerug is twelve kilowatts. Since we don't know how efficient their photosynthesis process is, the amount that gets converted into useful energy is unknown. At night, when the illumination is coming from light reflected from Gargantua, the incident illumination drops to four percent of that during the day, or about a hundred and sixty watts. There is also a substantial infrared output from both Barnard and Gargantua that cannot be used for photosynthesis, but which does help somewhat in keeping them warmer than their surroundings."

"We humans expend hundreds of watts while active," reasoned Deirdre. "And the nodes are about our size. If these creatures can store up energy by making new flesh during the lighted hours, they then have it to use to stay warm during the dark times."

As the *Dragonfly* headed away from the lander, Richard and Deirdre kept their viewscreens focused on the surface below, searching for interesting features in the monotonous landscape of acre after acre of blue-green icerugs.

"The average size of the icerug areas is dropping as we get closer to the city region around the Manannán geyser," Josephine reported. "Their areas are now closer to one thousand square meters."

"Might be getting more energy from the geyser and less from photosynthesis," remarked Deirdre.

The infrared scanners methodically swept the terrain, measuring and recording the varying temperatures of the icerug surface. Deirdre and Richard monitored the infrared image on their console screens, watching for a telltale flat yellow region that would mean a lake formed by a local hot spring. Suddenly they spoke simultaneously: "There, off to the left!" The *Dragonfly* banked smoothly and started to descend as Arielle circled around the lake, looking for a good spot to land.

"Look you, how none of the icerugs go up close to the shore," observed Deirdre.

"If the ice along the lake shore is like the ice shelves around Antarctica, those are dangerous places to be," replied Richard. "If a large ice floe breaks off, an icerug could be torn in two—or find itself stranded on a rapidly shrinking iceberg with no way to get back."

Below them, the glacier ice around the lake shore was obviously very thick, rising sheer some three meters from the water. The extreme edge of the cliff was irregular and sharp, suggesting that pieces had broken off abruptly rather than been worn away. Floating in the lake were pale blue-green icebergs and large flat-topped ice floes that had obviously calved from the icy shoreline. Arielle took the little plane slowly along the cliff-top shore, looking carefully for an area smooth enough to land. With a pleased grunt, she veered into a circle and steered the *Dragonfly* into a gentle descent onto a wind-slicked slope, which rose at the far end. Using her VTOL fans, she settled the *Dragonfly* slowly into the snow, ready to lift again if the landing struts didn't find support. The snow cover wasn't thick, and they settled smoothly onto the hard ice underneath. Even as Arielle began the routine of closing down the engines and securing the plane ready for takeoff, Deirdre and Richard were up out of their seats, Deirdre to stow Foxx in her exploration suit, and Richard heading for the rear to help Shirley with the flouwen.

"Just wait and stay still until I unhook you!" said Shirley to the three harnessed flouwen. Little Red was not a patient creature, and in his eagerness to get out was beginning to surge awkwardly within his harness.

"We have to have Richard outside the airlock to help you down," Shirley reminded them. Richard quickly put on his exploration suit, helped Deirdre check hers, and the two ducked through the airlock, and then out onto the surface of the snow. They stared around them in the dim silence, listening to the moan of the icy wind through the *Dragonfly*'s landing struts. Barnard's light was bright enough, in this clear air, to sparkle redly on the dense snowpack, and Deirdre stamped, enjoying the brief glitter. Both people grinned, in quick appreciation of their strange surroundings, before turning to help the flouwen.

"Okay, Little Red, easy does it!" The strong shoulders of both humans carefully took most of the weight of the hundred kilo flouwen in a controlled tumble to the ground, and Deirdre assisted him upright with a cheerful "Upsy-daisy!" before turning to catch Little White.

◊Near the water! I can tell,◊ said Little White, ◊even inside this suit. Must we really keep these things on?◊ It was unlike Little White to complain, and George looked at the creature with sympathy.

"We talked over the need for the suits very thoroughly, you know," he said gently. "Not only does it make it possible for us to know exactly where you are at all times, it protects both you and the water from any mutual pollution."

Shirley clucked in sympathy. "It really *is* important, but I know how you must feel—it'd be like swimming in an old-fashioned bathing costume."

Deirdre said nothing, her mind automatically rejecting the analogy. Flouwen and human sensations were so alien to each other that comparisons were worse than useless. "You'll be able to get along just fine, Little White. Here comes David, and he'll be explaining how your communication link will work."

David emerged from the lock, just as Josephine

opened a cargo door in the bottom of the *Dragonfly* and lowered a small amphibious crawler to the ground. Since it didn't need a large cargo hold and long-lasting power supply, this crawler was smaller than the exploration crawlers—only one meter long and a half-meter wide and high. Its name, *Babble*, was painted in bright red on its side. It crawled out from under the airplane's belly on its finned treads, equally effective for travel on ice or water. David jumped down beside *Babble*, and began to explain its workings to the aliens.

"*Babble* will be going into the water behind you three, and will always be trying to stay with you. Of course, since you can swim much faster than it can, even in those suits, it won't be able to always keep up, but it will soon catch up with you when you stop to explore something."

☆Not going to wait for it,☆ grumbled Little Red.

"Of course not," said David patiently. "It's just your message center. See, this bubble underneath is its sonar dome. It'll be listening to your messages from below sent through the sonar transponder in your suits. When it gets them, it transmits the message by radio through this antenna on top, up to the commsats, and thence to Joe, Josephine, James and us. We can answer you, too, and the messages will go by radio up to the commsats, then down through the radio antenna, out the sonar bubble, and down to you. When you aren't actively sending messages back and forth, you'll be hearing its 'ping!' every six seconds tracking you, but you don't have to answer, it's just following along."

"These flipper treads on the side help it to swim through the water," said Shirley. "It can even move the crawler over the ice, if it has to. Rather like having a water beetle for a pet!"

☆Pet dumber than usual,☆ said Little Red rudely.

Deirdre was amused; Little Red's sulks were not going to obtain his freedom from the hampering suits and the communications relay crawler, but they were entertaining. David, however, reacted in defense of his ingeniously contrived radio link; the crawler had been engineered on Earth and modified by Caroline and Shirley for this mission, but the high reliability multiredundant multichannel communications software that would maintain contact with the flouwen despite underwater sonar channel fading and wave noise was his own.

"Not at all like a pet," he said. "It's a two-way radio, that's all, but one made just for you, and for this place, and these conditions. Even under the ice, you'll never be alone!" There was a brief pause, after those triumphant words.

◊Hunh,◊ said Little White dubiously. Little Red's response was a wordless snort. David's suit computer made no attempt to translate it.

Arielle had scrambled out of the *Dragonfly* last, and the nine living creatures stood in silence, surveying the eerie beauty in front of them. Tiny wavelets lapped soundlessly at the snow beneath their feet, and farther out, chunks of brash ice of all sizes and shapes floated on the quiet surface, forming a disjointed mosaic whose pattern constantly and slowly shifted. Farther out yet, the shrinking icebergs, greenish-gray in the red light of Barnard, increased the perceived perspective of distance; their dwindling masses fooling the human eye into thinking they were very far away.

Shirley and Richard moved swiftly to fasten a winch to a jury-rigged A-frame derrick that was long enough to swing the winch out beyond the jagged cliff-face. David switched on the programmed personality that was *Babble*, and nodded approval as the calm little voice began.

"In the water, over the ice—I splash along, crawl along, follow Little Red, follow Little Purple, follow Little White, not worry, not trouble, just follow and talk and listen, and chatter and listen, and babble and listen, and call and listen, and talk . . ."

Deirdre had been helping Little White adjust the amplification on the transponder in his suit. The crawler's voice amused her—but Little White spoke in obvious dismay.

◊All the *time* that thing going?◊

Firmly though she refused to succumb to anthropomorphism, Deirdre felt quick sympathy for Little White, and hastened to reassure the flouwen.

"No, no, it's just blethering, now, so David can test it out. As soon as you're away it'll only be the ping signal, unless you call for more."

Little Red, too, had stopped, to turn almost menacingly towards the little crawler, but David was finished checking *Babble* out, and it stopped talking, so he resumed his ponderous progress toward the edge of the lake.

George and Richard hoisted the hundred kilo crawler easily between them in the low gravity of Zulu. Walking over to the brink of the ice, they hung it from the hook at the end of the cable and stepped back to join the others.

Carefully maneuvering the lines and the winch, Shirley and Richard swung the crawler out and over the edge, to lay it gently upon the surface of the water. As the lines were released and removed, the flipper-treads on either side of the machine began their slow and steady motion.

"Off I go, into the water. *Ping* and listen . . ."

Little White and Little Purple edged close to the rim of the snow-covered ice, and the humans came up to assist them. Attaching a line to a lifting point on the flouwen's backpack harness, they used the winch to lower Little White's cumbersome bulk into the water. Spreading out the baggy suit into a flattened shape that was suitable for swimming through the water, Little White dove below the surface with a happy-sounding sigh. Little Purple soon followed, and the two humans turned to reach for Little Red.

Little Red, however, had quietly moved back, away from the shore, and was standing, waiting—for all to notice.

"What is it, Little Red?" asked Richard in surprise. "Aren't you going to let us lower you . . ." Then he grinned in comprehension. Portentously, dramatically, Little Red tilted to one side in the round-bottomed suit and began to move, rolling over the ice faster and faster, his head whirling around and around at dizzying speed while his pseudopods pushed on the ice to make himself go faster. By the time he reached the edge of the ice, his speed was sufficient to propel him out over the water with a triumphant shout, and he cannonballed into the water with a tremendous and satisfying splash that sent a geyser of water up onto the shore. The drenched humans chuckled; such obvious joy was a delight to see, and the drops rolled harmlessly off their suits.

"Water warm!" was the first communication from the flouwen, already nearly invisible deep under the clear dark water.

"Only someone brought up in an ocean made out of an ammonia-water antifreeze solution would think that ice-cold water was warm," remarked Richard dryly.

The little crawler set off busily after the flouwen, its treading flippers churning smoothly. Watching it move across the surface, the humans could follow the direction the flouwen were taking, down below. Meanwhile,

Babble was transmitting back the comments that the flouwen were making.

◊Water feels warmer than home, even through suit,◊ commented Little White. ◊Not bad, but when we get closer to the hot vents, we may be glad we have suits on, so we don't lose ammonia.◊

Shirley and George exchanged a pleased look—the comment was as close as Little White was likely to come to a compliment.

☆Find coelasharks! Come *on*!☆ roared Little Red, and the small crawler's amphibious tread splashed up a froth of foam as it headed rapidly off into the lake and was soon lost to sight of the watching people on the shore.

SPEAKING

Back at the lander, Barnard was just setting behind some low clouds hanging over the leading pole horizon when Sam got to his feet, wincing just a little as his back straightened. He had been kneeling on the cold basalt for nearly a half-hour, driving a corer through the stone to extract a pristine sample of rock from a location deep beneath the possibly contaminated surface, while leaving behind, in an even deeper pilot hole, a thermocouple probe to measure the temperature gradient through the rock.

"Uff. A little cold and a little gravity—sure makes a difference to the old knee joints and backbone, doesn't it?"

Thomas agreed, as he raised his ever-present electro-camera to take a snapshot of Sam holding his prize—a cylinder of fine-grained dark gray rock with crystallites of shiny augite and greenish-yellow olivine embedded in it. The electrocamera chittered as it stored the picture away in its memory.

"It helps to keep moving. I've now been completely around the perimeter of the knob and have a set of shots that should give us a close-up panoramic view of our surroundings that'll complement the long-distance one I took from on top of *Victoria* earlier today. In the process, I got a lot of shots of icerugs carpeting the ice, and a few nodes, but they seem to be staying well back from the rock."

The two of them started toward the lander as the deep red sunset faded and the sky darkened, lit only by the half-moon of Gargantua. "Well, how does it look, Sam? This landing site we're on—is it just another bump of rock, or what? And how come we seem to be in sort of a hole, with ridges of ice all around us?"

"Well, it's basalt, that's for sure—and that means it's a lava knob. It's probably come from a small lava extrusion, a couple of thousand years ago. It can't have been much longer, since it's still warm enough to melt snow. The heat must also melt back the glacier ice, causing this depression we're in. Once I get this sample back to *Prometheus* to put through an isotope ratio analysis, we should be able to pin the age down to a few hundred years. Meanwhile, as soon as the thermocouple probe stabilizes and I can get a reading of the temperature gradient, I'll be able to figure out its cooling rate. That ought to help me pin down the date it was formed. But, it would be helpful to have some idea of how big the knob is."

"I paced it off," said Thomas. "It's nearly circular, and about four hundred and twenty meters in diameter—plus or minus about twenty meters depending upon which diameter you take."

"But we've no idea of how deep down it goes," said Sam. "I'd like to talk with the icerugs again—and see how much they can tell us of their local geology."

The two men returned to the lander, where Cinnamon cycled them through the airlock.

"Nice paperweight," remarked Cinnamon, as she saw Sam's prize. "Little lacking in color, though."

"What do you mean?" retorted Sam. "Its got lots of color. See . . ." He pointed at various spots on the dark gray cylinder. "Greenish-gray, bluish-gray, reddish-gray, blackish gray, and grayish gray. David'd see more, of course."

"Well Cinnamon, what have you been doing while we've been out playing in the snow?" asked Thomas, as he handed his helmet to the Christmas Branch. "Do you have our hot chocolate ready?"

"I want marshmallows in mine," added Sam.

"You can order your own from the galley imp," replied Cinnamon. "Although I doubt you'll get real marshmallows no matter how you ask. As for what I've been doing, the Christmas Branch and I have opened up the sick bay into the sleeping bay region that the *Dragonfly* crew vacated, and I've checked out all the medical equipment."

"Did you get the remaining four bunks rearranged, too?" asked Sam.

"Yes. You'll be able to sleep horizontally tonight," said Cinnamon.

"If we can figure out when 'tonight' is," said Thomas. "These fourteen-point-eight-hour days are going to make scheduling sleep periods difficult."

"Since it's easier to fall asleep when you go to bed late, rather than early, I suggest switching to a thirty-hour biological day," said Cinnamon. "Stay up through a Zulu day, a Zulu night, and another Zulu day, then sleep through the next Zulu night."

"Sounds fine to me," said Thomas cheerfully. "Plenty to see and do. We'll keep busy, all right."

"You can also take catnaps while you're on watch,"

added Sam, who was nominal commander of the four-person contingent assigned to *Victoria*. "Josephine can wake you up if you're needed. And—speaking of watch duty—you're on for the next four hours."

"But aren't we going to visit the icerugs again?" asked Thomas. "I wanted to go and take some more pictures."

"Next time," said Sam.

"Then take one of my cameras and get some shots for me," said Thomas, while wondering to himself which of his precious electrocameras to trust to Sam.

By the time they had gathered back down on the engineering deck to put on their exploration suits, Katrina and the Christmas Branch had loaded sampling tools, collection bags, and various items of portable analyzing gear into two large backpacks and one small one. With the help of Josephine's Christmas Branch operating the winch, the three explorers were lowered down to the surface, Cinnamon and Sam riding down first, with Katrina and the three packs following. Although dimmed slightly by the high, thin snow clouds, Gargantua was approaching full-moon phase and the night was bright enough to travel safely.

"Here you go, Sam, and this one's yours, Cinnamon." Katrina quickly strapped the smaller pack on her own back.

"Taking it a bit easy, Katrina?" said Sam, easing the burden onto stiff shoulders.

"A little," she admitted. "But I think it's fair enough. If I tried to carry the one I gave you, Sam, I'd never make it up to the top of the ridge."

Cinnamon smiled agreement as she shouldered her pack; better to have their diminutive biochemist bouncing along in the lead, rather than struggling to keep up.

"I can't wait to get samples of all the icerugs so I can compare them with the samples that we got last time."

"Slow down, Katrina," said Cinnamon. "You don't just march up to new acquaintances and start cutting pieces off them!"

"But we've so little time!" said Katrina.

"We'll do it right," said Sam decidedly. "Start with the general and proceed to the particular. If we go tactfully, we'll get a lot more information than if we antagonize any . . . body."

Cinnamon was surprised at his attitude—she had not thought Sam would be this careful in his dealings with aliens. Sam, however, was a pragmatist: it worked better to ease living creatures along, heading them gently in the direction one wanted to go; this worked with humans as well as longhorns. It was only rocks one could safely split open with a carefully placed wallop.

"Are you going to be our . . . speaker to the aliens, today?" Katrina asked, curious.

Sam considered. Cinnamon, remembering with a smile George's spur-of-the-moment orations of yesterday, said, "If you are, better polish up the fancy phrases, Sam! Somehow I don't think they'll come as easy to you!"

"Sooner him than me," said Katrina ruefully. "I really am so anxious to probe, I know I'd blurt out something clumsy. Cinnamon?"

"I'm no good at speeches, but I feel—something friendly with these creatures. I think I could talk *with* them, but not at them."

"I'll start out like George did," suggested Sam. "But I'll keep it brief and see if we can lead into the three of us splitting up so we can learn more, quicker. If they resent that, we'll yield, but let's each one try to get kind of friendly with one of them."

"Good luck chatting up the aliens," came Thomas' voice over their suit imps as he monitored their progress over their imp links. He was also having Josephine store the images that were being captured by the video cameras in their helmets. As they talked, the humans had left the rock dome, climbed up the small ridge of ice, and approached the intersection where the aliens they had met previously had been. The exploration crawler, *Splish*, was there, waiting. A light snow was beginning to fall, and the whispery rustle it made as it touched the frozen surface was all the sound they heard as they stood, rather awkwardly, and looked around. At their feet was a place where three wedge-shaped segments of icerug carpets met—turquoise, azure, and jade in color. Off in the distance they could see the nodes of two of the icerugs next to each other at the far corners of their carpets, talking with a few of their neighbors occupying the areas on that side of their bodies. The body of the third carpet, the turquoise one that belonged to Gray-Mote, seemed vacant, with no node visible anywhere on the triangular carpet, one hundred meters on a side.

Soon, as they watched in fresh amazement, two of the improbable creatures they had met the day before started over their velvety naps to greet them. Then, from nearby, another node seemed to rise up out of a turquoise-colored depression and arrived first. The creature spoke instantly, in tones of such benevolence that the humans relaxed even before the translated words of welcome sounded in their helmets.

"Greetings! Greetings! Greetings!" emanated the repeated sound from the visibly vibrating turquoise sides of Gray-Mote's head.

"Make sure you get lots of pictures," Thomas reminded Sam over their imp link. "Those video cameras in your helmets are all right for data recording, but you can't blow the images up very far before the pixels start showing."

Watching Gray-Mote's approach, with Thomas' camera clicking and chittering quietly in his hands, Sam tacitly agreed with Cinnamon's instincts. This node, with the curious mote in the center of an iris of silver-gray and its ornately embroidered cape, was obviously a creature of some authority, as befit a physician in the community and leader of the local association. In their previous encounter, Sam had not noticed the device that Gray-Mote now held in its slender turquoise tentacle, holding it up in front of its enormous eye. With a slight jolt, all the humans recognized at once that it was a monocle, constructed of ice in a lens of carefully polished curvature, and held in an ornately engraved frame. Through it, the gray eye inspected them all in turn, while the alien repeated the greeting in a bass that rumbled through their helmets like a drumroll.

Yellow-Star arrived at this point, and they saw how clearly the starlike design shone in the green center of its eye, even as it reiterated the welcoming sound. Accompanying Yellow-Star was a node they had not met before. Its iris shone a brilliant blue and it rode on an azure carpet.

"This is Blue-Stare," introduced Yellow-Star. "The master mason for our local association."

Sam spoke first, as his suit-imp used its speaker cone to translate his words into the booming tones of the icerug language.

"Greetings to you, Gray-Mote. Greetings to you, Yellow-Star. And greetings to you, Blue-Stare. We thank you for your presence. We wish to hear more about you, to learn more about you, to see more about you."

Fervently Sam hoped the variety of terms would indicate harmless interest. Apparently, they did, as all three nodes began speaking almost at once and addressing their messages separately to the humans confronting them. Sam struggled briefly in an attempt to listen to all the conversations, but gave up quickly, noticing only that Cinnamon and Gray-Mote were moving slowly off in one direction, with Cinnamon examining Gray-Mote's monocle, making sure that the video cameras in her helmet recorded it from every angle at close distance, while Katrina had drifted off to the side of Yellow-Star's carpet, followed by the caped and beribboned node showing her how its harp-drum instrument worked by playing her a ballad, accompanied by its deep bass voice.

Sam's interest was aroused when he learned that Blue-Stare was a mason, and he hoped the icerug could tell him more about the rock formation on which *Victoria* had landed. He soon learned that the mason knew "Big Rock" quite well.

"By our measurements, the top portion of the large warm rock here at the surface is about four hundred meters in diameter. Do you have any idea how deep it is, or if it gets much wider under the ice where we cannot see it?"

There was a delay, as *Splish* carried on a side discussion with the alien to make sure they both agreed on the conversion of meters to icerug measurement units and back again. It was amusing to Sam to see the robot and the alien making spanning gestures as if they were describing the length of a fish that had gotten away—the robot with its shiny metal manipulators and the icerug with its fuzzy azure tentacles.

Blue-Stare rolled its eye back around to Sam and resumed its booming tones, with Sam's suit-imp making the translation. "Big Rock rises 920 meters high out of the ocean bottom, and is approximately oval in shape there, some 650 meters in one direction and 580 meters in the other."

Sam was startled. "You're sure about that?"

"For a long time, I and the others around Big Rock have encountered the rock at various depths while we have been excavating our . . ." There was a pause while the translation program in Sam's suit computer attempted to find the right word, and was finally rescued by Josephine figuring out the appropriate word from the context. ". . . tunnels through the ice." The booming alien word for "tunnels" seemed to echo in Sam's ear, and then he realized that Cinnamon and Gray-Mote were using the same word. Her next question to the icerug physician brought a reply to which Sam listened intently.

"Yes, I am pushing tunnels continuously down, through the ice in all directions and into the ocean water below. I line them with my body, searching for tiny . . . bits of useful chemical compounds," Cinnamon's translation program lamely concluded.

"Trace elements?" guessed Cinnamon.

"That translates correctly," was Gray-Mote's grave response.

"How do you dig the tunnels?" asked Cinnamon.

"Certain chemical compounds in our bodies have the capacity to dissolve the ice; ammonia is the principal one. The digging portion of our flesh nearest to the ice exudes the ammonia and converts the ice into liquid ammonia-water, which the flesh then absorbs and passes back to the main body along with any nutrients that are in solution. Our body thus forms a long tunnel through the ice which is lined with our own tissue, which then sprouts finer tunnels in all directions, searching for more trace elements. The water that is produced from melting the ice in the tunnels is disposed of down a long waste tunnel that penetrates through the ice into the ocean water beneath. Of course, only the water and other waste products are expelled. The ammonia is retained for reuse, while the trace elements are used to make new flesh."

"Your tunnels are like roots!" concluded Cinnamon. She hesitated after the word, but the translation was apparently acceptable to Gray-Mote. "Your root tunnels gather the water and minerals and send them to your carpet, which uses photosynthesis to put them together to form more tissue. Just like a plant on Earth."

"Out here in the country, where there is plenty of unworked ice, our bodies have no difficulty growing and spreading farther, with all the nutrients coming from the ice and with the light from Barnard."

Meanwhile, Yellow-Star had finished playing his ballad for Katrina, and they now moved slowly back to the others, where Katrina joined in the conversation about the tunnel structure of the aliens under the ice.

"That's fascinating, Cinnamon!" said Katrina. "And in addition to being a plant, it's an animal, too, because it gathers and eats other plants and animals. It's marvelous how these icerug bodies are made!"

"They are ideal," replied Gray-Mote solemnly.

"We cannot, however, travel wherever we please, as the humans seem to be able to do," remarked Yellow-Star. "We are bound by our root system to the ice of Ice, while the humans can travel from world to world, seeing strange things that we will never see." Sam could almost sense a wistful tone as the normally booming voice quieted to nearly a mumble, as Yellow-Star realized the limitations that its ice-bound body placed on its soaring spirit.

"I still think it's marvelous," replied Katrina cheerfully. She turned to look again at Yellow-Star. "But there's something interesting that happened—when we were over there. . . . " She pointed a short distance away. "My friend Sam accidentally stepped backward onto your carpet while you were singing your ballad to me. I saw him, but you did not, since your eye was looking at me. But, although you did not see him, your eye instantly blinked when he stepped on you, and you turned to look in that direction. Did you sense that pressure?"

"Of course."

Katrina turned to look at Cinnamon to explain why she thought the incident was interesting. "The distance was nearly twenty meters away and the eye response was instantaneous."

"Pretty fast reflex action," murmured Cinnamon, thinking.

The voice of Thomas came over the imp link from *Victoria*. "I've had Josephine pull back from memory that segment of Katrina's helmet video record. In one frame, I can see that Sam's heel has not yet touched Yellow-Star's carpet, while in the very next frame it has touched it, *and* Yellow-Star's eye has already started to blink."

"The reaction time is less than one video frame!" said Cinnamon.

"One sixtieth of a second—seventeen milliseconds," added Thomas. "Way faster than a human."

"Then it can't be ionic conduction," said Katrina. "It must be electronic conduction. I must remember to make an electrical conductivity measurement on the tissue samples once I get them under the microscope."

Katrina, carefully patient, soon coaxed small samples of flesh from Blue-Stare to compare with the samples of the others she had collected yesterday. Again, she had her biopsy punch out, but it wasn't needed. The icerug just budded off a small portion of flaccid flesh, which Katrina popped into a sample bag.

"We want to thank all of you for the tissue samples, and Gray-Mote in particular for answering all my questions," said Cinnamon. "We have learned a great deal about your physiology."

"Certainly," replied Gray-Mote. "And now, may I ask some questions of my own about your bodies?" Then Gray-Mote asked a brief series of probing questions regarding human physiology: what their internal structure was, what they ate, how they disposed of waste, why they were wearing protective suits; their answers were brief but accurate, and the alien accepted them politely.

"I noticed there were no questions about reproduction," added Cinnamon. "It must not be a polite subject to discuss with strangers."

"I'm also glad that they didn't ask us to reciprocate by giving them a sample of our flesh," said Katrina. "I wouldn't mind missing some hair and fingernails, or even a little blood, but that's it!"

Meanwhile, Sam was using his geologist's pickax to chop yet another fragment of stone free from the ice, and talking simultaneously to the alien and the rock. "All right. Out you come, you sparkling little bit of—" he paused to look at it carefully "—granite, aren't you?" He tapped it with the point of his pickax. "Hardness about six, I'd say." He handed the stone to *Splish*, who turned it around and around in front of its video eyes to obtain a good record of its appearance, and then extended its manipulator over its back to deposit the find in its cargo hold. "Do you find a lot of stones lying about, Blue-Stare?"

"Yes, especially after big eruptions, when there are many new rocks thrown out by the water. Those that don't fall on us sink quickly down through the new snow to the hard ice below, so we look for useful bits as soon as the eruption is over."

Sam looked up at the sky. Through the thinning clouds, he could see that Gargantua was approaching the full-moon phase and the shadow spot of the moon they were on had started its nightly trek across the gigantic globe that filled a fifth of the sky. "The night is nearly half over. It's time for me to take shift duty and let Thomas come outside and play explorer," he said. He added another curious bit of glinting rock to the crawler's storage bin. "*Splish* and I will take this assortment back to the lander," he decided. "Give me something to analyze while I'm monitoring the comm console."

Katrina interrupted. "If you don't mind, Sam, I'd like to take the next comm shift duty on *Victoria*. I'm really anxious to put these samples of icerug flesh under the tunneling array microscope. I'll take your bits of stuff for you. Come along, *Splish*!" Quickly, before Sam could object, she marched off, stepping carefully over the ragged drifts of snow.

Sam, glad that he would be able to continue talking with the icerugs, turned to look at the aliens, who were gathered around Cinnamon, talking. He grinned. Cinnamon's gift for listening appeared to exercise a universal attraction.

Gray-Mote was speaking. "It is only our usual local association meeting held between night-middle and day-start every fourth-day, and there is nothing momentous we plan to discuss. However, you are most welcome to attend with us and observe."

Thomas, busily donning his suit back on *Victoria*, heard the icerug comment and muttered to Sam over the imp link, "Right. Out of the sky come—simultaneously, mind you—'The Jelly Blobs from the Planet Rocheworld' and 'The Two-Eyed Stilt-Walkers From Outer Space,' and they have 'nothing momentous to discuss.'"

Cinnamon bowed slightly at the invitation—Reiki had showed her this most formal acknowledgement of equals—and said, "We would be most interested in attending your local association meeting, and will come as soon as the third person in our party, Thomas, arrives." It didn't take long for Thomas to cycle through the airlock, scramble down the Jacob's ladder in the low gravity, and trot past Katrina and *Splish* on their way back to the lander.

As Thomas arrived at the intersection where the areas of the three icerugs met, panting slightly under the weight of the cameras and equipment bags he was carrying, Yellow-Star glided away on its jade carpet, following the boundary between it and Gray-Mote. "I'll see you at the entrance to the association meeting hall."

"You three can come with us," said Blue-Stare, opening a narrow path on the ice between its azure carpet and Gray-Mote's turquoise carpet. The humans hurried along the path in single file, running awkwardly in the effort to keep up, while the nodes of the two icerugs slowed their pace to stay with them. Sam wished suddenly for his skis—he'd not thought of them in years, but the Christmas Bush could probably construct something for him.

"Where are we going?" panted Thomas.

"It's a meeting, of some sort. Find out when we get there, I guess," was Cinnamon's breathless reply. After traveling a hundred meters or so, they came to an intersection of six icerug bodies of various different blue-green hues. Nodes of four other icerugs were there to be introduced to the humans.

"This is Smooth-Brown, the teacher for the area," said

Blue-Stare, introducing a heather-colored node with an eye of deep, dark brown with almost no streaks or flecks in it. "This is Lavender-Blue, my apprentice; Green-Ring, the butcher; and Five-Arm, communicator between our local association and the next one leeward." Further ahead, the humans could see more of the alien nodes in a procession through the light snowstorm toward a depression in the ground at the further vertex of Smooth-Brown's heather carpet. One of them was the recognizable jade-colored node of Yellow-Star, traveling along the far side of Smooth-Brown's area.

As the three humans and the six icerugs traveled together down the path along a boundary between Smooth-Brown's heather carpet and Lavender-Blue's teal one, the humans slowed to study the curious fashion in which the nodes of Blue-Stare, Green-Ring, Five-Arm, and Gray-Mote traveled after they had left their own home carpets. Along the meter-wide path of open ice between Smooth-Brown and Lavender-Blue lay four narrow trails of carpet, about ten centimeters wide, each connected back to the vertex of the individual's triangular area: azure for Blue-Stare, moss for Green-Ring, spruce for Five-Arm, and turquoise for Gray-Mote. There was a twenty-centimeter wide path of clear ice left for the humans to walk on. The pedestals of each icerug moved smoothly along its trail of similarly-colored flesh, which widened to accommodate the pedestal as it went past, while the neighboring trails automatically shrank in width, when touched, to make room. The nodes of Lavender-Blue and Smooth-Brown, of course, traveled on their own carpet bodies which bordered the path. Cinnamon stopped to bend down and look closely, and then she walked on with the others.

"They get very close," she said. "But none of them touch each other."

"What happens at intersections?" wondered Sam. All three paused at the next intersection and peered closely at the multicolored trails as they met, some of them crossing each other. "Look, the spruce-colored one tunnels down into the ice to go under the others," said Thomas, his gloved finger pointing to the reappearance on the other side of the path of the spruce strand. "But it still manages not to touch them." He quickly photographed the curious tangle of colored trails. The unasked query of how a two-meter-high node could pass through a tiny tunnel was answered as the spruce pedestal of Five-Arm, following its spruce trail along the path, simply picked up its leading edge, and in a flowing motion "stepped" over the intervening trail of a different color and resumed its glide along its own trail on the other side of the crossing tunnel.

"The flesh just disconnected from the trail and connected again on the other side!" said Cinnamon in amazement.

"'Pears to me these things have a skin like the flouwen," said Sam. "More like a liquid than a membrane. Sure is different from our skin, which is flexible enough, but not so loose you can tear it off and then fasten it somewhere else whenever you want to."

The humans, after watching Five-Arm pass, raced to catch their guides, who had stopped to wait for them at the underground entrance to the meeting hall.

"It will be pleasant to be indoors, out of the snow," remarked Blue-Stare to Sam, casually, "although it will cost us some energy since we must provide our own light." A concave depression formed itself in the head portion of Blue-Stare's node and began to emit a blue glow, which shone in the direction the eye was looking.

The humans slowed their steps, seeing ahead of them an oval opening in the side of an ice bank, into which a number of icerug nodes were gliding and disappearing. As each icerug node started down the tunnel that led underground, their bodies too began to emit a glow from the head portion of their node, illuminating the path before them. With senses alert, the humans followed them into the tunnel, unhooking permalights from their belts to light their own way. Since the tunnel was tall enough to admit the icerug nodes, it was taller than the humans, and smoothly sided with solid ice. The angle of the floor sloped downward steeply, and the booted feet of the humans began to slide. Trying not to step on the multitude of colored trails leading downward, Cinnamon lost her balance, clutched vainly at the hard-frozen walls, and sat down hard in the center of the path. She gasped, and the two men beside her grabbed her arms and attempted to lift her to her feet. In the process, they all fell and began to slide helplessly down the tunnel. They finally arrived at a level surface in a headlong tumble, and looked around.

From their undignified position, they were able to see that they were in a large cavern, whose walls and ceilings were apparently made of dressed stone arches supporting blocks of carved ice, which had been arranged into geometric designs made up of triangles and hexagons. Light from the nodes of two dozen icerugs illuminated a scene of quiet peace, as the strange alien eyes were turned in mild curiosity toward the untidy little heap of humanity.

Sam's long legs felt as clumsy as a colt's as he struggled to his feet. Once more upright, Cinnamon felt her breathing slow, and she looked about her with amazement. Thomas' camera was in action again, and he walked without hindrance through the crowd of aliens, stepping carefully over any of the colored trails that he saw. Sam and Cinnamon followed, with growing confidence as they observed that even an inadvertent step directly upon a trail seemed to cause no distress to any of the nodes. Sam, conscious of his duty as nominal commander of the home base party, put in a call to the lander.

"Katrina? Josephine? Can you hear me?" A reassuring reply came quickly back.

"I have been monitoring you constantly," came Josephine's cool reply. "You really should have checked with me before you went underground, you know."

"How is the connection?" asked Sam, properly chastened.

"Perfect," replied Josephine. "The signal strength is down about six decibels, but I have thirty-two in reserve. The ice, being well below freezing, transmits the radio channels from your suit quite well—even the video images from your helmet cameras are noise-free."

"And very interesting they are, too," added Katrina.

With their communications secure, the beauty of the room began to fascinate the humans; the constantly shifting lights on the icerug bodies, and the light reflecting from the large glistening icerug eyes, glittered from the icy faceting of the walls like a pastel kaleidoscope and was mirrored in the ceiling curving above them. Around them, the sound of icerugs speaking to each other was like the familiar murmur of any congregation, benign and soothing, but deep in tone, like a group of pipe organs talking softly to each other. In approximately the center of the room was a raised area. Judging from the number of icerug nodes who glided up and down from it steadily, it was not a position of honor as much as a platform for being seen while addressing the group. As each icerug left the platform, it retracted the trail which it had laid on its way up.

Thomas slowly scanned the room, counting. "Twenty-four," he finally concluded. "Just exactly the number there should be."

"Why do you say that?" asked Cinnamon, puzzled over Thomas' certainty.

"When I was looking at the panoramic views that I took from the top of *Victoria*, I realized that the triangular bodies of the icerugs 'tile the plain.' They aren't perfect triangles by any means, but close enough so that their overall pattern has a long-range hexagonal symmetry. So, at each vertex of its body, an icerug has five neighbors to speak to—for a total of six—as we saw when Blue-Stare and Gray-Mote introduced us to Green-Ring, Five-Arm, Lavender-Blue, and Smooth-Brown. Since this meeting hall is at a vertex, there are six icerugs that are nearest to the meeting hall, and eighteen icerugs that are next nearest, for a total of twenty-four—just the number that are here."

Their physician acquaintance, Gray-Mote, now glided to the center of the raised platform and spoke, its resonant voice reaching easily to the edges of the big room. The murmur of voices ceased, but Cinnamon noted with interest that throughout the ensuing discussion interruptions were frequent, brief, and apparently not resented. Although Gray-Mote was the leader of the gathering, it did not dominate the discussion, but acted more as a moderator where all the speakers held equal status.

Gray-Mote introduced the human visitors with a kindly oratory, and several eyes rolled to survey the newcomers briefly. Thomas lowered his camera and stood, slightly abashed at being the object of public scrutiny, while Cinnamon and Sam turned slightly to be back-to-back. They all felt relieved, if somewhat humbled, when it became apparent that their presence was of no real interest. These creatures were very much concerned with their own affairs, and proceeded in an orderly fashion.

There was a brief and amicable discussion of some shift in territorial arrangement between several icerugs, followed, to the surprise of the humans, by a song, led by the bard Yellow-Star on its harp-drum, but joined in by all the others. The vibrations of the blended voices filled the hall with almost tangible sound. Cinnamon, at first transfixed by the beauty of the song, quickly made sure that her suit-imp was making a stereo recording that she could play back later. The icerugs seemed to enjoy their own concert immensely, and Thomas was able to catch with his camera some of the gentle swaying of several nodes in apparent rhythm. The sounds of the song were allowed to die away fully before another node glided to the center of the dais. It was Five-Arm, whom Blue-Stare had introduced as the "communicator" with the leeward local association. Judging from Josephine's literal translations, Five-Arm was reporting on the activities and decisions of another icerug community some distance away, but of which the speaker was also a part. The report consisted mostly of numbers, growth statistics, and shipments of flesh to the city, and was listened to attentively and with evident approval.

Sam muttered to Cinnamon, "It's just like a farmer's grange meeting on Earth!"

Her reply jolted him: "No, it's not. You're making an assumption, not stating a fact." Tacitly, he admitted the truth of that.

Still, he sensed what he would almost have dared to call an intense communal interest in the next speaker, an icerug which Josephine referred to as Big-Lump.

Accompanied by a much smaller node, Big-Lump moved up onto the viewing platform on its verdant trail, two tentacles gently pushing the emerald node of the little one ahead of it, its dark blue eye with a single green streak blinking rapidly. Big-Lump absent-mindedly rubbed at the large lump on the side of its head with a third tentacle.

"I have brought a young one for your taste and approval."

The room quieted. Then one by one, the other icerugs glided forward, looked the newcomer carefully in the eye, murmured some sort of comment, and then touched the young one's head or pedestal with a probing tentacle tip.

"They aren't taking a bite, so they might be tasting with their tentacles," guessed Cinnamon over the imp link. Finally the last icerug withdrew.

"You have now all tasted this youngling. I have already taught it a few words, which was extremely easy to do, as the youngling is eager to learn and tries very hard to please me. I suggest it would be a worthy addition to this association."

Josephine's translation seemed to be much briefer than the alien's speech, for which the humans were grateful. It was becoming apparent that the icerugs were fond of speaking, and of using elegant and flowery phrases in an idiom which did not translate well into English. It would have been confusing to the visitors if Josephine had attempted to include all the local references.

Throughout the long discussion of the youngling which followed, the humans heard only that its adoption into the community was accepted, and the selection of a name for the newcomer was thoroughly talked out. After many comments from the assembly, Big-Lump spoke again.

"I have been calling the little one Green-Streak, because of the streak of green color in its otherwise blue iris. There was another Green-Streak once in a distant association, but that person died many years ago. I think the youngster should be given the name Green-Streak, and I further suggest that Green-Streak be given the area which used to belong to Eager-Blink." While these statements were being commented on, the humans struggled to understand the implications of the speech.

"Died?" whispered Cinnamon, excitedly. "If Josephine got that right, then these creatures are mortal—unlike the flouwen, who are essentially immortal unless they rock up to think through a mathematical problem that takes forever to solve. Must be because their nodes have differentiated cells, whereas all the cells in the flouwen are the same. Josephine, it's important that we somehow find out their life-span, and the various causes of death. . . ."

"They are giving Green-Streak someone else's territory. So territory is assigned by the local association, if I follow that right," said Thomas. "Wonder what happened to Eager-Blink?"

Sam listened intently. Despite Cinnamon's admonition, he felt that extrapolating from context was the only way he would learn how this strange community functioned. He was rewarded when the next to speak alluded casually to the absent icerug.

"I understand from the information passed to us by Yellow-Star, the communicator to the association inward, that Eager-Blink is doing well at the Center for Engineering Studies—its interest in architecture is still strong, and Eager-Blink will likely stay in the city indefinitely. I, too, believe the area which Eager-Blink extracted itself from, in order to journey to the city, would be appropriate for this Green-Streak."

"If all are agreed, then," concluded Big-Lump, "the youngling will stay with me in my area for some sixteen

four-days, to assimilate more of our ways and customs.
Then, when it is ready, I will install it in Eager-Blink's
area and have it attend Smooth-Brown's primary school
for tutelage." Agreement to this proposal was reached,
although only after, as nearly as Cinnamon could judge,
every icerug present had spoken to the question.

The final item on the agenda, as Sam rebelliously
thought of it, was the singing of several more songs. The
newest member of the association seemed to listen to the
song with great interest and swayed a bit in time to the
rhythm, but took no part, nor did its sponsor encourage it
to do so. When the vibrations of the last deep note
ceased, the icerugs began to move in leisurely fashion
toward the tunnel.

Cinnamon moved quickly to intercept Big-Lump and
the youngster. At closer range, Cinnamon could discern
the tumorlike bulge in Big-Lump's head region, which
must have given the verdant icerug its name. She hoped
the tumor was benign, then realized that it probably was,
since Big-Lump had most likely been named when very
young, as Green-Streak had been.

Blue-Stare joined them and she started to ask questions. She knew that among civilized societies on Earth
questions about reproduction would not be tolerated, but
her scientific training as well as her curiosity urged her to
make the attempt. Carefully approaching the sensitive
subject, she spoke to Big-Lump sweetly, trusting
Josephine to make sure that her suit computer translated
her questions tactfully.

"Please. Do tell me more about this fine youngster.
How long has it been with you?"

Big-Lump answered readily. "It was some three four-
days ago that I found it, out on the ice to the north of my
area."

Startled, Cinnamon exclaimed, "You found it? Out on the ice?"

"Yes. I had pushed a trail out onto the ice plains north of me to look for food and stones that might have fallen on the ice during the last large eruption of Manannán. Although I didn't find any food, I did find this youngster in a snowdrift. It didn't taste bad, so I let it follow me home. It seems an agreeable little fellow, and it settled down quietly in my area, so after a few four-days, I decided to bring it to this assembly for approval."

Cinnamon's mind strove to accept this "found under a cabbage leaf" explanation of icerug replication, but failed. She turned to ask the physician Gray-Mote her next question, risking offense in her determination to learn more.

"This young one . . . have there been other young ones? And are they all foundlings—not created by icerugs—simply adopted after being discovered under some snowdrift?"

Josephine's voice came over Cinnamon's imp link as Cinnamon's suit-imp was using its wobble-film to boom out her translated words to Gray-Mote. "I didn't include the phrase 'not created by icerugs' in my translation."

Gray-Mote, however, seemed unperturbed by Cinnamon's curiosity. "Oh, yes. Younglings are found occasionally. Usually while we are out gathering."

Cinnamon was finally forced to ask the question more directly. "I hope you realize that I am ignorant of your ways and customs, and I may ask questions that you may choose not to answer. If this question disturbs you, do not answer. Please, if young icerugs are found, where do they come from?"

Gray-Mote, seemingly unperturbed by the blunt question, answered her readily. "There have been many theories discussed by those at the Center for Medical Studies about the origin of young icerugs. The most accepted one is the theory of 'Void-Filling Spontaneous Generation.' It is well known that no youngsters ever appear in the city, or even out in the country where the ice is fully covered by coverers-of-the-ice. They only appear in the ice plains, where there is a void of coverers-of-the-ice. The theory of Void-Filling Spontaneous Generation hypothesizes that nature abhors a void, especially a void of coverers-of-the-ice, and so spontaneously generates new youngsters to fill the void. So far, the theory has shown itself to be correct."

"Have those at the Center for Medical Studies come out to look at the ice plains themselves to make sure that these new youngsters are really spontaneously generated and not formed by some other mechanism?" asked Cinnamon, trying not to be critical, for spontaneous generation of lower animals such as worms and flies had been believed by human scientists only three hundred years ago back on Earth.

"No. Of course not," replied Gray-Mote. "They are too rooted in their own areas at the center to think of travelling around like a wandering bard. They depend upon the observations of those of us here on the periphery of the nation, as passed on to the city by the communicators between associations. I believe, however, that the theory is correct, for I myself, many cycles ago, when I was using a stretch of Big Rock to warm myself on a sunny day, found a relatively large youngster wandering in from the distant ice fields. It had the wrong taste, however, so I ate it."

The two icerugs had continued to move slowly toward the tunnel, not disturbed by Cinnamon's questions, but obviously ready to go their own ways. To Cinnamon, the combination of the innocence and appalling savagery of the supposedly intelligent and civilized aliens was enough to discourage her from further queries. She, too, was ready to return to her own kind, to talk over this unsatisfactory explanation of icerug reproduction with Deirdre and Katrina. Suddenly she grinned to herself: their reactions to the new information would certainly be interesting!

When Cinnamon arrived back at *Victoria*, however, it was Katrina who had the most interesting news about the icerugs.

"The icerugs and flouwen are related!" exclaimed Katrina, as Cinnamon joined her in the small area on *Victoria* that served as combined laboratory and sick bay. "Their cellular structure is the same. In both of them, the basic cell is shaped like a fat dumbbell—two knobs connected by a thick neck. I haven't had time to do any detailed scans yet, but the images from the tunneling array microscope show that both the icerug and flouwen cells have complex semirandom patterns on their surfaces that serve as both the genetic code and the long-term memory for the creatures. *And*—" she continued, still punching icons on the screen as the imaging continued "—they use the same basic genetic code patterns, indicating that the flouwen and icerugs definitely have a common genetic ancestor. The same goes for the coelasharks."

She looked up at Cinnamon and pointed at the screen. "This is a scan of some coelashark muscle tissue that Little White brought back. The cells here in the muscle tissue have specialized and changed basic shape by joining into long strands of knobs, but the basic coelashark cell is also double-knobbed and uses the same basic genetic code pattern, so icerugs and coelasharks have a common genetic ancestor."

"How closely related are they?" asked Cinnamon.

"Not close at all," said Katrina. "Again, I haven't had time to get detailed maps of the genetic patterns in order to run comparisons, but just a quick scan shows a major difference. The coelasharks have two sets of genes, each slightly different from the other, one set on one knob of the cell and the other set on the other knob. That makes them diploid. The icerugs, however, have only one set of genes: the patterns on the two knobs of their cell are the same. So, they are monoploid while the coelasharks are diploid—that's a major difference which indicates that they are not closely related at all."

"On Earth, a diploid genetic structure usually indicates a more complex and therefore a more advanced life-form," said Cinnamon. "Yet the icerugs seem to be much more intelligent than the coelasharks."

"Since they only need one knob of their cell for reproduction," said Katrina, "perhaps they use the other knob for thinking—changing the patterns on the cell surface to store long-term memories. Anyway, even though distantly related, they *are* related."

"If that's true, then following the pattern on Earth, probably all life on Zulu is related to each other—and thence to the flouwen," mused Cinnamon.

"So far, they are," said Katrina. "The sample of small-fish and the boardweed that Gray-Mote gave Little White also show a double-knob cell structure."

"I wondered how it happened? Did life from here go to Rocheworld, or the other way around? Rocheworld does come pretty close to Gargantua once every three orbits."

"The geyser here throws lots of biological material from Zulu into space," said Katrina. "And the interplanetary waterfall between the two lobes of Rocheworld is an obvious method of moving life from that world into space."

"It could also be something as prosaic as a large meteorite hitting either planet and throwing into space a chunk of dirt or ice with microbes in it."

"We'll probably never know," said Katrina. "But in any case, the life-forms on Zulu and Rocheworld have the same ancestor."

Sam came into the lab to see what they were talking about so seriously, and his entry caused Katrina to remember her other exciting piece of news.

"Sam!" she exclaimed. "Remember how the icerug Yellow-Star jumped when you stepped on it?"

"Yes?" said Sam, puzzled. "You two said something about super-fast reflexes."

"The reflexes were super-fast because the signals were carried by a superconductor! The icerug nervous system consists of specialized nerve cells that grow long threads which connect to other nerve cells. The threads have a poor conductor for a surface layer and a strong and flexible metal-organic polymer inside that's a room-temperature superconductor! The microscope has a heated stage, and I ran it up to a hundred celsius—as high as it could go—and I still measured zero resistance through a five-centimeter strand—the longest I could tease out."

"That's fantastic!" enthused Sam. "A room-temperature superconductor that is also a strong and flexible polymer would revolutionize electrical technology back on Earth. That discovery alone might easily pay Earth back for the entire cost of our mission."

Katrina turned to look at Cinnamon. "You said that you had something interesting to tell me about the icerugs. What is it?"

"Nothing really important," replied Cinnamon, slowly. "You can read it in my report—which I'd better get to work on."

SUBMERGING

Quietly and rapidly, the flouwen submerged, luxuriating in the slow surge of the ocean around them. As the humans had promised, the signals from *Babble* soon became only an occasional faint blip of sound at regular intervals—easily ignored. The three quickly discovered that swimming in the strange suits was a different matter altogether from the freedom to which they were accustomed. However, they soon adapted to the new sensation.

☆Takes work to swim in this bag,☆ grunted Little Red.

◊But, being more compact, the glide is longer,◊ demonstrated Little White, forging ahead. The blobby, awkward-looking shapes increased their pace with practice, and with powerful lunges headed toward the depths.

Although the light filtering down from the surface provided a weak amount of illumination, the superb sonar of the flouwen gave them a bright and clear picture of their surroundings, the highly flexible glassy-foil fabric of the suits allowing the sonar pulses from their bodies to penetrate into the water. Little Purple, emulating one of his favorite humans, commented frequently on what they were "seeing" as they swam along. His observations were converted by David's software algorithm into a high-reliability communications code, and redundantly transmitted over a number of channels by the sonar transmitter on Little Purple's chestpack back to *Babble*, to be transmitted up through the commsat links to Joe on *Dragonfly*, who devolved the code to reconstruct the message and pass it along to David, while copies were sent to Josephine on *Victoria* and James on *Prometheus*.

⌐Water getting warmer. No sign of anything moving. Tide is moving against us. Wait. A funny echo . . .⌐

☆Big!☆

◊Stop!◊

The three flouwen attempted to stop simultaneously. Their normal techniques, however, failed in the clumsy suits, so that instead of the easy cessation of motion they expected, there was a collision of the three, which distracted them. By the time Little Red had stopped blaming the other two, the large distant echo had vanished, but the three explorers now proceeded more slowly, surveying all the areas around them.

⌐Sea bottom now in range. Large crater down below. Not deep. Full of plants. Inside crater hear bubbling sounds of vent field. Water getting warmer as we go nearer. Funny echo again.⌐

Little Purple stopped transmitting, and all three stopped seeing around them with their sonar pings, and instead switched to looking through the lenses built into their helmets. Down below them, illuminated by the reddish light trickling down from the surface above, a large and powerful form undulated around the rim of the crater, sleek and silent as a snake. It was a giant coelashark, larger than either a human or a flouwen bud.

☐Big. Four legs, with fins on the ends. Four tentacles, stubby too, coming from beneath, below mouth. Tentacles carry sharp stone. Moves in s-curves, sideways.☐

The coelashark's attention seemed to be concentrated on the warmer, plant-choked waters inside the crater, and it did not notice or pay attention to the silent bulk of the three aliens above it. The coelashark moved slowly, effortlessly, but with a steady rhythm that seemed in no way idle; it was watching the plants for something and waiting with a purpose. It swam off and disappeared around the opposite side of the seaweed bed, but the flouwen stayed quietly where they were, also waiting and watching. After some time the coelashark reappeared. It stopped to sharpen the already sharp point of its stone on a rock and continued its patrol of the vent field, its attention still directed inward, and passed.

With tacit mutual consent, the flouwen kept sonar silence to prevent being observed, swam over the edge of the crater to the inside, and began to drop slowly downward. Behind, they could hear the approach of *Babble*, its treads making a great deal of noise as it splashed across the ocean surface above them. Thankful this time for the presence of the noisy machine, the flouwen were able to use *Babble*'s pings and tread noise to keep track of the large coelashark, while saving their own sonar chirps to scan things nearby.

Suddenly, they stopped. A sound was rapidly increasing through the water, as though some creature was approaching them from out of the plant cover, screaming as it came. They watched as two creatures approached, swimming in frantic haste. The larger of the two was a coelashark, only a quarter of the size of the one they had already seen, and it was hotly pursuing another, still smaller, which was making the noise. The victim had lost its tentacles, and some dark fluid flowed like smoke from a puncture in its side, but it never slowed in its desperate flight outward toward the rim of the crater. As the flouwen watched, both little coelasharks virtually exploded, hit full on by the huge predator that had circled back. The screams stopped, and nothing was left of the encounter but the languid motion of the satiated coelashark and the rapidly dissipating trace of the dark film of liquid.

☆Good hunting, two at once like that,☆ said Little Red in admiration. The flouwen resumed their advance.

The seabed above which they were slowly floating was rough and littered with small rocks. A small and furtive movement among them caught Little White's attention. Carefully he slowed and brought his sonar to a focus on the pebbles. The little scuttling creature was now still and indistinguishable from the stones all around. Patiently, silently, the flouwen waited. There were a few tiny shiftings among the litter, and then several quick darts, as the strange living rocks jetted a brief distance, and then sat immobile.

⬜Little pebbles squirt,⬜ observed Little Purple aloud. ⬜Squirting pebbles look almost like real rocks.⬜

Little Red gave one of the squirting pebbles an exploratory prod. It dug itself into the seabed with such speed and force that in less than two seconds it had disappeared.

☆Probably good to eat,☆ said Little Red. ☆For somebody.☆ As they continued toward the warmth, more and more of the little animals became visible. Acting faster this time, Little Red used a pseudopod to capture one of the squirting pebbles and stuffed it in a sample bag to take back to Katrina.

Tiny fronds were the next form of life to appear to the

flouwen. They too became more numerous as they advanced from cold water to warm, and they also became larger. Soon they spotted clumps of tough and spongy grasses. The blades were thick, varying in color from palest blue to a rich forest-green, and were as resilient as leather. At David's urging, the flouwen gathered samples and bagged them. Nestling concealed within the largest clumps, only leaving when Little White disturbed them, were a variety of small, wormlike creatures. They wriggled frantically when disturbed and raced to dive without hesitation into the next available tussock.

As the water temperature continued to rise, the fronds of the plants became thin and flat, and extended into many-lobed leaves, waving gently in the drift of the tide. The roots of some of these were digging into the seabed rock, where they apparently hardened, forming fragile-looking, lacy structures which looked like coral and were every bit as hard. The flouwen, after careful inspection and bagging of a representative sample, stayed warily clear of these, but continued to probe busily into the heart of all the weedy plants along the way. Out of one, thus dislodged, shot a very small coelashark, but its precipitous dive into the next cluster was a mistake; apparently the denizen of this neighbor was another coelashark, slightly larger than the first. Instantly the two babies were locked in combat. Little Red, curious, interfered in the fray by holding the larger firmly to the seabed; the tiny one, with this advantage, promptly bit through the throat of its adversary with dispatch and began to eat as fast as possible, hauling the victim down into the grass clump with savage, twisting jerks.

The surrounding water was now slightly less clear. Little Purple had dutifully recorded a description of the opacity, and comments began to come back in over

Babble from David, who was listening intently from his post on *Dragonfly*.

"Possibly a type of plankton, clouding the water. Better take a sample of seawater for Katrina to look at."

The seabed was becoming more thickly covered now, and even the gentle passage of the aliens disturbed swirls of unidentifiable muck. The thick and spongy grasses began to give way to large areas of taller weeds of several different sorts. One of these showed long flat leaves, two or three centimeters thick, nearly twenty centimeters wide, and tens of meters long. They swayed heavily in the currents, pushing against other weeds which rose like vertical snakes, a couple of centimeters in diameter. The dense forests of these bottom-dwelling plants obscured the floor of the ocean, but the flouwen were able to see many tiny creatures of varying shapes moving within their shelter. The heat had increased greatly and the flouwen were getting uncomfortable.. Little Purple's laconic descriptions continued, and up above, David mentally pictured the seaweed growths below.

"How tightly are the plants fastened to the seabed?" he asked. "Try to pull one free, Little Red." Little Red tugged at one of the slender stalks, and it came free with suddenness, dislodging several of its broader-leaved neighbors in the process. It took some effort on the part of the flouwen, but they managed to tear off samples of both plants that were small enough to fit into the sample bags. The uprooting action had revealed several darting shapes, frantically rushing into hiding.

☆Three little coelasharks, chasing whole group of tiny swimmers. Swimmers all move together, blue on one side, green on the other.☆ David recognized the pattern of schooling fish, although whether or not these bicolored creatures were fish at all was unknown. The flouwen watched with interest as the coelasharks tore into the little group, decimating it until a desperate burst of speed shot the remaining members of the school out of sight. Little Red managed to capture one of the injured swimmers in a sample bag.

☐I can see hot water plumes from central vents now,☐ said Little Purple, picking up the doppler-shifted return signal from the rapidly rising turbulences. ☐Getting too hot. Lots of weeds here. We not go closer but swim around vent.☐ The flouwen turned, to keep the vent to one side of them, and pushed through the water between the waving tendrils and leaves. From time to time, they stopped and descended to push the plants firmly apart and take samples of the animal and plant life. Each time they found they had disturbed numerous small creatures; however, as Little Purple reported, they no longer saw any little coelasharks.

☆Little flippy things. More little squirting rocks, much smaller. Lots of little worms.☆

☐Water getting warmer again, change direction,☐ reported Little Purple, while his suit and *Babble* automatically recorded the new position.

☆Big rocks here, less weed, lots of small rocks piled up.☆ Little Red dislodged the top of the nearest heap of stones. They rolled downward, and the familiar shapes of life appeared momentarily, vulnerable until they found new hiding places within the crevices and crannies of the mound.

☐Still no little coelasharks,☐ mentioned Little Purple.

"Try moving into slightly cooler water," suggested David. "Perhaps the hotter temperature is too much for them." The flouwen moved out, and wandered around and among the vents irregularly spaced about the field. As they reported, the teeming plant life nearest the vents only concealed the tiniest sorts of animals; only in the cooler depths could they find the larger animals, like coelasharks.

"Perhaps as they get larger," David mused out loud to Joe, "their surface to volume ratio shrinks, and they find it harder to keep their insides from getting too hot, so they need to stay in cooler water." At David's suggestion, the flouwen headed out again to cooler water. They found only a few animals, and just two coelasharks, well hidden in holes within some large rocks. One of the coelasharks, nearly thirty centimeters long, obviously resented their intrusion, but was too cowed by their much larger size to launch an attack. It took out its frustration by attacking one of the other animals that the flouwen had disturbed, a large flat ribbonlike creature. It chased the ribbon-fish outward into the clearer, cooler water away from the vent field, the flouwen watching the chase with their sonar. Suddenly, the coelashark turned tail and dove for its hole under its rock, while behind it the weak sonar return from the ribbon-fish was replaced with a very large return signal. All of this was carefully relayed to David, who was becoming alarmed.

"You've got inside the big coelashark's territory, that's good," he said calmly. "Now the tricky bit may be getting yourselves out. *With* your suits intact." The flouwen paused to consider what he had said. Unafraid on their own account, they recognized the desirability of preserving the well-engineered suits. Shirley had assured them that the glassy-foil was nearly impossible to cut or tear, and had shown that a knife-point could not penetrate it, but the flouwen were not anxious to try it out on coelashark teeth.

◊This way?◊
☐Straight up?☐

☆Between two vents?☆

David caught only hints of the consultation going on below. Decided now, the flouwen moved smoothly and steadily off at an angle, following the trace of slightly cooler water that flowed off between the warm areas of two of the active vents. They were unsuccessful in their attempted escape. The giant coelashark spotted them, and screaming belligerently, it attacked; "My territory! You are my food! You cry from fear—and I shall kill you now, tear out your guts, spill your blood, rip open your throat . . ."

◊All yell at head now!◊ Little White commanded the other flouwen as the creature rushed at them. Shaping their bodies into shallow dishes, they each generated a high pitched sonar scream that shot through the thin glassy-foil fabric of their suits into the water and was focused onto the head section of the approaching coelashark.

The fury of the coelashark was swept away on the piercing, destroying wave of sound that blasted from the flouwen, focussing on the flesh of the animal, exploding its eyes, numbing its brain, and vibrating chunks of flesh from its lips. Quickly, the flouwen surged past the dazed coelashark into cooler waters and paused to send sonar pulses back to see if it was recovering from the attack. They saw, apparently appearing from nowhere, three medium-sized coelasharks converging on the remnants of the predator. Biting and swallowing with savage speed, they spared no time or breath for speech until the giant coelashark had been ripped into large chunks. The three then turned on each other. Powerful tails flipped agile bodies, tentacles jabbed at eyes with pointed stones, and finned feet struggled to maintain each animal's equilibrium, while the jaws lunged and tore, searching for a vital hold. The flouwen watched dispassionately as, by chance, two of the sharks managed each to get a firm grip on the third. Within seconds they had torn it practically in two. The larger of the two then struck with speed and power at the throat of the other. The smaller one was not much smaller, however, and was quick to respond. Two tentacles deflected the thrusting jaws for an instant, and although they were bitten off close to the body, the smaller animal had gained a precious chance. All four fins, on the ends of the stubby legs, swirled and pushed to send the coelashark shooting backward, into the warmer water, where it slid hastily into a crevice and hid. The victor coelashark seemed about to pursue, then hesitated, and hung irresolutely in the water, turning its large head first toward the three flouwen, waiting and watching, and then toward the escaped and hidden enemy. Tentatively, it advanced in the direction of the flouwen, thrusting its sharp stone before it, but a warning blast of sound from them stopped it.

"*My* territory now! All food in this territory is mine!" There was a hint of triumph in the voice, and Little Red was curious enough to communicate with the killer.

☆You have won?☆

"You know it! You saw it! I have killed those two! No one is left bigger than I am! I rule this area now, and any who show themselves I will devour! That goes for you, too, whoever you are! Whatever you are!"

Little Purple said peaceably, ⬜You cannot harm us, and we do not wish to harm you. We have only come to see how you live.⬜

"And it'll be the death of you!" screamed the coelashark, advancing once again. A repeat of the sonar warning interrupted the action, and the coelashark hung back, screaming threats and insults. The three flouwen began to move with deliberate slowness into the cooler waters away from the coelashark, which stayed where it was, still raging. When they were out of sight, the flouwen sent a sonar signal back and found that the coelashark was swimming off at a tangent. A few more minutes of observation at that distance told the flouwen that the creature was circling, first slowly and then with increasing confidence, the vent field which fed that area with its life-giving heat and mineral-laden water.

"It's about time for us to come and pick you up," said David from the *Dragonfly*. "I'll see you shortly at the spot where we left you off."

The flouwen, with their sample bags full, headed silently back in the direction from which they had come, *Babble* paddling noisily behind, trying to keep up.

VISITING

With the flouwen launched, George was anxious to proceed with a visit to the icerug city, Windward. The humans worked quickly to ready themselves and the *Dragonfly* for departure, while leaving no trace of their visit upon the icy shore but their tracks in the snow. With considerable satisfaction, Deirdre helped Richard and the Christmas Branch stow the ropes and telescoping poles they had used to lower *Babble* into the water in the belly hold of the airplane.

"That's the way it should be, it is that," said Deirdre, as she climbed into the airlock and turned to look around. "Nothing taken and nothing left. Come, observe, report, and leave—clean and scientific!"

Richard took one last walk around the airplane to make sure they had picked up everything. Suddenly, a strong jolt ran through the ice, knocking him off his feet. It was followed by a loud rumbling crack that sounded somewhat like a distant giant breaking a tall tree in two like a matchstick. Richard picked himself off the ground and ran for the airlock where Deirdre was waiting for him, his feet unsteady as the ice beneath them tilted back and forth slowly.

"The ice shelf we're on has just turned into an iceberg! Let's get out of here before it decides to turn turtle!" He leaped into the open door.

"I'm in, Arielle!" shouted Richard. "Take off and get to altitude!"

Before the outer airlock door had completely closed, the large electrically driven fan engines in the wing roots of the airplane had started spinning, and Arielle coaxed the *Dragonfly* into the air like an overladen rocket.

Once they were safely high above the ice and held up by the VTOL fans, Arielle smoothly shifted from fan lift to jet thrust, and the airplane climbed in altitude and away from the icy shore edge along the open water of the warm lake where the flouwen had submerged. Richard looked back out the small porthole in the outer airlock door. He could now see a jagged line of open water where once there had been solid ice connecting their landing spot to the shore.

"A nice big flat ice floe," he remarked. "I guess we weren't really in danger after all."

Arielle turned the *Dragonfly* until they were headed directly toward the distant cloudy blur of Manannán geyser, with its thick telltale column of condensing moisture rising kilometers into the air. Through the clouds could be seen a rooster-tail spray of windblown water droplets from the geyser in the middle. The boiling jet was half a kilometer high and growing higher with each geyser pulse.

Shirley, at the science console, looked at a graph of the predictions for tidal forces on her screen. "Zuni is approaching conjunction, while Zouave is not far behind. Not a true triple conjunction—more like a two-point-seven-tuple conjunction. The ocean surface should rise about nine meters in the next two hours, then drop again." Richard, still dressed in his suit underalls, strode down the narrow corridor, swivel-hipped past David's console chair, and stood looking over Shirley's shoulder, sipping on an algae-shake he had picked up from the galley imp.

"The rising tide is probably what caused that ice floe to break off," he said. "We should now get plenty of action from Big Berth . . . Manannán. There's going to be a lot of hot water thrown up into the air in the next few hours."

"That's not good," said George from the copilot seat. "Those are ripe conditions for causing a plane to ice up."

Arielle was already alert to the problem, and the small pilot kept constant check on the icing indicators, while changing course to take the plane well to windward of the distant geyser. As they left the small open lake where they had put the flouwen and moved toward Manannán's much larger lake off in the distance, the crew were examining and commenting with fascination upon the changing terrain. Although David could have observed from his console by watching the color video input from the visual imagers set in the eyelike side domes of *Dragonfly*, he went forward to the flight deck where he could look out Arielle's side cockpit window from the jump seat behind her.

"Look at that jade-colored one—with the paler ones on either side!" David's ability to see the slightest variations in color helped him to delineate the regular patterns unfolding below. Deirdre, fresh from a shower and back in her trim brown coverall, came forward with Foxx to take the jump seat behind George.

"They're definitely triangular, d'you see?"

With the clue, the humans all began to pick out the

repetition of shape, even though some of the blue-green fields were so closely alike in color that distinction was difficult. Richard and Shirley, their heads close together as Richard stared over Shirley's shoulder at her console screen, enjoyed trying to pick out the boundaries of each irregular formation, while simultaneously enjoying their own closeness. Richard was supporting himself on his hands placed close on either side of Shirley's console table. The heavy warmth of Shirley's breasts brushing against his forearms as she reached to bring up new views on the touch-screen, recalled casual liaisons of years past, and Shirley, relaxing in this carefree moment, delighted in reminding Richard. Up front, oblivious, George and Deirdre commented on the increasing number of icerugs visible below.

"We ought to take some sort of count," speculated George. "The icerugs seem to congregate in certain areas and not in others, so a map of population density might be a good thing to make."

"That's going to require a survey, an aerial survey, of a great deal of territory, will it not?" asked Deirdre.

"Umm," replied George. "Anything really accurate would be more than I'd care to undertake, at least on this mission. But an overview of at least the inner pole area, and perhaps a visual estimate of the population around each geyser, might prove enlightening to us—and maybe even the icerugs."

Deirdre didn't automatically approve of attempting to enlighten the aliens, but she knew well how population trends can illustrate trends in environmental changes. An accurate map of the native population density would be valuable base-line data for future research studies. As they flew closer to the large lake—tens of kilometers in size—the area that each icerug occupied became smaller, and the pattern shifted from the general hexagonal arrangement of triangles that they had noticed out in the country to more complex shapes.

"There seem to be certain centers of importance," said David. "Instead of a point being surrounded by six equilateral triangles, it is surrounded by dozens or even hundreds of narrow isosceles triangles, all meeting at the same vertex point, as if it were necessary for all those icerugs to be in communication with each other at the same time."

"Could be the icerug equivalent of a parliament," suggested George. "Or a factory with a production line—although I doubt it. The types of items that we have seen the icerugs carry are more like those produced by craftsmen than a production line—still, you never know. . . ."

"Here's something interesting!" said Shirley, as she changed the zoom on the right-hand dome visible imaging telescope. They could now see an enlarged image of a long snakelike strip made of two slightly different blue-green colors adjacent to each other.

"If those are two icerugs lying side-by-side, then they are the *longest* icerugs I've seen yet," said George, copying her screen. "They must go for five kilometers or so."

"Look," said Richard, his finger on Shirley's touch-screen producing a green indicator spot on George's screen. "They meet up with another pair of long icerugs here."

Shirley increased the zoom, and soon they could see objects moving along the twin strips.

"It's a living conveyor belt!"

On one strip there were lumps and parcels of various sizes and shapes moving rapidly along, while on the neighboring strip, similar objects were moving in the opposite direction. Shirley's fingers flicked over the icons at the side of her screen, then touched one of the strips, which lit up with a yellow border surrounding it. Soon Joe replied through her imp, "Area of strip indicated is forty-four hundred twenty-four square meters. Average width of strip not quite one meter, length four-point-eight kilometers."

"That's about the same area as one of the triangular icerugs out in the country," remarked Deirdre. "But this one seems, perhaps, specialized."

"I wonder what other specialty body shapes they can assume," mused Richard. "Do they have driller icerugs, or mining icerugs, or water company icerugs, or sewage disposal icerugs?"

"Telephone line icerugs?" ventured David. "If they changed width to a strip a millimeter across, four thousand square meters would stretch . . ."

Joe responded with the answer: ". . . four thousand kilometers, David, lad. One-quarter o' the circumference of the moon. More than enough to reach from one geyser community to another."

It was obvious that the central portion of Windward was concentrated on the lee side of the geyser lake, in the direction where the prevailing winds from the leading pole of Zulu would blow the spray from the geyser. The dangerous ice-shelf shores of the lake were barren of icerugs, although a few "brave" specimens extended a small portion of their bodies out onto the thicker parts.

The *Dragonfly* flew through a small upward-billowing cloud rising from the warm waters below, temporarily blocking the view. Suddenly, the *Dragonfly* swerved to the right and continued in a wide circle, until the plane was heading away from the big geyser. "Wings icing. I try again." Arielle's voice was firm and unworried, but the others fell silent, looking out at the incredibly slender wings that carried them. David quickly left the jump seat and returned to his computer console, where he flashed terse questions at Joe concerning the geysering pattern of Manannán, as determined from previous recordings of the geyser action under similar tidal conditions, and assimilated the computer's brief answers into his predictions. He was going to check his conclusions with their geologist, Richard, but when he glanced over at the absorbed couple at the science console, he decided to make the decision on his own. He broadcast his recommendation through all imps.

"In fifteen minutes, there will be a respite—perhaps a half hour in duration, when the geyser activity will be less. The tides from Zuni and Zouave will be canceling each other slightly because of their different phases, and the pulsation period of the geyser will simultaneously be at its minimum. According to Joe, during that period, Arielle should be able to touch down, drop an exploration crew off, and go again, with minimal chance of icing up. She can return safely a few hours later, when the two conjunctions are over and the geyser has settled down again."

As he spoke, Arielle took the *Dragonfly* back again toward the center of all the geyser activity. "I take another look." Her eyes flickered, searching the ice-shelf shore of the lake for a safe place to land that was near the center of the city. George, anxious to succeed in his plan to land and meet with the more sophisticated members of this alien civilization, left his copilot seat and started back to the rear to put on his exploration suit. He passed Richard and Shirley, and automatically registered their closeness. As he walked on, he quickly inserted this fact into his various options.

"Right—they're at that stage. I don't give a damn, but we're short of time on this mission and I'll need both of them sensible. I'll have to break it up. They can wait."

He returned shortly in his exploration suit, minus his helmet. He reached the copilot's seat and zeroed all his attention in on the information appearing on his screen. Arielle grunted and flicked a long fingernail out the side cockpit window on her left before swinging the *Dragonfly* back into another big circle. George had just time to see what she had been pointing at before it swept from view. It was a large circular area along the Manannán lake front ice shelf, which looked both relatively flat and empty of icerug bodies.

"Next pass, if ice stays off wings, I try there." Arielle's few words gave George a clear, quick picture of her scheme, and he began to take action.

"David. Stay with the plane and monitor the activities of the flouwen. Richard and Deirdre, suit up to go out with me. Shirley, stay with the plane and design a mapping survey of the inner pole area. You can start with a population density map of the icerug nation around this geyser, as accurate as you have time for, before picking us up again. Arielle, take us down when ready."

The crisp commands sparked everyone. Joyfully, Deirdre headed to the rear to put on her suit again. Richard and Shirley arose more slowly, but Richard's mind sprang quickly to the prospect of exploring more of this world, and Shirley fastened on the two concerns of a new task to perform and the customary but vital one of assuring the safety of the crew in their suits. Soon, Richard was going through the checkout of his suit panel, grunting as Shirley punched each check button.

Arielle found her planned landing site again, and soon the *Dragonfly* cut its jets and started a slow glide toward the bare spot of ice between the lake shore and the center of the city. The icerugs had obviously cleared out from the area so the plane could land. There was a light snow falling from the upper clouds, but the geyser had slowed down, as predicted, and there was no icy rain accompanying the snowfall. Where they were heading, there were dozens of narrow isosceles triangles of colorful carpets arranged in a circle, their apexes pointing at the round patch of clear ice. The nodes of each icerug were placed well back from the landing area.

In the back of the airplane, as the three explorers entered the inner airlock door, Richard's eyes met Shirley's through the intervening visor of his suit; both grinned, and Shirley kissed the visor lightly, then instantly buffed away the tiny trace of lipstick she had left on the surface.

"See you later," they said together.

Deirdre caught the exchange, noted it, and forgot it. She moved into the airlock behind George, excitement mounting within her, although Foxx, perched on her shoulder, reflected Deirdre's calm outward composure.

The time Arielle was willing to spend on the ice was short; so George, Richard, and Deirdre, having made sure that they had all the items that had been planned for this meeting stowed in their chestpacks, waited in the closed airlock, ready to leave as soon as the plane landed.

Arielle assessed the landing site. To David, watching from the copilot seat beside her, the field seemed full of boulders and ice ridges—much more so than it had appeared from above—but Arielle coolly brought the large plane to a hovering halt on its VTOL fans, and rotating it about its vertical axis, maneuvered the long wings between the threatening masses and lowered it down near the icy surface.

Reluctant to come to a complete halt, Arielle hovered

while George, Deirdre, and Richard opened the airlock door, jumped onto the ice, and ran out from under the wing and toward the front of the plane where Arielle could see them. Once they were safely in view, the tiny pilot smiled brightly at them through the thick cockpit window, waved good-bye, and the *Dragonfly* lifted and swiftly flew away.

The three explorers turned to look around. The almost hasty decision he had taken, to land at this early opportunity, left George feeling that the last few moments had been hectic. In startling contrast was the composure of the large alien node confronting him, with its yellow-gold eye in the middle of its peacock-colored carpet. The majestic-looking icerug node looked as if it had been standing there, immobile, for hours, as the fine granules of lightly falling snow slid down over the fantastic colors and shapes of its ornate attire.

At the base of its eye stalk was a wide collar of shining gold medallions alternating with bushy rosettes of brightly colored red lace. From the collar fell a long white cape covered with more red lace rosettes with long strands of red ribbons fluttering from them. Around the narrow "neck" region below the globular head and above the four tentacles was a neckband, again with shining gold medallions alternating with rosettes of red lace, from which draped more ribbons which fell down between the four tentacles. The ribbons partially covered a number of pouches and artifacts that hung down below the tentacles where they could be easily grasped. Surrounding the "waist" region below the four tentacles and above the pedestal was a belt, again with medallions and rosettes. Hanging from the belt was a white skirt that covered the pedestal of the icerug node. The skirt design repeated the gaudy rosette and ribbon motif of the cape. Using one peacock-colored tentacle, the icerug lifted a large monocle and looked through it, its eye looking even larger through the lens.

The nodes of the other icerugs surrounding their landing site were well back at the far end of their carpets, apparently deferring to the elaborately dressed greeter. All the icerug nodes were clad in a kaleidoscopic variety of costumes. The humans started over the bare ice toward the greeter, and the yellow-eyed alien glided simultaneously across its peacock carpet to meet them.

"All these icerugs seem a lot better dressed and decorated than the country ones," remarked George through their private imp link.

"That's so, and much good it does them," said Deirdre coolly. "Nothing I see of warmth or protection, only grand to look at."

George and the icerug node met at the edge of the icerug's carpet. George was not a small man, but the eye of the icerug towered over him. George cleared his throat, wondering if he should speak first, and regarded the imposing alien with some awe.

"Greetings to you, strangers, from the Governing Council of Windward City, of which I, Golden-Glint, am Presider!" The long rolling thunder of this speech was smoothly rendered into human words and tones by the translation programs in their suit computers. The humans stood silent, studying the fine peacock shimmer of the Presider, surmounted by a yellow eye with a strong sparkle of golden color that flickered as the alien continued to speak.

"We have heard of your arrival in a far distant region of ice near our nation's perimeter. We have studied and discussed reports of you, your flying machines, and your actions, brought to us through the Conveners in contact with that region. We have decided, unanimously of course, to invite you into our great city to show you of its wonders." There was a great deal more, mostly of a self-laudatory and rather pompous nature, but so benign in character that George had leisure to compose the opening sentences of a speech for the visitors. He recalled formal presentations on Earth, and resolved to use as many oratorical garnishes as he could remember; Reiki had mentioned once that among cultures with a love of speech-making a short answer is tantamount to an insult.

George did his best, but eventually found himself running out of things to say. ". . . and so, hearing of the marvelous wonders to see, and things to learn in your wonderful city, we resolved to travel here for a brief time, hoping to see something of its . . . erm . . . marvelous wonders." The sheet of glassy-foil in the hands of his suit imp boomed out the icerug translation of George's last few words and fell silent.

And we're wasting the time we have, thought Richard. *Cut it short, George!* Thankfully, he saw the icerug bodies ahead of them begin to move their carpet edges apart, opening a clear path of ice for the humans to walk on, while Golden-Glint indicated with a graceful sweep of three of its tentacles that the visitors were to accompany them.

The procession moved quickly. The icerug seemed to move effortlessly, and the humans marched as fast as was comfortable.

"Ahead, you will observe the Grand Portal. This is the main entrance into our Great Meeting Hall."

They were approaching the decorated opening of a tunnel going down into the ice. This tall entrance portal was constructed of beautifully polished and elaborately carved rocks, closely fitted together. As they descended along the gleaming icy path lined with hundreds of threads of icerug flesh, Richard noted and commented to the others through their private imp link, "There, at the bottom of the walls. Those are nickel-iron meteorites—very strong building materials if you can get them. And there, up above, the composition of the arch changes to volcanic rock—light, but still strong. Look how high that arch is!"

They were all impressed with the size of the entrance hallway. The ceiling above them, vaulted with rock and roofed with what looked like bars of ice, soared higher than the entryways in many medieval cathedrals. They finally entered a gigantic room with the roof supported by stone arches rising from thick stone pedestal bases.

"It's the low gravity here, I guess," murmured Richard. "Even with all the mass of ice and snow on top, they can still build these tremendously tall and wide arches."

Deirdre said nothing, her whole attention caught by the spectacle around her. Hundreds of icerug nodes were in the gigantic meeting hall, which still seemed almost empty, so vast were its spaces. Each icerug was emitting a spot of blue bioluminescent light from a dished-in portion of the spherical head section of their node, and all the soft blue "spotlights" were pointed in their direction. The light from all those concave spots was also reflected from the stone walls, polished to a mirror sheen, and in addition, was reflected off all the eyes on the ends of the eye stalks, focused upon the visitors. Deirdre was reminded of a field of sunflowers, with herself as the sun, and was enchanted. George, less happily, remembered his first graduation ceremony and hoped he wouldn't trip.

Accompanied by the Presider, the humans moved to a clear floor area seemingly set aside for them. There was nothing upon which a human could sit, or even lean; all three were resigned to this, and adopted a relaxed stance they could maintain indefinitely. Golden-Glint was speaking again; they caught the glitter of something held by two of the alien's tentacles. It was a small sheet of ice that Golden-Glint held in front of its concave illuminator while "reading" from it with its large eye, occasionally glancing up to look at the humans or the attentive audience. The humans watched, fascinated, as the upper edge of the sheet apparently melted and was absorbed by the tentacle holding it from above, while the speech was being read. Golden-Glint finally concluded:

"We know you will enjoy hearing our Orchestra and Chorus from the Center of Musical Studies. They shall perform for you now."

Amazed, the humans realized that a large segment of the surrounding crowds was arranged in orderly rows, each individual holding a small sheet of rock between two tentacles. Some of the others held curious objects which were revealed to be musical instruments; varieties of chimes could be seen, and all sorts of drums. There were also strange shapes mounted with taut strands, which were plucked or bowed. All three humans wished suddenly that David were with them. The rest of the musicians constituted a large chorus, and the music which burst forth from this alien combination was wonderfully deep and compelling to Deirdre.

"Fond I am of the low bass tones," she murmured to the others through their private imp link, "but I never before heard a song where the highest note in it was middle C!" She listened with delight; for the first time she forgot her professional determination to distance herself emotionally from this alien life-form. Richard and George were studying the various instruments intently, memorizing as many different structures as they could see, to relate later to David, and hoping that the video monitor cameras in their helmets had enough resolution to capture the details of construction.

"That chime is surely icicle-based, and the drum-frame is either ice or some sort of rock," remarked George through their link. "But what is the drum-head made of? From the pattern, it looks like snake skin or fish skin, but it's too large for that."

Similarly Richard was trying to analyze the uniform sheets every musician held. "They must be thin slices of rock, that's exactly what they look like, and they're covered with tiny squiggles. Can it be they're reading from them?"

Richard enjoyed the performance, although he was not as absorbed in it as Deirdre; rather, he was hoping that the concert would be brief, so that some of the many questions occurring to him could be asked. George was thinking the same, and when the music ceased he started to speak, only to stop, a little embarrassed, as Deirdre applauded enthusiastically, with her gloved hands. The men copied her gesture then, and the icerug orchestra visibly rippled, whether from amusement or curiosity it was impossible to tell. At any rate, it gave George a moment to rephrase his sentences more formally.

"That is truly splendid music. There are those among us who also make music; their instruments, and the sounds they make, are vastly different from what we have just heard. It illustrates to us how much we can learn, and are eager to learn, from you. We thank you for the pleasure of your music. Rather than interrupt any further the activities of your day, might we perhaps speak with just a few individuals—scientists or craftsmen—who would be willing to explain to us something of the objects that we are seeing?"

There was no evidence of displeasure in the response of the alien. Deirdre abruptly recalled herself to reality: human values and reactions had no place among these creatures. While the concert resumed behind them, Golden-Glint escorted the humans from the hall, through an adjacent tunnel and into a much smaller room. Keeping a mental map, Richard surmised that the walls of this under-ice cathedral were many meters thick, and that while they were actually in the first room outside the hall, the rock-lined ice walls were so thick that little of the booming music penetrated here. George noticed this also, and recalling the physical throbbing of the alien drums, speculated with interest on the acoustics of the vaulted ceilings. Deirdre was meanwhile trying to sort out the tangle of colored strands over which they were walking. There seemed to be fewer of them here than in the main tunnel entrance.

As they entered the small side room at the end of the tunnel, Golden-Glint said, "Here you shall meet with a few of our scientists, those who had time to spare to talk with you."

Once again the humans noticed that the aliens had no expectation of anything of much interest coming to them from these interviews; the icerugs were willing to discuss themselves, apparently finding that reason enough to talk. Separately, each human made a quick mental inventory of what they had brought with them in the way of "trade goods," hoping to arouse a little curiosity in the icerugs. George waved a questioning hand at a small stack of music plates.

"It is puzzling to us even what sort of material these things are made from. When you . . . erm . . . Sir Presider, were greeting us so eloquently, the sheet you held appeared to be dissolving as you spoke."

"Of course," agreed the alien. "It was not an important speech, so I simply wrote a few notes upon a page of ice I generated from my own fluids. Then I reabsorbed it. Water ice makes a very satisfactory material for such short-term use—strong, readily available, clean, easily inscribed upon, and instantly disposable. Things which must be used many times, like those music plates, are written on thin sheets of stone." The casual phrase startled the human ears.

"*How* do you write in stone?" asked Richard. "Have you metals?" The Presider fluidly waved a peacock-colored tentacle in the direction of the small cluster of icerug nodes waiting for them, the red ribbons hanging from its neck band fluttering in response to the motion.

"That, and other questions you may have, will be answered by our distinguished scientists from the Center of Scientific Studies. May I introduce the illustrious and eminent scientists, Eclipse, Bright-Eye, and Dark-Star, all venerable experts in their respective fields. You will now please excuse me; I have other duties to attend to." The Presider glided rapidly away in a flutter of red ribbons, and the alien identified as Eclipse spoke, its "voice" several tones higher than that of its leader. Eclipse's skin was a soft beryl in color, and the node was wearing a cape of what looked like white linen cloth, finely woven and fancifully embroidered with designs in different-colored threads.

"Writing on stone is no more difficult than forming the stone into useful shapes in the first place. It is simply a matter of body chemistry, although it takes a great deal more time, dissolving stone rather than ice. Writing— here, I shall show you—goes quite quickly indeed."

Eclipse, obviously named for the semicircular segment of dark gray in the rim of its yellow iris, glided to what looked like a bookcase that had been carved into the solid wall of the room and picked up one of the stone tablets stacked there on one of the shelves. Then, with a swiftly extended tentacle, the alien added a few characters to the squiggles that closely filled the sheet of rock.

"I merely exude a small amount of . . ." There was a pause as the translation program in their suits conferred with Josephine through the commsats overhead to get the proper translation through context of the conversation. ". . . acid that dissolves the rock, and then reabsorb the resulting solution." There was a pause as the tentacle used for the writing pulled back from the rock sheet, shrank down, and pulsated a few times, while the eye of the node rotated to look down at the tentacle.

"Mmmmm. This rock is quite tasty." Eclipse then rotated its eye back again until it was looking at the humans, the concave light on its head following the motion of the eye, and continued. "A similar process, using fine threads of flesh, is used by the stone masons to cut rectangular blocks of rock from the bedrock beneath for use in constructing our buildings, and for use by the platemakers who slice writing plates from those blocks for record-keeping purposes."

George moved closer so he could see what Eclipse was doing. He could barely discern the tiny, intricate designs, and he watched, amazed, as Eclipse's tentacle tip moved across a bare portion of the stone, leaving a string of finely engraved symbols behind.

"The characters are so tiny!" said George, impressed. "Wouldn't take much acid to engrave them."

"The large size of their eyes means they can see quite small features, George," Deirdre reminded him quietly through their imp link. "Their vision is far superior to ours. I wonder— Cinnamon had me bring along one of her posters to give to the icerugs—shows humans without suits. Think you it would be interesting to share at this time?"

"That's why we included the poster on this foray," replied George. "Eclipse and the others are supposed to be various kinds of scientists. Let's see if any of them are interested in human physiology."

Deirdre drew the poster in its tube from her chestpack and unrolled the slender cylinder before the alien's eye. It was an innocent scene, romantically pastoral in the Maxfield Parrish tradition. It showed a young man and woman strolling through an exotic meadow holding hands, wearing no spacesuits and indeed, very little else. The icerug scientists gathered close with the first haste the humans had noticed from them, and tentacles reached out to touch the paper, feeling dexterously along the edges and smoothly over the flat surface.

"This is a most unusual substance," boomed Eclipse. "The picture is mildly interesting, although the colors used are strange—but what is this picture plate made of? Can you return it to the shape of the small container?"

"Indeed, I can," said Deirdre, demonstrating. The room throbbed with the low tones of several icerugs speaking at once, and an air of excitement grew. The probing tentacles were still careful with the poster, but Deirdre thought it wise to show them the frailty of the new substance. "Look you, it is light and easy to write upon with many tools, but it will tear." She slowly ripped a small corner from the bottom, and extended it to Eclipse. "It is much more fragile than rock or ice. But it is larger and thinner and lighter than anything we know—large maps and charts could be made upon it.

"Is it an element only obtainable from your world?"

asked Eclipse, holding the fragment of paper up before its large yellow eye in a beryl-colored tentacle.

Deirdre searched her mind for the basics of paper manufacture, while George was puzzled that the picture itself was of such little interest to these creatures.

"Paper is made of small fibers. They can be practically any sort of fiber, such as the fibers that make up the threads used to weave your cloaks. If you have plant fibers, like those in seaweed, you can make paper—it is simply a process of making a mesh frame, filling it with a thin layer of pulp . . . slurry . . ." She hesitated as her imp warned her that the translation program did not include those words, and Deirdre stopped, seeing the difficulty. With the marking pen she used for labeling sample bags, she sketched on the back of the poster a simple box frame with a screen stretched across it, and above it, a number of layers of criss-crossed threads.

"Paper's so easy," murmured Richard. "I'm surprised they've not got it already, especially since they make thread to weave cloth."

"You need a slush of threads and water to make paper," said Deirdre briefly over their private imp link. "Difficult to imagine here, isn't it, how to form a slurry at below freezing temperatures?" Still, she persevered. Showing Eclipse the diagram, she started to explain it.

"You start by mixing fine fibers in a container of liquid water. You use a device like this, which passes water, but holds onto the fibers, to extract the fibers from the water to form a thin mat. You press the water out of the mat and dry it with heat. It must be dry, not frozen. . . ."

It was enough. The advanced intelligence of the alien had already sorted several possibilities. Eclipse raised its beryl tentacle, which was still holding the torn-off bit of paper.

"This will help, when I have looked at it under a microscope. I shall go now, and with my assistants shall work on trying to duplicate this . . . paper." Hearing the human word, spoken in the deep bass voice of the alien, startled Deirdre. She turned to George, who was attempting to give Dark-Star a description of how his braided safety rope was made.

George had cut off a section of the rope and unbraided a strand of the superstrong polymer monofilament line. Dark-Star's tentacles instantly reached to touch and flex and tug on the strong line, while questions came faster than George could respond.

"It is a single long thread, made by extrusion . . ." His translation program complained, and he tried to simplify his explanation. "A heat-softened compound of the right chemicals is forced through a hole of fine diameter, into a cooling bath, where it hardens into a long thread. Sometimes the compound used is a sticky substance that is forced through the hole into a chemical solution that causes it to change into a hard substance.. . ." George was dismayed to realize that that was about the limit of his knowledge of monofilament lines. There was a moment's delay, before he remembered Josephine's inexhaustible references and tapped into them. Unfortunately, they were all too technical to be of much help in his explanation, designed as they were for the use of the Christmas Bush. However, a few understandable phrases—along with another quick sketch by Deirdre of a rather basic extrusion machine— seemed adequate for Dark-Star.

"Coelashark bones and fins, from which we make glues—they have a chemical structure that might be adapted to this purpose. And compounds from seaweed—they are many and varied—we still find new uses for them. Perhaps you would want to see where we work with them?"

As George, Dark-Star, and several other icerugs moved out of the room, Richard noticed that with their withdrawal the light in the room diminished considerably. Glancing about him, Richard saw that, apart from the glowing spots on the heads of the creatures themselves, no light was available. Of course, since the concave spots shifted around on the spherical head to illuminate the direction that the single eye was looking, there was always enough light for each icerug. Almost as though following his thoughts, the icerug referred to as Bright-Eye bent its large eye with its light blue iris slightly toward Richard.

"As you can see, this room becomes dim without a large group of us present."

Bright-Eye itself was lighter in color than its peers—a rather soft aquamarine, and the swirling woven cloak with the intricate designs was the same shade as its velvety body. "Is your own vision augmented by such light that we cannot see it? Or perhaps you can see without light?"

Richard decided not to admit any human weakness, simply as a precaution; however, he reached for the solar-rechargeable permalight hanging from his belt to show Bright-Eye that humans also had a means of illumination—although it was artificial rather than natural.

Meanwhile, Deirdre rolled up Cinnamon's poster and stowed it in her chestpack. If the icerugs were not interested in having the picture, Cinnamon would certainly want it back. She understood Richard's reticence and was not as critical as she might have been about his decision to display advanced Earth technology in the form of the permalight. She watched silently as he played the light about the room, illuminating the farthest corners. The bright white light beaming from the flashlight was much more powerful than the weak blue bioluminescence of the glowing cavities formed in the icerug bodies. Bright-Eye and the remaining icerugs drew closer to handle the little torch, turning it off and on as children might.

"Is this a part of your head, which you can separate and carry?" Richard forbore to answer the question directly, but began to dismantle the instrument. "It is a machine that we make from various metals and chemical compounds. See, the bulb here contains a fine filament, made of tungsten metal. When electricity passes through it . . ."

"That word was not translated."

The two humans paused, initially dismayed. Deirdre was now concerned that they were interfering with the alien culture's development. If the icerugs knew nothing about electricity, perhaps too much had already been shown to them. Richard, however, was undaunted and began considering how the icerugs might possibly make a device similar to a flashlight, for they certainly didn't need to know all about electricity to do so. Without glass for a bulb to hold a vacuum, however, it looked impossible. Still, a long sliver from a nickel-iron asteroid with a high melting point and a reasonable resistance might glow a bright Barnard red color in the reducing atmosphere of Zulu for some time, if fed by a carbon-iron battery. As Richard related his ideas to Bright-Eye, the alien's superior intelligence ranged widely, considering what it knew of the materials available to it. As it cogitated, its eye wandered higher and higher until it was looking straight up in the air in deep thought, the top portion of its spherical head glowing in a circular halo around its aquamarine eye stalk.

"You say fine fibers of metal are needed to carry this

electricity from one place to another. Perhaps gold or mercury would be easiest to form into these . . . wires. And the generation of energy in something called a battery, using sheets of metal dipped in water containing salt or acid. . . . If indeed this electricity exists, I should be most interested in experimenting with it. A curious fact we have long pondered, regarding metals, is that when we hold two dissimilar ones at the same time, our tentacles experience an extremely sharp and bitter taste."

As clearly as possible, the humans speculated aloud on various combinations and experiments that might prove fruitful, while the alien's mind absorbed everything and said little. Finally, Bright-Eye spoke.

"We must go to the laboratory, and plan a logical series of trials. Would you care to come along?" Both humans assented eagerly and set off behind the quickly traveling alien, relaying to Josephine their progress so George would know where they had gone.

Bright-Eye moved swiftly down a wide, stone-arched tunnel, along the flat ice floor covered with the skein of icerug threads. The alien seemed disinclined to talk as it moved, and both humans were grateful, as they were moving at a pace which would have made conversation difficult. When they turned into yet another tunnel, this one hewn out of polished ice, they sped up yet again. The humans saw that the floor of this tunnel now contained only one wide band of aquamarine—evidently this was Bright-Eye's own territory, and they were now running at such speed that stepping on the velvety ribbon of flesh was unavoidable. Richard puffed out an apology, but the icerug emitted only a sound which their translator interpreted as, "It means nothing." The alien slowed its speed, then, as though it had observed the effort the humans were making in order to keep up while walking on the slippery flesh. They had traveled nearly a half kilometer along this deep solitary tunnel, lit only with the glow from Bright-Eye, when Deirdre stumbled and muttered something about "moving sidewalks." Richard too found it suddenly difficult to keep his feet, as the colored band on which he was walking seemed to twist and jerk.

Neither person was alarmed; both assumed this jerky motion of the icerug path was yet another manifestation of icerug physiology. Bright-Eye, however, had stopped dead, and the glow from its midsection increased to illuminate the entire tunnel, while its node sank down into its supporting stalk.

"Icequake!" boomed the deep voice of the alien in obvious panic, its eye rolling around in all directions as it scanned the tunnel walls. Then they all heard the ominous creaking, screaming, crackling sounds of frozen substances under tremendous pressures. Chunks of ice spalled from the walls and ceiling.

"The tunnel is collapsing upon us!" Booming incoherently, the icerug seemed to melt before their eyes, shrinking down on its pedestal in a desperate effort to protect its head and eye from being crushed.

"Get down!" yelled Richard, as the top of the tunnel started to push down on the top of his head. Bright-Eye was now lying flat upon its own carpeted path, its eye stalk contracted until its eye was resting beside its larger globular head. The tough sixed-lobed nictitating membrane of the eye was closed tightly shut over the vulnerable eyeball. The ice itself was echoing, in grotesque parody, the groaning sounds of the terrified icerug.

Richard had heard those sounds from ice before, from icebergs and glaciers, as they deformed and stretched, before succumbing to the irresistible forces that shaped them. What chance had puny humanity against such elemental power? Deirdre was alarmed, he saw, but she had no real inkling of the tremendous danger they were in. The humans, first stooping, and then kneeling in the slowly contracting ice tunnel, were forced to the floor along with the icerug by the slowly collapsing ceiling.

"Deirdre! Make an arch!" gasped Richard, crawling toward the vulnerable eye and head of the alien and curving his body over them. Deirdre slithered over to cover the icerug's eye, and interlinking one arm and one leg with Richard's, added her strength to his, endeavoring to use their combined muscles and bones in a probably futile attempt to resist the deadly, increasing contraction of the ice.

"Increase suit pressure!" shouted Deirdre to her suitimp, and Richard understood. Instantly, both people demanded pressure increases within their carefully engineered suits, and soon— yawning violently to alleviate ears popping with pain—they were answered with many atmospheres of internal suit pressure. The tough glassy-foil suits stiffened, swelling until the elbow joints were locked and rigid. The pressure from the ice above grew. Foxx's small body trembled and chittered against Deirdre's throat; however, at a soft command, the animal was still.

The entire head of Bright-Eye was now glowing in fright, and in the weird blue bioluminescent glow, Deirdre was amazed to see her gloved hands slowly sinking into the ice. She knew that even with the stiffened sleeves of the suit helping to keep her elbow joints from bending, the bones in her wrists and forearms weren't strong enough to do that. Once her arms had penetrated into the ice above her elbows, however, the ice froze about the suit material, adding support. The same thing was happening to Richard. They were both sinking into the ice. But instead of her torso crushing down on the vulnerable eye of the icerug they were trying to shield, Bright-Eye's eye and head sections seemed to sink into the ice, too, until finally Deirdre's chest was supported by the icy floor of the tunnel, while Bright-Eye's eye was safe in a cavity in the ice below her. Deirdre was now completely encased in ice and could no longer even move her helmet to look around.

At this point the distressed sounds of moving ice ceased, and the three felt all motion within the now shrunken tunnel stop. The sudden silence registered in Richard's mind, and he felt a surge of hope; they were still alive, although in such perilous circumstances he could hardly comprehend them. Trapped, cut off from everyone, and surrounded by unyielding ice meters thick—they had little chance of escape.

Less knowledgeable about the severity of their situation, Deirdre attempted to relax her quivering muscles and assess their predicament.

"Right, Richard, make an arch, you said, and that we've done. A fine, sturdy one, too! How long will it take to dig us out, d'you think?"

"Assuming they find us," said Richard, trying to sound calm.

"Only a small segment of the tunnel has collapsed," said the booming voice of Bright-Eye, slightly muffled by the close proximity of the ice close around them. The voice of the alien was now steady and sure, and devoid of panic. "I will have us out shortly."

The humans' view of their surroundings vanished in a blur of aquamarine, as Bright-Eye enveloped their inflated suits with ice-dissolving chemicals from its own body. Then, in the same way that it had melted away the ice under the humans's stiffened hands and feet, and from under its own head and eye to form safe cavities in the ice, the alien set to work dissolving the constricting ice around them, melting it away with amazing speed, and depositing the resultant water into the ocean below through its distant waste tunnel. It was less than an hour later when the humans again stood upright, their suits restored to normal pressure, with Bright-Eye standing tall beside them, poised on its pedestal on its ribbon of aquamarine.

"I owe you my life," it said. "I owe you flesh. My students owe you flesh. My Center owes you flesh. My nation owes you flesh." Deirdre was slightly appalled at this, wishing that her suit translator could find another word than "flesh." Deirdre picked up a word that the translation program had used. "Students?" As all three creatures proceeded slowly along the tunnel, feeling almost a comradeship after their shared danger, Bright-Eye explained.

"I and my laboratory are part of the Center of Scientific Studies. I seek new ways to use the natural materials we have available, and new combinations and uses for the products which we make ourselves. I have young icerugs about me, to learn what I can teach them, and they of course have ideas of their own. They help support me with their flesh, and the rest of my need for flesh is provided by the Center of Scientific Studies, from that which they collect routinely from their portion of the assessments levied by the Governing Council. My students are many, just now. For your acts of preserving the life of their teacher, they will be willing to provide you with some of their flesh whenever you wish it."

Richard and Deirdre exchanged a look, but could think of nothing to say. Fortunately, the widening tunnel they were traveling along soon opened into a spacious room, lined with shelves of reading plates and filled with strange equipment. The functions of some of them were instantly recognizable from their shapes, while others were so strange that neither human would have hazarded a guess at its purpose.

"A grand analytical balance, with a double-pivot knife-edge suspension system," said Deirdre, pointing to a double-pan scale, complete with stacks of graduated weights lined up before it. "Very accurate, that'll be."

Bright-Eye's booming tones called a sort of greeting to the several icerugs in the laboratory, each busy with its own eye directed at some task. They collected about the newcomers, and at the conclusion of Bright-Eye's introduction of the two humans, and a narrative of the recent rescue by them, each of the students declared its debt of flesh. The apprehensive humans were relieved to discover that this was apparently simply an acknowledged debt that could be called in at any time; no alien actually presented them with a portion of itself. Bright-Eye was eager to have its students see and understand the flash-lights of the humans. Both humans produced their permalights and turned them on. They noticed that the icerugs turned to avoid the light coming directly into their own eyes.

"Their eyes are more sensitive than ours, and well I know I don't like one of these shining right in my own eyes, indeed," murmured Deirdre. After that, both humans were careful to direct the powerful beams onto the floor, or the work at hand, rather than the aliens themselves. Demonstration of the tool led to explanation and analysis. The quick intelligences of the aliens soon led them to discussion of how they could construct such a device with icerug materials. Various substances were brought, manipulated, and discarded.

Richard found that the icerug laboratory did have an oven of sorts, well insulated from the freezing cold room by blocks of volcanic tuff and heated by endothermic chemical reactions. It could reach a few hundred degrees, high enough to carbonize seaweed, bone, and flesh, but not high enough to melt any metal except mercury.

"With sheets of carbon made from seaweed and nickel-iron sheets from an asteroid, and a little concentrated ocean water or dilute acid, like you use to dissolve rock, we can make a battery," said Richard. "Then all we have to do is try different carbonized threads and nickel-iron slivers until we find the right length and thickness to make a good, long-lasting incandescent filament."

It didn't surprise Richard that a carbonized thread of seaweed fiber turned out to be the best filament. Until tungsten filaments came along, that had been close to Edison's conclusion, too. Edison had found that the most practical and least expensive filament for an incandescent lamp was a piece of tough bamboo fiber baked until it was black.

Richard was going to reconfigure one "hand" of his suit-imp to act as a combination voltmeter and ammeter, but soon found that was unnecessary. Just as the early pioneers in electricity had learned to do, the icerugs soon found they could "feel" the amount of voltage generated by a battery by the strength of the "taste" produced in the tips of their tentacles when they put them across the battery terminals. At Deirdre's insistence, Richard didn't access Josephine's electrochemical tables to suggest different elements for the battery, but let the icerugs experiment for themselves. With surprising speed, the icerugs soon fitted together a crude but working battery-powered light of their own, and then set immediately to improve the power and life of the battery, using the tiny glowing filament itself as a rough indicator of the strength of the electrical current flow. Fortunately, they could see well into the infrared, and so could observe significant changes in the heat radiation emitted from a filament that looked completely black to the eyes of the humans.

While the students worked away at their tasks, Deirdre studied the workings of an intricate instrument near her made almost entirely of ice, within a framework of carefully shaped and polished stone. The beauty of it reminded her of sculpture, but she knew, almost instinctively, that it must be a form of microscope. One of the students, seeing her interest, quietly indicated the tiny but finely shaped discs of ice which served as lenses, and the large condensing lenses that focused the concave light from the observer's body onto the sample being observed, and with a thrill of delight she recognized that a peculiar-looking piece of gleaming bone was a focusing knob.

Meanwhile, Richard and Bright-Eye completed assembly of yet another trial flashlight, and one of the younger aliens reached a tentacle to connect it to the now refined source of battery power. With what the humans felt to be satisfaction and pleasure, the icerugs contemplated their glowing handiwork raptly. However, almost immediately, they began its disassembly, booming quietly between themselves.

Their suit-imps at this point chimed simultaneously, and Richard and Deirdre glanced at each other. It was a simple time signal, indicating they should begin the trek back to rejoin the *Dragonfly*, which would be flying in shortly. With surprise, each noted the other was worn with fatigue, mutual concern therefore making it easier to speak to Bright-Eye of their intention to depart. The

alien left its students at once to lead them swiftly back
along the tunnels with their ever-increasing bundles of
varicolored strands, then up to the surface via an exit tunnel not too far from the Grand Portal. Here in the city
the ice was smooth and polished underfoot, and the two
humans were soon walking briskly through the narrow ice
corridors between blue-green icerug bodies toward
George's waving arm in the distance at the landing field.
In the sky above, the *Dragonfly* could be seen descending from the sky as Barnard started to rise over the
horizon.

"Let's get a move on," called George through their imp
link. "The flouwen have already been picked up by the
Dragonfly and are ready to be taken back to the lander so
they can get out of their suits and freshen up."

"Sounds good to me," said Richard, breaking into a
ground-covering lope.

RAINING

The *Dragonfly* returned to the *Victoria* and went through the usual routine; the humans climbed the ninety rungs of the Jacob's Ladder to the airlock door, while the flouwen rode up on the winch elevator. From the airlock, the flouwen were sucked back into their tank, to empty their waste vacuoles into Josephine's efficient sewage treatment system, which could cope with anything but heavy metals, and to refresh every cell with clean, freezing-cold ammonia water.

⊓K-k-k-keeeek-k-k-k⊓ exclaimed Little Purple with pleasure, as he placed his purple-colored body about the jet coming from a nozzle in the top of the tank and expanded himself out into a purple balloon. Filled almost to bursting, he slowly let the refreshing liquid percolate through his thinned-down body.

☆My turn!☆ complained Little Red, trying to push a red pseudopod between the neck of the purple balloon and the jet nozzle. Little Purple continued to expand until the ballooning sides of his body touched the cylindrical wall of the habitat on all sides. Then, closing off the intake hole, in order to trap the bodyful of clean fluid inside, he finally moved down to the center of the tank and let Little Red have the jet. Meanwhile, the patiently waiting Little White went to the habitat taste-screen, to put into Josephine's extensive memory his recollection of the flouwens' observations during their exploration trip.

Little White wasn't the only one providing input to Josephine. Many of the humans—those not taking showers or eating—were also busy at touch-screens. Some were adding comments to the video pictures taken by their helmet monitors and automatically transmitted back through the commsat links. Others were relating experiences and thoughts inadequately captured on either video or audio, while others were making recommendations for the next excursion.

The three who had visited the city center, George, Deirdre, and Richard, carefully edited and annotated their experiences. They, of course, knew that their comments were simultaneously available to the imps of the rest of the crew, and comment and speculation about their reports became general. Later, Deirdre took David aside to tell him in more detail of the alien concert.

He questioned her: "So all the instruments were percussion, or variations of stringed instruments?"

Deirdre thought. "That's right enough," she agreed. "Such big drums I've never seen, and deeper notes than I could be sure I was hearing, perhaps just feeling with my body. And all sorts of stringed shapes, with the strings being plucked, and hit, and played with various bows. Chimes there were, too, long hollow cylinders of ice, and arrays of resonating disklike ice shapes like cymbals, but played with a soft mallet like a gong, and a marvelous sort of xylophone, with long bars of solid ice over hollow resonating chambers."

"But no wind instruments, not so much as a whistle?"

"Not one," said Deirdre. "And look you, David, how could there be if the creatures do not breathe? They have no lungs to store air, so their mouths are used only for eating."

"Pity, though," said David absently, and Deirdre looked at him sharply.

"Hold, David. Their music is wonderful, and contents them, I've no doubt. Would you be giving them a synthesizer, or some such daft thing?" David grinned wickedly into the burning green eyes at the thought of an icerug confronted with the keyboard of one of his highly complex sono-video synthesizers.

"Since they can't blow with their mouths . . ." mused David, "then any kind of wind instrument is out—even bagpipes." The image of an icerug in a kilt playing a bagpipe jumped into both their minds, and a wry smile dimpled the corner of Deirdre's mouth to match David's wide grin at the thought. "But not *all* wind instruments. Did you say that their chimes used long hollow cylinders of ice?"

"I did that," replied Deirdre, a little concerned. "You'll not be meddling, will you now, David?"

"Of course not!" David assured her as he turned away. He went to a console and pulled up the video images taken by the helmet cameras during the concert. He found the frame that he was looking for and had Josephine carefully measure one of the instruments. Then he sought out George and spoke eagerly to him.

"Shirley and Arielle have designed a survey routine for obtaining a good population density map of the entire inner pole geyser ring. I've set up a computer routine with Joe to carry out that procedure. On the next outing, instead of monitoring Joe, I'd like to go with you to the city to see this orchestra. The music you transmitted was full of peculiarly interesting sounds, and I'd like to know exactly how they were produced."

"I don't see why not—if Arielle, Shirley, and Joe are sure they don't need you aboard the *Dragonfly*," agreed George. He paused to recall what had been planned for the next few Zulu days. "Let's see . . . we plan to return to Windward in about twenty hours, just before the next Zuni conjunction. The conjunction tide will be assisted by the Barnard tide, so it should be larger than normal, and Richard wants to see the geyser reaction at close-hand. We'll remain there about seven hours—until the tide turns and the geyser subsides, so Arielle can bring the plane in to retrieve us without danger of the wings icing up. That seven hours should give you plenty of time to learn about their musical instruments."

And twenty hours will give me time to have the Christmas Branch make something to take along, thought David as he turned to leave.

Richard and Deirdre, after a friendly dinner with the rest of the crew in the viewport lounge on *Victoria*, spent half of the intervening twenty hours in deep sleep in their bunks aboard the *Dragonfly*. Bodies that had been stressed beyond the norm by the icequake needed rest. Richard gratefully shut out all distraction with white noise generated by his imp, while Deirdre had always had the gift of sinking into untroubled slumber within seconds of wishing to do so. Foxx drowsed while her mistress slept, but was eager and active the instant she awoke and headed purposefully for the galley.

Sometime later, Arielle, on watch in the pilot's seat on the *Dragonfly*, lifted her head to sniff sharply. Since the weather was good, and the airplane was resting safely on the ground, she had no hesitation in leaving her post abruptly in pursuit of the tantalizing aroma. When she got to the galley, she found she had to stand in line.

Deirdre's round brown loaves of Irish soda bread, stuffed with pseudo-currants, were all ready to cut. When Deirdre was in the mood to make omelets, as well, meaning when she was as hungry as she was now, it was simply a question of how many toppings one cared to add to the creamy scrambled algae-egg base—tiny bits of real ham, two kinds of grated algae-cheese, and chopped green onions, tomatoes, peppers, and mushrooms from the hydroponics deck on *Prometheus*. Steam rose from the fresh wedges of hot and fragrant bread, and the omelets came just seconds apart from the two hot skillets Deirdre alternated, skillfully, on the small stove.

"'S wonderful, Deirdre," said George rather thickly through a big bite of bread and algae-butter.

"Sets you up for the day," acknowledged Deirdre, taking a generous bite of her own cooking.

Replete, George outlined the upcoming day's plans. George had been promised a visit with the Presider to one of the intermediate level meetings, to see how this extraordinary civilization was governed. Deirdre would go with David to visit the musicians, while Richard hoped to meet with Pink-Orb, the icerug astronomer and expert on tidal phenomena, to observe and measure the geyser eruptions at close range.

"From what I've heard so far, this is the most leisurely government that ever existed," remarked George. "Seems to be just meetings. Some of them vertical in the chain of command, and some of them horizontal between adjacent areas at the same level. The Presider spoke of doing nothing but attending one meeting after another, but never said anything about any action being taken."

There were dissenting noises from several voices, and

Richard summed them up: "Oh, I don't know, sounds pretty normal to me."

The four explorers were soon busily arranging the contents of their chestpacks, belt pouches, and suit pockets. Richard and Deirdre carefully checked every item they had carried the day before, to be sure that there had been no damage done by the icequake. Aware that Foxx would be confined in her suit for some hours, Deirdre sent the little animal flying about the cabin, exercising small muscles so that they would be content to stay still, then directed it to its litter box in the storage area of Deirdre's bunk. As the russet body shot back from the bunk area onto Deirdre's shoulder, it sailed past Shirley in the weak gravity, and she made a half-hearted grab for the tiny animal— missing.

"Doesn't that get to be a nuisance, having to pack extra water and all, to take her along?" she asked.

"Not to me," was the cool reply. Arielle watched the small animal's acrobatics rather wistfully; she had seen Deirdre asleep, with the soft fur draped limply over her throat. No wonder she could slumber so deeply, with that hair-trigger guardian so close. David's chestpack was bulging unwontedly, and Richard watched, curious, as yet another peculiar object was stuffed in.

"Is that a saw I see, David?" he said.

"Never know when it mightn't be useful," David replied. Deirdre's ears pricked up. David had some project in mind, but was not divulging it—now why was that? She mulled over the thought briefly, and gave it up. Too many other things to think about, and her own hours among the icerugs were too precious to her to waste in thinking of her fellow humans.

The last things loaded were the three flouwen in their drysuits. Thomas and Cinnamon winched them down

from the airlock on *Victoria* and helped them into the airlock on the *Dragonfly*, where they would stay until they
reached the shores of Manannán Lake. They had
explored the smaller lake earlier and had found an underwater connection between the two. Today they would
repeat their surveys in the larger lake, while at the same
time observing the geyser action from underwater.

"Make sure you stay well away from that geyser when
it starts spouting!" warned Cinnamon as she shut the
outer airlock door on the three flouwen. "You might get
hurt."

☆Geysers can't hurt me!☆ bragged Little Red.
☆*Nothing* can hurt me!☆

◊You were torn in two, once,◊ Little White warned.
◊Next time you could be in many pieces.◊

⊓Pieces so small you couldn't put yourself together
again,⊓ added Little Purple.

Instead of retorting, Little Red, for once, was silent,
perhaps thinking of the long period when two large
pieces of himself had remained separated back on
Rocheworld, each piece thinking he was the only Roar-
ing☆Hot☆Vermillion. Then the humans had come and
had enabled his two pieces to join up again into a single
whole personality, with two divergent memories of that
long period of isolation from himself.

Once the three flouwen were on board, Arielle
smoothly launched the *Dragonfly* from the icy surface,
and headed for the icerug metropolis. It didn't take long
for her to find a bare spot on the distant shore, far from
Windward City, where the flouwen could enter Manannán Lake easily. Even *Babble*, lowered down from the
cargo hull underneath the *Dragonfly*, had no problem
entering the water from the low ice shelf. The flouwen

slipped into the water during the waning hours of daylight, and the seven and a half hour "night" on Zulu began, well lit by the large half-moon Gargantua hanging permanently in the sky above.

The airplane took off and Arielle, again avoiding the swirling clouds with masterly precision, flew the plane with its long and slender wings toward the icerug city.

"Look for a plum-colored carpet right about there along the shore front," said Richard, pointing with his finger at the map on the touch-screen. Arielle noticed the green splotch on her navigation display and the plane tilted slightly as she changed its heading.

"There it is!" said David, who had picked out the slightly more purplish-blue-green plum shade from all the rest of the blue-green carpets.

"Going down! Get ready to hop!" said Arielle. As she spoke, the plane dropped with the smoothness of an elevator, to hover a half-meter above the surface. George, David, Deirdre, and Richard jumped out onto the ice and walked to the edge of the plum-colored carpet.

"Strange color, is this," mused Deirdre. "Should be more blue-green for the best sunlight absorption. The reddish color might be due to a recessive gene."

Pink-Orb's node soon appeared, gliding swiftly straight for them. "Greetings! Greetings! Greetings! No doubt you have come to this spot to observe the approaching eruption of the great geyser-god Manannán. My mathematical models have predicted that the tide will be higher than normal, so the resulting geyser eruption will be well worth the seeing. In fact, I have been allocated this area on this side of the lake so that I may accurately measure the height of each eruption." Pink-Orb held up a device made of pieces of shaped, polished, and engraved slivers of fine stone, with lenses and mirrors on it.

"A quadrant!" exclaimed Richard. "Like a sextant, but covering ninety degrees instead of sixty."

"How can you be so sure?" asked Deirdre. "It may look like a quadrant, but it could be anything—even a musical instrument— for all you know."

"Form ever follows function," said Richard, pulling his own sextant out of his chestpack. The iris in Pink-Orb's eye widened as it saw the metal device, and soon the two scientists were comparing the similarities of their two instruments.

"How do you use it?" asked Richard.

"When a geyser eruption starts, I place the telescope in front of my eye and adjust the angle-arm on the quarter-circle until the image of the top of the geyser is on the fine line inside the telescope, while at the same time observing on the same line, either the horizon with this mirror in this position, or if the horizon is not visible, the center of the bubble with the mirror in this position. After the sighting is complete, I can read the angle from this engraved scale on the quarter-circle. Knowing the angle and the distance to the base of the geyser, I can use angle tablets to calculate the height of the geyser."

"Quarter-circle and angle-arm are obviously their terms for the arc and index arm, and the device even has a bubble level to create an artificial horizon. It's definitely a quadrant, Deirdre," concluded Richard.

Deirdre was satisfied.

"What do you use for the liquid in the bubble level?" asked Richard.

"A light oil with a very low freezing temperature," replied Pink-Orb. "We get it from one of the internal organs of the coelasharks."

Coela-liver oil, thought George.

"I, too, have come to observe and measure the

approaching eruption with my sextant," said Richard. "And while the others will probably watch the eruption when it occurs later on tonight, they also have other tasks."

"We had better get moving," said George, heading for the Grand Portal of the Great Meeting Hall, just visible a kilometer away around the lake. David and Deirdre followed, leaving Richard with Pink-Orb.

"You mentioned mathematical models," said Richard to Pink-Orb. "Does that mean you can predict the conjunction times of the various moons and the height of the tides?"

"Very accurately," replied Pink-Orb. "My model includes the orbital parameters of all the major moons of Gargantua and their tidal effects on Ice. It also includes an elastic model of the rocky core of Ice so that I can separate the core tides and their phase delays from the ocean tides. It also includes a model of the geyser itself, which has its own response delays and resonances. This particular eruption will be larger than normal, since the Sun-God is in the same part of the sky as the Near-God and their tides will reinforce each other."

"That will be some time from now," remarked Richard. "Around midnight."

"Yes, but there are no clouds in the sky now, so I shall use the time to measure the positions of the minor moon-gods that are visible. With enough measurements, the errors average out, enabling a more precise calculation of their true orbits to put into my mathematical model. But I can't do it with this instrument. Much too small and inaccurate. Would you like to see my telescope?"

"Certainly!" replied Richard with alacrity.

"Step on my carpet and I will take you there," said Pink-Orb. "It is near the center of my area."

Richard stepped on the plum carpet and instinctively assumed a slightly bent-knee surfer's stance, as he felt himself lifted and borne off on a wave, while Pink-Orb's node glided along beside him. He could easily see the figures of George, David, and Deirdre trudging along the far side of Pink-Orb on their way into the city, but no sign of any telescope.

"I don't see any telescope. Do you?" he muttered over their private suit-to-suit imp link.

"Be patient, and learn," Deirdre cautioned him over the link. "And remember not to be interfering—no suggesting ways to make it bigger or better."

"I'll try," promised Richard, trying to maintain his balance on the slippery surfaced wave. After they had gone a hundred meters on Pink-Orb's elongated isosceles-triangle carpet, they came to a strangely depressed region, perfectly circular and about thirty meters in diameter, with a pointed bulge in the middle, as though there were a short pole sticking up from below the surface.

"Here is my observatory," said Pink-Orb with pride as they glided up to the edge of the depression and stopped. "Let me uncover it for you." As Richard watched in astonishment, the carpet covering the depressed area opened and withdrew, exposing an open mesh of ropes that covered a deep hemispherical pit. In the center of the pit was a gigantic open-work telescope supported by a massive mount. The support for the rope canopy rose from the top of the mount. As he watched, the flesh around the periphery of the pit pulled the rope canopy to one side, allowing the telescope beneath a clear view of the skies.

"Wow!" exclaimed Richard as he took in the size of the telescope. "What a monster! The main mirror is nearly two meters in diameter and the focal length must be twenty meters or so."

The voice of Josephine came in over Richard's imp. "It is similar to the large telescopes Sir William Herschel used to make in the 1700s. But significantly larger than any Herschel attempted. No doubt the lower gravity of Zulu compared to Earth makes it possible."

Pink-Orb started to describe the various features of the telescope. "The mirror is made of mercury, warmed until it was liquid, then allowed to freeze while under constant rotation. By keeping the telescope shaded when not in use, it stays cold enough to keep the mercury frozen."

"That would give you a perfect parabola," said Richard with admiration. "Just what you need for a good telescope. Much better than grinding lenses, like Herschel did. That only gives you a spherical surface, which then needs to be laboriously figured into a parabola. I see it's on an azimuth-altitude mount."

"Yes," replied Pink-Orb. "I use this telescope for accurate position measurements of the moon-gods with respect to the background stars. I have another telescope nearby on a polar mount for use during longer periods of observation, when searching for transient weather features on the major moon-gods."

"How do you rotate it in azimuth?" asked Richard. "That mount must weigh a couple of tons!"

"In this manner," said the node of Pink-Orb. Far below, portions of its body rose up off the bottom of the pit and pushed against some posts built into the base of the telescope. The massive mount started to turn slowly. "It floats on a thin film of oil."

Pink-Orb began to go down a spiral ramp around the inside of the pit, and Richard found himself following the node down the spiral while standing on a level platform made of plum-colored velvet. "We have some hours yet before the conjunction. Let me show you the azimuth and altitude rulings. They are the finest ever made on Ice."

As George, David, and Deirdre approached the Grand Portal, they met the Presider, in its elaborate ribboned cloak and skirt, advancing to meet them across its peacock-colored carpet. With ceremonial dignity, the Presider welcomed George, and was still talking as the two of them started off to the first "meeting." It was a regional meeting of the one hundred or so local association leaders of the Inner North Northwest portion of the nation. The meetings were led by the Convener of that region, while the Presider usually attended as an observer.

The sounds of musical instruments led David and Deirdre through the Grand Portal and into an anteroom that looked like a storage and repair area for musical instruments, with many tools and devices for holding, shaping, and assembling various musical instruments. Off in large side tunnels were storage areas with different drums, harps, chimes, and strange resonating devices. In one corner was what looked like "useful junk"; scraps of patterned drum skin, hollow cylinders of ice chipped at the ends, cracked "boards" of cross-plied, compressed, and dried seaweed that served as the icerugs equivalent of wood, chipped beams of polished stone, and many coils of gut and fiber string, slightly frayed in spots.

There were two icerugs in the anteroom, apparently tuning the musical instrument between them. Their large eyes turned to look at them. The taller node lifted a monocle of ice with its cyan-colored tentacle, through which the wide band around its iris shone like silver. The smaller icerug's eye was an almost colorless light blue, in contrast to its carpet covering, which was a vivid electric blue-green.

The cyan-colored node spoke first, in the characteristic booming voice of the icerugs.

"I am named Silver-Rim, and this is Clear-Eye. You, the human called Deirdre, were here before. You . . . applauded . . . our music by striking the ends of your appendages together to make a sharp noise. It was a strange thing to see, and new to us. I understand that it was meant to be a complimentary gesture; therefore we accept it."

Deirdre noted, with interest, that there was no implication in these words of either humility or gratitude; an accurate delineation of these aliens should include that fact. David's eyes had already fastened upon the huge, fantastically carved stone frame before him, with its thick, regularly spaced strings fitted so close together that human fingers would have fumbled over them.

"Greetings," he said, mindful of George's instructions. "I am named David. I was told of your fine performances yesterday and wanted to see, and hear for myself, your splendid instruments. That is a truly beautiful instrument, and a most unusual sort of harp. I imagine you obtain tones of extreme depth from such a . . . fine instrument." David felt unsure of himself as he struggled to spout the fulsome phrases the aliens seemed to expect. Fortunately, Deirdre took over.

"Careful words they like, David, but not blarney!" To the icerugs she spoke directly: "David is interested in music, and makes it for his own pleasure and ours. May we ask a demonstration of some of your instruments?"

Clear-Eye moved behind the giant harp without a word and reached two tentacles towards the ropelike strings. With strength and speed, the appendages plucked half a dozen of the central strands, which quivered as they filled the ears with a deeply throbbing chord. Amazed, David bent nearer, studying the strings, which more nearly resembled cables. His fingers itched to touch them, but he forbore to do so without an invitation, which was not forthcoming either then or later.

"I've never heard such a bass note from a string— sounds more like a drum. May I ask what these strings are made of?"

"These thickest ones in this . . . size one harp, are made from the gut of a coelashark. It is the largest harp in our orchestra." The computer translation of the instrument's name was clumsy, thought David, but probably as accurate as was possible in the circumstances. Making noises of genuine admiration, he moved along the wall to the next instrument, a tall and extremely narrow sort of drum. Without being asked, Clear-Eye thumped its surface with a tentacle balled up at the end into a very efficient mallet, and the resultant boom created pleasant reverberations in the humans.

"Wow!" was their mutual reaction, and the icerug craftsmen took them into the tunnels to show them more of the instruments stored there, playing each of them briefly. Deirdre was struck by the artistry of construction and looked closely to verify her opinion that each was unique—a one of a kind creation. The surfaces, of natural materials, were polished to a high sheen, but retained the grain, patterns, and whorls of stone, skin, and dried seaweed.

David, after hearing so many variations of sound in the lower registers, asked curiously, "Do you sometimes use other ranges in your music? Those in the soprano?" He stopped when his imp said that the word was not easily translatable, and remembering these creatures's skill with mathematics, repeated the question, substituting vibrational frequencies for musical terms. "Those notes which involve vibrations of one thousand cycles per second or higher?" This, the computer could easily convert into vibrations per icerug time units.

In answer, Silver-Rim reached for a very small harp, gleaming and unique like the others. The tentacles stroked it lightly, and tones of about the middle range jangled pleasantly.

"We can make notes higher in pitch than these, although some of those listening to the music are unable to sense them. The smaller of the ice-tube chimes contribute a good high note, when it is wanted." The alien tapped on the shortest one of a circle of long tubes of ice hanging at regularly spaced intervals around a central pedestal. The tubular bell gave off a ringing note.

"It provides an accent to our singing, but of course our own voices are mostly in the range below . . ." There was a pause as Josephine converted the response into human units. ". . . two hundred fifty cycles per second."

"And middle C is two hundred sixty-two cycles," mused David. He turned to look at Deirdre. "You should sing for them, Deirdre! Let them hear some of your soprano trills," he said without thinking. A green glare shot through the opposite helmet.

"I should not," she said flatly.

Hastily, David turned to the two aliens.

"I understand that you do not use wind to make music of any sort. Because we can produce winds with our mouths, we have long been turning breath into varying notes, using our voices, or mechanical devices such as whistles and pipes and—"

Deirdre interrupted, "Those words are not going to translate. David, what are you thinking of?"

David began to remove the odd assortment of objects he had brought along in his chestpack and laid them out upon a nearby work surface. He walked over to the "useful junk" area.

"May I use some of these materials?" he asked before touching them.

"Certainly," replied Clear-Eye. "They are not materials that we would use to construct concert instruments, but they are useful for repair."

David picked up three of the chipped hollow ice cylinders that had once been tubular bells. He gave a soft whistle of relief when the outer diameter of one of the chipped cylinders just fit into the larger end of the conical device which he had brought along. His measurement of the video images of the chime cylinders had been correct.

"Is it a new technology you are introducing?" asked Deirdre sternly.

"Just a whistle," replied David. "If my head wasn't inside a helmet, I would blow into it and show you. See, here at the narrow end is where I would blow, and here on the side is the notch that causes the interruption of airflow which makes the vibration, and this is where the sound comes out. Certainly a whistle is not high technology. The only difference between this and a regular whistle is its size and this sliding valve for cutting off the air."

"If you can't blow it, and the icerugs can't blow it, then why are you showing it to them?" asked Deirdre suspiciously.

"There's more than one way to blow a whistle," replied David. "And besides, it's not going to be a whistle." Ignoring Deirdre, he picked up the saw he had brought along and cut the chipped ends off the hollow ice cylinders, using a tape measure to make their lengths exactly correct, while differing in length. He used the tiny lasers in his suit-imp to fuse the ice cylinders into the larger ends of the three whistlelike devices the Christmas Bush back on *Victoria* had constructed for him.

Then, he picked up some dried seaweed "plywood" boards, sawed them into shape, and assembled them into a box. Using the hand-awl and circular file tools on his Swiss Army Mech-All, he cut three holes into the top, into which the smaller end of the conical whistles fit tightly. The three tubes now stood upright out of the box, one short, one medium, and one tall.

"It's an organ!" said Deirdre, fascinated.

"Not yet," replied David. "It needs a source of wind for the wind chest, and they don't have electrically powered rotary blowers here on Zulu, so we'll improvise a bellows instead." He reached back into his chestpack and pulled out a sheet of all-purpose tough plastic. "This stuff is flexible and impervious to air. I imagine coelashark skin would work even better."

Deirdre watched, as curious as the aliens, as David skillfully cut, shaped, and folded the pieces of plastic and glued them between two triangular pieces of seaweed board, one with a hole in it. He closed the hole in the top board with an intake valve flap made of thicker plastic, and fit the exit nozzle of the bellows tightly into a hole in the side of the wind chest below the three pipes.

First making sure the sliding valves under the three pipes were closed, he separated the two boards of the bellows on their hinge. The air rushed in through the large intake hole and the flap valve closed to his satisfaction. He pressed gently on the handles and was relieved when he felt back pressure, indicating that the bellows, wind chest, and valves were all airtight.

Mentally crossing his fingers, he opened all three slid-ing valves under the pipes and pressed down hard on the bellows. Deirdre winced at the discord that sounded from the three pipes, while the two aliens moved back sharply on their carpets.

"Close, but so wrong! I was trying for a C major chord. I should have done them one at a time!"

Although the aliens had been surprised, they immedi-ately returned, bending over the ugly contrivance. Silver-Rim's tentacles reached out, then stopped.

"You may touch it," said David generously. The humans watched in silence as the alien tentacles prodded the flexible plastic on the bellows, felt delicately within the valves, and then closed the valves on two of the pipes and pushed firmly on the bellows. The sound which emerged was not pretty, but was at least a single, more or less coherent tone. Clear-Eye and Silver-Rim began a careful examination, pushing the bellows frequently to produce sound. Amazed, David saw that they had almost instantly learned to produce the same force upon the bag each time; their tentacles apparently were more sensitive to pressure than fingertips.

Having tuned tubular ice chimes, they realized that the tones of this musical instrument also depended upon the length of the tubes, and used their tentacles to melt away and add ice to the ends of the tubes until they had tuned the device to a harmonic chord.

Then David put one gloved hand over the open end of one of the pipes and motioned for Clear-Eye to push down on the bellows again. As the alien did so, the pipe emitted a tone that was an octave lower in pitch. The bodies of the two aliens emitted a "rowf" noise—whether in surprise or pleasure Deirdre never found out.

"A stopped pipe produces a sound that is an octave

lower in pitch than an open pipe of the same speaking length," explained David as he stepped back to let the icerugs repeat his experiment themselves.

Once the icerug craftsmen had satisfied themselves that they understood the construction of the valve and whistle mechanism, they left the device David had made, went to their storeroom and, selecting some very long hollow ice tubes, began to make, out of ice, a whistle and valve for each one.

David bent closer to see, and Clear-Eye obligingly extended its handiwork towards him. With dexterity and skill, the alien was indeed shaping the ice as easily as an earthly potter worked with clay. Meanwhile, Silver-Rim had been identically busy, producing a shorter pipe.

"It looks like they'll have no problem making pipes, but what concerns me a little is the bellows bag," he said, looking along the shelves and in the junk area. "To make an organ large enough to be used in the Grand Meeting Hall would require a gigantic bellows. Coelashark skins might be too expensive to use."

Clear-Eye pulled loose the bellows from the wind chest and extended it to David, while at the same time Silver-Rim removed the three pipes.

"This has been most interesting," said Silver-Rim. "Your demonstration is clearly understood. Using air in this way might not have occurred to us for a long time, and we shall want to try many things with these sustainable new tones. This flexible substance of yours we return, as perhaps it is as valuable to you as coelashark skin is to us. Something so simple as a . . . bellows to move air, we shall, of course, construct out of a more readily available material."

"What sort of material?" asked David.

In answer, Silver-Rim pointed to Clear-Eye. "Observe."

The human's gaze slid down the considerable length of the alien to rest upon the thickened area of electric blue carpet that had formed to one side of its pedestal. With growing understanding, they saw a bulging fold of the stuff take shape and turn into a large and flexible pocket—a wind chest made out of living icerug flesh like the air bag of a bagpipe. The ends of the five pipes, three made by David and two by the aliens, fitted into this living bellows-bag with instant facility. The icerug expanded its own flesh to take in a large quantity of air, and then compressed the pocket, while opening the sliding valves under each pipe with caution, and the clear notes of the ice-pipes sounded again in a perfect noble chord. Deirdre smiled with pure pleasure.

"Well done," she said quietly. "I cannot fault you, David. The use of air is all you truly had to offer, here, and they'll be doing much with that."

"We shall indeed," agreed the listening icerugs, who moved off into the depths of their storerooms.

The humans, reminded by Josephine of the impending eruption, turned and left the room, although David looked back just once, longingly, at the huge cable-strung harp. Outside, in the increasing light from Gargantua, they rejoined George and Richard at the edge of Pink-Orb's carpet. Pink-Orb was explaining what would happen.

"As you see, it is approaching the middle of the night. The Sun-God is behind Ice and the Night-God is full in the sky. We cannot see it, but the Near-God is also over the outer hemisphere of Ice and lining up in the sky with the Sun-God. You can see its black shadow moving slowly across the face of the Night-God, approaching the center. You will soon see another shadow."

As they watched, a black spot appeared on the right

side of Gargantua. It was nearly three times as large as the slowly moving shadow of the Near-God moon, Zuni, and moving twice as fast.

"That is the shadow of Ice," said Pink-Orb. "The moon-god we are on. When the shadow of Ice and the shadow of the Near-God meet near the center of the Night-God, the tide will be at its peak. But even before that time, there will be geyser activity as the tidal pull of the Near-God and the Sun-God stretch the ground below the ocean bottom." Pink-Orb stopped speaking and raised its quadrant to measure the height of the water column, while Richard imitated the motion with his own sextant.

Roaring with a life of its own, the restless waters rising in the distance surged upward, bubbling and falling back only for an instant before rising ever higher. Incalculable volumes of water rose in a powerful upward-thrusting tower, thick vapors swirling around as it climbed swiftly. Fringes of water fell from its sides, as most of the rising column was hurled toward the sky in a thundering torrent which the eyes, both human and alien, observed in awe as it rose above them. Still higher and higher it gushed. The top temporarily disappeared into the clouds, then reappeared above them, heading for space. Around them the sleetlike rains from the falling spray began, drenching the icerugs and deepening their colors. In the dim red light of Gargantua, the falling downpour glowed like rubies before splashing onto the frozen ice or the spongy surface of the icerug.

"Uff!" A sudden cry from Pink-Orb startled the humans.

Deirdre and the others, who had been totally mesmerized by the gigantic waterspout, looked around in bewilderment.

"What happened?" demanded George. Pink-Orb's reply was reassuringly elated.

"A coelashark has landed on me! It is quite a large one, so I shall bring it here to explore it for ripe vermicysts, and you may see it." David watched the node expectantly, but the others, already accustomed to the strange mobility of the icerug's surface, turned to gaze out over the distant stretches of the carpet. Far away, a plum-colored mound arose in the vast carpet and moved toward them like a small and specialized wave, bearing a legged fish upon its crest that was as large as a human.

"I'd not fancied they could be so large!" exclaimed Deirdre.

"This is a particularly prime one," said Pink-Orb. "Some coelasharks are ejected by every large eruption, and although this was only a moderate-sized outpouring, I was fortunate. More will fall at the occasion of the maximum high tide, when both the Near-God and the Far-God are lined up with the Sun-God."

The humans were transfixed: George was trying to imagine a larger geyser than the one they had just witnessed; David was staring at the weird, motionless specimen of sealife before him; Richard was grappling with the idea of a rain of coelasharks; and Deirdre was studying every detail of the huge fish, puzzled why its mouth was still twitching.

"Is it truly dead?" asked Deirdre.

"Yes," said Pink-Orb. "The fall always kills them, but fortunately their strong jawbones and skull protect the delicious vermicysts in their cheeks. They are an irresistible delicacy, although possibly not attractive to you." Deftly and with surprising strength, two of Pink-Orb's tentacles forced open the wide mouth of the coelashark, exposing rows of extremely sharp-looking teeth. Both cheeks of the inside of the coelashark's mouth were inflamed and swollen.

"Looks like it bit its cheek," said Richard.

"The inside of the cheeks of the coelashark head that Little White brought back were smooth and white," said Deirdre. "These cheeks look like they have something like a cold sore infection or a boil about to come to a head."

"The swelling is so bad I bet it couldn't even chew," Richard added.

With two tentacles holding the jaw open, Pink-Orb's other two tentacles pressed on the inflamed cheek tissue, which broke open with a gush of fluid, revealing a translucent oval-shaped object.

"Ah! A delicious vermicyst. Here, you may look at it while I get the other one." Pink-Orb handed the cyst to Deirdre to hold while it reached back in the coelashark's mouth to pry loose the vermicyst from the opposite cheek. The humans handled the flat little cushion carefully, although it was apparently constructed of a tough, semitransparent membrane.

"Somewhat like 'mermaid's purses'—egg cases of rays or dogfish," said Deirdre. "Except there are no tendrils at the corners. Look you—through it—against the light. . . ." She held the cyst up, and shone her permalight behind it. They could see what looked like tiny tadpolelike worms within, wiggling furiously. Deirdre, with some sotto-voce commands to her chestpack computer, zoomed her helmet video camera in on the strange treasure until she had captured a high-resolution image of the tiny creatures inside the cyst. She wanted very much to keep the cyst and its worms for later analysis, but the icerug was obviously waiting for her to give it back.

"What are those little creatures inside the cyst?" asked

Deirdre. The icerug paused, with the vermicyst raised to its mouth.

"We have no knowledge of what the contents of the vermicyst actually are," said Pink-Orb. "We do know that they are so wonderfully good to eat that they are usually consumed on the spot—as this one will be." So saying, the icerug's mouth opened, exposing small but extremely efficient-looking teeth. The vermicyst was popped inside, over the teeth, and swallowed whole, without chewing, like a human eating an oyster. Pink-Orb soon finished savoring the tidbit and was looking at the remaining vermicyst.

"I should enjoy eating the other one, but I dare not. Although superbly delicious, vermicysts are so rich in their nature that consuming more than one frequently produces . . . illness. I shall be able to trade this one, while it is still fresh, for a set of reference plates of mathematical integrals. And the rest of the coelashark I shall transport to the butcher for storage in my food locker. Since the conjunction period is over, I shall now return to the Center of Scientific Studies to report my latest findings regarding the accuracy of my calculations in predicting the dimensions of this eruption. The others at the Center will also be discussing their work, and of course, the Convener of the Center always has a great deal to say, and says it at great length, unlike my own brevity. There will be another large eruption, similar in size to this one, in not quite two days. It will occur just before midnight. Will you be returning to view it?"

"Two Zulu days," replied Richard, thinking it over. "That's about thirty hours. Yes. I'll certainly be here. See you a few hours before the conjunction."

The node moved off, with its precious delicacy secure in an elegant pouch suspended from its neckband, while a plum-colored wave bore the dead coelashark swiftly in another direction, but not before Deirdre had obtained permission from Pink-Orb to take some samples using a biopsy punch. Off in the distance, the humans could see the *Dragonfly* flying in to take them from the ice shelf. Their next stop would be the other shore to pick up the flouwen. Then they all would head back to *Victoria* for a well-deserved rest and a decent meal instead of suit snacks.

FLUSHING

Returning to *Victoria*, the exploration crew was met by Cinnamon, Sam, and Thomas, who already had lowered the winch in preparation for hauling the flouwen aloft to the airlock. The flouwen were bubbling over in their eagerness to report on what they had seen on their trip to the seamount vent beds.

"The coelashark was *walking*?" Cinnamon and Deirdre were startled by Little Red's words as he began to pour them out even before reaching the comfort of the habitat. Little White continued while the red flouwen was sucked out of his suit.

◊Pull of water getting stronger and stronger—we work hard to stay and watch. There was very large coelashark, next to its vent bed. When geyser started spouting, coelashark sink!◊

⊡That's right!⊡ Little Purple took up the excited account. ⊡It gave off bubbles and sank to bottom. Then it drop sharp rock, pick up heavy rock, and walk on leg-fins.⊡

"Maybe picking up the rock helps it to fight against the

271

current," suggested Cinnamon. "So that it's not swept up by the geyser."

◊But,◊ argued Little White, ◊why did it leave vent bed and go *toward* geyser?◊

"What!" exclaimed both humans.

☆Yes!☆ shouted Little Red through their imps from inside the habitat. ☆We saw it! Holding on to heavy rock, moving slow, but toward geyser!☆

⊓We did not follow it far,⊓ said Little Purple. ⊓Current too strong for us. It did not come back.⊓

◊Another coelashark, smaller, took over vent,◊ finished Little White.

Cinnamon and Deirdre continued to question the flouwen closely about the strange, apparently suicidal advance of the large coelashark towards the geyser, but learned nothing further. They sat together in the lounge, speculating.

"Sounds like it deflated a swim bladder, that bubbling business," suggested Cinnamon.

"And then resorted to another means of locomotion," puzzled Deirdre. "Slower, but safer—more controlled. Except that it persisted in heading toward danger!" The two fell silent as they tried to puzzle out the meaning of this strange behavior.

Deirdre, still thinking, stretched long legs out to prop her boots up on the ledge under the large viewport in the lounge. Through the window she could see a large storm in the distance, coming in from the leading pole. The *Dragonfly* would be grounded until it passed. Outside the window, forty meters below down on the ice, the *Dragonfly* had all its lights on. Arielle could be seen in the cockpit window, taking Joe through a preventive maintenance checklist, while outside the airplane, Shirley and Richard were screwing hold-down anchors into the ice and tying *Dragonfly* to them with strong duralloy cables.

It felt good to Deirdre to be out of the confining exploration suit, and both she and Foxx were relaxing muscles weary with tension. Katrina entered the lounge with her morning-shift coffee, and Cinnamon described to her the strange coelashark behavior. She, too, found it inexplicable, and they had again fallen silent when George came up the passway and headed purposefully for the galley. He paused when he saw them and looked at them oddly.

"Well, Deirdre looks as tired as I feel, but I must admit, it's a real pleasure to see people sitting and not saying anything!"

"We're not particularly gabby!" protested Katrina. "Usually," she qualified.

"Didn't mean to say you three talk all the time," agreed George, "but the icerugs do! I never heard such a crew. It's a perfectly good way to run a country—I was really impressed with their logic, and the discussions were all calm—but my God! They never shut up! Talk! Talk! Talk!"

"What was it? A debate or something?" asked Cinnamon.

"No," said George, dropping into the reading chair by the viewport window. "It's apparently just how they run things. Any little problem that arises is talked over until everyone agrees. Today, it was all about assigning some territory which became available when an icerug died. Everyone around the area had plenty to say, and they all listened to every word, and then others were brought in, and then the whole matter was put off for a time to allow everyone to think about it for a while!"

"Well, but new territory, that sounds pretty important to me—proper to get full agreement on it," argued Katrina.

"Yes." George laughed. "But it turned out this discussion has been going on for something like a hundred days, long before we got here! And they're now just about almost ready to begin to think about maybe coming to a decision . . . anytime now!"

Cinnamon chuckled, but her interest had been caught by the earlier fact.

"The icerug died? How?" she asked curiously.

"They mentioned that lightning had struck the node," said George. "From the way they spoke of it, I gathered that it's quite a rare occurrence, since they normally go down into their tunnels when a storm approaches. But they seem to accept death as inevitable, especially when a node becomes very old. Also there are other accidents that can happen."

"Like an icequake," Deirdre reminded him.

"Like an icequake," George agreed. "There is also the possibility of starvation. A good part of the meeting was taken up by a report by an icerug that seems to be an ambassador of sorts, called a slender talker. It reported on the status of a community immediately to the north that is in dire straits. Their geyser failed some time ago, and the icerugs there are dying of malnutrition. What intrigued me is that there was no expression of sympathy or compassion in the discussion of the icerugs at the meeting—only a desire to keep the others at a distance. There was even a vague reference to the possibility that there might be what sounded to me like some sort of a conflict or war. They didn't explain, or dwell on it long enough for me to get much idea of what they were talking about—just a word in passing, talking about things that happened long ago, or might possibly happen in the distant future. . . . Listen to me," he said in disgust. "It's catching. I'm becoming as talky as an icerug."

Cinnamon politely denied that, then asked if the icerugs had a hierarchy of any sort, or if everyone just spoke in turn? George felt that the latter was the case, and began a description of the speeches. Deirdre quietly slipped from the lounge; she was ravenously hungry, and she knew the galley was well stocked with an assortment of seafood. Within a very short time, she had put together a large and creamy seafood stew, thick with chunks of 'ponics-fish fillets and tender bivalve meat from the clam-muscle tissue growth, Blue Oyster Culture. Cinnamon had cloned the tissue sample from a Pismo Beach clam and had puzzled Nels with her choice for the name. He'd groaned, but accepted the pun when she played him some of the old songs of the Blue Oyster Cult, a 1970s rock group. The sauce was fragrant with fruity white wine from James' chemical synthesizer and herbs from Cinnamon's spice bed on *Prometheus*. It was the sort of dish best made for a group, and along with Deirdre's fresh hot biscuits, it was profoundly appreciated. Sam, in particular, enjoyed it.

"You know, I never tasted seafood until I left the ranch when I was twenty-one, but when I did—never could get enough of it," he said, helping himself to thirds.

Arielle swallowed quickly, to say, "This not the real thing, Sam—you should taste Canadian lobster! Not bad, though," she added, reaching for another biscuit. Deirdre smiled to herself. As usual, there would be no leftovers to worry about. After such a hearty meal, sleep came even more quickly to the four explorers who had been out in their suits. They were asleep in their large bunks on the *Dragonfly* long before the others had completed their routines. Shirley and Arielle, who had enjoyed the easy duty inside the *Dragonfly*, checked over the suits stored on the *Dragonfly* with Joe and the suit-imps, ensuring that every subsystem was checked, and that the suit fabric was intact and the glassy-foil had not been pierced by a micrometeorite or scratched by a sharp rock. As always, Shirley took this particular task seriously. Richard's suit was the final one to be examined, and as she spread it out for inspection, a faint aroma of sweat caught her nose.

Arielle's own nose wrinkled slightly: "Richard work hard today, I guess," she commented. Shirley shrugged, but as she and the Christmas Branch restored the suit to its customary pristine condition, she became increasingly quiet. Then she yawned aloud, and said, "Well, that's enough for me for today! See you in the morning, Arielle."

Arielle murmured something about waiting for her clothes to dry, but grinned wickedly as she watched the tall blonde walk casually up the corridor of the *Dragonfly* to the crew sleeping quarters and pull the privacy curtain open. Shirley turned to look back as she closed the curtain and caught the grin. She stared coolly, and quickly stepped within. Arielle snickered, and turned to check on the status of the microwave clothes dryer. She would wait until her pajamas were dry and hot before going to bed. Her thin body was always cold at the temperatures the rest of the crew found comfortable. The dryer finally chimed and she pulled out the pink bunny suit, complete with elastic cuffs and booties. It was warm and soft, and she clutched it close as she listened to the noises of the ship. She was waiting to hear Shirley start her shower, so she would know it was safe to part the privacy curtain. Instead of the shower, however, she heard sleepily murmured half-objections from Richard, before the Sound-Bar door on his bunk closed down and shut them off.

*   *   *

At breakfast the next morning, Richard and Shirley behaved towards each other with careful friendliness, but even such a temporary liaison resulted in the heightened awareness of each other which periodically affected the humans. Their differences in appearance, their emotions, their own desires suddenly seemed to become noticeable again, after long days of dormancy.

The passing storm was increasing in intensity, but during a lull, the four members of the crew who slept on *Victoria* put on their suits and joined the six on the *Dragonfly* for a communal luncheon, leaving the flouwen and Josephine in charge of the lander. They hurried through blowing snow and rising winds as the cloud-darkened day grew pitch-black with the arrival of the noontime eclipse. When they entered the airplane, they could hear the hull humming from the vibrations of the tie-down cables. Once they were all together inside, it was like being trapped in a snowstorm at a ski lodge during the holiday season—all the comforts one could want and no work to do.

For David, of course, the reaction was to create a sono-video composition on the computer console; some of it wild and stormy, some of it calm and soothing.

"I call it 'Ice Storm,'" said David. "It's based on the weather conditions outside. Let me play this first section for you."

Soon, a group gathered around David's console to watch the computer-generated video scenes, while listening to the music through imp-earphones. The showpiece began with a stark scene of slick ice stretching to the horizon, reflecting a black star-studded sky. It wasn't set on the inner pole of Zulu, since there was no Gargantua in the sky. The music which accompanied the slow panning motion over the stark landscape was equally stark, with eerie auroral choruses, staccato icy crackles, and tinkling stellar bells. A storm then loomed over the horizon, accompanied by deep threatening chords and shrieking banshee wails which grew louder and louder as the screen filled with images of driving snowflakes, first small, then larger and larger, until a single snowflake image covered the whole screen as it rushed past the viewer at high speed. The snow turned into hail and the rattle of the striking ice pellets grew so loud that they drowned out the howling wind. . . . The screen turned black and the music stopped.

"That's all I've done so far," said David. "Give me another hour or two and I'll have the next part done."

Deirdre liked David's show, but it had the unexpected effect of making someone who was normally cool almost cranky. Thus, when Sam's hints for the prospects of some of Deirdre's famous fresh hot waffles were accompanied by a warm and tender smile, Deirdre not only glared, she growled, and Sam retreated hastily.

David's exciting music reawakened in Thomas and Katrina the urge to dance; this was an exercise they both enjoyed on *Prometheus*, where there was plenty of room, and where the lack of gravity made it simple to carry out dramatic dance variations. They had Joe play some dance music through their imps and began dancing while the others tried to get out of their way. It was difficult to move freely in the confines of the *Dragonfly*, however, and they had to be content with a few brief jigs and polkas up and down the narrow corridor, trying to avoid bumping into the console chairs as they twirled between them. It was fun for both of them, but only for a few minutes, and Katrina sighed, envious yet again of Arielle's dainty grace. George sighed also; this forced day of rest already seemed long. He fervently hoped that the aroused tensions discernible around him would dissolve by the time of tomorrow's excursions. And, gradually, in their own ways and times, they did. Cinnamon tuned out David's complex and sometimes disturbing compositions by retiring behind the Sound-Bar door of one of the bunks to listen again to her own favorites through her imp earphones, humming, and Deirdre vented her rare upset in a satisfying argument with Richard on the wisdom of introducing new ideas, however innocuous, to the icerugs. By the dawn of the next Zulu day, the humans were physically rested and mentally restless; all were eagerly contemplating the morrow's chances for discovery, but the storm was still raging outside.

After dinner, the crew divided, with those assigned to *Victoria* following a safety line through the driving snow as they made their way back. The extra room in each vehicle felt luxurious, now, and the regular routines of study, report writing, and analysis came as welcome and pleasant work. These were not people much accustomed to indolence.

Finally, the storm ceased. A full Earth day had passed, nearly two Zuni days, and it was time for the second Barnard-assisted Zuni conjunction tide. Barnard's nearly four-meter tide would be in a different phase with respect to the eight-meter conjunction tide, but the maximum tidal height should be well above eleven meters, as it was on the previous Zuni conjunction.

Quickly they prepared to lift off again in the *Dragonfly*. Cinnamon replaced George on the *Dragonfly* crew, George having decided to visit the regional Convener and learn about the icerug's form of government from that viewpoint.

After dropping off the flouwen and Cinnamon at the entry point on Manannán Lake where *Babble* was waiting for them, and David and Deirdre at the entrance to the Grand Portal, Arielle flew the airplane to Pink-Orb's territory, and used the VTOL fans to hover over the snowdrift-covered plum-carpeted area—but Pink-Orb was not in sight. Richard stepped out of the airlock onto the carpet, knowing that the Pink-Orb node, wherever it was underneath the acre of flesh, would instantly know he was there. The carpet, however, felt strangely flaccid under his feet.

Richard waited, but instead of Pink-Orb's node coming to him, he found himself being carried along the carpet by a plum wave, although much more slowly than before. The traveling wave took him down a tunnel, and after many turns, each turn carrying him deeper, he was deposited in a small room. Pink-Orb's node was there, its eye dull and listless, its pedestal bloated, and its body node barely giving off enough light to see by.

"I apologize for not coming to greet you," said Pink-Orb in a deep-pitched, sickly growl. "But I could not."

"What's the matter?" asked Richard, concerned.

"I'm sick," said Pink-Orb. "I guess I'm getting too old to handle even a single vermicyst. Now . . . I have been warned by the researchers at the Center for Literature Studies that you humans have a taboo about speaking of bodily waste functions. In fact, your formal language contains no word that actually describes the true purpose of the room where you go to carry out those functions. All the many words that you do use for that room are euphemisms. Since you and I are scientists, however, I presume I can safely ignore that taboo?" Pink-Orb paused, waiting for an objection from Richard, then continued on. "I have what you humans call diarrhea."

"Oh!" said Richard, smiling. "And this is your water closet."

"More like an outhouse in operation," replied Pink-Orb. "For I must supply the water out of my own body." A ripple passed through its bloated pedestal and the pedestal deflated as Richard heard a gush of water. "I am on top of a tunnel melted down through hundreds of meters of ice, which reaches down to the ocean under the ice," continued Pink-Orb. "It is lined with that portion of my body which serves the function of extracting nutrients and essential bodily fluids, while disposing of wastes and excess water."

"Sort of like our gut," said Richard.

"Exactly," said Pink-Orb. It gave another exhausted groan and Richard heard another flush of water.

"I was going to suggest that you and I watch the upcoming geyser period together. . . ." said Richard.

"Some other time," said Pink-Orb. "There will be some equally large tides in about forty-five days. We can watch then."

"I understand. I'll return at that time," said Richard. "Now how do I get out of here?" But before he could turn, a plum wave formed and carried him off up the sloping tunnel. Behind him, he heard another groan, followed by the sound of rushing water.

The first of the geyser eruptions was starting as Richard came to the surface. After riding to the edge of Pink-Orb's carpet and walking out onto the ice shelf, he set his feet firmly on the ice, turned on his position transponder so the commsats could record his exact latitude, longitude, and altitude to less than a centimeter as the ice under him rose and fell with the tide, and raised his sextant to catch the height of the top of the geyser.

Hurrying down the Grand Portal tunnel behind David, Deirdre passed an entrance to a large side chamber. She noticed a multitude of icerug threads leading into it and interpreted their meaning: a group of icerugs had gathered within. Curious, she took a quick look into the chamber and stopped, transfixed. One end of the large room was covered, from floor to ceiling, with a gleaming, glistening array of pipes of ice, all different lengths, solidly frozen together into a gigantic sheet. Her eyes wandered along the topmost edges of this amazing creation, where the end caps were carved into sparkling diamonds, and then down the swooping lengths to the base, where the notched "mouths" cut in the sides of the pipes were embellished with geometric carvings.

Underneath the multiple banks of pipes, enclosing the foot of each pipe, was a billowing cushion made of the velvety carpet of an icerug, in the cyan shade of blue-green that Deirdre recognized as that of the icerug Silver-Rim, lifting and billowing and quivering as though it breathed. She was so intent on this marvel that she didn't notice the throng of icerug nodes standing quietly around her on either side of the door, until the blue body-light of one of them caught her attention and she turned to see them. She then saw the node of Silver-Rim, standing quietly to one side of the organ, its eye concentrated on the stone plate it held in front of it. The cyan carpet inflated, then the portion of the carpet under the longest pipe twitched to let the air flow in.

At the first sound from the pipe, Deirdre forgot all about the icerugs about her; she didn't even notice David coming into the anteroom to stand beside her. For the sound was a note, a tone so deep she thought it might be the floor throbbing beneath her. It went on and on, steady and soft, and then, as the pulsating beat continued, more and more tones joined in one by one, low but ris-

ing, forming chords which changed and then swelled
again, the notes still rising through a song like a thousand
human voices and still upward to an ethereal chorus as if
the aurora had been turned into sound. Then, descending, the chords changed, shifting and blending, now
softening to a single pure note, now enlarging to a multi-
tongued chord that reverberated in every body. The hair
on Deirdre's neck was erect, and Foxx quivered on her
shoulder, as the incredible voice of that mighty organ
echoed in the vault and filled every niche with beauty.
Motionless, humans and aliens stood entranced until,
with a final melodic whisper, the instrument was silent.

In the waters below the ice shelf, the flouwen were
busy. In their previous survey of the vent fields around
Manannán geyser, they had made a cautious long-range
survey of the entire area using sonar. Now that they had a
map and knew what types of life-forms existed in different regions of the lake, they began collecting samples of
the smaller fauna and flora, sealing them up in plastic
bags and taking them to Cinnamon, who inspected them
briefly and put them away in insulated carrying boxes,
while the flouwen went back for more. It was soon obvious that the life-forms found beneath the thick ice under
Windward City were significantly different from those
found beneath the ice of the empty shore.

⬜Many holes in ice,⬜ Little Purple was explaining to
Cinnamon. ⬜Out of holes flows much water, rich in
tastes.⬜

"Those might be the waste vents of the icerugs," said
Cinnamon.

☆Taste like Creepy⊗Stink!☆ complained Little Red.

◊But Creepy⊗Stink is good to eat,◊ reminded Little
White. ◊There are many things—seaweed, sponges,

fishes—that are found only around vents. They like vent water.◊

"Please get samples of the water from around the vents," Cinnamon requested the flouwen. "There may be tiny things in the water that can only be seen under a microscope."

☆Back soon!☆ said Little Red, as the three flouwen took another quantity of sample bags and swam off, moving gracefully despite their constricting drysuits. They came to the edge of the ice shelf and swam under it. The light from Gargantua faded away into blackness—but that didn't bother the flouwen. The sharp sonic pings from their bodies illuminated the sea around them and the ice above them with a searchlight of sound.

⌷That vent over there very active,⌷ remarked Little Purple as he shot off a focused beam of sound in the direction of the jet to draw attention to it.

◊It is emitting again—very heavily,◊ remarked Little White.

☆Something come from vent!☆ exclaimed Little Red, picking up speed and sending focused chirp after chirp into the water, as he closed in on his target. A quick swoop of the sample bag and the prey was captured. The other two flouwen came to examine the prize with their sonar pings.

☆Tiny!☆ complained Little Red. ☆Not worth catching!☆

⌷Very tiny,⌷ agreed Little Purple. ⌷But different from other things. Looks like tiny worm.⌷

◊The human Cinnamon asked us to look for small things,◊ Little White reminded them. ◊We shall take it back.◊

Katrina and Deirdre bent over the sample bag, one of

the many lying out on their improvised examining table at the base of *Victoria* while Richard, Cinnamon, and Sam were winching the flouwen back up into the airlock. The tiny inhabitant of the bag was still moving, although not as vigorously as when Little White had first given it to Cinnamon. The ocean water within the bag was starting to freeze in the frigid air, and both humans were anxious to learn all they could from the minute life-form before it expired in this hostile environment.

"Very similar, it is, to the worms in the vermicyst that I obtained enlarged video images of," said Deirdre thoughtfully.

"We can take similar-sized pictures of this fellow and compare them," said Katrina. "Look, it's nearly motionless with cold, let's get it into an insulated container until we've got some good pictures."

The small biologist bounced up the Jacob's ladder carrying the insulated box, while Deirdre collected the rest of their gear and followed more slowly. Her thoughts were busy, exploring possible life-cycles, untrammeled by convention. Learning of the bizarre and complex interaction on Earth between certain insects, flowers, lizards, and trees had long ago made Deirdre aware that an individual creature could have an unbelievably roundabout dependence on other creatures.

"I talked some more with the flouwen," reported Cinnamon as she helped Deirdre out of her suit, "trying to pin down exactly where they caught the vent worm. They remember exactly where they were at the time, and they and Josephine pinpointed it with respect to underwater surface features. The active waste vent was right under the area of ice occupied by Pink-Orb."

In the small but efficiently organized lab space aboard the *Victoria*, the three biologists used an optical microscope to look at the worm found near Pink-Orb's waste vent.

"It's a single-celled creature," said Katrina, as she adjusted the focus on the microscope. "Has the typical double-knobbed cell structure of all the creatures on Zulu, except that one knob has specialized into a large tail so it can swim about."

"There is a distinctive banding structure on the tail," said Cinnamon. "That should help in the comparison."

"Now to pull up the enlarged video image Deirdre got of the worm in the vermicyst," said Katrina. Soon the two images were side by side on the screen.

"The banding structure is the same on both worms," said Cinnamon.

"So," said Katrina, pointing to the two enlarged images on the console screen. "Pink-Orb ate the vermicyst worms in this video image, and later the worm in this microscope image—with the *same* banding pattern— shows up near Pink-Orb's waste vent. If not a certainty, it's a reasonable conjecture that this vent worm passed through Pink-Orb's interior."

"It's hard to tell because of the poor resolution of the video image, but the head of the vent worm looks a little larger," remarked Deirdre, not quite sure.

Katrina, however, was positive. "I think that's just an optical illusion because of the liquid in the cyst. There is no question about the banding pattern though. They are identical. That vent worm came from the cyst Pink-Orb took from the dead coelashark."

"With dire results for Pink-Orb," Cinnamon added wryly.

"Oh, now, wait you there," cautioned Deirdre. "They've known for long that the vermicysts are not good for them— remember?"

Cinnamon nodded. "That's right, Pink-Orb said it couldn't resist eating the one, although it was so . . . rich," she recalled. "But what I'm really curious about is its presence in the coelashark. The flouwen watched a *mature* coelashark walk deliberately toward the geyser." Her emphasis on the word made the others think.

"And the icerug said the mature ones were the ones infected with cysts," said Katrina thoughtfully.

"Hmm," mused Deirdre. "So small a scrap of life. But it might—just possibly—have real power."

"What?" Katrina looked up quickly. "What power are you talking about?"

"The vermicyst came from the swollen cheek of a coelashark that had very likely committed suicide by letting itself be drawn into the geyser. The vermicyst had a life-form within, which survived a fall which killed the coelashark outright. Protected by the cyst and the coelashark's body, that life-form did not immediately freeze to death in the cold air out on the surface. It was quickly found by an icerug, prized loose because of its exquisite flavor, and immediately swallowed, but not chewed, thus quickly finding its way into the warm body of an icerug—perhaps to be digested—perhaps not. Next, Richard reports that those icerugs that swallow vermicysts have a tendency to diarrhea. And now this small specimen was found—according to Little White—near the waste vent of an icerug, a vent showing unusual activity. How now if this worm were a deadly parasite which infected a coelashark, drove it to suicide, enticed an icerug to consume it, and then forced the icerug to discharge it through its waste vent—unharmed—so it could infect another coelashark?"

This was an unusually long speech for Deirdre, but its import was what startled the others.

There was silence.

"I don't know," said Katrina firmly, "but I feel the icerugs should be informed. Perhaps, if they don't eat any more of them, the infection cycle will be interrupted. George says there's the equivalent of a Surgeon General in the city, the Convener of the Center for Medical Studies. The Medical Convener, at least, should be told about all this."

"Truly I disagree," said Deirdre. "It's interfering, again!"

"But only with a small bit of information about their own world," said Cinnamon reasonably. "And you're not ordering, or insisting—you're just passing along an observation we've made of a connection between coelashark deaths and icerug illness. And, tell you what, Deirdre," she added suddenly, "*you* be the one to tell the icerugs! That way, you can word it as carefully as you like!"

Deirdre considered. She had never tried to be an ambassador, having little respect for those who manipulated people with words. But she cared intensely about learning all she could of this strange world, and surely, talking with the Convener of the Medical Center might reveal facts which the aliens took for granted. And, besides, this mission certainly was better entrusted to someone as reticent as herself, rather than a well-meaning, kindhearted Katrina. She stood up, and started for the passway leading up to the control center on the flight deck of *Victoria*.

"A word with George, first," she said. "And if he agrees with us, it's me off to have a word with the doctor. But just a wee one, mind you!"

George concurred with the biologists' decision, and on their next visit to Windward City, Deirdre marched briskly between the icerugs, following George's directions to find the Convener of the Center of Medical Studies. She deviated from the path only long enough to take another quick look at the imposing ice-organ, silent now in the large anteroom. The pipes looked strange, hanging down from the wall with their bottoms open to the air, with no wind chest or complicated air valves and sliding stop arrangements underneath. All of that apparatus on a key organ was replaced by a single icerug body that "blew" air with its body into each organ pipe when and as required. The thought of how quickly these alien intelligences had grasped David's crude model and extrapolated this sophisticated wonder impressed upon Deirdre, yet again, the necessity of dealing with the highly intelligent icerugs with great care.

Accordingly, when she found the Convener at the Center for Medical Studies, she proceeded slowly, talking in general terms of admiration while she looked the creature over thoroughly. The node of this icerug was of substantial size, and the orb of its large eye was of a cool green, which struck both human and alien as familiar. It was a shock to Deirdre to see an eye so similar to her own in color, but she rallied quickly, noting with scientific detachment that the icerug's illuminating region glinted softly on the short, flared cloak it wore of an almost copper hue, which hung down over the ultramarine pedestal. As the formal greetings continued, Deirdre stared thoughtfully upward into Green-Eye's countenance and decided to approach her subject with a question.

"As you and your fellows are aware of the mishaps which can occur after ingesting the chance-found vermicysts, why is it that the practice persists?"

"Severe diarrhea, you mean," said the Convener matter-of-factly. "Yes, that is the customary result. It can be extremely debilitating, particularly in older members of society, and can lead to complications, although these are fortunately rare. But to return to your question; it is impossible to describe the flavor of something to one who has never partaken of it, but I can assure you that once tried, it is irresistible indeed. In fact, the curious part of the experience is that ordinarily, one cyst is sufficient; few feel compelled to eat both of the delicious objects."

"The observations of our friends the flouwen lead us to believe that there might be a connection between the apparently suicidal behavior of the coelasharks and those same wee worms which arrive, alive, here on the surface," said Deirdre carefully. "It might possibly be a wise precaution to refrain from consuming the morsels altogether, until such time as more is known."

"That is a logical suggestion, especially since the effects of eating a vermicyst are often unpleasant—and one I have considered recommending myself," responded Green-Eye. "However, it is difficult for me to urge abstinence upon my patients when I cannot practice it myself."

Deirdre wondered, briefly, if the vermicysts were addictive, in the earthly sense of the word, but further talk revealed that no icerug deliberately set out to find a vermicyst; it was simply welcomed as a rare treat.

"I suppose, over time, the vermicyst has gradually acquired and perfected its unique flavor," she speculated aloud, "as part of its own evolution." There was no immediate reply after the suit-imp had translated the last word using its glassy-foil speaker and Deirdre looked up, surprised at the lack of response.

"The translation your talking machine used for that last word was a short phrase that is completely meaningless to me," said the tall icerug. "The phrase was 'modifications occurring during successive reproductions.' Each of those words means something to me, but the phrase as a whole is meaningless. What is . . . evolution?" The human word sounded ominous when spoken in an icerug's deep tones.

Alarms went off in Deirdre's racing mind. Had she blundered into a taboo subject? Warily, she chose her words. "Evolution, to the scientists of our world, is a theory that the changes which occur from generation to generation in a species are due to modifications which are favorable to reproduction of that species." She felt a trifle helpless, hoping that Josephine's translation would not be taken ill. Instead, the alien seemed still unsure of what she had said.

"Theories, of course, we use," said Green-Eye. "They follow hypothesis and experimentation. And modifications are performed every time one improves a tool or artifact. But—generation? And, the meaning of the translation given to the word reproduction does not seem to imply the making of an object identical to another, but instead the formation of a copy of an object by the original object itself. Can you elucidate further?"

Still feeling her way cautiously, Deirdre decided to begin with simplistic, general life-forms and avoid the dangers possibly inherent in discussing the icerugs' own sex life. Accordingly, she began with the lowest form of Zulu life she could recall that could be seen under an icerug optical microscope. It was a single-celled algae which lived in the ice near the shores of the warm lake where the ice was not as cold as it was elsewhere on the moon. When present in sufficient numbers, it colored the ice blue-green. She was heartened when the quick intelligence before her seemed to understand.

"We have occasionally observed such things." The icerug's description indeed seemed to be the same, and Deirdre proceeded confidently.

"Now, when this wee creature is mature, and is ready to create replicas of itself—"

"How can it do such a thing? Why should it?" In apparently genuine bafflement, the icerug began to ask questions so basic that Deirdre floundered and stopped to reflect. A few more questions brought forth the information that all observations of the algae had been on frozen specimens, brought in from the dangerous ice shelves to the safety of the icerug laboratories, which, of course, were kept at below freezing temperatures to keep the ice lenses in the microscopes from melting. The reason for examining the algae had primarily been to determine why the ice turned green, and once that had been determined, no attempt had been made to culture the tiny life-forms, so the icerugs had never seen them replicate.

Deirdre now wished, rather desperately, that she hadn't brought the matter of evolution and reproduction up, but she was too honest to try to avoid an explanation. Slowly, she explained the essential processes of procreation, and the amazed icerug learned for the first time of life's varied methods of reproduction. Deirdre started with the budding of simple cells, and progressed in as orderly a manner as she could through the complications of evolution, describing the value of sex and its mixing of genes. Frequently, she was forced to backtrack, to explain terms to the alien; "cloning" presented little difficulty, but "buds" and "shoots" and differing "sexes" did, and she was limp after an hour's talk.

Fortunately, the icerug's native intelligence far surpassed hers, and it was able to absorb data and arrive at its own conclusions instantaneously. Deirdre was immensely relieved to see that nothing of what she had said appeared to disturb Green-Eye's sensibilities; the alien was simply curious and interested. She decided to explore, tentatively.

"Would you be willing to tell me, Green-Eye, if one of the processes we have been discussing is the manner in which young icerugs come to exist? I have not observed differing sexes among you, but I am ignorant of your world, and wish only to learn more. Please tell me if that is a question I may not ask."

"Why not?" was the calm reply. "No, all you have said is most interesting, but we icerugs do not utilize any such means of . . . reproducing . . . ourselves that you have mentioned." The new word was used with a note of satisfaction. "Young icerugs come to us from the far plains of ice outside our nation. A few of them are unacceptable to us and are consumed, but when one is pleasing to one of us, the rest have no difficulty in accommodating to its presence, and it is welcomed and raised among us."

"And, the ones consumed, they resemble normal icerugs in all respects save taste?" Deirdre had observed cannibalism in far too many species to be upset by it, and it seemed unimportant to this alien.

"Yes. I have not actually seen any younglings myself, as I left my outer association for higher studies at an early age and have been here ever since. I and my fellows at the Center for Medical Studies have long since settled into our roots here. The discovery of younglings, far out on the plains, is reported through the fine network of Conveners on the periphery of our nation."

A thought struck Deirdre. "And do those out on the periphery of the nation come across other animals or plants or living beings?" The startling reply was quick and firm:

"No. There are many different plants and animals in the ocean, but there are no other living creatures on the ice except coverers-of-the-ice."

This was something which Deirdre had to pause to think about. Certainly the humans had seen no other plants or animals, no birds, insects, even grasses or mosses. The icerugs had been given no opportunity to observe reproduction and evolution—except, of course, among themselves. Although there was a great variety of life around the volcanic vents beneath the sea and under the ice near the icerug waste vents, as related by the flouwen, these were obviously beyond the ken of these terrestrial creatures, who only saw dead and rapidly freezing specimens of animals and plants thrown out by the geyser. Even their imaginations would be limited, having never seen another form of active life but themselves.

Staring up into the green orb, so disconcertingly like her own, Deirdre finally dared to ask the basic question:

"Can you speak, then, of how and where the young icerugs come from?" She held her breath, and then listened with growing dismay, as the alien spoke in its usual calm rumble.

"Careful and lengthy observation of the known facts has preceded the general acceptance of the Theory of Void-Filling Spontaneous Creation for the appearance of younglings. Never, in all our long history, has a single youngling appeared within the city. Never, in all our long history, has a single youngling appeared even far out in the country where the ice is covered with the bodies of those that collect sunlight to produce flesh. They appear, if ever, *only* in the distant ice plains, where no coverers-of-the-ice live, and where there is a total void of life. From careful experimentation in our laboratories at the Center for Scientific Studies, using pumps to evacuate thick-walled containers, we observe that, when a void exists, something rushes in to fill it. Complete emptiness is unnatural. Nature abhors such voids. Therefore, on those empty ice plains, nature spontaneously erupts, occasionally, and creates a new coverer-of-the-ice, a youngling. Unlike the eruptions of our geyser, we have so far not been able to predict such events accurately, but there is no doubt they occur, because the younglings appear."

Codswallop! thought Deirdre. But she knew there was a time when spontaneous generation had been a widely accepted theory on Earth, and spoke gently. "And has no one ventured forth upon those ice plains to see, to explore any other possibility of creation? Perhaps a bit of budding, from some traveling icerug?"

"No. There is no need for such a futile journey to be made, when the reports of our distant leaders and Conveners are so accurate, and also so similar to each other. From what you have said, lower creatures might come to exist by different methods—such as this sex method you spoke of. But for icerugs . . . I am sure our Theory of Spontaneous Generation is correct in every respect. It has been held by my teachers before me, and never once failed."

To Deirdre, listening intently, there was just a hint of self-doubt in the final words, but she dismissed the thought. She knew that the icerugs must reproduce in some more prosaic manner, but without any genuine information on the subject, it was better dropped. However, Green-Eye had apparently absorbed Deirdre's explanations of reproduction and successive generations so rapidly that now the alien had thought of more questions to ask. In particular, it was curious about the flouwen, and Deirdre carefully explained, as vividly as she could, the swirling dance of amalgamation between three or more individual flouwen which resulted in a young flouwen—a combination of budding and sexual union. Even as she was speaking, she was struck by the incredible differences between flouwen and icerugs; yet, according to the similarities of the genetic patterns on their cells that Katrina had obtained, they were, in some manner, related. She puzzled over that, deep in thought, as she walked back and met the *Dragonfly* again.

Thankfully climbing out of her exploration suit, she immediately went to find Cinnamon and Katrina and related the whole of her interview, with all the questions it had created. As she spoke, the eyes of the other two widened, but she hurried on.

"So then, when it was asking about why it was better to have a wide choice of genes, and I was telling it about survival of the fittest—"

"Deirdre!" gasped Cinnamon. "*You* told it all that? All that totally new, foreign, unexpected information?"

"What were you thinking of?" cried Katrina. Deirdre was thunderstruck, and collapsed onto the sofa.

"I can't believe, now, it was me doing all that talking. Me, interfering, pouring out, unasked—not that any of it was untrue, mind! But ah, I should never . . ." She gulped, genuinely distressed.

"Ah, well." Cinnamon sighed. "You didn't actually tell it that its theory was rubbish, did you? And, maybe now that it has heard a few facts, it will start to find out the truth on its own."

"I cannot know whether to hope that happens or not," said Deirdre miserably. "It was unforgivable—but it was wonderfully interesting!" She brightened, unable to refrain from sharing with the other biologists the strange facts she had learned. Together they speculated again on the truth of what it was that happened out on those empty plains of ice that produced young icerugs, but they could only wonder.

CIRCUMNAVIGATING

"We've been here at the inner pole for a month," announced George one day at dinner. "A month of Earth days and fifty Zulu days. It's time we looked at some of the rest of this world."

"But there's still so much to learn here," protested Katrina. "I have an appointment to visit Smooth-Brown's classes tomorrow to be the show-and-tell object while it teaches the young icerugs about humans. I hope at the same time to learn more about how they teach their young."

"We're going to have to leave *some* things for the follow-on missions to do," answered George. "After all, our job is to explore and find, not stay and investigate. We've still got more moons around Gargantua to visit—Zuni, in particular. But right now I want to visit more than just one icerug city. Besides, you can still keep your appointment—you're scheduled to be one of the four on *Victoria*, while the rest of us go off in the *Dragonfly*." He turned to look at Shirley. "I'd like to leave tomorrow if possible. What needs to be done to make the *Dragonfly* ready for a three-week journey away from *Victoria*?"

"It already carries enough frozen food for ninety days, but that's for the six humans," replied Shirley. "We'll need to stow aboard food for the flouwen, check out the plumbing arrangements that allow the airlock to be turned into a temporary flouwen habitat, and load up some consumables tanks with ammonia water. But that shouldn't take more than a day. Give me a work crew of four and I'll have it done in half a day." She looked around for volunteers, but everyone seemed to be avoiding her eyes.

"Arielle and Deirdre should be starting their sleep shifts so they will be fresh when we take off," said George. "Richard, Cinnamon, and I are assigned to the *Dragonfly*, so we are obvious candidates for the work crew." He looked around the lounge and Sam raised his hand.

"The rocks and ice around here can wait another day."

"Let's get going, then," said Shirley, handing her tray to the galley imp and starting down the passway to the engineering deck below. She stopped to look back at George. "I may need you to move the *Dragonfly* a little closer to *Victoria*. The transfer hose for the ammonia water may be too short."

It was only ten hours later when the various tasks had been accomplished, and the *Dragonfly* was ready to go as a fully self-supporting vehicle. The exploration crew that was to go off on the long journey in the airplane— George, Arielle, Cinnamon, Richard, Deirdre, Shirley, and the three flouwen—were all on board. The humans had switched to a rotating shift schedule so that the *Dragonfly* was operational around the clock. Shirley and Cinnamon were now on sleep shift, while George and

Arielle flew the plane, and Richard and Deirdre operated the science and engineering consoles.

"I want to visit one of the other icerug communities around the inner pole," said George. "Since we can't visit them all, we should make our choice carefully."

"Here is the population density map of the inner pole region," said Deirdre, bringing the map up on her console touch-screen. George copied her screen onto his copilot console. Deirdre touched various spots on the screen as she continued talking, and as she did so, a green splotch showed up on George's screen.

"There's Manannán Geyser Lake next to Windward City," Deirdre started. "Where we are now. It lies between the inner pole and the leading pole. Manannán is the biggest geyser, but Sam and Richard are sure that has nothing to do with its position. There are eight other active geysers, each about the same distance from the inner pole as Manannán."

"That's because the tidal strains on the crust are a maximum at that distance from the inner pole," interjected Richard.

Deirdre touched an icon on the perimeter of the touch-screen to increase the color intensity, and the blue-green colors of icerug bodies leaped into prominence. "Around each geyser is an icerug city, while between the cities lies empty ice." She pointed to a lake where the hues of the surrounding icerug bodies seemed dim.

"There used to be a tenth geyser, now inactive, although pictures taken during the passage of the flyby probe fifty-five years ago show that it was quite active in the past. Cinnamon, Katrina, and I felt it's that city we're wanting to visit. There seems to be a falling off in both numbers and color strength. And, there's signs that the size of the community has gone down while others around it are still thriving. We suspect it may be because the geyser has died away. The icerugs there seem to be trying to compensate by spreading out, to increase their photosynthesis intake, but they may need whatever it is the geyser gives them to prosper."

"Sounds like a good choice," said George, looking at the map. "At least it will be different from Windward City."

Arielle copied the map onto her screen, looked at it with a practiced eye and grunted. "Be there in hour."

Since the first stop was only an hour away, the flouwen, resting quietly in the airlock, stayed in the drysuits which they had donned to make the transfer from *Victoria*.

☆Boring!☆ complained Little Red as he looked through the porthole in the inside airlock door at the interior of the *Dragonfly*. The red flouwen was getting quite expert at interpreting the visual images that were focused onto his red flesh behind the large lenses built into his helmet, but he could see little through the small porthole window except the suit lockers on the other side of the engineering section. Occasionally, the Christmas Branch would pass by, its colorful laser diodes sparkling brightly, busy on one task or another. He watched as the computer motile put some human clothing into a hole in the wall and shut the little round door. Little Red wondered idly if that was a hole to dispose of waste, like the hole that James and Josephine had taught the flouwen to use in their habitat tanks on board *Prometheus* and *Victoria*. Little Red then felt a sinking and rocking motion, similar to what he would feel when a large wave went overhead in his home ocean.

◊We are lifting off,◊ said Little White, looking through the porthole in the outside airlock door.

☆Feels good!☆ exclaimed Little Red with satisfaction, as he adjusted easily to the rhythm.

They soon arrived at the city immediately north of Windward City, with its nearby geyser lake quiescent and choked with ice floes.

"Land us on the ice shelf near the center of the city, Arielle," said George.

"No danger of wings icing up this time," she replied, banking the *Dragonfly* in a large circle. Shirley and Cinnamon were still sleeping soundly, although Shirley— ever sensitive to the sounds of the machine she had helped design—shifted uneasily in her sleep as the flying hiss of the *Dragonfly* changed to a hovering hum, and then finally to the quieter noise of a plane sitting on the ground, engines running.

After Arielle had landed, she stayed at the controls while Richard, George, and Deirdre helped the flouwen out of the airlock and into the lake, their communicator *Babble* paddling along behind them.

"The major things you three are to look for are *differences*," George reminded the flouwen through the radio-sonar communication link that *Babble* supplied. The flouwen had illuminated the ocean below them with sound as they had entered the water, and the sonar returns were starting to come back in.

☆Nothing *but* differences!☆remarked Little Red.

❒No motion . . . anywhere!❒ added Little Purple.

◊There seems to be no life-forms of any kind anywhere nearby,◊ reported Little White in more informative detail. ◊Any motion of any animal, or even moving seaweed fronds, would be easily seen by us because of its doppler shift. Everything has been eaten.◊ The translation stopped, and Joe's voice came over the imp link.

"The words Little White used were: 'Everything has been eaten.' But since there is no word for death in the flouwen language, I presume from the context they should be translated, 'Everything is dead.'" George, aware that the nearly indestructible bodies of the flouwen were essentially immortal, so they had no concept of death, once again was forced to face his own mortality.

◊There is nothing here,◊ said Little White. ◊We will go elsewhere.◊

☆Something move! Far off! I go see!☆ said Little Red.

⌐I go see too!⌐ called Little Purple.

"Be back in five hours!" George called through his imp, the paddle treads on either side of *Babble* moving into high gear as the communications amphibian attempted to keep up with the flouwen, now swimming at high speed.

The three humans headed inland toward the center of the city. For safety reasons, and to supply a high quality radio relay link for *Babble* and the suited humans outside, Arielle took the *Dragonfly* aloft and hovered over the city on the VTOL fans.

As the humans looked around at the city center, they could see several ornate above-ground structures which indicated some important buildings were below under the ice, but many of the structures seemed to be in disrepair. Between them and the lake front were a number of icerug bodies of various colors of pale blue-green. As the humans approached the icerugs, their suit-imps climbed out, each holding a circular piece of glassy-foil to produce the low bass notes of the icerug language. An ornately dressed icerug node with a distinctly oval eye moved forward across its malachite-colored carpet to greet them. As the node grew closer, Deirdre could see that its cape, although elaborate, was torn and shabby. The icerug looked carefully at each of them in turn, its oval eyeball rotating as it did so.

"Welcome, wonderful beings that fly from star to star, and world to world, and moon to moon, on beams of light. I am Oval-Eye, Prime Speaker of Northward City, and I welcome you to our proud but deeply distressed community. We have heard much about you and your machines through our slender talker who connects to the slender talker of Windward City. When I heard and saw your flying machine approach our city, I summoned all the available Speakers, so that they can meet with you and carry the news of our discussions to all in our nation."

The Prime Speaker and other members of the greeting party moved together toward the cluster of buildings and started underground, George checking the status of the commsat links as they moved under the ice. Soon they came to the Northward City equivalent of the great meeting hall. There were a number of icerugs there, but nowhere near as many as attended the meetings in Windward City. Their finery, too, was sparse and worn-looking. After introducing the humans to the assembled Speakers, the Prime Speaker questioned the visitors.

"Some say you must have magic, to be able to fly through the air and between worlds. Have you magic enough to wake our god, Panapan? The great geyser has been asleep for far too long. Our city is suffering greatly." George glanced quickly at Richard, who shook his head fractionally and added a comment through their private imp link.

"Once a geyser like this gets clogged up and quits, not even a nuclear bomb will get it going again in the same place. At best it would resurface kilometers away—which wouldn't help this city much. I'm afraid they're doomed."

"We have no magic," replied George to Oval-Eye

through the translator imp. "We do know how to build machines to travel through air and space, but they are not magic. Someday you will be able to build similar machines, I am sure. I am afraid, however, there is nothing we can do to help you reawaken your geyser."

"Is it vital to you, then?" asked Deirdre, trying to think of a way around the icerug's plight. "You use the good of the sunlight, that we know; surely you can make new flesh thereby."

"Those coverers-of-the-ice which are on the outskirts of the city do just that," conceded a nearby icerug, whose coloring was almost as pale as slate. It had been introduced as Pale-Gray, the Speaker of the Medical Guild, and the light gray eye which gave it its name regarded them steadily.

"They try very hard to keep us here in the center of the city fed with shipments of new flesh, but it is not sufficient. And a peculiar fact is that the flesh they send is increasingly poor in quality. It lacks flavor, and is singularly unsatisfying."

"Sounds like a mineral deficiency," said Deirdre quietly over their imp link. "A fruit tree, on earth, can seem to do well, given sunshine and water. But if the soil is lacking certain minerals, it's fruit is so poor as to be worthless. The geyser, bringing up all the richness of the sea, must provide these creatures with vital elements."

She then turned to address the Prime Speaker. "And how are the youngling icerugs faring under these conditions?"

The Prime Speaker paused before speaking. "We in the center of the city do not ever see younglings, they only appear at the outskirts of the city." Its oval eye rotated as it looked away from the humans to address the assembled Speakers.

"What news have any of you from your local group Pedestalers about newfound younglings? Are they suffering from the poor quality food also?"

After lengthy discussions it was learned that no new younglings had been found out on the ice for many cycles—since shortly after the geyser had died. This news was of some surprise to the assembled Speakers—who were far distant both physically and organizationally from the icerugs out on the frontiers—but then, they were normally concerned with more important matters.

The news didn't surprise Deirdre. Although she didn't yet know how icerugs reproduced, it was understandable that poorly fed icerugs would have difficulty producing viable children. She did wonder, however, why the news was of so little interest to the council. A zero birth rate would be of great concern to any Earth government.

It now struck the humans that the hall was unusually dimly lit, although all of the icerugs were using their lights. The walls of the building were as richly carved as those of Windward City. At the extreme temperatures they stood in, there was little change to be effected by lack of attention. But the floor, which in the other nation was kept polished to a highly reflective surface, was here uneven and dull; these icerugs apparently had lost quite a bit of their customary energy, and they simply laid their trails as they needed them, without smoothing the surface as they picked them up again. The gloom of the building was reflected in the gloom of the reports from the various Speakers. Icerugs in the inner city were, for the first time in their experience, feeling the effects of cold. Their energy was increasingly devoted to keeping from freezing.

"My Crafts Guild members and I have no strength to manufacture goods to sell," said a tall icerug the color of

seawater on a cloudy day. "This means we have nothing to
trade for flesh from the country. We are gradually dimin-
ishing and there is nothing we can do to stop it. We must
do something!" There was an instant chorus of assent,
which was a shock to the humans. In the comfortable
debates they had witnessed before, no two icerugs ever
spoke at once or raised their voices.

"And we know what we must do, don't we?" growled a
very old-looking icerug. "It has been done before, when
circumstances were desperate. And they're desperate
now. Desperate enough for war!"

The Prime Speaker spoke more calmly. "None of us—
even you—Elder Green-Orb, can recall war. What I have
read of it tells me that there are tremendous losses on
both sides of a war. Even if we won, many of us would
die."

"What difference if we die in battle or of slow starvation?" asked the tall sea-colored Speaker of the Crafts
Guild. "My neighbors on both sides have died already.
They were older than I, but certainly not ill. Their tunnels and workshops are there for the taking, but none of
us have any use for them. We are shrinking steadily, while
those well-fed creatures in Windward City are growing
larger every day. They *must* send us their surplus—they
have flesh and coelashark meat to spare!"

"If they refuse to feed us their excess, we'll make a feast
of the loathsome beasts themselves," muttered the elder.
"I'd enjoy nothing more than twisting the eye off their
Presider myself and eating it, before starting in on the rest,
dead or alive." The humans listened with growing dismay
as the rest of the reports continued, with no word of
improvement or hope. Each successive Speaker, indeed,
ended its report with some mention of a bitter
determination to wrest supplies from the wealthier city.

Suddenly Green-Orb, who had been watching the humans steadily, interrupted the complaints with a question.

"How valuable are you, travelers, to the icerugs of Windward City? Perhaps we could trade your . . . safety, for an ample supply of coelashark meat." The prospect of being held hostage stunned George, and Richard tensed himself warily.

Deirdre had not lost her detachment, however, and said coldly, "We have no value to either you nor any other icerug. Our species of being is so alien to yours, we are worthless, as you are to us." Inside her helmet, Foxx sat stiffly erect, and reacting to the tension she felt in her mistress, her sibilant hiss curled around and through the woman's words. The Prime Speaker intervened with calming words and began what gave the promise of being a more traditional, lengthy icerug speech, full of vague generalities. No one glanced at the humans as they slowly moved toward the entrance, and the speech was still going on when they left. Deirdre, always sensitive to mood, felt uneasily that the speech would come to an abrupt end as soon as the humans were out of hearing; if indeed violence was to be considered, and she was very much afraid it was, the icerugs would not want these alien humans to hear anything of their plans. The snow crunching beneath their boots was the only sound as the crew walked through the dwindling city past triangular living areas only half-filled with pale icerug flesh, and between deserted buildings and tunnel entrances without life or activity visible.

George, Deirdre, and Richard climbed back into the airlock on the *Dragonfly* and stayed there while Arielle made the short trip across the lake to where they had put the flouwen in the water. Cinnamon's voice spoke through their imps. "Joe has collected some preliminary reports from the flouwen through the comm link. And they're not cheerful ones. Let me play back some of them for you." The crew listened to the grim account.

◊All volcanic vents quiet. No living things left but coelasharks.◊ That was Little White's steady voice.

☆But coelasharks doing fine!☆ enthused Little Red. ☆They *huge!*☆

Little White continued with its report. ◊No hot water from vents to keep coelasharks away. They eat everything around vent. Nothing left but rocks, and big coelasharks chew them too, looking for food inside.◊

It was soon obvious that the cessation of hot water activity from the volcanic vents had exposed all the vulnerable plants and small animals to the full fury of the coelasharks, who had left nothing uneaten. The surviving coelasharks were now hungry, battle-scarred, and larger and meaner than ever.

⊓Here come two coelasharks, yelling,⊓ came a later report from Little Purple. ⊓Talking⊗Sticks listen for you. I tell what they do.⊓ The imp on Little Purple's suit passed on the underwater sounds and Little Purple's narration. The listening humans could then picture the events which followed, both by the flouwen's brief words and the coelashark's screams. The two coelasharks under observation by the flouwen were desperately hungry, and feinted at each other with their sharp-pointed rocks.

"Great bag of guts, I'll poke out your *other* eye!"

"Not while I've got teeth left to tear you apart, you cringing coward!"

Human eyes might have missed the rapid motions, but the flouwen's sonar sensed the sudden closing with great precision.

⊓One lost most of tail. Stuff coming out of hole in other one's belly.⊓

Little Purple was interrupted by a shout from Little Red. ☆Here comes trouble!☆

The humans heard great screams of rage and pain, and Little Purple described, with commendable detachment, several more of the veteran coelasharks who had kept this skirmish under careful scrutiny and now saw their chance. With brute savagery they ripped and tore the flesh of the two wounded battlers. In seconds, the last scrap of their bodies had been gulped down, and the number of surviving coelasharks was reduced by two.

⌷Soon only one coelashark be left. Then what?⌷

"You'd better come back now," Cinnamon called to them. "We're coming to pick you up."

By the time the *Dragonfly* landed, the flouwen were already waiting for them, while *Babble* could be seen making its way back over the surface of the water, its progress hindered by the ice floes choking the slowly cooling lake.

As Cinnamon and Deirdre helped the flouwen out of the water and into the airlock, they asked the flouwen further questions.

"Were there any coelashark young?" asked Deirdre.

☆No!☆ replied Little Red with certainty. ☆All eaten!☆

"Were there any signs of mating behavior?" asked Cinnamon. "Sometimes desperate circumstances trigger sexual activity."

◊No unusual activity,◊ replied Little White.

⌷Only activity of coelashark seems to be eating,⌷ added Little Purple. ⌷Everything. Especially each other.⌷

"I cannot see the sense in it," declared Deirdre.

"Evolutionary sense, you mean," agreed Cinnamon.

"These creatures just get older and larger, eating each other up. No breeding, no young. It's a dead end for them."

"And they don't think of leaving," wondered Deirdre. "Nor trying to swim away to a better spot."

"From what the flouwen said earlier," remembered Cinnamon, "they have just enough intelligence to have a language, but not enough to put it to any good use. Maybe it's time they became extinct."

"Seems a bit hard—not that I'm caring, of course," Deirdre added quickly. "Only, they're still floppin' out on the ice and dying over at Windward City. And that seems pointless, too." They were glad to abandon the topic while they helped the clumsy flouwen into the airlock, then passed through themselves, leaving the airlock to the flouwen to use as their habitat tank.

"That was a depressing visit," said Richard as he removed his suit. "I wish we could do something for those people; they are really suffering."

"It's not people they are, it's icerugs, I'll be reminding you," said Deirdre firmly. "And how is it you know that they are suffering? Plants, which is, scientifically speaking, what they are, cannot register pain."

Once George was free of his helmet, he used his imp to talk to Arielle up in the cockpit.

"Since we're already on the north side of the inward pole, Arielle, let's head for the north pole."

"North pole next stop," replied Arielle, and the *Dragonfly* lifted into the air on its VTOL fans, and soon the sounds coming through the hull changed from a feathery hum to a high-pitched whistle as the nuclear jet cut in.

George came forward to talk with Arielle and Shirley. Shirley was at the science console, setting up a mapping program for the science imaging instruments on the scan platforms looking out of the bulbous side windows on the airplane.

"From what Joe can make out from the maps taken from orbit, there is nothing between here and the north pole but ice," said Shirley without looking up. She punched some little used icons around the side of the touch-screen. "But now that we know what the life-forms look like, I'll insert some 'interest operators' into the monitor program to look for 'interesting' groups of pixels."

"Good idea," said George. "You never know. There might be the warm water equivalent of an oasis somewhere out on this desert of snow." Swiveling past Shirley's chair, he came up to the flight deck and slid into the copilot seat. Automatically, as soon as he touched the seat, his pilot's training made him scan the skies thoroughly all around.

"What's the ETA?" he asked.

"Since less than four thousand kilometers, we be able to do it in four hours," replied Arielle. "But I flying low and slow. We not be back this way again, so I optimize cruise for best mapping data, not best speed. Eclipse coming up soon, too. I'll put us in circle for those ninety minutes so we don't have gap in the map." She touched her screen, and a copy of her flight plan appeared on George's console. "We get to north pole in about twelve hours unless we hit weather."

"How does the weather look, Joe?" George asked his imp.

"Clear for the next eighteen hours," came the reply.

"Then, if it's okay with you, Arielle, I'll hit the sack and take over when I wake up," said George.

"Fine," replied Arielle with a cheerful smile. "Not tired. Most of the time above Northward City, I put Joe on autopilot and watched old movies."

"And ate!" snorted Shirley. "If I ate *that* much I wouldn't even fit in a flouwen drysuit, much less my regular one."

"Speaking of flouwen suits," said George. "If it's going to be that long before we need the airlock again, perhaps we could let them out of their suits." He turned to his imp. "Cinnamon? Could you please set up the habitat for the flouwen?"

"Sure, George," came the reply. "I'm sure they'll appreciate the freedom."

"I'll be getting some of their food to put in the airlock," said Deirdre from inside the privacy curtains. "Richard is hogging the shower again."

"Good thing Joe has plenty of heat from the nuclear reactor for making hot water," muttered George, feeling the itchy places on his skin underneath the creases of his underalls. It would feel good to squirt them hard with the shower's fine spray.

Deirdre went forward and opened a freezer compartment in the food locker opposite the galley. She picked out three bags. One contained long green-blue fronds, another lumps of orange-colored jellylike flesh, and the third what looked like large dark purple slugs.

"Fine variety," she decided, after looking at the labels. "Slender grass for salad, filet of rogue for the main course, and creepy stinks for dessert." She took them back and opened the inner airlock door.

☆I come in and help fly airplane!☆ announced Little Red, trying to push his way into the main cabin.

"Later. It's time for your swim now!" announced Cinnamon brightly, trying to block the way of the large drysuited alien.

"A swim and lunch!" added Deirdre, adding her pushes to that of Cinnamon, while holding up the food bags. Distracted by the sight of the food, Little Red allowed himself to be pushed back into the airlock, and the two women shut the door and locked it.

"Start habitat cycle, Joe," said Cinnamon through her imp.

Joe, having used its Christmas Branch earlier to make the necessary changes in its plumbing and valve connections, emptied the air out of the airlock, being careful to save the oxygen and ammonia, while dumping the nitrogen and carbon dioxide outside. Simultaneously, it pumped in icy ammonia water from the consumables tanks that normally held air for use by the crew on airless planets. The minute the water started to flow, the flouwen unzipped their drysuits, flowed out of them onto the floor, and began to play in the jet, while the suit-imps hauled the drysuits up into nets hanging from the ceiling. Joe also signaled the flouwen that the drain connection had been opened, and the flouwen took advantage of the opportunity to empty their waste vacuoles before starting their meal.

☆Creepy⊗Stink too hard!☆ complained Little Red.

◊You must be more patient, subset of Roaring☆Hot☆Vermillion,◊ chastised Little White. ◊Let it thaw first. Here, have some Thin⊗Grass to eat while you wait.◊

⬜K-k-k-k-eeeeeee-k-k-k,⬜ said Little Purple, ignoring the food for now, while enjoying the cooling freshness of the jet.

Their antics were watched by Cinnamon and Deirdre, peeking through the airlock window.

"Little Purple likes showers as much as Richard does," said Deirdre. She heard the sound of the bathroom door opening, and moved quickly through the privacy curtain and into the bathroom, catching a glimpse of a hairy leg with four toes just disappearing into a commodious upper bunk as she did so. The bunks on the *Dragonfly* were big enough to sit up and get dressed in, which made life easier for all concerned, since the main corridor between the engineering section in the back and the science section near the front went right through the crew quarters, and there was lots of traffic back and forth through the privacy curtains.

As the *Dragonfly* flew north, Barnard rose early and traveled through the sky to Gargantua, which had moved from its spot overhead toward the southern horizon. Barnard then disappeared behind Gargantua in its normal noonday eclipse. When the eclipse darkness arrived, Arielle put the plane into a wide circular holding pattern, and let Joe hold it there while she got a quick snack and took a one-hour nap. Shirley activated the infrared imagers in the two science scan platforms that looked out the bulbous "eye" ports on either side of the nose, but found no hot spots in the darkness that might indicate an oasis in the lifeless ice below.

After the eclipse, Arielle resumed their northward course, and the daylight, instead of ending three hours after the eclipse, stretched on and on, as Barnard neared the horizon but never set. George awoke and took over as they approached the north pole. As he sat down and automatically scanned the sky, he had to squint his eyes slightly against the red sun hanging just a few degrees above the horizon.

"Here we are in the land of the midnight sun," he said. "The scenery is about as barren and uninteresting as the scenery at the Earth's north pole."

"Or the north pole of Ganymede," remarked Richard. "But you're looking at it with the wrong eyes. To me it's very interesting. Below that crust is millions of years of climatic history, compressed into layers of ice containing trapped air bubbles and dust particles and various isotopes that can tell us what has happened to this moon in the distant past. I want a sample—" his finger pointed at the touch-screen "—from right here."

"The north pole," replied George, looking at the green blob on his navigation display. "Of course. We should be there in half an hour." He spoke to his imp: "Deirdre?"

"Deirdre is now on sleep shift," replied Joe. "Shall I connect you with Cinnamon?"

"Please," replied George, and when the connection had been made, he added, "Richard will be needing to use the airlock in about an hour. Please get the flouwen back into their drysuits and the airlock emptied out."

"Right," came Cinnamon's reply back through his imp. "But Little Red will be wanting to help you fly the airplane."

"That's okay," replied George. "I'll put him in the copilot seat and let him operate the display—but I'll deactivate the controls—that'll keep him occupied and out of the way."

George landed the airplane at the north pole without incident.

"What's the weather prediction, Joe?"

"James predicts a few mild snowstorms, but no high winds for at least two days."

"Great!" exclaimed Richard. "I should be able to get at least a kilometer-deep core in that time."

"Where are you going to put a kilometer-long ice core?" exclaimed Cinnamon.

"In Joe's memory," replied Richard, heading for the airlock.

After they landed, everyone not asleep put on suits to go outside. George helped Richard haul the electrically powered coring machine out from the storage hold underneath the airplane, while Shirley pulled out a power cable connected to the *Dragonfly*'s electrical power system. Before he started the machine, Richard explained how it worked to Cinnamon.

"It's not really an ice coring machine that cuts out a core and brings it to the surface to be analyzed. It's more like a mole with an analysis machine built into it. This millimeter-sized cylindrical cutter in the very nose cuts a core and passes it back through a sophisticated analyzer that continuously measures the ice's density and opto-electrical properties, then melts the core to extract the air and dust, and analyzes those. The data collected is then passed back up the power cable. I start it out by using a coring tool to make a hole for the mole to start in." He demonstrated using a sharp edged cylindrical tool that quickly cut a half-meter deep hole in the packed snow. "I then put the mole in the hole—it's a snug fit—and these screw treads along the side push it forward, while these sharp rotating teeth in front cut up the ice, pass the chunks up through these channels, and out the rear. If it encounters a rock, it backs up—you can see that there are cutters in the rear, too—starts another hole at an angle, and works its way around the obstacle and continues on down, sending back data as it goes. The real trick was getting ten kilometers of power and data cable in this storage canister at the end. It's all done optically through a very low loss optical fiber and high-efficiency electro-optical and opto-electric converters." He started the mole up, and it soon was out of sight.

"What happens when it gets to the bottom?" asked Cinnamon.

"I can either leave it there, or have it climb out, either back up the hole it made on the way down, which is the fastest way, or upward through pristine ice to get a confirming set of data. I won't decide which option until I see how fast it is penetrating through this ice, or George or the weatherman warns me that my time is running out."

Once the mole was on its way down, and Shirley and her helpers had anchored the *Dragonfly* down with ice anchors, there was little else to do except watch Barnard circle around the sky, eight degrees above the horizon. When the noontime eclipse occurred, with Barnard going behind Gargantua, cut in half by the horizon, the crew went back into the plane, and the flouwen habitat was restored.

Later, Deirdre found herself idly staring out the cockpit windows at the darkening sky, swirling with another snowstorm. All of the humans were apt to do this; the sight was mesmerizing. The snowflakes changed shape with the force of the wind, ranging from clusters held together by sleet, to fine, tiny particles like diamond dust, now drifting into huge mounds, now swirling in miniature cyclones, now blowing horizontally. Trying to imagine how cold it would feel on her skin, Deirdre shivered and turned away from the bleak landscape. Although the *Dragonfly* was comfortably warm inside, Deirdre's long reverie by the window had left her feeling chilled, and she headed purposefully for the galley. Pausing only to get a cup of hot tea, she put Joe to work on some puff pastry. The galley imp was capable of producing a fine, thin sheet that, in the hot oven, would burst into delicate layers of crispness. Deftly, Deirdre wrapped the unbaked pastry around a rich filling of chunks of real meat from Chicken Little, fragrant mushrooms, and crisp bits of onion, moistened with a clear sauce redolent of wine from James' chemical synthesizers. The aroma of the little triangles, baking to a rich brown, brought the crew in plenty of time to savor them hot, with a bit of freshly mixed mustard. Deirdre called the little pies "bridies," and the crew loved them. They were improved even further by their contrast to the forbidding landscape outside.

The ice at the north pole must have been fairly clean of micrometeorites, because the mole never encountered one. The only excitement came after two Zulu days, when, four kilometers down, the mole broke through into the ocean under the ice. Fortunately, it was able to back up in time, and after turning the mole around, Richard had it climb back up, taking more data on the way.

After the period of relative inactivity, the crew was eager to go. The mole was resupplied with a new power cable package and stored under the hull, the anchors were lifted and stowed away, and Arielle was in the pilot's seat. As it had been continuously since they had arrived, it was still light outside.

"Where next?" asked Arielle, turning to look at George in the copilot seat.

"The leading pole," said George. "That's where all the atmosphere and water molecules that the geysers throw into space fall back again onto Zulu. We want to get samples at as high an altitude as we can fly."

"*Dragonfly* can go all the way into space on its jets," Arielle reminded him.

"We want to save the monopropellant for real emergencies," replied George. "Like the ascent module on *Victoria* not working. Just fly us there at a good mapping altitude, and when we get close, we'll take it as high as it will go on the atmospheric bypass jets."

Arielle lifted the *Dragonfly*, Shirley started the mapping routine, and George pulled up the northern hemisphere weather map obtained from the statite *Colin* hovering above and shifted it to cover the region from the north pole to the leading pole. The map was full of strong, tightly coiled cloud features.

"We're in for a stormy experience," he said with obvious concern.

"Maybe we should try another pole first," suggested Shirley. "Perhaps the weather around the inner pole will be better later."

"The weather around the inner pole is always bad," replied George. "Because of all the infalling air and water vapor at the leading pole, it's a region of constant high pressure, high humidity, and relative warmth—the kinetic energy of the infalling molecules heats up the air. As the warm high pressure air mass spreads out onto the rest of the planet, it cools, precipitation starts, and storms are bred. It's a continuous process—one storm front after another. Waiting won't do any good, so we might as well go now."

It was a terribly bumpy flight. Everyone stayed belted in either a seat or a bunk, and the flouwen had an occasional breaking wave in their habitat tank. Shirley complained that they were losing mapping data, but a number of times Arielle had to climb above the clouds because there was no way around them at lower altitudes. Finally, they approached the leading pole region and the air became calmer. The sky was clear overhead, and Gargantua was on the horizon, cut in half by the skyline. Barnard had just set and the visible half of Gargantua was fully illuminated. It was a picture of quiet calm.

"We're in the permanent center of the storm," remarked George, now in the pilot seat. He took the plane up as high as he could coax it to go, until the controls became mushy. He wished Arielle were not on her sleep shift, because she could have got a few hundred more meters out of the plane.

"Deploy atmospheric sampler scoops," he commanded Joe, and the plane wiggled slightly in protest and drifted lower in altitude as its aerodynamic properties were changed.

"The composition looks pretty much as you predicted," reported Richard from the science console, as he watched the data build up on his screen.

"Except I now have real numbers to put into my atmospheric model," replied George. "I presume you want an ice core sample?"

"Of course," replied Richard.

"Then down we go," said George, turning the *Dragonfly* into a slowly descending spiral. As he descended, the illuminated portion of the half-hemisphere of Gargantua visible above the horizon became thinner and the night grew darker, as Barnard circled around during the night. Finally Gargantua was no longer a source of light, but instead was a large gray-black blank spot on the eastern horizon of the star-studded sky. There was no light except that from the stars and the distant quarter moon of Zouave. George thought for a while about landing on the ice using his wing lights, but decided discretion was the better choice and put the *Dragonfly* into a circular holding pattern until the sun rose. Sunrise was forty minutes late, as Barnard finally rose from behind Gargantua. The eclipse, which occurred at noonday on the inner pole, occurred at daybreak here at the leading pole.

After four days at the leading pole, a frustrated Richard finally had to give up with only a few kilometers of core data taken because of multiple encounters with stones. It didn't take a very large micrometeorite to clog up a millimeter-sized coring tube.

"The seasonal ice layers are extremely thin here," remarked Richard as he looked at the data. "In some cases, large sequences that we saw in the north pole data are missing, as if there had been no deposit during that period, or the surface was evaporated away at a later time."

"It *is* warmer here than anywhere else on the planet," George reminded him.

"But why are there so many rocks?" Shirley asked. "We didn't run into any in the north pole core."

"It *is* the leading pole," remarked Cinnamon. "Naturally you would expect more debris to fall in on this hemisphere."

"That's part of it," said Richard. "But I suspect the real reason is that while lots of snow and meteorites fall down onto the surface over time, the snow evaporates away, while the rocks don't, so pretty soon you have built up a high density of rocks. I give up. Let's go somewhere else more profitable."

"And where there is something for the rest of us to do other than watch Richard's moles dig holes in the ice," muttered Shirley.

"The next stop is the outer pole," replied George. "The orbital survey cameras have identified a number of icerug colonies there, so we should all have plenty to see—including the flouwen."

They headed westward, passing bumpily again through the storm belt around the inner pole. The further west they went, the lower Gargantua sank on the horizon. They finally left it behind, and as a result, when nighttime came, it became pitch-black, but Arielle kept the plane boring through the darkness.

"The icerugs at the outer pole shall be living a different schedule to the inner pole icerugs," mused Deirdre. "They'll have to shut down completely at night, while the ones at the inner pole just slowed down, since they still could see, though their energy intake was lowered."

"That would be one of the things we'll have to ask them about," agreed Cinnamon.

They didn't get to ask them anything. Arielle had slowly, and carefully, and quietly, landed the *Dragonfly* on the outskirts of a prosperous-looking icerug city. A greeting party of George, Cinnamon, and Deirdre had exited the airlock—George deciding that including the flouwen on this first meeting would be too confusing. Each member of the greeting party had their suit-imp outside on their shoulder, holding a large speaker cone of glassy-foil in their glittering fingers, ready to boom out the icerug words as the humans spoke. The humans had marched up to a vertex where three of the icerug carpets met and waited. George looked up at the sky to see that *Prometheus* was hovering above them. The crew on the spaceship would be watching the meeting through the video cameras in the helmets of the exploration party. The three icerugs first looked at them from a distance, then together they ventured up enough nerve to bring their nodes to the edge of their carpets. One of them gave a lengthy speech, but instead of an automatic translation of the speech, there was only silence from their imps.

"I am unable to translate," Joe finally had to admit.

"Do you mean to say you can't understand a word?" asked George. "Did you ask James to help you out?"

"It is comparable to asking someone to translate Swahili after having been trained to translate Japanese," came James' voice over their imps.

"These outer pole icerugs are as distant and isolated from the inner pole icerugs as are Africa and Japan," remarked Deirdre. "It is not surprising there are major differences in language."

"If you start talking while pointing at people and things, I can start building up a new vocabulary," suggested Joe.

"I'm afraid we don't have time for that," said George regretfully.

"The reason we were able to communicate with the other icerugs so quickly is that *Splish* and James had spent the necessary time beforehand learning the language," Cinnamon reminded him. "What we need is another *Splish*."

"We have one—*Babble*," said Deirdre.

"That's a good point, Deirdre," said George, thinking. "We are going to have to leave the visiting of these outer pole icerugs to the follow-on mission, but we can make their life easier by leaving *Babble* behind to maintain contact so James and these icerugs can learn to speak to each other."

"We'll be wanting first to use *Babble* with the flouwen in the ocean," reminded Deirdre. "Although we cannot ask these icerugs for samples of themselves, the flouwen can surely get bits of the plants and animals around the volcanic vents here. At least we'll learn if there are differences between the inner and outer pole underwater ecosystems."

So, after a baffling exchange of sounds, the humans and icerugs parted.

As expected, the flouwen found the ocean similar to the ocean around the Manannán geyser, and returned with many bags of samples. The flouwen were willing to tackle a coelashark, but George forbade it.

"Richard will want to measure the next big tide and geyser action anyway. That is bound to eject some coelasharks, and all we have to do is get to one of those thrown out on the ice before the icerugs do."

Back on the *Dragonfly*, Richard checked with the tidal tables for Zulu. "The next good-sized tide will be in three Zulu days. It will occur at high noon here on the outer pole. Zuni will eclipse Barnard, and their two tides will add up."

"And three days should give you enough time to take another ice core sample," said George with a sigh. "Too bad you need the *Dragonfly* power supply. It would be nice to use the time to fly around and get mapping data of the rest of the geysers around the outer pole."

"It'll give me time to modify *Babble*," said Shirley. "I'll want to add a video camera and a touch-screen so James and the crew on *Prometheus* can do more than just talk with these icerugs." She walked down the corridor toward the engineering section in the back. "I'll also need to leave it some spare parts so it can fix itself."

As before, when a geyser eruption was expected, everyone wanted to watch. Sleep shifts were juggled and nudged, and preparations made. Deirdre shared Arielle's opinion that a good show was made even better by ample refreshments, and expertly blended various tasty ingredients into spreads for the crisp and wholesome but bland crackers that James seemed proud of. She also assembled several spicy sauces, perfect for dipping small hot crunchy portions of "crab" cakes and "sausages." Four of the crew wedged themselves comfortably into the cockpit area and the jumpseats behind to watch the beginning of the eruption, while Deirdre and Richard went outside; Richard to measure its height, and Deirdre in silent determination to miss nothing, if she could help it.

Shirley had activated the radar in the nose dome of the airplane to scan the geyser during the eruption.

"If a big object like a coelashark gets ejected, we should be able to track its trajectory with the radar and calculate its approximate landing point. If it's far enough outside the icerug city, then it's fair game for us."

All of them were in position well in time. Foxx sat quietly on her mistress' shoulder; Deirdre enjoyed having her small presence to talk to. Now, as the distant waters began to rise up, the woman was too breathless to speak at all. The sky above was clear, and it was strange not to see the giant bulk of Gargantua taking up a large part of the heavens. Barnard rose higher, rapidly catching up with the fingernail moon of Zuni high overhead. The dark orb of Zuni was four times bigger than the distant sun.

The rising column of water seemed to take on a life of its own. It almost seemed like some strange god, pulsing with vitality as it thrust upward. No wonder the icerugs regarded it with awe. Higher and higher the giant waterspout climbed, glinting and sparkling redly in the light from Barnard, and as it froze into droplets at the summit, the turbulent upward rising winds driven by the geyser began to catch the vital moisture and fling it outward in all directions. Barnard finally caught up with the now dark Zuni at the zenith and disappeared behind it. In the two and a half minutes of total darkness that resulted, the geyser reached its full height of fury, the distant rumbling, gushing sound overwhelming them, the frozen snow beneath their feet shaking with the mighty roar. Barnard came out from behind Zuni to illuminate the peak of the rising column of water, now reaching through the upper atmosphere and out into space. Richard was intent, periodically measuring the height of the geyser top with his sextant and calling out the results to his imp for later analysis, while Deirdre simply watched, and now had to blink away tears of gratitude for the privilege of beholding this wonder. Not until the waters had subsided, as swiftly as they had risen, was she able to move and return to the ship.

"That was great! I'm really pleased. I was able to get a good set of data this time. Quite a show, huh?" Deirdre could only nod, once, before hurrying off, and Richard shrugged. "Just can't impress that girl," he thought.

As Richard and Deirdre cycled through the airlock, they were surprised that no one, not even Shirley, was there to help them out of their suits. Helmets in hand, they went forward. Everyone was gathered around the communications console, which showed the worried-looking face of Katrina.

"Something strange is happening here," she said. "When Thomas looked out the viewport window during his mid-shift meal at midnight, he saw that the nearby icerugs were gone!"

"Gone!" repeated George, concerned. "That *is* strange. I don't like it. I think perhaps it would be best if we came straight back and rejoined forces, then find out what is going on."

"My coring mole is on its repeat journey," said Richard. "We don't need to stay here for my sake. We can cut it and go— I've got more."

"Then let's head back to base," said George, starting for the cockpit.

"Shucks," said Cinnamon. "I was really hoping to find a whole coelashark to dissect—hopefully one with some vermicysts in it."

"It'll have to wait," said George gruffly.

WARRING

As the *Dragonfly* sped back toward the *Victoria*, Deirdre discovered to her own surprise that she was eager to meet again with the icerugs of Windward City. Carefully avoiding the thought of any sentiment, she was hoping that the icerugs would have made some progress in figuring out their own life cycle, and that she could learn something about it. She still regretted her own "interferin'," as she privately regarded her explanation of evolution to the icerug; however, if she had aroused the creature's curiosity, it might perhaps prove fruitful.

George radioed to the *Victoria* as they neared.

"Glad you're nearly here," said Katrina. "Thomas and Sam have been out looking around. They didn't learn much, but there must be some kind of serious trouble here, and without the *Dragonfly* we can't go find out what it is."

"What kind of trouble?" asked George.

"That's just it, we don't know," said Katrina, her concern clear in the transmitted words. "All the adult icerugs have left the area around us, abandoning the young ones and leaving them to shift on their own. Even the local teacher, Smooth-Brown has left. But there's been no sign of any disasters, major eruptions outside the normal tidal cycle, or storms." The crew aboard the *Dragonfly* were silent, considering this information. Arielle turned to George.

"Fly by city center on way?"

"Good idea," agreed George. "Probably can't tell much from the air, but it can't hurt." The slender plane turned gently to the right, and headed for the center of the icerug city. The human eyes stared eagerly down at the bleak landscape below, and as the first icerugs came into view, there were exclamations of surprise. Instead of the large, triangularly-shaped blue-green carpeted fields covering the ground, great sections of the ice now lay uncovered. On the northern side of the city, they could see some icerug carpets, but they were arranged in long strips to form a kilometers-long tapered blue-green band of icerug flesh, with the wide ends of the carpets based in fields around the city, and the narrow ends close together and all pointing off into the distance toward the north. Far out on the horizon to the north of the end of the tapered band, another darkened blue-green band was visible, and without a word, Arielle turned the little craft in that direction. As they neared the strange formation, they began to see what it was.

"More icerugs! In those peculiar strips!" David's far-sighted eyes picked out the elongated pointed shapes of the icerug bodies.

"The carpets are like spears," said Deirdre. "I know they're not spears, but the shape of them is spearlike. And they're all pointed at the city." Arielle swung the *Dragonfly* in a wide arc above the line of tightly grouped icerugs, and then headed back to *Victoria* directly.

"As soon as we drop off the flouwen, we'll head right back to the city and find out what's going on," commanded George. "Maybe this is an icerug ceremony of some kind."

Back at *Victoria*, the flouwen returned to their habitat tank. The humans, however, were anxious to learn what was happening and soon were back in the air. Arielle floated the plane gently down on the ice shelf near the center of the city.

"We'll plan on a short visit this time, Arielle," said George. "I'd prefer that you not go all the way back to *Victoria*. Keep circling nearby, unless you hear from me. We might want to leave sooner than we've done before." Arielle grinned.

"Make quick go-away?" she asked.

"I think it's 'getaway' you mean, but yes, that's the idea." As the little plane hovered, the humans jumped to the surface, their boots kicking up a fine dust of frozen snow. They marched quickly, without talking, increasingly concerned at the sight of the changes around them. No icerug nodes stood talking or moving about their own affairs in the normally busy environs of the city center. In the distance, through the blur of gently falling thick snowflakes, they could see occasional bright flashes of light and hear loud icerug voices. Puzzled and alarmed, they hurried on and rounded an icy wall, confronting an open area of ice which served the aliens as a central forum. Five icerug nodes were fighting furiously, and while three of the nodes were attached as usual to a track of carpet which led off to their body in some distant field, the other two nodes had no extended carpet, only a wide skirt of velvety flesh around the thick pedestal. The three normal nodes, hampered in their movements by their trailing carpets, were stabbing and slashing at the two more mobile nodes with crude halberds, poles of dried seaweed stalks topped with combination spike and axe heads of sharp stone. The outnumbered pair had stone knives in each tentacle and darted around and over the carpets of the others with lightning quickness, slashing at their opponent's heads and eyes as they whirled past. They were all bellowing, and the speed and ferocity of the two strange nodes almost seemed to equalize the battle. One of the halberd wielders finally worked its way around behind the conflict and struck savagely at the knife-wielding tentacles, severing a number of them in a series of short, powerful chops. The two carpetless nodes, now nearly helpless, still fought to wrestle their opponents with unbridled fury, even trying to bite their foes with their tiny mouths. There was no attempt to surrender or plead for mercy or even to flee, which the more mobile nodes could easily have done. It was obvious, though, that the mobile nodes were rapidly becoming exhausted. With roars of triumph, the three carpeted icerugs surrounded them, and stabbed and chopped viciously with their pole axes until their foes were only scattered chunks of flesh upon the scratched and gouged surface of the formerly polished ice. As the victors straightened, Richard saw with amazement that one of them was his companion of a few weeks ago, Pink-Orb. He spoke to it, amazed.

"I can't believe what I saw! What is going on here? Who were those icerugs without carpets?" The three aliens approached slowly, and Katrina exclaimed.

"They're hurt!"

Deirdre and Richard recognized the other two then, but only just. Silver-Rim's great shiny eye was dimmed, apparently cooked to a coagulated white on one side, while Eclipse had lost the ends of three tentacles. As the humans looked, they could see the strange fluidlike skin of the icerugs begin to clot over their oozing slash wounds. The clots were soon covered with a fresh surface of velvety skin-covering, leaving lumps where wounds had been.

"Greetings, Richard." Pink-Orb's voice was weak, and it apparently hurt to vibrate the wounded tissues of its clot-dotted head portion, but the alien spoke as coolly as ever to the humans, nothing of the savage fighter showing in its manner. "Those creatures we have killed were some of the advance warriors of our enemy. We are at war." The flat statement silenced the humans briefly.

"War with who? Icerugs like those two—were?" George glanced at the remains and looked away. Pink-Orb exchanged a brief sentence or two with its companions, who moved off together at high speed, heading toward the distant sounds and lights. Pink-Orb addressed George without the customary icerug verbosity.

"War with invaders. Their own geyser, far to the north, has failed. The first we knew of their approach was when an advance party of carpetless warriors erupted from a tunnel they had made, deep within the ice, penetrating below our city center. They attacked instantly, and killed our Presider and many others. By now, the others of us fighting below the surface have killed or driven back the carpeted icerug nodes that carried these carpetless ones through the tunnel. But there are still many of them loose in the city."

"You really had no warning?" asked George.

"None. We knew they were starving because their geyser had stopped, and we suspected that they might some day come to drive us away from Manannán, but we did not have any warning of this attack until they were among us. The tunnel avoided all our own construction below the city with great care. It was a dreadful day. Many of us have been wounded, some very seriously, in the fighting. Two things have aided us: the invaders must travel a long distance, and the carpetless ones have little endurance. They must constantly eat to keep up their strength. Also, we were fortunate that the Convener of the Center of Historical Studies kept a museum of ancient weapons. They may be old, but the edge of a venerable axe is still good! And, of course the Convener has the history plates that tell us all about those weapons, so we are rapidly making more."

George was aghast. "You are making *more* weapons?"

"Certainly." The reply was grimly cold. "The invaders arrived armed only with crude stone knives and spears, and fire poles—long staffs with a ball of blazing pitch at the end to sear an eyeball. Our history plates tell us how to make poison gas to flood the invader's tunnel and kill all those there, machines that throw flame to a great distance to singe the carpets of an invading army coming over the surface, and flash bombs to blind the foe. When blinded, the enemy are even more vulnerable, and we shall overwhelm them utterly. I must go to search out more of the advance party." Pink-Orb glided away without another word.

"We must stop them! We must get them to talk, negotiate, use reason!" Katrina was incoherent with dismay.

"I can't believe such civilized creatures really mean to totally destroy each other," said George. "Pink-Orb must have been exaggerating. Let's go further along this way. But until we know more, we'd best stay out of the way as well as we can."

Richard spoke quietly. "I didn't hear, in anything Pink-Orb said, the slightest desire for peace."

Deirdre nodded. "It's most careful observation we must be making, just now. And most scientific detachment, Katrina. This is no time to interfere!" The little group raced as silently as possible toward the sounds ahead and climbed up on a convenient ice wall to survey the action below.

It was another battle of the carpeted icerugs with a group of carpetless invaders, not a large one, but of such ferocity the humans could only watch in horror. Pink-Orb had rejoined its associates, and the three were part of an uneven line advancing with small, flashing bombs exploding before them. The invading icerugs, which were undistinguishable from the defenders to a human eye except for their lack of carpet, resisted bitterly.

Two opposing nodes fell upon each other's upraised whirling blades, and then separated, desperately wounded. With a final burst of energy, one hurled another flash bomb at its opponent and got it full in the eye. The screams of both were ghastly, and the advancing victor, whom the humans recognized as Silver-Rim, closed brutally with its victim, slashing and stabbing. Katrina whimpered as the blinded icerug retaliated wildly, attacking until the ruthless blows of Silver-Rim killed it and chopped it into quivering chunks. Deirdre fought to remain calm.

"You'll be noticing, Richard, there is no call for mercy, and none given?" she said.

Richard spoke with some difficulty. "Yes, I see that. The blinded icerug made no motion of surrender." The battle continued, and George was shocked to observe that it was all aggression; there was no move to assist a fallen comrade, rather a total commitment to destroying the enemy. And the enemy, at least in this particular savage encounter, was annihilated to the last specimen. The victorious defenders stood, absolutely alone, upon the field, and then began slowly to collect their dead and wounded in silence. The gentle snow continued to fall upon the slaughtered, and the humans roused themselves, deeply disturbed by what they had witnessed.

George was especially bothered. "When humans fight wars, they hate the enemy soldier and all he stands for, but once he's injured and no longer a threat, it's international law that he be treated well. He is, after all, a fellow human."

"But these are not humans," Deirdre reminded him. "And they should not be judged according to human standards. Besides, although we may not ken what it be, there is probably a reason for their behavior."

"Besides," objected George, "what's going on doesn't make sense from either a political or military point of view."

"What do you mean by that?" asked Richard.

"As we have seen from the air," replied George, "there is plenty of room around Manannán geyser for more icerugs. Windward City occupies the best location, on the downwind side, but the vacant sections of the shore aren't that bad. From a political point of view, it would have been wiser for the Presider of Windward City to let the Northward City icerugs occupy part of the unused lake shore than to let things escalate into a total war with heavy casualties. From the military point of view, the invader's tactics are wrong. What they want is the fallout from the geyser, so they need territory—territory under the geyser. They should have crept onto the unused lake-front territory, set up a perimeter defense, and waited, growing stronger all the time, daring the Windward City icerugs to attack. Instead, they launched a full-scale attack at the center of the city, complete with the icerug equivalent of berserkers, with the primary intention of killing as many of the Windward City icerugs as possible, no matter what the cost in casualties. It is almost as though both sides were unable to comprehend the concept of sharing."

"Perhaps that concept is alien to them," said Deirdre coolly. "Humans are highly social, with cultures designed around sharing. Although the icerug communities may look like social organizations, they are not human, and you should not expect them to function similarly."

George began relating, for Josephine's benefit, his impressions of the battle they had witnessed to go along with the video images that their helmet cameras had recorded, as the humans headed back to meet Arielle. The listening crew were appalled at what he had to say, and Cinnamon queried him in disbelief.

"You mean these gentle creatures, who make such lovely music, who have been so polite to us, who live in such beauty of their own creation—they actually slaughtered each other without mercy?"

"With absolute savagery," answered George somberly. "Without hesitating a second. There was no thought behind what I saw, it was just butchery."

"I thought this was a real civilization, Cinnamon," Katrina transmitted sadly. "But I'm afraid I was wrong."

"I was, too," admitted George. "I fell into the old anthropomorphism thing, finding parallels with humankind at every step. That was a mistake. These creatures have no humanity in them."

"That's right," said Richard definitely. "They are purely and simply—alien." They had reached the landing site now, and the *Dragonfly* was hovering silently.

"*True*, damn it!"

The barked words sounded like a gun-blast, and the

crew spun around to stare in amazement at Deirdre. She stood apart, angrier than she had ever been before. Her words were scorching, and no one there had ever imagined the lilting voice was capable of such venom and fire.

"*Alien*, ye've said it, and *I've* said it, and it's a fine word that. An honest word, and it doesn't mean less than human, or more than human, it means *different* to human! And ye should thank whatever gods your small minds pray to that they're *not* human! Think you it's a thing to be proud of, indeed? These ignorant creatures know nothing of torture, have you seen that? They dinna torture, nor enslave, nor harm any living thing, not for reasons of race, or greed, or lust, nor all the reasons any self-respecting human dictator can—*and has*—found expedient! They dinna kill nor maim nor imprison minds or bodies in the blessed name of religion, which *all* human religions have found expedient! Nor do they do any of those things for the foul reason so many humans do—because their wicked souls *enjoy* inflicting pain on other people, on enslaved animals, on small things that have no words! I have tried, *most* of you have tried to keep from thinking of the icerugs as intelligent, unemotional, but funny-looking *people*, and we have all failed! We are *wrong*! And full well ye know it! They are not, nor shall they *ever* be human, and may the universe forgive us for coming here and meddling and then—*damn* it to hell!—*condemning* them for their behavior! *Shame* be on your human heads!"

The fiery green glare suddenly sparkled and softened as Deirdre's eyes filled with tears. She pushed through the little crew of stunned people and hurried into the airlock. Nobody had anything to say. Richard followed quickly, removed his suit and headed thoughtfully for the shower. He saw that Deirdre had the same intention and was coming toward him wrapped in a towel. They both stopped, and then Richard stepped back, with a brief nod, and got out of her way. Deirdre smiled and walked silently into the shower, closing the door firmly behind her.

DIVING

As the war continued, the humans stayed aboard *Victoria*.

"I feel strongly that we must not interfere," said George. "And I can't see us just strolling about, observing and commenting, but taking no part in the action."

"And you'd be in the way," added Deirdre dryly. "Might even be a bit . . . painful, perchance." George said nothing. The crew's safety was his prime responsibility, and he took it seriously. For several days, as they stayed aboard their two vehicles and studied the data and samples they had collected, the crew could hear occasional battle noises, which had now grown to loud explosions. They never became accustomed to them, and everyone winced at the sounds. On the fourth day, silence fell, and lasted. Shirley sent a query to *Splish*, which had remained immobile on the ice shelf lakefront near the city.

"The icerugs in my field of observation are no longer fighting. They are moving slowly and are filling up their respective territories. There are no more loud voices."

"Perhaps this means there is peace now!" said Shirley eagerly.

Splish's mechanical reply was precise. "Peace is not a word the icerugs have in their dictionary. They have probably annihilated the enemy and the war is over for that reason."

This came as a shock, even after all they had seen. But all were anxious to know the condition of the formerly friendly icerugs, and Thomas and Richard volunteered to investigate. George agreed, but insisted on going along. For the first time in the long history of their explorations, he also insisted on supplying each of them with a weapon. It was a recoilless hand launcher for laser-beam-riding rocket-propelled explosive bullets—accurate in any gravity field from zero to five gees.

"Keep it concealed in your chestpack—unless you need it—and I'm pretty sure you won't. But in the aftermath of war, sometimes situations become . . . uncertain."

The three men were dropped off on the lake front ice shelf, Arielle keeping the *Dragonfly* aloft above them. They were cheered by the sight of icerug nodes active again upon their carpets, although there were many empty areas.

"There's Pink-Orb," said Richard, pointing to the plum-colored carpet. "But the node is not coming to greet us. I'll give a shout." The friendly deep hail from the glassy-foil speaker cone of Richard's suit imp seemed to surprise the alien, who turned slowly in the center of its carpet. Another call from Richard, and Pink-Orb moved in their direction, slowly. To their horror they saw that the beautiful large pink eye of the alien was gone, replaced with a blob of scar tissue on the end of the eyestalk. The node moved cautiously, stopping frequently to reorient itself.

"Thomas and George are with me, Pink-Orb. Is there any sight left to you?" asked Richard anxiously. The alien gave a forlorn-sounding moan.

"None at all. My other wounds, though deep and serious, are healing rapidly. But I will never see a star or moon again. Fortunately, my last blow killed the invader. It was one of the last of them, I think." The alien's voice was firm and cool now, and Thomas, who had only heard about the savage battles, was stunned.

"Were there no survivors or captives at all?" Thomas asked.

"What are captives?" asked Pink-Orb curiously. That stopped Thomas.

George asked, "What about the Presider, Golden-Glint? And the musicians Silver-Rim and . . ." He was going on, but Pink-Orb waved a tentacle in protest.

"The Presider was one of the first killed, so I know of that death. Of the rest, I only learn as I am told, from my nearby neighbors. My career here in the city as an astronomer is at an end. I shall have to retire to the country, where it is easier for a cripple to live. I hope to be out there in time to benefit from the season of high tides, which is due in the next twenty days. The expected deluge should produce a rain of rich foods for me."

"Will we be unwelcome if we go into the city to see the damage done by the battles?" asked George.

"No one is ever unwelcome in our city, unless they mean harm," said the alien gravely.

"Like the old warning: 'Trespassers Will Be Eaten,'" muttered Richard. But he could feel only respect and compassion for this profoundly wounded alien intelligence and offered, "Shall I visit you at your new location, at the time of the quadruple conjunction? I could describe the sight to you, and we could compare data."

"That would a generous gift to me," said Pink-Orb. "One which I cannot repay. . . ."

"We are sharing knowledge," said Richard. "Information is valuable only to those who can use it. We, ourselves, have much to learn, always."

Pink-Orb seemed satisfied with Richard's vague words, and they agreed to meet at the time of the middle and the largest of the five upcoming eruptions. The three humans then continued into the city, looking around for traces of the war. There were surprisingly few.

"Actually, the buildings and all look in pretty good shape," said Thomas. "I guess ice is not going to be affected by anything less than a bomb or fire. But you said they had both of those?"

"Yes, but they were only intent on each other's bodies," stressed George. "They didn't seem to be trying to take or hold territory. You didn't see them, Thomas. It was not like any battle of the sort we know. It was just a series of mutual assassinations, single-minded murders every one."

They encountered several icerug nodes moving through the city on their carpet threads, all of them bearing lumpy scars covering new wounds and moving with difficulty. It was also apparent how much fewer there were of them; only individuals, intent on their own affairs, none of the gossiping clusters that had previously made the city center hum with their deep voices. The three humans grew more and more depressed, but continued their walk. They entered the Grand Portal and went down into the room of musical instruments. Here, George was delighted to see Silver-Rim; Deirdre and David would be glad to know the musician had survived, although it had lost a tentacle.

"Yes, my other injuries will mend, but for me the loss of a tentacle is severe indeed, and will affect my music.

Fortunately, the other tentacles will stretch, so I shall be able to adapt. My greatest loss is Clear-Eye. The invaders butchered my brightest student in one of the first attacks. We had no idea of danger until we found ourselves in the middle of a battle."

Thomas was struck again by the lack of emotion in these sentient creatures. Silver-Rim's report was factual, but not grief-stricken. This was borne out in further conversation; the injured icerugs would heal, would grow new flesh and incidentally devour every trace of their enemies. The areas and tunnels belonging to those in the city who had been killed would be taken over and utilized in an orderly manner.

"Then we shall be able to resume our normal activities," concluded Silver-Rim. "I shall send word through the Conveners that I can accept a new pupil. Some of the younglings in the country escaped the war and will be eager to come to the city. And, of course, in the interval between the high tides, new younglings will appear. We shall survive as we always have."

After a few more words, the humans left, sobered by the toll the brief conflict had taken on the icerugs and still puzzled by the necessity for it, but on the whole reassured. Back on *Victoria*, George stowed their weapons, feeling rather humble. Thomas and Josephine then presented the rest of the crew with a schedule for the upcoming maximum high tides.

"There is going to be a series of five high tides and geyser eruptions. They happen every one hundred eleven-point-five Zulu days, when Barnard, Zouave, Zuni, and Zulu all line up in a quadruple conjunction. We were in space looking down at the top of the geyser the last time this happened. It was at noon, when Barnard was in eclipse behind Gargantua. This upcoming conjunction will occur at midnight, when Barnard, Zouave, and Zuni are all over the outer hemisphere of Zulu, and this time we'll be underneath the geyser, looking up."

"Have we really been here over a *hundred* days?" exclaimed George.

"A hundred Zulu days," Thomas replied. "Over two Earth months."

Arielle's first concern, as always, was with the safety of her airplane. "I take *Dragonfly* west—out of fallout," she announced firmly.

"Although *Victoria* should be safe this far out in the country, I wish I could move her, too," replied George. "But she'll just have to ride out the storm."

Cinnamon, Deirdre, and Katrina, however, were eager to know when, between surges, it would be safe for them to go out collecting.

"Your suits will protect you against small debris," Shirley warned. "But a hundred-kilo coelashark, falling at terminal velocity, will be bad news. You'd better plan those trips carefully!"

The view of the first eruption from the viewport window of the *Victoria* was eerily beautiful, seen from a distance, but lacked the spine-tingling awesomeness of the sight close up. Still, Deirdre watched all of it, until it was time to suit up and go out hunting.

"We'll head out onto the distant ice where the icerugs don't go," declared Katrina. "That way we'll not deprive them of any food." Deirdre thought grimly that lack of food was not one of the icerug nation's particular problems just now, but she agreed. The three humans stayed within sight of each other as they moved away from *Victoria* into a changed countryside. The frozen drifts and scoured, icy hillocks glittered with freshly fallen snow.

Scattered about were tiny bits of weed, broken shells of minute beauty, stalks of seaweed from twig-size to tree-size, strange sea creatures of every size and shape, and, inevitably, coelasharks. They found a large mature specimen just twenty minutes after leaving the ship, and they pounced upon the beast with glee.

Carefully avoiding the multiple rows of extremely sharp teeth, Katrina pried open the jaw, and Cinnamon extracted the vermicysts and dropped them into the sample bag Deirdre was holding. Then, as they had agreed beforehand, Cinnamon, their ichthyologist, carefully sliced open the great belly of the creature to expose the interior. The three biologists stared eagerly at the glistening vitals, Cinnamon exposing them with careful slices, while Katrina used biopsy punches, scalpels, and shears to take samples and put them into bags that Deirdre carefully labeled. All of them regretted that limits of space prevented their carting back the whole coelashark.

"Built much like an Earth fish," remarked Cinnamon. "Mostly swimming muscle."

"But look you, Cinnamon, at how these grand thick fibers support the wee short legs. Considerable strength there."

Cinnamon nodded in agreement and reached inside with a gloved hand. "This is probably the gut, but what's this pouch here after the stomach?" She squeezed it. "Pebbles inside. Possibly a gizzard for grinding up the big chunks that the teeth bite off." She poked around some more. "Gills here. Where's the heart? Hmmm. Looks like three hearts. Take one for a sample." Katrina cut out and bagged a heart, while Cinnamon poked lower.

"This must be the flotation bladder, but it's completely deflated."

"I wonder. Did it collapse because of the fall? Or did the coelashark empty it on purpose earlier?"

"Here's something blobby that's full of blood—probably functions like the kidney or liver or both. I'll take a sample of that, too."

"But is it male, or female, or neither?"

"I don't see a recognizable reproductive organ," puzzled Cinnamon. "But I may be looking in the wrong place. In a male octopus, the sex organ is in the tip of one of the eight tentacles—like having a penis for a finger. For all we know, this coelashark could have a penis in its right front flipper." At the thought, she looked carefully at the construction of all four legs of the coelashark. They were identical. Katrina cut one leg off, and Deirdre bagged it after looking at it carefully.

"The bottoms of the feet are rough and show cuts, as though they've been abraded recently."

Together, and working with practiced ease, they thoroughly dissected the fast-freezing flesh, but without finding any clue as to the animal's sexuality. Lastly, they cut off the head and used a battery-powered bone saw to cut it in half down the middle to reduce the weight, while keeping representative samples of the brain, eyes, and hearing organs.

"Terrible small brain cavity," remarked Deirdre as she bagged the half head, with its half of a brain showing.

"More bone than brain," agreed Cinnamon. Finally Deirdre stood up.

"Right. We've got bits of the beast in plenty, but nothing that seems to be involved in reproduction. Perhaps one of the organs we're seeing is not what we think."

Together they loaded the samples into an insulated carrying case and started back to the *Victoria*, leaving the remains of the coelashark on the ice. No icerug was in sight, and soon the still-falling sleet and snow covered the stiffening carcass.

On the way back, Deirdre's long sight glimpsed another large object some distance away, and she hurried over to examine it. A little closer, she slowed down; the object was evidently another coelashark, but this one was in poor condition.

Must have been ejected a few weeks ago, thought Deirdre. *Decay is advancing nicely.* The body of the fish had softened in outline and looked pulpy. There was a sort of greenish-brown, seaweed-colored pus oozing from several places in the flesh, and only a biologist would have used the word "nicely." She looked at the spectacle with detached interest and curiosity, and then the hair on the back of her neck tingled with the strangest of thoughts: how, in this land of perpetual snow and frost, could the coelashark be decaying? With scrupulous care, she collected a sample of the pus and a portion of the less rotten flesh, then returned to the others. As they hurried back to *Victoria,* she presented them with the question that was baffling her: why was the coelashark decaying at all? The bits and pieces of the one they had dissected were already freezing solid, but the isolated specimen she had found, untouched for some time, was rotting. Cinnamon was as puzzled as Deirdre by the phenomenon, but Katrina put it aside.

"We'll know a lot more when I can get these samples under the tunneling array microscope," she assured them confidently. "We'll get all the answers then."

Deirdre shook her head. "It's a touching faith you have, in your equipment, Katrina. And terrible good it is, too, on showing us *what*. Yet it's at a bit of a loss, is it not, at telling us *why*?"

David monitored their transfer through the airlock.

Deirdre handed him her collection of sample bags to store in the Christmas Branch's cold storage container while she took off her exploration suit.

"This looks like a bag of gacky pus," remarked David, holding it up to the light. "I've never seen an uglier color in my life."

"It *is* pus," said Deirdre coolly. "And to a biologist, no color is ugly."

As the time for the expected largest eruption neared, the three biologists talked with the flouwen about the advisability of another expedition to the sea bottom.

"We'd like to have you watch the behavior of the coelasharks," said Cinnamon. "To try to understand how many of them are affected by the worms and commit suicide. The parasites can't make *all* the coelasharks do it, or soon there would be no hosts for future generations of worms. There must be some coelasharks that are resistant and engage in reproductive behavior—and the time of the highest tides might be the trigger—as it is for many ocean dwellers on Earth. Perhaps you can catch them in the act."

"But it's really dangerous," worried Katrina. "The big coelasharks are very strong, but *they* get caught in those eruptions and killed."

☆Coelasharks DUMB!☆ scoffed Little Red.

⬜Yes, they are,⬜ agreed Little Purple. ⬜Mean, and strong, but stupid.⬜

"You must keep in contact through the sonar-radio transponder link at all times," insisted Katrina. "And take extremely good care not to get into a battle with the coelasharks. Even if you didn't get hurt, it might distract you from the danger of the eruption."

"Besides, you've a serious job to do down there," said

Cinnamon soothingly. "We want you to watch the coe-lasharks who *don't* go near the geyser and see if any of them are pairing off, or chasing each other without trying to bite, or producing eggs, or small replicas of themselves."

The instructions and warnings continued while the flouwen were suiting up. Thomas and Josephine had calculated that the *Dragonfly* had just two hours to take the flouwen to the lake, put them in the water, and fly to safety beyond the reach of this highest eruption.

Arielle was adamant about the timing of this mission. "Fish, rocks, seaweed, all *kinds* of junk fall out there! I not like dents in *Dragonfly*!" The flight to the seashore was uneventful, and as the humans and flouwen exited the airlock, they paused briefly to look at the flat dark water. Its surface was covered with brash ice, pocked with small irregular plates of frozen sleet. A fine, powdery mist of ice-dust blew around them in the wind, and when a small clot of the stuff hit the water, it melted slowly and reluctantly. There was no fresh snow falling, just then, but the eruption would change that. Still chattering cautions, Katrina helped the others ease the flouwen into the sluggish water, while Shirley and Sam threw an expendable sonar-radio transponder out into the lake.

"And mind you keep sending those reports! I want to hear your voices every minute!"

☆Tired of hearing *yours*,☆ said Little Red rudely, but Little White said, ◊We understand. Report begins when we get there,◊ and Katrina was satisfied with that.

The flouwen checked their communications link through the transponder and then headed for the depths. The humans reboarded the *Dragonfly*, which headed off to a safe distance, with the biologists keeping contact with the flouwen through the commsat link to the transponder.

*   *   *

Back at *Victoria*, Richard suited up and went out across the basalt knob to visit Pink-Orb, who had moved out near the knob to be closer to his human colleague. It was nearly two hours to midnight, and Gargantua was approaching full moon phase. On the illuminated face of Gargantua was a circular shadow moving slowly toward the center of the giant planet. Richard made his way to the area that Pink-Orb now occupied and stepped onto the carpet to let the alien know that he had arrived. He could hear a deep rumble from off in the dimly lit distance, and his suit-imp translated it for him.

"Richard. You have come as you promised. I will meet you in the middle of my carpet."

Richard felt the carpet lift beneath him, and bending his knees slightly to keep his balance, he was borne off on a wave. Soon he could see the central node of the icerug coming toward him, gliding over its rolling sea of flesh on its pedestal. As the human and the alien came together, the alien reached out to touch Richard with a tentacle, as if to reassure itself that Richard was really there. It was the first time that Richard could recall an icerug touching a human. Instead of letting go, the icerug held onto Richard's hand as the ugly lump on the end of its eye stalk stared blindly upward at the massive planet hanging overhead.

"Has the shadow of the Far-God appeared on the face of the Night-God yet?"

"Yes," replied Richard. "Zouave's shadow has started across the surface and soon will be one-third the way toward the center of Gargantua."

"Then shortly we should see the little shadow of the Near-God appear," said Pink-Orb with certainty.

Shortly after, Richard saw a tiny bite being taken out of

the giant planet. "Here it comes," he said, as the bite turned into a circle. "It's only a little more than half the size of Zouave's shadow. But it's moving a lot faster."

Manannán geyser, which had been grumbling noisily off in the distance, now raised its gushing tower higher. Richard was tempted to pull his hand loose from Pink-Orb's tentacle to get his sextant, but forbore for the alien's sake.

"Where are the two moon shadows now?" asked Pink-Orb some time later.

"Zouave's shadow is now nearly two-thirds the way to the center, while Zuni's shadow is one-third," reported Richard.

"Then look for another shadow," said Pink-Orb. "That will be the shadow of Ice."

The shadow of Zulu quickly moved onto the now fully illuminated face of Gargantua and headed toward the center, rapidly catching up with the slower moving shadows that had preceded it. The phrase "Racing with the moon . . ." came unbidden to Richard's mind.

"Zulu's shadow is significantly larger than Zouave's," remarked Richard. "I thought Zulu was slightly smaller in diameter than Zouave."

"It is," replied Pink-Orb. "But you forget that Barnard is not a point source of light. The shadows of the moons you see on the Night-God are cross-sections of the umbra—the shadow cones behind each moon where Barnard is in total eclipse. Although Ice initially forms a shadow cone with a smaller diameter base than the Far-God, it is closer to the Night-God, so its shadow cone is cut closer to its base, which produces a larger shadow."

"Oh!" said Richard, finally realizing what the professor had been trying to teach him in that "Astronomy for Geologists" course he had taken long ago.

The geyser now sounded a full-throated roar that continued to grow louder and louder as the rising spout of boiling-hot water shot higher and higher from the surface and into the upper atmosphere. Billowing steam clouds occasionally blocked the view overhead, but through the clouds Richard could see the conjunction rapidly coming to a climax.

"The three shadows are all approaching the center," he reported. "Their shadows are beginning to merge . . . they are just one elongated shadow now . . . *conjunction!*" His exclamation was nearly drowned out by the steady roar from Manannán. Richard's hand hurt, and he suddenly realized that Pink-Orb had been squeezing it hard in excitement. He squeezed back, and Pink-Orb, realizing that it had been holding onto the human all this time, quickly released its grasp. Richard reached out, gently took the tentacle back into his hand, and proceeded to narrate the rest of the three-moon eclipse to his blind companion.

Deep in Manannán Lake, the three flouwen swam strongly to the rocky bottom, keeping up a running commentary on things they spotted of possible interest to the listening biologists.

☆*Lots* of weed, here. Hot water bubbling up through sand. Weeds full of funny little fish. All tail and eyes, not much mouth.☆

"Weed-dwellers, I guess," said Cinnamon. "In relative safety, so they don't need much but eyes and tail."

⫍Small coelashark, there under rock,⫎ mentioned Little Purple. ⫍Came out of hole, but went back quick.⫎

"A solitary?" questioned Deirdre over the comm link from the *Dragonfly*.

⫍Wait. I look close.⫎

The flouwen used a handy bit of stiff weed to poke exploratively into the recess.

⌐Just one. No sign of egg-things.⌐

Little Purple had been curious about eggs, and Deirdre had explained to the flouwen that eggs could come in peculiar shapes. The suit-clad aliens continued their search and met several small coelasharks circling a thick tuft of sea grass. They paused to watch and detected within the weeds a fat round-bodied creature somewhat like a newt. It was obviously the prey of the small coelasharks, and the only question was if one of them could succeed in taking it without injury from its competitors. Suddenly, the largest of the three darted in and seized the small lizard in its teeth, gulping frantically as it fled for safety. However, taking advantage of the fact that the captor's teeth were occupied, the disappointed pair lunged after it and bit viciously at the flailing tail.

☆Hunh! These things *never* cooperate!☆ observed Little Red. ☆They *always* fight!☆

As they wandered closer to the major volcanic vent fields on the side of the underwater sea mount that surrounded Manannán geyser, the water around the flouwen began to move up slope.

Simultaneously there came an announcement from Katrina: "The next eruption is beginning. Be sure to place yourselves in a secure position." The aliens moved to find something interesting to watch during the eruption. Little Purple was lucky enough to spot a rough-faced rock with holes in it, in which two coelashark heads were visible. They seemed unaware of each other, but Little Purple intended to stay close by to see if the pair engaged in any kind of mating behavior.

Little Red watched the approach of a large coelashark with a missing right rear leg. As it moved into the region of stronger currents, the coelashark sank to the floor of the ocean, picked up a ballast stone with its tentacles, and proceeded on three stubby legs. Little Red remembered seeing that behavior before and decided to follow discreetly, picking up a ballast rock of his own as he did so. Perhaps this walking mode signified a behavioral change related to reproduction.

Little White found a solitary coelashark in a small enclosed haven among the rocks, waving its tail in determined passes over the surface. Having been warned by Cinnamon to look for this "nestmaking" behavior, Little White wedged himself between two rocks and settled down to watch. Through the water, the rumbling sound of the erupting geyser grew louder.

Gradually and slowly, but with never a pause in the increasing tug, the upslope flow of the water pulled on all the myriad creatures of the sea floor. Uprooted tufts of grass and weed began to tumble slowly along, and small, darting fish began to work at heading away from the current. Little Purple, secure behind a barrier of rock, saw the two coelasharks he had been observing withdraw deeper into their sanctuaries, still paying no attention to each other. Little White's tail-wagging specimen suddenly twisted head to tail, and the savage mouth opened and seized the desperately wriggling legged shellfish which had tried to escape by burrowing into the sand.

◊Not egg-laying. Just more eating,◊ concluded Little White through his suit-imp.

The large three-legged coelashark still continued its ponderous march up slope, and Little Red thought himself unobserved, until the massive head suddenly swerved and shot a bitterly hostile glare at the flouwen.

"When you're close enough, monster, I'll tear you apart!"

Little Red recoiled, but only for an instant. ☆Ho! *You* the monster! Even uglier than the others, with only three legs!☆ Swapping insults was something Little Red secretly enjoyed, and he increased his speed to continue the exchange.

"I lost a leg, but the other lost more than that! I was hungry that time. Nothing was left but a blob of bloody water. And, speaking of bloody blobs . . ." The four tentacles dropped the ballast rock and the coelashark suddenly lunged at Little Red, who slithered adroitly out of reach. The tug of the water was strong now, and the coelashark's three legs dug into the sand in the effort to control its pace as it regained its rock. Little Red's powerful body flexed within his suit as he strove to stay equal with but not too close to his adversary.

"Brainless blob! One good slurp and you'll be part of my gut!"

☆Stupid *and* ugly! All mouth and no brains!☆

To either side of them, small coelasharks occasionally appeared, in frantic flight from the steadily increasing pull of the geyser. But the big coelashark, with its flouwen escort, continued to move steadily up the seamount in the direction of the geyser. Little Red had mentally shelved the question of why any of the coelasharks avoided this lemminglike march, determined to find a way to make the foul-mouthed creature reveal, in some fashion, why it was so bent on suicide.

☆Got worms in your ugly mouth! They crawling and itching? Hunting for your brain?☆

The coelashark ignored Little Red's words and continued to plod upward. The time of the peak tide was close at hand, and the geyser burst into its full-throated roar. The upslope current surged stronger and Little Red was in the process of exchanging his ballast rock for a larger one, when suddenly the coelashark said calmly, "I must go." The giant fish deliberately dropped its ballast rock and allowed itself to be drawn rapidly up slope into the geyser.

Little Red, surprised by this behavior and hampered by his suit, fumbled the exchange of rocks he had been attempting and found himself with no ballast at all, being drawn helplessly up slope behind the coelashark.

☆The geyser! I'm caught in the geyser! Help!☆ Hearing the cry for help, the suit-imp activated the combined sonar and radio distress signal mechanism on the flouwen's drysuit.

Little Red realized that the pace at which he was being sucked up the submarine mount meant he had only seconds before he would be drawn into the boiling hot water of the geyser itself, and he must save himself if he could. He unzipped his suit and poured himself free, leaving the signaling device to continue its alarm. Once in the familiar coolness of the sea, Little Red assumed his most efficient swimming shape and headed both down slope against the current and outward toward the surface, trying to get to the surface layers of water forming the cooler shell of the spout. Perhaps he would be lucky enough to break out of the geyser column at a point where he could surf down the side to safety.

With growing alarm, he realized the returns from his frantic sonar chirps indicated that while the surface of the water was only slowly getting closer, the sea bottom was rapidly getting further away. He was rising rapidly up inside the geyser! Desperately, Little Red fought his way to the surface and burst into the alien air. Blind now, his sonar useless, and his vision lenses left behind in the suit, he had no idea how far up he was, but he knew he was falling—and falling—and falling.

He spread himself into a canopy, hoping to catch enough of the thin air to slow his descent. Dismayed, he felt his speed increasing. He could only hope that the suit was broadcasting his plight.

"Emergency Message!" Thomas's imp shouted in his ear. Coming over the emergency channel into *Victoria*'s communication center was the repeating, mechanical voice of a suit-imp.

"Mayday! Little Red needs help! Mayday!"

Thomas activated the radio direction-finders on the console before him and instantly understood the problem when he saw that the suit was broadcasting from a point nearly a kilometer above the lake.

"All personnel! Emergency! Look upward along the geyser! Little Red was caught! Watch where he falls!"

"I see him!" shouted David from the viewing lounge below. "My God, it looks like he's . . . hang-gliding!"

"I see him, too!" called in Richard from his position on Pink-Orb's carpet. "He's going over me at about a half-kilometer up. He should land on the ice somewhere beyond *Victoria*."

Although Little Red had spread his considerable mass almost tissue-thin, and had used the slight amount of lift that he thus obtained to get himself clear of the geyser, he could not capture enough air to slow his descent much. Little Red, with his superior IQ and intimate knowledge of fluid flows, knew all about hydrodynamic instabilities forced by steady flows between fluids of different densities, and knew exactly what was happening to his dense fluid body as it started to flutter uncontrollably in the increasingly strong wind passing by it, and knew precisely when he would start to break up into blobs and even roughly how big the pieces would be—but there was nothing he could do about it.

The body of Little Red fell to the surface in dozens of blobs of red jelly scattered widely over the crusted snow. The blobs were not large enough to be intelligent, so the personality of Little Red was gone. Fortunately, the blobs were sentient enough to protect themselves by rocking up their surfaces to prevent liquid loss, while conserving the ammonia from those tissues inside the hardened surface. The outside layers of cells soon froze, but the ammonia-water mixture bathing the cells in the inside of each blob had a freezing point that even the coldest night on Zulu could not reach.

Arielle flung the *Dragonfly* in the direction of the distress signal at top speed. Shirley activated the infrared scanners in the viewports on each side, and she and Joe looked for telltale warm spots on one side of the plane, while Sam and Joe looked on the other side.

"I see a number of small warm spots on my side," reported Sam. "In a large oval-shaped region, about a half-kilometer wide and a kilometer long."

"How many spots?" asked Shirley, not really wanting to know.

"Forty-two large ones," replied Joe.

"Drop us off here, Arielle," said Sam, putting his finger on the touch-screen in front of him. "Then go get the others."

Arielle glanced at her navigation display, with its green blotch indicating the place, grunted assent, and the *Dragonfly* headed for the spot.

"We'll need something to carry the pieces in," said Katrina. "I'll get out the large size sample bags."

"After we get in the airlock, have the airlock imp squirt a little ammonia-water in the bags. It'll help keep the pieces alive," added Cinnamon.

"We'll be needing something bigger to recombine all

the pieces," added Deirdre. "I'll break out a rescue bag. That should be big enough."

The *Dragonfly* fluttered to a halt and disgorged five suited figures, who spread out away from the airplane, which lifted into the sky and headed for the lander on the distant horizon.

At the *Victoria*, George, Thomas, and David quickly suited up and slid down the winch rope to the surface, while Richard stretched his long legs to cover the ground between Pink-Orb's area and the waiting *Dragonfly* as fast as possible. They clambered into the open airlock and the plane took off again immediately. Inside the airlock, an imp was securing a partially open rescue bag to some handholds and squirting in ammonia-water.

Once at the site, they joined the others, spreading out methodically in hopes of reaching the shattered alien while its fragments still survived. Arielle went aloft, where Joe operated the infrared scanners and directed the search crew through their imps. Very soon there was a triumphant shout from Richard.

"I've found a big chunk!"

He put the crusty blob of red jelly into the sample bag, where it quickly dissolved in the ammonia-water. Sheets of dead surface tissue fluttered to the bottom of the bag, but most of the red blob was now fluid and active.

☆WOW! FLY!☆

"And it's alive!"

That put new heart into the others; they knew that Little Red could be restored, a small piece at a time. Bit by bit, directed by Joe from above, they picked up more blobs. Soon they each had one or more, and Arielle dove down to the surface and flew along the search line. As she hovered to a halt near each searcher, the living contents of the sample bags were emptied into the waiting rescue bag, where they instantly joined together, becoming more and more Little Red as the blob of red jelly grew in size.

☆I fly!☆ came a reasonable imitation of Little Red's voice out of the rescue bag.

"You crashed, is more like it," replied Cinnamon, as she dumped her second bag into the waiting container. "There are still dozens of pieces of you scattered all across the countryside."

☆Find me! Find all of me!☆ the red blob called out. Then after a long pause, a much quieter voice asked, ☆Please?☆

"Reiki's lessons on *Prometheus* must have sunk in," muttered Cinnamon, but the magic word worked, and she returned to the cold and tedious task of searching the ice with new vigor.

It would take time, and the collection of many more of Little Red's blobs of tissue to restore the alien to his former strength and intelligence, but it would be done. The humans headed out to the farther reaches of Little Red's calamity to find and rescue still more of his shattered flesh. The force of his crash had spread his body over a wide area, and the humans were soon out of sight of each other, although all could see the *Dragonfly* overhead.

Bending over, intent upon the ground, Deirdre was suddenly shocked to see booted footprints in the snow in front of her! Her Irish bones knew an instant of superstitious fear, and then she laughed. She was standing in the area of the snow they had come "fishing" in previously—for freshly killed coelasharks. Now, as she looked about, she saw again the shapeless lump of the decaying coelashark—she had left a marker there to investigate later if she had the chance. She walked over to inspect it and was startled again. There was no trace of coelashark, decaying or otherwise. But there *was* an icerug! It was the smallest she had yet seen.

Quickly she looked about her, searching for this infant's parent, but there was nothing in sight. With luck, she would have time to inspect the little one carefully before its guardian returned. She began the soft wordless crooning that worked so well to calm a frightened animal, from a panicky Rocheworld rogue to an agitated Foxx in free-fall. Slowly, the clutching tentacles of the icerug node stopped their searching gyration and fastened firmly around her gloved hand, and the eye regarded her with seeming interest.

With the other hand, Deirdre gently probed the dense velvety foliage of its carpet and lifted up its edges. This tiny icerug seemed to be completely unattached to the ice.

"Hey there, little one . . . where's your mum, hmm? Left you out here . . . huh? Didums? Wuzza wugga icewuggy . . ."

As she made absentminded baby-talk, she delicately and slowly handled the alien, peering closely at the fine fibers that gave it its velvet texture. They were each a greenish-brown seaweed color, but the whole collection of them seemed darker, due to the light-absorbing properties of the fiber array. The single large eye of the node portion was more brown in color, like kelp. Finally, she straightened, wincing a little as her chilled backbone moved erect.

"Well, better go find more of Little Red . . . keep cool, little one."

With a final pat to the surface of the tiny icerug, she strode briskly away over the crusted snow, feeling with pleasure the warmth returning as she stretched her long legs. As she searched the snow ahead of her for red blobs, moving her head from side to side in a deliberate search pattern, a movement behind her caught her eye, and she turned abruptly.

What was that? A dark shape on the ice, small, but moving, and coming closer. With mounting dismay, Deirdre realized the small icerug was following her!

"Oh, drat the thing. . . ." She stopped, and the small icerug silently flowed up to stop at her feet, its large brown eye looking at her hopefully.

"Here now, get off with you! Daft beastie." No hint of gentleness now in the singing voice, only coldness and dismissal. "Off! Off with you! Back to mama! Or whoever! Sssscat!"

Deirdre turned and started to move away as fast as she dared over the crusted snow.

Wwaaoo! Wwaaoo!! Wwaaoo!!!

Behind her, a hideous deep wailing arose, like a warbling fog horn, and she stopped, uncertain. Quickly the icerug caught up with her and the dreadful noise it was making quieted.

"Damn! As if I didn't have enough to worry about! I've no time for baby-sitting carpets. Go home, blast you!"

She moved off again, but it was instantly evident that there was no way she could escape the small creature which seemed to have imprinted itself upon her. She stopped and glared fiercely into its one huge eye, but it only seemed to take this as encouragement and wrapped itself around her legs, gazing up at her trustfully.

"Blasted terry cloth mutant," she muttered under her breath. "An' they say you all are sentient beasties."

She reported her predicament to the *Dragonfly* through the comm link.

"I would really like to get a sample of an infant icerug,"

came Katrina's voice. "Can we come and pick you both up?"

"It may be small, but it's too big to fit into the airlock," replied Deirdre.

"Besides," added George, "our primary responsibility is to finish collecting the rest of Little Red."

"Well, I'm of no help, now, with this blasted creature always under my feet," complained Deirdre.

"We're almost done," suggested Sam. "Why don't the rest of us continue the search for Little Red, while Deirdre walks the baby icerug back to the rocket. We'll meet her there."

Deirdre agreed, although the prospect of spending hours alone walking across this slippery and unfriendly terrain was not attractive.

"And heaven knows what will happen if this carpet's mum finds out I've run off with her child. . . ."

EXPLAINING

Thomas, having pumped the diminished Little Red out of the rescue bag and into the flouwen habitat on *Victoria*, was venting the spilled ammonia-water out the open airlock door, when he looked down and saw Deirdre at the base of the Jacob's ladder. Thomas slid down the winch line to stare at Deirdre's curious companion.

"Where did you get *that*?" he asked.

"I found it alone out on the ice, and it followed me here," was the terse reply. The brief answer was so chilly it did not invite further questions, but Thomas broke into gleeful laughter.

"*That* old story!"

"Obviously the immature specimens of the icerug species exhibit the imprinting instinct common in many Terran species, particularly those whose young must be mobile at an early age," came the retort, in tones so cold Thomas was shunted back to years and light-years ago, when a similar voice had caught him daydreaming and asked that since he seemed to know so much already,

367

perhaps he would care to demonstrate the next problem on the board.

"Erm, yes, right," he stammered, "Of course." Deirdre went in the *Dragonfly* to get out of her suit and put Foxx into her cage. Soon, however, at everyone's insistence, she had to suit up again and go back outside, where the small icerug was warbling loudly and trying to get inside the airlock door.

"Poor widdle thing!" Thomas was saying to the icerug as she exited the airlock. "Awl awone out in da cold. Mommy will be coming soon. . . ."

"A stupid creature, indeed," Deirdre muttered as she exited the airlock, forgetting how the suit-imps magnified everything that was said. No one could be sure whether she meant the alien or Thomas.

Now she sat stonily on an upturned sample container while the icerug rumbled about her feet. One by one, others of the crew came out to view the tiny icerug and, to her ire, congratulate Deirdre on her "new baby."

The minute David saw the creature, he blurted in astonishment, "Say! That icerug is *exactly* the same ugly color as that gacky pus sack you brought back last time! Couldn't you find something prettier?"

Deirdre was surprised that David saw a resemblance in color, but she didn't question his judgment—the whole crew knew that David's color sense was as true as his pitch sense. Instead, she turned to Katrina, the last to arrive to see the young icerug.

"Katrina?" she said. "I found this icerug in the same place where I picked up the bit of pus from the decaying coelashark. *And*, David says they have exactly the same color. I think we might compare a sample of this wee beastie with that pus sample."

As Katrina approached, the young icerug shuffled around, making room for her. Katrina knelt, and while gently stroking the icerug's carpet, she teased out a small portion of the velvet flesh until it was attached to the main carpet by only a thread. The huge brown eye watched her trustingly, then the six-leaved nictating membrane blinked as Katrina gave the carpet a spank while simultaneously snipping through the thread with a pair of scissors—but the infant didn't utter a sound.

"What have you named it?" she asked, gently ruffling the fur where she had caused the injury.

"It's not to be named. It must go back to its mother, or tribe, or whatever the icerugs have."

"With its seaweed-colored carpet and its kelp-colored eye, I think you should call it Kelpie," said Katrina, standing up with her now-filled sample bag, and tickling the alien with her boot.

"Huh," was Deirdre's reply. According to Celtic mythology, Kelpies were sea sprites who tried to drown unwary travelers. *This* kelpie was trying to freeze Deirdre, instead. When daylight came, Deirdre led the infant across the knob to the local association of icerugs nearby. It was with immense relief that she saw the infant instantly transfer to Smooth-Brown, the teacher for the local association, and Deirdre was able to drift away and return to the *Dragonfly*.

When Deirdre emerged from her shower, Katrina had some news for her.

"The gene patterns on the baby icerug cells are *identical* to those on the pus cells! That baby icerug seems to have spontaneously generated itself from a dead coelashark! Maybe the Surgeon General was right!"

"Daft, y'are," reproved Deirdre.

"Maybe icerugs lay their eggs in dead coelasharks, like wasps do in caterpillars," suggested David.

"An idea, that," said Deirdre. "For we know that coelasharks have something in them which forces them to turn into dead coelasharks. Something that quite likely came from an icerug. The worms in the vermicysts."

"I see!" exclaimed Katrina. "The icerugs send out zygotes—embryo icerugs—which infect the coelasharks, driving them to suicide, so the zygotes can have enough food to grow up into big new icerugs."

"But that cannot be the whole story," objected Deirdre. "Why then do the icerugs remove the vermicysts whenever they find a dead coelashark—and *eat* them? Why don't they just leave the dead coelashark alone to turn into a new icerug?"

They discussed their findings with Cinnamon on *Victoria*.

"We need more facts," concluded Cinnamon. "Up until now, we've concentrated on collecting samples, not analyzing them. I think we'd better start looking closely at some of our samples and comparing them—especially our samples of icerugs, coelasharks, and worms. Maybe there's a link we're missing."

"The sample of pus had some coelashark tissue in with it," said Katrina. "I'll take a look at that."

"And I'll use the microscope here on *Victoria* to take a look at the worms in the vermicysts we collected," said Cinnamon.

"And I'll be cooking something to eat," said Deirdre. "Let me know what you find."

The bleak surroundings turned her thoughts to soup, and quickly she sizzled tiny bits of onion and pseudobacon in algae-butter until they were fragrant. They had long ago learned that small pieces of the mock-foods tasted closer to the real thing than did large chunks. She chopped potatoes into neat cubes, cooked them rapidly, and added them to the pot along with algae-cream, which she insisted on calling "top o' the milk," and stirred and simmered the mixture until it was thick enough to stand a spoon in upright. Then she added lavish amounts of real chopped clam meat from the Blue Oyster Culture. Deirdre ground fresh pepper over her creamy chowder, and ladled generous bowls for herself and the others. The hot, richly satisfying meal awoke generous thoughts in Richard, and he had the Christmas Branch pack portions in an insulated carton for the crew on *Victoria* and take them over to put in the galley.

It was Cinnamon who reported back first. "Whatever those worms are in the vermicyst, they certainly *aren't* icerugs. They don't have the right cellular structure. They only have a one-knobbed basic cell structure, with a large banded tail growing out of the cell for swimming about."

"Strange, is that," replied Deirdre, coming forward to look at the image of Cinnamon's worm on the science console screen. "Everything else on Zulu has a two-knobbed basic cellular structure."

"Perhaps I chose a defective one," said Cinnamon. She directed the imp in the microscope stage to replace the worm with another one. "Nope," she said, as the image built up. "Another one-knobber instead of two."

"A half-sized cell instead of a whole-sized one," remarked David, who had a copy of Cinnamon's screen on his console.

"Hmmm," added Cinnamon. "Am I right, Josephine? Is the genetic pattern on this one different?"

"Very observant, dearie. It *is* different."

"But, look there, the band pattern on the tail is the same," said Deirdre. "That would indicate a common genetic heritage in the tail-banding gene. Look at another one."

Scanning a number of worms from the vermicyst, the biologists learned that there were two kinds of worms, and only two.

"Half-sized cells that come with two different genetic messages," Deirdre mused.

"That certainly sounds familiar," said Cinnamon. "I'd better take a look at the genetic patterns of the coelashark that harbored that vermicyst."

Taking a sample from the liverlike organ of the coelashark, she gave it to *Victoria's* Christmas Branch, who took it to the micro-surgical stage. There, a single cell was teased out and transferred to the microscope stage. Cinnamon then set up the desired scan pattern on her screen, and Josephine started scanning the tunneling array across the surface of the cell.

"That'll take a while," said Cinnamon, getting up and heading for the galley. "I think I'll have an early lunch."

❐I watch scan,❐ said Little Purple from the flouwen habitat tank. On his taste-screen was a copy of Cinnamon's screen.

Cinnamon was halfway through a bowl of chowder, listening to "Don't Fear the Reaper" through her imp earphones, when a crackly flouwen voice exploded in the middle of the second chorus.

❐It is *same*! Worm and coelashark *same*!❐

Cinnamon twisted one hand next to her earphones, and the music of Blue Oyster Cult faded away. Still carrying the bowl, she went to the science console where Josephine was proceeding with the imaging scan. The screen showed only a small portion of the surface of the coelashark cell, with more detail showing up slowly as the tunneling array microscope moved across the surface.

The high-resolution screen showed a complex pattern on the surface—the genetic code of the coelashark. As she sat down at the console, Josephine brought her and Deirdre up to date.

"Little Purple believes that the genetic code pattern on this liver cell is identical to that on the worm."

"I would suspect that all life-forms on Zulu have similar patterns for many of their functions, so it isn't surprising that the patterns would be *similar*," said Cinnamon. "How does he know they're *identical*?"

☐I remember,☐ said Little Purple with confidence. ☐This bit is pattern for length of leg. It is same on worm. Worm and coelashark same.☐

"You remembered?" exclaimed Cinnamon, stunned again by the magnitude of the intelligence of the flouwen. "Is he right, Josephine?"

"Yes, dearie. The genetic pattern on the single-knobbed cell of the worm is identical to *one* of the knobs on the double-lobed cell of the coelashark."

"But how about the other knob?"

"That is identical to the worms in the vermicyst who have the other genetic pattern."

"So," remarked Deirdre, her green eyes wide with discovery, "one wee worm is just like one half of a coelashark cell, while the other is just like the other half. The coelashark has a diploid cell carrying two different copies of the genetic pattern, while the wee worms are monoploid—carrying only half of the genetic information of the coelashark."

"The worms in the vermicyst are the *sperm* of the coelashark," exclaimed Cinnamon.

"Or *eggs*," corrected Deirdre. "Or something neither sperm nor egg. We cannot assume earthlike attributes for alien creatures."

"What's going on?" asked Sam, who had wandered by.

"We've found the sex organ for this coelashark," replied Cinnamon. "It's the vermicyst." She quickly explained what they had learned.

Sam chuckled, "So when an icerug eats a vermicyst, it's like a cowboy eating a 'prairie oyster.'"

"But," said Cinnamon, "we don't know how it is used, or where it goes into the receiving coelashark, or how it produces more coelasharks, or why it makes icerugs sick, or why icerugs eat them in the first place."

"Perhaps the icerug contributes by disseminating the sperm cells over a wide area," suggested Sam.

"Questions we have," Deirdre concluded. "Facts are harder to come by. The truth may be far stranger than we can guess."

Katrina finally looked up from her console, where she had been imaging the cells of the coelashark that had produced the pus and the infant icerug.

"I've learned something else that may help. It took me a while, since I chose the wrong half of the coelashark cell to scan first, but now it's clear." Deirdre's screen blinked as the image she had been looking at was replaced by the contents of Katrina's screen. There were two images of two double-knobbed cells.

"On the top of the screen is a cell from the pus, which is exactly the same as a cell from the baby icerug that Deirdre caught."

"It caught me," objected Deirdre.

"On the bottom of the screen is a cell from the coelashark that produced the pus and the baby icerug. Note that both patterns on the two halves of the icerug cell are the same, as is typical for an icerug cell, while the patterns on the two halves of the coelashark cell are different, as is typical for a coelashark cell. *But* . . . the pattern on one half of the coelashark cell is *identical* to the baby icerug pattern. So, the genetic pattern that defines what an icerug is also exists in the coelashark cell—at least half of it. That baby icerug *did* spontaneously generate itself—from its dead parent."

"Or half-parent," remarked Deirdre. "Curiouser and curiouser. Well, that explains where baby icerugs come from—they don't come from momma and papa icerugs—which is why the icerugs know nothing of reproduction. But, then, where do baby coelasharks come from?"

☆Look at worm I find!☆ interrupted Little Red from the habitat tank on *Victoria*. ☆It not have one knob. It have two!☆

"He's right!" exclaimed Deirdre. "It did have two knobs. Where is that vent worm?"

"I've got the image in memory," said Katrina. "Let's see . . . what did I label it?"

"I've got it, luv," said Joe helpfully, and instantly a two-knobbed worm appeared on their screens.

"That worm *is* different from the ones I looked at from the vermicyst," said Cinnamon. "Mine have a one-knobbed cell and this vent worm has two."

☆Worm is baby coelashark!☆ said Little Red.

"I was saying at the time the vent worm had a larger head," said Deirdre. "But it was hard to be sure since the video enlargements had such poor resolution. The beasties are mostly tail anyway."

"It *did* have identical banding on the tail," said Katrina.

"Which shows that it came from the vermicyst I videoed," said Deirdre. "But this wee one has had something added to it. Perhaps added during its trip through Pink-Orb."

"We have a sample of Pink-Orb's flesh," Katrina said. "I never got around to scanning it, though. I assumed it would be similar to the other icerug samples I had already scanned. It's in the storage locker on *Victoria*."

"I'll get it out and take a look," said Cinnamon. A short while later, a cell from Pink-Orb was teased out onto the microscope stage, and the tunneling array microscope started to produce an image below the image of the two-knobbed vent worm.

☆Same!☆ burst out Little Red.

"How do you know?" exclaimed Katrina in surprise. "The scan has just started."

☆Remember pattern.☆ Manipulating the icon on the edge of the taste-screen in the habitat tank, Little Red circled a small area on the two-knobbed worm. Josephine expanded the circled area. Sure enough, the genetic pattern of the two-knobbed vent worm was identical to the pattern the microscope had just obtained from Pink-Orb's cell. It wasn't long before they also determined that the genetic pattern on the other half of the vent worm cell had come from the dead coelashark that had fallen on Pink-Orb, and from which Pink-Orb had obtained the vermicyst.

"The vent worm's genetic parents were *both* an icerug and a coelashark," remarked Katrina, slightly bewildered. "But because of its diploid gene structure, it was destined to grow up as a coelashark."

"Somehow . . . some way . . ." concluded Deirdre, "Pink-Orb fertilized that worm. No wonder eating a vermicyst was pleasurable. Evolution would ensure that it was so."

"What's all the excitement?" asked Richard from the galley, yawning widely as he sugared his morning-shift coffee heavily.

"Sex," said Deirdre.

"Kinky sex," said Cinnamon over the imp link.

"Kinky rococo sex," added Katrina.

"Sounds interesting," said Richard, taking a seat on a galley stool. "Tell me all about it."

"So," concluded Deirdre, "if a mature coelashark with ripe vermicysts lands on an icerug, the icerug swallows one of the vermicysts. Then, either the icerug 'fertilizes' the worm, or the monoploid worm takes a knob from an icerug cell. In any case the single-knobbed, monoploid worm becomes a double-knobbed, diploid worm, which is evacuated unharmed through the gut of the icerug into the ocean, where it grows into a coelashark."

"So that's how baby coelasharks are made," said Richard. "Now, how about baby icerugs?"

"If the coelashark lands on empty ice and dies, each of the single-knobbed monoploid worms in the vermicyst grows from a single-knobbed cell into a double-knobbed cell, but genetically it remains a monoploid since it has only one set of gene patterns. The cells multiply then, as blobs of undifferentiated slime, until one of the cells has consumed the coelashark *and* its cyst-mates, and turns into a big pool of pus made of double-knobbed cells. At that stage it is not too different from a flouwen."

☆I not pool of pus!☆ objected Little Red, who had been listening from inside the flouwen habitat.

Deirdre continued. "The cells begin to differentiate, and specialize, forming an icerug node, and the pool of pus turns into an icerug."

"And that's how baby icerugs are made," mused Richard. "So the coelasharks and the icerugs are related."

"Truly, icerugs and the coelasharks are not two different species—despite their vastly different structures. They are just different aspects of the same species."

"Like males and females," suggested Richard. "Which is the male and which is the female?"

"More like caterpillars and butterflies," suggested Katrina.

"Neither," said Deirdre firmly. "They are their own example—an alien example—as we should accept without forcing them to fit our own notions."

"I wonder . . ." mused Richard, "which came first? The icerug or the coelashark?"

When the three biologists explained to George what they had discovered about the complex interrelated sex life of the icerugs and the coelasharks, he was fascinated.

"Well, that sure explains a lot," he said. "Why the coelasharks committed suicide, and why the icerugs didn't know about reproduction. Now that we know the reason they behave as they do, they don't seem quite as alien as they used to." He paused to think some more and shook his head. "Nope. They are *still* alien. I don't understand the war they had—if you want to call an all-out frontal suicide attack and genocidal annihilation a war."

"Although other reasons there may be, alien and unique, there is a partial biological reason for that behavior," Deirdre replied. "The icerugs are monoploids and do not mix genes directly with other icerugs through joint sex. Other icerugs are competitors for food and, unknowingly, sex partners. So, there would be a genetically driven tendency to eliminate other icerugs instead of cooperating with them."

"Unless the other icerugs were very closely related, so that you shared many of the same genes, as is probably true for these physically isolated geyser communities," added Cinnamon.

"I see . . . I think," replied George. "But how does an icerug tell if another icerug is related or not?"

"Taste," said Katrina. "Remember the tasting ceremony that the local association held for the foundling Green-Streak? If the little icerug had failed that test, it would have been dinner instead of the latest addition to the local nursery school."

"We don't know that," reproved Deirdre. "Although I admit that it is a logical supposition."

"What we need to do," said Cinnamon hopefully, "is convince the icerugs to trade vermicysts between nations. The hybrid vigor from outbreeding would benefit all the icerugs, and in a few generations, everybody would taste the same and there would be no more wars."

"And thanks to the meddling, but kind-hearted humanfolk, the icerugs would live happily ever after," said Deirdre sarcastically.

The three biologists decided to go together to explain to the icerugs of Windward City what they had learned about them and their relationship to the coelasharks. Deirdre felt that self-knowledge about the way their species reproduced would be welcome to the aliens. Katrina and Cinnamon hoped that the information would lead to exchanges of vermicysts between nations and ultimately a more peaceful coexistence, but Deirdre's sardonic references to "happily ever after" had convinced them to keep their suggestions along that line to a minimum.

Accordingly, they presented themselves to Green-Eye, the Convener of the Center of Medical Studies, who gathered together a number of the lecturers at the center and their students. They all listened politely to Deirdre's commendably brief description of their own life cycle. Cinnamon felt an aura of disbelief when Deirdre began, but sensed an exciting change in the attitude of the icerugs as Katrina displayed microscopic images and other pictures on electrorase prints. Oddly, the really convincing pictures were the color photographs of the decaying coelashark oozing pus and the infant icerug. The icerug scientists studied them carefully, their highly discriminating color sense enabling them to see that the pus and the infant were the same color. This made it easier for their acceptance of the microscope images of the individual cells taken from both, showing that they had identical genetic patterns—and that the decaying coelashark had indeed changed into an icerug.

They had more difficulty with the idea of being part of the reproduction of the coelasharks, however, since the biologists had no photos to show them, only microscopic images of "virgin" worms taken from a vermicyst, and the single "pregnant" worm that Little Red had captured near Pink-Orb's waste vent.

"So, somewhere in the body of an icerug, the wee creature from the vermicyst is changed from a single-knobbed cell, with only half of the genes needed to make a coelashark, to a double-knobbed cell with a full complement of coelashark genes. The second half of the gene set is obtained, in some unknown fashion, from the icerug as the worm passes through. We cannot fathom how, or where, or when, it is done."

Cinnamon interpolated, "It is a mystery! Perhaps with further study, you can discover the answer."

"The altered worm leaves your body," continued Deirdre, "and swims to the sea floor. Here, the worms who survive grow large and strong, and live out their lives as coelasharks. As they mature, vermicysts form within them. At the correct biological time, coinciding with a massive geyser eruption, the coelasharks move instinctively toward the event which will cause their own deaths—but ensure the survival of their kind."

"And that works, for them," said Cinnamon, "because if you icerugs find the vermicysts and eat them, there will be more coelasharks. But it works for you, too, because if there are too few icerugs clustered around a geyser, the coelashark does not land on an icerug and so the vermicysts stay inside. The little worms then survive on their own, consuming the dead coelashark and each other until the last grows into an infant icerug."

"Which you find, and raise, and add to the community, thus increasing the icerug population!" said Katrina triumphantly.

There was a long silence as the icerugs considered what the three humans had told them. Finally, Green-Eye broke the silence. "You have presented a very interesting conjecture. It will most certainly provide for lengthy discussions in our Center of Medical Studies meetings for many cycles to come."

"It seemed extremely involved and convoluted to me," objected one of the more beribboned and elder lecturers. "The Theory of Spontaneous Reproduction is a much simpler explanation for the origin of younglings than this conjecture that the humans have hypothesized."

"It isn't a conjecture! It's the *truth*!" whispered Katrina, upset. Joe was wise enough not to translate her words for the aliens.

"Hush," warned Deirdre. "The idea is there, let the creatures develop it or no, as they will!"

The last several days of the mission were filled with small but important duties, and all of the crew were busy. Reports, videos, further consultations with the icerugs on points of culture and function—and, for Deirdre and

David, the poignant joy of hearing, once more, the huge pipe organ, looking like it had been made of crystal and sounding more majestic than anything on Earth. The whole crew stood, awed, as the mighty notes swelled and echoed through the Great Meeting Hall during the farewell ceremony. The new Presider, a sapphire-colored icerug with an eye to match, stood with them, as did Green-Eye. When the music ended, the humans, flouwen, and icerugs looked at each other, and George spoke a brief farewell.

"We'll see you again before we go," said George, "but as we are all here at once, I should like to thank you for all you have taught us."

"We are glad of your visit," responded the young Presider seriously. "We have learned things from you. We can now enjoy music from this grand instrument, certainly a vast improvement upon your primitive model. We know how to make paper, although it is usually too much trouble. The batteries we have also constructed, although they are heavy and are only used on our occasional trips deep below the surface. And we are interested to hear your conjectures about our origins, although even if the discussions at the Center for Medical Studies eventually conclude that they are true, they won't make much difference to our daily lives." There was a pause.

"And that's *all*?" Shirley asked, dismayed. But Deirdre's heart sang again. They had interfered, but not too much.

Back on *Victoria*, Shirley, George, and Katrina, with Josephine's assistance, were readying the Ascent Propulsion Stage of the rocket for takeoff and discussing the disposal of the *Dragonfly* airplane.

"I know it was designed, deliberately, to be used for exploration and then discarded," complained Shirley, "but it seems wasteful, even though I've taken every removable scrap out of it." She had, indeed, on the grounds of "you never know," even removed such items as light fixtures, fan motors, and analytical instrument modules from the workwall, and stowed them in the overflowing storage compartments of the *Victoria*. "We're still throwing away a perfectly good computer in Joe, and all the flying capability of the plane."

"I know," said George. "And I did have one idea. Now that we've seen that the icerugs can operate independently of their carpets, it wouldn't be too difficult to teach them how to interact with Joe and fly the airplane."

"Yes!" interrupted Shirley. "That's terrific! They can use the plane to go to foreign cities, trade vermicysts back and forth to promote international harmony, and find out more about the rest of the planet!"

"Of course, without the support of their carpets, they'll need to take along a lot of food," said Katrina.

"And there's a lot more to flying a plane than just turning on the computer," said George more cautiously. "I'd hate to have them get caught in one of the storms here and crash. And the thought that they *might* would haunt me."

"It wouldn't take much time to put a complete instruction program into Joe, would it?" asked Katrina eagerly. She liked the idea of leaving the icerugs some really tangible gift.

"Actually, there's more to it than that," said Shirley seriously. "There *is* a nuclear reactor in the tail. Although it's well shielded, it still emits a significant amount of radiation, and the longer they run the plane the worse it gets, and we have no idea how sensitive they are to radiation."

"And I've just thought of something else," said George firmly. "Or, rather, someone. Deirdre."

Katrina's enthusiasm for the project slumped.

"We stay with the original plan," said George. "Joe will fly the plane to a distant, uninhabited part of the planet, like the south pole, and stay there. The icerugs will be told it is there, and if they ever develop enough technology to find it and use it, they'll be ready. But we won't just hand it over—that would be irresponsible." The others knew George's feelings about responsibility and were resigned. Katrina, indeed, decided not even to mention the idea to Cinnamon, and especially not to Deirdre—no sense in asking for trouble!

George settled into the communications console for a consultation with *Prometheus*. Jinjur's face appeared on the screen, and she sounded eager to have the explorers, especially George, return.

"We've monitored all your reports, of course," she said. "And studied all the images. The icerugs and coelasharks both look to me like something out of a nightmare! You'll be glad to leave those genocidal killers and baby-eaters behind, eh?"

George protested, "No! They're wonderful, the icerugs—amazingly creative, and gentle—you forget they're not really human . . . and, of course, that's a mistake. But I really learned to admire them. How's Nels doing?" he asked, to change the subject.

"Fine!" answered Jinjur, and chortled. "You won't believe those new legs he's got, George. They're long and strong—beautifully muscled—and the man is now nearly six feet tall. But the funny thing is that his legs are as *hairy* as . . . as a hobbit! Long, gold-colored fur all over them, even on his toes! But he doesn't care—he's totally thrilled and refuses to wear long pants or shoes, just marches proudly around in shorts, beaming from ear to ear!"

George laughed and shook his head in amazement,

rejoicing that the experiment had worked so well. Suddenly, he was eager to get back to the giant spaceship and all the people he had been separated from for so long.

In the lab section on the engineering deck, the three biologists were carefully organizing their collection of specimens, putting small amounts of representative tissues in insulated cases for permanent storage aboard *Prometheus*, and putting aside most of the tissues to discard here on their native world. George came down the passway ladder to tell them Jinjur's description of Nels. Typically, Katrina giggled. Deirdre considered the picture and smiled, and then forgot it—she'd probably not even notice the new legs. But Cinnamon was thoughtful— would this change the man's personality? And if so, how? She had several private hopes.

"It's pleased the flouwen will be, then." Deirdre recalled that it was the flouwen's vital analysis of Nels' genetic map which led to the limb-growing process.

"How's Little Red? Calmed down, I hope?"

"Yes, thank goodness," said Cinnamon. "What with his accident, and then the refusal of the coelasharks to listen to him, I think he's about fed up with this world. But, then, all three of them are ready to go. It's hard for them to be so idle, cooped up in that small habitat tank, while we get the ship ready."

Katrina snorted. "I think they handle it very well," she said tartly. "When I last spoke to them, they asked me a question about the human genome, and Little Red was quite rude when I didn't know the answer!"

"What'd he say?" asked Deirdre curiously.

"Never mind," said Katrina stiffly. "Now, with Josephine's help, I'll fold up the analytical bench into the workwall, if you two want to do something else."

Cinnamon turned to take the unwanted tissue samples to the airlock, while Deirdre climbed up the passway ladder to the galley to inspect the remaining foodstuffs. There were ample provisions for their last hours here—although most of the high-protein snacks had gone—probably into Arielle, thought Deirdre. There was still a supply of rich material, in the form of chemically synthesized chocolate and algae-butter, and soon Deirdre had transformed these into a magnificent chocolate cake, dense and dark, still warmly fragrant as she glazed the top with a thin clear frosting. "To keep it moist," she told herself, "although why I'm thinking that will be a problem . . . " as she looked at the faces that seemed to be constantly drifting casually by the galley door. Later, sitting in the view lounge, George outlined their plans over large chunks of the confection, accompanied by cold algae-milk.

"We leave at seventeen-hundred," he said. "David and Arielle? Joe should have flown the *Dragonfly* to the South Pole by now. You'd better check in with Joe through the commsats and take him through the shutdown procedure."

Arielle smiled sadly, and put down her portion of cake, barely nibbled. "Hate saying good-bye," she said.

"We all do," said George kindly. "But I'm looking forward to seeing Nels' legs! And Jinjur says John is completely well, too. They're all getting interested in our next target, Zuni—the reports from the landers are exciting!"

"I remember seeing one of the early pictures," said Thomas. "It's going to be a colorful world: blue oceans, green islands, and sandy beaches. It'll be a real break after this colorless place. I've just gone through my electropix collection, and it looks like I could have done the whole damn series in black and white."

"And my recordings of the icerug music sound like I had only the bass response control turned up," remarked David.

"The ice core sample variations were in a narrow range, too. Indicating a very stable climate," said Sam. "Highly important to the creatures who live here, but peculiarly uninteresting."

"It really is an alien world," said Shirley carefully, with a glance at Deirdre. "Stranger than anything I ever dreamt of. But I'm glad I had the chance to see it."

Deirdre's green eyes lifted, and she stared long into Shirley's. Then she nodded. "Forever grateful I'll be, to have walked on that surface," she said, the soft lilt making the words almost a song. "Time out of mind, I'll not forget that dark beauty, changing and terrible. And the creatures *of* that world, and right for it. I was there, and the memories of it will travel with me for all the rest of my days."

Jinjur's strong voice, coming in over their imps from *Prometheus* high above them in the sky, broke the silence which followed. "Memories are fine, but what I need are written reports. The Phase III reports on this portion of the mission are due for transmission back to Earth in one month. Do you have your first drafts done yet?"

Technical Report BSE-TR-70-0342
December 2070

BARNARD STAR EXPEDITION
PHASE III REPORT
VOLUME I—EXECUTIVE SUMMARY

Submitted by:

Virginia Jones, Major General, GUSSM
Commander, Barnard Star Expedition

INTRODUCTION

This Volume I is the Executive Summary of the information collected to date by the Barnard Star Expedition, especially the more recent information gathered during Phase III of the expedition, which included a landing on the surface of Zulu, the innermost large moon of the giant planet Gargantua. This Executive Summary contains a brief condensation of the extensive amounts of technical material to be found in the companion volume, Volume II —Technical Publications. Volume II, as well as similar publications that followed Phase I and Phase II, contain a series of technical papers on various aspects of the mission, each of which runs to hundreds of pages, including tables. These papers are intended for publication either in archival videojournals or as scientific or technical monovids, and contain extensive amounts of numerical data as well as many specialized terms that would be understood only by experts in those particular fields.

For the benefit of the reader of this volume, who is assumed to be interested only in a brief summary in non-technical language without extensive numerical detail, the more precise specialized words and phrases used in the technical papers have been replaced in this summary with common words, and most of the numerical data have either been eliminated or rounded off to two or three places. In addition, to assist those readers of this Executive Summary who may not have read the previous Phase I and Phase II summaries, pertinent background material from those reports has been included here.

The three major topics covered in this Executive Summary are covered in three sections:

Section 1. The performance of the technical equipment

used to carry out the Barnard Star Expedition and the recent mission to the surface of Zulu, the exploration target of Phase III.

Section 2. The pertinent astronomical data concerning the Barnard star planetary system, with specific emphasis on Zulu, the innermost large moon of the Barnard planet Gargantua.

Section 3. The biology of the aliens discovered in the Barnard system, specifically our exploration companions, the flouwen from the Barnard double-planet Roche-world, and the alien life-forms recently found on Zulu.

SECTION 1
EQUIPMENT PERFORMANCE

Prepared by:
Shirley Everett—Chief Engineer
Anthony Roma, Captain, GUSSF—Chief Lightsail
 Pilot
Thomas St. Thomas, Captain, GUSAF—Chief
 Lander Pilot
Arielle Trudeau—Chief Aircraft Pilot

Equipment Configuration at Launch

The expedition sent to the Barnard star system consisted of a crew of twenty persons and their consumables, a habitat for their long journey through interstellar space, and four landing rockets for visiting the various planets and moons. Each rocket also carried a nuclear powered vertical-takeoff-and-landing (VTOL) exploration aerospace plane.

This payload, massing 3000 tons, was carried by a large reflective lightsail 300 kilometers in diameter. The payload lightsail is of very lightweight construction consisting of a thin film of finely perforated metal stretched over a sparse frame of wires held in tension by the slow rotation of the lightsail about its axis. Although the lightsail averages only one-tenth of a gram per square meter of area, the total mass of the payload lightsail is over 7000 tons, for a total mass of payload and lightsail of 10,000 tons. Light pressure from photons reflected off the lightsail provides propulsion for the lightsail and its payload. The lightsail used retroreflected coherent laser photons from the solar system to decelerate the payload at the Barnard system, while, for propulsion within the Barnard system, it uses incoherent photons from the star Barnard.

At the time of launch from the solar system, the 300-kilometer payload lightsail was surrounded by a larger retroreflective ring lightsail, 1000 kilometers in diameter, with a hole in the center where the payload lightsail was attached. The ring lightsail had a mass of 72,000 tons, giving a total launch weight of lightsails and payload of over 82,000 tons.

Interstellar Laser Propulsion System

The laser power needed to push the 82,000-ton interstellar vehicle at an acceleration of one percent of Earth gravity was just over 1300 terawatts. This was obtained from an array of 1000 laser generators orbiting around Mercury. Each laser generator used a thirty-kilometer diameter lightweight reflector that collected 6.5 terawatts of sunlight. The reflector was designed to pass most of the solar spectrum and only reflect into its solar-pumped laser the 1.5 terawatts of sunlight that was at the right wavelength for the laser to use. The lasers were quite efficient, so each of the 1000

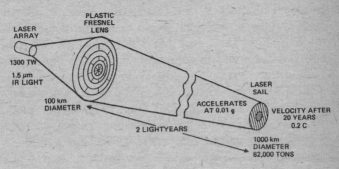

ACCELERATION PHASE

LASER
ARRAY

1300 TW

1.5 μm
IR LIGHT

PLASTIC
FRESNEL
LENS

100 km
DIAMETER

2 LIGHTYEARS

ACCELERATES
AT 0.01 g

LASER
SAIL

VELOCITY AFTER
20 YEARS
0.2 C

1000 km
DIAMETER
82,000 TONS

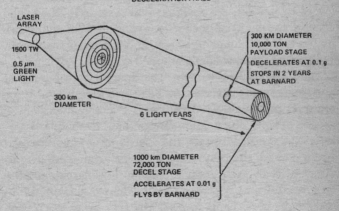

DECELERATION PHASE

LASER
ARRAY

1500 TW

0.5 μm
GREEN
LIGHT

300 km
DIAMETER

6 LIGHTYEARS

300 KM DIAMETER
10,000 TON
PAYLOAD STAGE

DECELERATES AT 0.1 g

STOPS IN 2 YEARS
AT BARNARD

1000 km DIAMETER
72,000 TON
DECEL STAGE

ACCELERATES AT 0.01 g

FLYS BY BARNARD

Figure 1—Interstellar laser propulsion system.
[*J. Spacecraft*, Vol. 21, No. 2, pp. 187-195 (1984)]

lasers generated 1.3 terawatts, to produce the total of 1300 terawatts needed to send the expedition on its way.

The transmitter lens for the laser propulsion system consisted of rings of thin plastic film stretched over a spiderweblike circular wire mesh held in tension by slow rotation about the mesh axis. The mesh was designed with circular zones of decreasing width that were alternately empty or covered with plastic film whose thickness was chosen to produce a phase delay of one half a wavelength in the laser light. This huge Fresnel zone plate, 100 kilometers in diameter, acted as the final lens for the laser beam coming from Mercury. The relative configuration of the lasers, lens, and lightsails during the launch and deceleration phases can be seen in Figure 1.

The accelerating lasers were left on for eighteen years while the spacecraft continued to gain speed. The lasers were turned off, back in the solar system, in 2044. The last of the light from the lasers traveled for two more years before it finally reached the interstellar spacecraft. Thrust at the spacecraft stopped in 2046, just short of twenty years after launch. The spacecraft was now at two light-years distance from the Sun and four light-years from Barnard, and was traveling at twenty percent of the speed of light. The mission now entered the coast phase.

For the next 20 years, the spacecraft and its drugged crew coasted through interstellar space, covering a light-year every five years, while back in the solar system, the transmitter lens was increased in diameter from 100 to 300 kilometers. Then, in 2060, the laser array was turned on again at a tripled frequency. The combined beams from the lasers filled the 300-kilometer diameter Fresnel lens and beamed out toward the distant star. After two years, the lasers were turned off and used elsewhere. The two-light-year-long pulse of high energy laser light traveled across the six light-years to the Barnard system, where it caught up with the spacecraft as it was 0.2 light-years away from its destination. Before the pulse of laser light reached the interstellar vehicle, the revived crew had separated the lightsail into two pieces. The inner 300-kilometer diameter lightsail carrying the crew and payload was detached and turned around to face the 1000-kilometer diameter ring-shaped retro-reflector, which was now acting like a mirror. The ring mirror had computer-controlled actuators to give it the proper optical curvature. When the laser beam arrived, most of the laser beam struck the larger ring mirror, bounced off the reflective surface, and was focused back onto the smaller payload lightsail as shown in the lower portion of Figure 1. The laser light accelerated the massive 72,000-ton ring mirror at one percent of Earth gravity and during the two-year period the ring mirror increased its velocity slightly. The same laser power focused back on the much lighter payload lightsail, however, decelerated the smaller lightsail at nearly ten percent of Earth gravity. In the two years that the laser beam was on, the payload lightsail and its cargo of humans and exploration vehicles slowed from its interstellar velocity of twenty percent of the speed of light and came to rest in the Barnard system. Meanwhile, the ring mirror continued on into deep space, its function completed.

Prometheus

The interstellar lightsail vehicle that took the exploration crew to the Barnard system was named *Prometheus*, the bringer of light. Its configuration is shown in Figure 2, and consists of a large lightsail supporting a payload consisting of the crew, their habitat, and their exploration

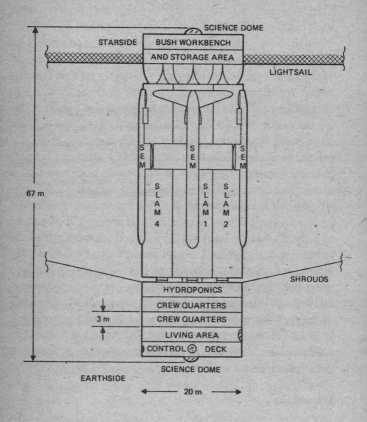

Figure 2—Prometheus

vehicles. A major fraction of the payload volume was
taken up by four exploration vehicle units. Each unit consisted of a planetary lander vehicle called the Surface
Lander and Ascent Module (SLAM), holding within itself
a winged Surface Excursion Module (SEM).

The largest component of *Prometheus* is the lightsail,
1000 kilometers in diameter at launch, and 300 kilometers in diameter during the deceleration and exploration
phases of the mission. The frame of the lightsail consists
of a hexagonal mesh trusswork made of wires held in tension by a slow rotation of the lightsail around its axis.
Attached to the mesh wires are large ultrathin triangular
sheets of perforated reflective aluminum film. The perfo-
rations in the film are made smaller than a wavelength of
light, so they reduce the weight of the film without significantly affecting the reflective properties.

Running all the way through the center of *Prometheus*
is a four-meter diameter, sixty-meter long shaft with an
elevator platform that runs up and down the shaft to supply transportation between decks. Capping the top of
Prometheus on the side toward the direction of travel is a
huge double-decked compartmented area that holds the
various consumables for use during the 50-year mission,
the workshops for the spaceship's computer motile, and
an airlock for access to the lightsail. At the very center of
the starside deck is the starside science dome, a three-
meter diameter thick glass hemisphere that was used by
the star-science instruments to investigate the Barnard
star system as *Prometheus* was moving toward it.

At the base of *Prometheus* are five crew decks. Each
deck is a flat cylinder twenty meters in diameter and three
meters thick. The control deck at the bottom contains an
airlock and the engineering, communication, science, and
command consoles to operate the lightcraft and the

science instruments. In the center of the control deck is the earthside science dome, a three-meter diameter hemisphere in the floor, surrounded by a thick circular waist-high wall containing racks of scientific instruments that look out through the dome or directly into the vacuum through holes in the deck. Above the control deck is the living area deck containing the communal dining area, kitchen, exercise room, medical facilities, two small video theaters, and a lounge with a large sofa facing a three-by-four meter oval view window. The next two decks are the crew quarters decks that are fitted out with individual suites for each of the twenty crew members. Each suite has a private bathroom, sitting area, work area, and a separate bedroom. The wall separating the bedroom from the sitting area is a floor-to-ceiling viewwall that can be seen from either side. There is another viewscreen in the ceiling above the bed.

Above the two crew quarters decks is the hydroponics deck. This contains the hydroponics gardens and the tissue cultures to supply fresh food to the crew. The water in the hydroponics tanks provide additional radiation shielding for the crew quarters below. In the ceilings of four of the corridors running between the hydroponics tanks there are air locks that allow access to the four Surface Lander and Ascent Module (SLAM) spacecraft that are clustered around the central shaft, stacked upside down between the hydroponics deck and the storage deck. Each SLAM rocket is forty-six meters long and six meters in diameter.

Surface Lander and Ascent Module

The Surface Lander and Ascent Module (SLAM) is a brute-force chemical rocket designed to get the planetary

exploration crew and the Surface Excursion Module
(SEM) down to the surface of the various worlds in the
Barnard system. The upper portion of the SLAM, the
Ascent Propulsion Stage (APS), is designed to take the
crew off the world and return them back to *Prometheus*
at the end of the surface exploration mission. As is shown
in Figure 3, the basic shape of the SLAM is a tall cylinder
with four descent engines and two main tanks.

The Surface Lander and Ascent Module has a great
deal of similarity to the Lunar Excursion Module (LEM)
used in the Apollo lunar landings, except that instead of
being optimized for a specific airless body, the Surface
Lander and Ascent Module had to be general purpose
enough to land on planetoids that could be larger than
the Moon, and have significant atmospheres. The three
legs of the Surface Lander and Ascent Module are the
minimum for stability, and the weight penalties for any
more were felt to be prohibitive.

The Surface Lander and Ascent Module (SLAM) carries within itself the Surface Excursion Module (SEM),
an aerospace plane that is almost as large as the lander.
Embedded in the side of the SLAM is a long, slim crease
that just fits the outer contours of the SEM. The seals on
the upper portions were designed to have low gas leakage
so that the SLAM crew could transfer to the SEM with
minor loss of air.

The upper portion of the SLAM consists of the crew
living quarters plus the Ascent Propulsion Stage. The
upper deck is a three-meter high cylinder eight meters in
diameter. On its top is a forest of electromagnetic anten-
nas for everything from laser communication directly to
Earth (almost six light-years away) to omniantennas that
broadcast the present position of the ship to the communications relay satellites in orbit around the planetoids.

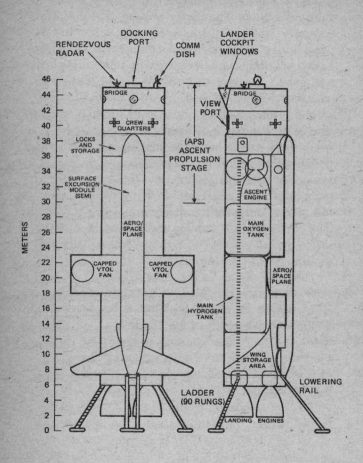

Figure 3—Surface Lander and Ascent Module (SLAM)

The upper deck contains the main docking port at the center. Its exit is upward, into the hydroponics deck of *Prometheus*. Around the upper lock are the control consoles for the landing and docking maneuvers and the electronics for the surface science that can be carried out at the SLAM landing site.

The middle deck contains the personal quarters for the crew with individual sleeping cubicles, a shower that works as well in zero gee as in gravity, and two zero-gee toilets. After the SEM crew has left the main lander, the partitions between the sleeping cubicles can be rearranged to provide a more horizontal orientation for the four crew members left in the SLAM.

The galley and lounge are the relaxation facilities for the crew. The lounge has a video center facing inward where the crew can watch either videochips or six-year-old programs from Earth, and a large sofa facing a large viewport window that looks out on the alien scenery from a height of about forty meters. The lower deck of the SLAM contains the engineering facilities. Most of the space is given to suit or equipment storage, and a complex airlock. One of the airlock exits leads to the upper end of the Jacob's Ladder. The other leads to the boarding port for the Surface Excursion Module.

Since the primary purpose of the SLAM is to put the Surface Excursion Module on the surface of the double-planet, some characteristics of the lander are not optimized for crew convenience. The best instance is the "Jacob's Ladder," a long, widely-spaced set of rungs that start on one landing leg of the SLAM and work their way up the side of the cylindrical structure to the lower exit lock door. The "Jacob's Ladder" was never meant to be used, since the crew expected to be able to use a powered hoist to reach the top of the ship. In the emergency that arose during the first expedition to Rocheworld, however, the "Jacob's Ladder" proved to be a good, though slow, route up into the ship. The airlock design, however, was found to be faulty. With the lock full of people, the outer door cannot be closed. Other than this flaw, the SLAM performed well on both expeditions to Rocheworld and the recent expedition to the ice-planet Zulu.

One leg of the SLAM is part of the "Jacob's Ladder," while another leg acts as the lowering rail for the Surface Excursion Module. The wings of the Surface Excursion Module are chopped off in midspan just after the VTOL fans. The remainder of each wing is stacked as interleaved sections on either side of the tail section of the Surface Excursion Module. Once the Surface Excursion Module has its wings attached, it is a completely independent vehicle with its own propulsion and life-support system.

Surface Excursion Module

The Surface Excursion Module (SEM) is a specially designed aerospace vehicle capable of flying as a plane in a planetary atmosphere or as a rocket for short hops through empty space. An exterior view of the SEM is shown in Figure 4. The human crew gave the name *Dragonfly* to the SEM because of its long wings, eyelike scanner ports at the front, and its ability to hover.

For flying long distances in any type of planetary atmosphere, including those which do not have oxygen in them, propulsion for the SEM comes from the heating of the atmosphere with a nuclear reactor powering a jet-bypass turbine. For short hops outside the atmosphere, the engine draws upon a tank of monopropellant that not only provides reaction mass for the nuclear reactor to work on, but also makes its own contribution to the rocket plenum pressure and temperature.

The SEM proved to be an ideal exploration vehicle for the conditions on Rocheworld. Rocheworld had two large lobes to explore that are equivalent in land area to the North American continent. Although there are excellent mapping and exploration instruments onboard, these have distance limitations, and two surface expeditions involving many long criss-cross journeys over both lobes were needed to fully determine the true nature of the double-planet. The general flexibility of the SEM design, which with its onboard semi-intelligent computer is capable of flying itself, is attested to by the fact that the flouwen are able to operate the SEM by themselves. The SEM also performed well on the recent expedition to Zulu.

A nuclear reactor could be a significant radiation hazard, but the one in the aerospace plane is well designed. Its inner core is covered with a thick layer of thermoelectric generators that turn the heat coming through the casing into the electrical power needed to operate the computers and scientific instruments aboard the plane. A number of metric tons of shielding protect the crew quarters from radiation, but the real protection is in a system design that has the entire power and propulsion complex at the rear of the plane, far from the crew quarters. Since the source of the plane's power (and heat) is in the aft end, it was logical to use the horizontal and vertical stabilizer surfaces in the tail section as heat exchangers. Because most of the weight (the reactor, shielding, and fuel) is at the rear of the plane, the placement of the wings on the SEM are back from the wing position on a normal airplane of its size.

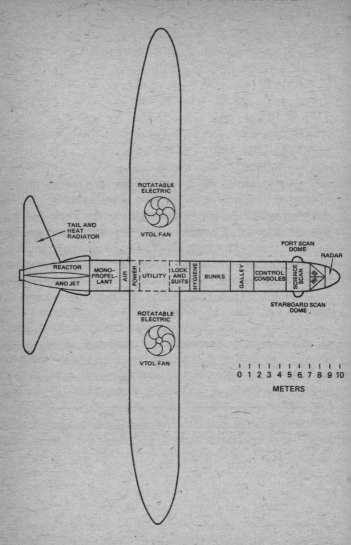

Figure 4—Exterior view of Surface Excursion Module
(SEM)

Although the SEM can use its rockets to travel through space, and can fly through practically any atmosphere with its nuclear jet at nearly sonic speeds, the components that made it indispensable in surface exploration work are the large electrically powered vertical takeoff and landing (VTOL) fans built into its wings. These fans take over from the more efficient jet at low speeds to lower the SEM to the surface.

The details of the human-inhabited portion of the SEM are shown in Figure 5. At the front of the aerospace plane is the cockpit with the radar dome in front of it. Just behind the cockpit is the science instrument section, including port and starboard automatic scanner platforms carrying a number of imaging sensors covering a wide portion of the electromagnetic spectrum. Next are the operating consoles for the science instruments and the computer, where most of the work is done. Further back are the galley and food storage lockers. This constitutes the working quarters where the crew spent most of their waking hours.

The corridor is blocked at this point by a privacy curtain which leads to the crew quarters. Since the crew would be together for long periods, the need for nearly private quarters was imperative, so the SEM was designed so each crew member has a private bunk with a large personal storage volume attached. Aft of the bunks are the shower and toilet.

At the rear of the aerospace plane are the airlock, suit storage, air-conditioning equipment, and a "work wall" that is the province of the Christmas "Branch," a major subtree of the robotic Christmas Bush motile that went along with the aerospace plane on its excursions. Not designed for use by a human, the work wall is a compact, floor-to-ceiling rack containing a multitude of housekeep-

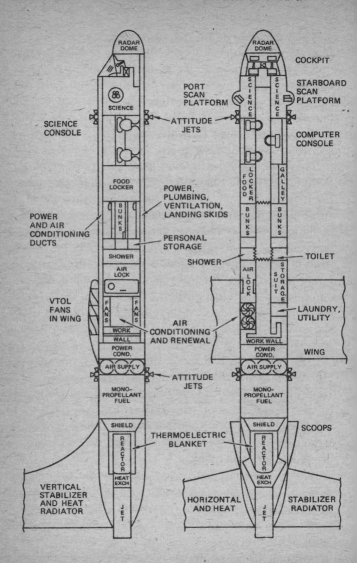

Figure 5—Interior of Surface Excursion Module (SEM)

ing, analyzing, and synthesizing equipment that the Christmas Branch uses to aid the crew in their research, and to keep the humans and the SEM functioning. Behind the work wall are the power conditioning equipment, the liquified air supply, and a large tank of monopropellant. All this mass helps the lead metal shadow shield in front of the nuclear reactor keep the radiation levels down in the inhabited portions of the aerospace plane.

Christmas Bush

The hands and eyes of the semi-intelligent computers that run the various vehicles on the expedition are embodied in a repair and maintenance motile used by the computer, popularly called the "Christmas Bush" because of the twinkling laser lights on the bushy multibranched structure. The bushlike design for the robot has a parallel in the development of life-forms on Earth. The first form of life on Earth was a worm. The sticklike shape was poorly adapted for manipulation or even locomotion. These sticklike animals then grew smaller sticks, called legs, and the animals could walk, although they were still poor at manipulation. Then the smaller sticks grew yet smaller sticks, and hands with manipulating fingers evolved.

The Christmas Bush is a manifold extension of this concept. The motile has a six-"armed" main body that repeatedly hexfurcates into copies one-third the size of itself, finally ending up with millions of near-microscopic cilia. Each subsegment has a small amount of intelligence, but is mostly motor and communication system. The segments communicate with each other and transmit power down through the structure by means of light-emitting and light-collecting semiconductor diodes. Blue laser beams are used to closely monitor any human beings near the motile, while red and yellow beams are used to monitor the rest of the room. The green beams are used to transmit power and information from one portion of the Christmas Bush to another, giving the metallic surface of the multibranched structure a deep green sheen. It is the colored red, yellow, and blue lasers sparkling from the various branches of the greenly glowing Christmas Bush that give the motile the appearance of a Christmas tree. The central computer in the spacecraft is the primary controller of the motile, communicating with the various portions of the Christmas Bush through color-coded laser beams. It takes a great deal of computational power to operate the many limbs of the Christmas Bush, but the built-in "reflex" intelligence in the various levels of segmentation lessen the load on the central computer.

The Christmas Bush shown in Figure 6 is in its "one gee" form. Three of the "trunks" form "legs," one the "head," and two the "arms." The head portions are "bushed" out to give the detector diodes in the sub-branches a three-dimensional view of the space around it. One arm ends with six "hands," demonstrating the manipulating capability of the Christmas Bush and its subportions. The other arm is in its maximally collapsed form. The six "limbs," being one-third the diameter of the trunk, can fit into a circle with the same diameter as the trunk, while the thirty-six "branches," being one-ninth the diameter of the trunk, also fit into the same circle. This is true all the way down to the sixty million cilia at the lowest level. An interesting property of the Christmas Bush is its ability to change size. Just as a human can go from a crouch to an arms outstretched position and change in height from less than one meter to almost three meters,

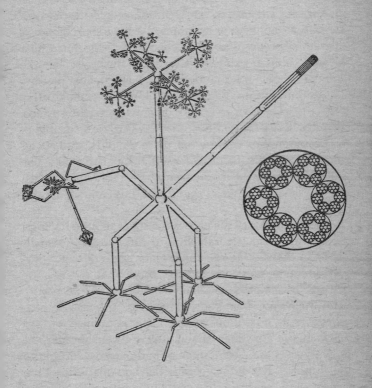

Figure 6—The Christmas Bush

the Christmas Bush can shrink or stretch by almost a factor of five, from a short, squat bush to a tall, slender tree.

The "hands" of the Christmas Bush have capabilities that go way beyond those of the human hand. The Christmas Bush can stick a "hand" inside a delicate piece of equipment and, using its lasers as a light source and its detectors as eyes, rearrange the parts inside for a near instantaneous repair. The Christmas Bush also has the ability to detach portions of itself to make smaller motiles. These can walk up the walls and along the ceilings using tiny cilia to hold onto microscopic cracks in the surface. The smaller twigs on the Christmas Bush are capable of very rapid motion. In free-fall, these rapidly beating twigs allow the motile to propel itself through the air. The speed of motion of the smaller cilia is rapid enough that the motiles can generate sound and thus can talk directly with the humans.

Each member of the crew has a small subtree or "imp" that stays constantly with him or her. The imp usually rides on the shoulder of the human where it can "whisper" in the human's ear, although some of the women use the brightly colored laser-illuminated imp as a decorative hair ornament. In addition to the imp's primary purpose of providing a continuous personal communication link between the crew member and the central computer, the imp also acts as a health monitor and personal servant for the human. The imps go with the humans inside their spacesuits, and more than one human life was saved by an imp detecting and repairing a suit failure or patching a leak. The imps can also exit the spacesuit, if desired, by worming their way out through the air supply hoses.

SECTION 2
BARNARD SYSTEM ASTRONOMICAL DATA

Prepared by:
Linda Regan—Astrophysics
Thomas St. Thomas, Captain, GUSAF—
  Astrodynamics

Barnard Planetary System

As shown in Figure 7, the Barnard planetary system
consists of the red dwarf star Barnard, the huge gas giant
planet Gargantua and its large retinue of moons, and an
unusual corotating double-planet called Rocheworld.
Gargantua is in a standard near-circular planetary orbit
around Barnard, while Rocheworld is in a highly elliptical
orbit that takes it in very close to Barnard once every orbit, and very close to Gargantua once every three orbits.
Rocheworld comes within six gigameters of Gargantua,
just outside the orbit of Zeus, the outermost moon of
Gargantua. It has been suggested that one lobe of Rocheworld was once an outer large moon of Gargantua, while
the other lobe was a stray planetoid that interacted with
the outer Gargantuan moon to form Rocheworld in its
present orbit. Further information about Barnard, Rocheworld, and Gargantua and its moons follows:

Barnard

Barnard is a red dwarf star that is the second closest
star to the solar system after the three-star Alpha
Centauri system. Barnard was known only by the star
catalog number of +4° 3561 until 1916, when the American astronomer Edward E. Barnard measured its proper

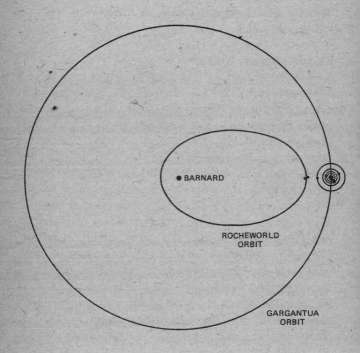

Figure 7—Barnard Planetary System

motion and found it was moving through the sky at the high rate of 10.3 seconds of arc per year, or more than half the diameter of the Moon in a century. Parallax measurements soon revealed that the star was the second closest star system. Barnard's Star (or Barnard as it is called now) can be found in the southern skies of Earth, but it is so dim it requires a telescope to see it. The data concerning Barnard follows:

Distance from Earth = 5.6×10^{16} m   (5.9 light-years)
Type = M5 Dwarf
Mass = 3.0×10^{29} kg (15% solar mass)
Radius = 8.4×10^{7} m = 84 Mm (12% solar radius)
Density = 121 g/cc (86 times solar density)
Effective Temperature = 3330 K (58% solar temperature)
Luminosity = 0.05% solar (visual); 0.37% solar (thermal)

The illumination from Barnard is not only weak because of the small size of the star, but reddish because of the low temperature. The illumination from the star is not much different in intensity and color than the illumination from a fireplace of glowing coals at midnight. Fortunately, the human eye can adjust to accommodate for both the intensity and color of the local illumination source, and unless there is artificial white-light illumination to provide contrast, most colors look quite normal under the weak, red light from the star (except for dark blue-green—which looks almost black).

Note the high density of the star compared to our Sun. This is typical of a red dwarf star. The diameter of a star is determined by a balance between gravity and internal light pressure, which in turn depends strongly on the

414 Robert L. Forward & Martha Dodson Forward

temperature. The internal light pressure of a cool red dwarf is much less than the internal light pressure of our warm yellow Sun, resulting in Barnard having a much smaller diameter and a resultant higher density than our Sun, despite having less total mass than our Sun. Because of this high density, the star Barnard is actually slightly smaller in diameter than the gas giant planet Gargantua, even though the star is forty times more massive than the planet.

Rocheworld

The unique corotating dumbbell-shaped double-planet Rocheworld consists of two planetoids that whirl about each other with a rotation period of six hours. As shown in Figure 8, the two planetoids or "lobes" of Rocheworld are so close that they are almost touching, but their spin speed is high enough that they maintain a separation of about eighty kilometers. Since their gravitational tides act upon one another, the two bodies have been stretched out until they are elongated egg shapes.

Although the two planetoids do not touch each other, they do share a common atmosphere. The resulting figure-eight configuration is called a Roche-lobe pattern after E.A. Roche, a French mathematician of the later 1880s, who calculated the effects of gravity tides on stars, planets, and moons. The word "roche" also means "rock" in French, so the dry rocky lobe of the pair of planetoids was given the name Roche, while the lobe nearly completely covered with water was named Eau after the French word for "water." The data concerning Rocheworld follows:

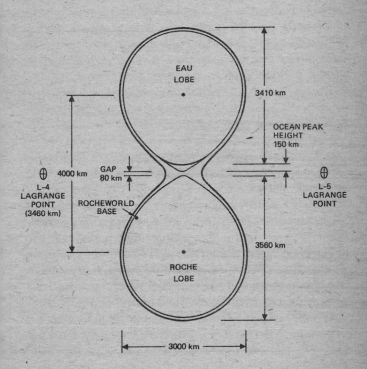

EAU
LOBE

3410 km

OCEAN PEAK
HEIGHT
150 km

GAP
80 km

4000 km

L-4
LAGRANGE
POINT
(3460 km)

ROCHEWORLD
BASE

L-5
LAGRANGE
POINT

3560 km

ROCHE
LOBE

3000 km

Figure 8—Rocheworld

Type: Co-rotating double planet
Diameters:
        Eau Lobe: 2900 by 3410 km
        Roche Lobe: 3000 by 3560 km
Separation: Centers of Mass: 4000 km
Inner Surfaces: 80 km (nominal)
Co-rotation Period = 6 h
Orbital Semimajor Axis = 18 Gm
Orbital Period = 962.4 h
              = 160 rotations (exactly)
              ≈ 40.1 Earth days
Axial Tilt = 0°

One of the unexpected findings of the mission was the
resonance between the Rocheworld "day," the Rocheworld "year," and the Gargantuan "year." The period of
the Rocheworld day is just a little over 6 hours, or one-
fourth of an Earth day, while the period of the
Rocheworld "year" is a little over 40 Earth days, and the
orbital period of Gargantua is a little over 120 days. Accurate measurements of the periods have shown that there
are exactly 160 rotations of Rocheworld about its common center to one rotation of Rocheworld in its elliptical
orbit around Barnard, while there are exactly 480 rotations of Rocheworld, or three orbits of Rocheworld
around Barnard, to one orbit of Gargantua around Barnard.

Orbits such as that of Rocheworld are usually not stable. The three-to-one resonance condition between the
Rocheworld orbit and the Gargantuan orbit usually
results in an oscillation in the orbit of the smaller body
that builds up in amplitude until the smaller body is
thrown into a different orbit or a collision occurs. Due to

Rocheworld's close approach to Barnard, however, the tides from Barnard cause a significant amount of dissipation, which stabilizes the orbit. This also supplies a great deal of heating, which keeps Rocheworld warmer than it would normally be if the heating were due to radiation from the star alone. Early in the expedition, both Rocheworld and Gargantua were "tagged" with artificial satellites carrying accurate clocks, and the planets have been tracked nearly continuously since then. The data record collected extends for over two years. The 480:160:1 resonance between the periods of Gargantua's orbit, Rocheworld's orbit, and Rocheworld's rotation, is now known to be exact to 15 places.

Rocheworld was explored extensively in landings made during Phase I and Phase II of the mission, and more detailed information about the double-planet and its interesting astrodynamics, can be found in the Phase I and Phase II reports.

Gargantua

Gargantua is a huge gas giant like Jupiter, but four times more massive. Since the parent star, Barnard, has a mass of only fifteen percent of that of our Sun, this means that the planet Gargantua is one-fortieth the mass of its star. If Gargantua had been slightly more massive, it would have turned into a star itself, and the Barnard system would have been a binary star system. Gargantua seems to have swept up into itself most of the original stellar nebula that was not used in making the star, for there are no other large planets in the system. The pertinent astronomical data about Gargantua follows:

Mass = 7.6×10^{27} kg (4 times Jupiter mass)

Density = 1.92 g/cc
Orbital Radius = 3.8×10^{10} m = 38 Gm
Orbital Period = 120.4 Earth days
        (3 times Rocheworld period)
Rotation Period = 162 h
Axial Tilt = 8°

The radius of Gargantua's orbit is less than that of Mercury. This closeness to Barnard helps compensate for the low luminosity of the star, leading to moderate temperatures on Gargantua and its moons.

Gargantuan Moon System:

There are nine major moons in the Gargantuan moon system. Their orbital and physical properties are listed in the following table. The five smaller moons are rocky, airless bodies, while the four larger moons have atmospheres and show distinctive colorings. All the Gargantuan moons are tidally locked to their primary.

Name	Solar Equiva-lent	Orbital Radius (Mm)	Orbital Period (h)	Mass (10^{20} kg)	Radius (km)	Surface Gravity (gee)
Zeus	Asteroid	4850	828.0	—	12	—
Zapotec	Mars	1650	164.3	4500	3000	34%
Zen	Oberon	1440	134.0	10	400	4%
Zion	Iapetus	1210	103.2	22	550	5%
Zouave	Titan	730	48.3	3100	2900	25%
Zuni	Earth	530	29.9	1500	1900	28%
Zulu	Ganymede	330	14.7	2100	2600	21%
Zoroaster	Asteroid	250	9.7	—	30	—
Zwingli	Asteroid	250	9.7	—	32	—

Figure 9 gives a comparison of the orbits of the four large moons in the Gargantuan system with the orbits of the four large moons in the Jovian system. The Gargantuan system is seen to be similar to the Jovian system, although a little more compact.

Jupiter		Io	Europa	Ganymede	Callisto
71		420	670	1070	1880 Mm

( )————————————o————————o—————————o———————————————o————

( )————————o————————o———————————o——————————————o————

98	330	530	730		1650 Mm
Gargantua	Zulu	Zuni	Zouave		Zapotec

Figure 9—Comparison of Gargantuan and
Jovian Moon Systems

Zulu

Zulu is the innermost of the large moons of Gargantua and was the objective of the Phase III planetary surface expedition using the third of the four landers available to the Barnard Star Expedition. Zulu is similar in many respects to the Jovian moon Ganymede, in that it consists of a rocky core completely covered with an ocean that is capped with a thick layer of striated ice. The pertinent data on Zulu is listed in the following table:

Mass = 2.1×10^{23} kg (136% Ganymede)
Radius = 2600 km (ave.) (100% Ganymede)
Density = 2.9 water (136% Ganymede)
Surface Gravity = 2.1 m/s^2 (21% Earth gravity)
Atmospheric Pressure = 820 mbar (81% Earth

pressure)
Orbital Radius = 330 Mm
Orbital Inclinations = 0° (w.r.t. Gargantua equator)
                      = 8° (w.r.t. Barnard ecliptic)
Orbital Period Around Gargantua ("sidereal day") =
  14.7 h
Gargantuan Orbital Period ("year") = 2890 h
                                   = 120.4 d
Illumination Period ("solar day") = 14.8 h
Axial Tilt   = 0° (w.r.t. Gargantuan orbital plane)
                 = 8° (w.r.t. Barnard ecliptic)

Zulu Tides:

Since the moon Zulu is so close to its large planetary primary Gargantua, the gravity tide from Gargantua is large and dominates the dynamics and shape of the moon. The major effect of the gravity tide is that Zulu, like all the Gargantuan and Jovian moons, is tidally locked to its primary, so that its "inner" pole is always facing Gargantua. Because of this tidal locking, the tidal forces from Gargantua, instead of having twice daily variations, stay fixed in position in the body of the moon and produce a permanent distortion of Zulu into a triaxial elliptical shape with six "poles."

First, Zulu has the usual "north" and "south" poles on its spin axis. Then there is an "inner" pole that always faces Gargantua, and opposite that, an "outer" pole that always faces away from Gargantua. In addition, there is a "leading" pole that faces in the direction of the motion of Zulu in its orbit and is where material from space falls in on Zulu due to the moon's orbital motion through space. Opposite to that is the "trailing" pole.

The triaxial ellipsoidal shape, due to the combination

of the gravity tide from Gargantua and the centrifugal tide from the rotation of Zulu about the planet, gives Zulu three significantly different diameters, depending upon the pole-to-pole axis chosen. The north-south diameter is 5108 km, the inner-outer diameter is 5478 km (370 km difference), and the leading-trailing diameter is 5200 km, making Zulu distinctly oval in shape.

In addition to the huge tidal bulge of many hundreds of kilometers produced in both the crust and ocean of Zulu by Gargantua, there is a tide produced twice a "day" (every 7.4 hours) by the star Barnard. The Barnard tide on Zulu is four times stronger than the solar tide on Earth, and causes a peak-to-peak variation in ocean level of 3.5 meters. In addition, there is a conjunction with nearby Zuni and a large "pulse" tide of about 8 meters lasting 3.4 hours out of every 29 hours (just short of once every two "days"), and a conjunction with more distant Zouave and a modest pulse tide of about 2 meters lasting 4.4 hours out of every 21 hours (about once every 1.4 "days"). Since tidal acceleration forces go as the inverse cube of the separation distance, the "pulse" tides from the two moons are short and strong during conjunction, but negligible otherwise. This is different than the tide from Barnard, which rises and falls rhythmically, like the tides on Earth.

High tide, when Zuni, Zouave, and Zulu are in triple conjunction, occurs every 549 hours, which is about 23 Earth days or 37 Zulu days. The magnitude of these high tides varies, since the alignment of the three innermost moons of Gargantua is more precise during some triple conjunctions than others. The high tides reach a maximum when Barnard is in alignment with the triple conjunction. This occurs every 1646.8 hours and produces a maximum tide of some 14 meters or 46 feet, which is equaled on Earth only at the Bay of Fundy, where the funnellike features of the bay accentuate the tidal height.

Geysers:

Zulu is slightly more massive than Ganymede, indicating that it has a thicker rock core and a proportionately thinner ocean. Unlike quiescent Ganymede, however, Zulu is as active as Io, but instead of sulphur volcanos it has water geysers. There are hot spots on Zulu where periodic streams of hot water shoot tens to hundreds of kilometers up through the atmosphere and into space. As would be expected, most of the geysers are associated with the two tidal bulges on the "inner" and "outer" poles, in a ring around the bulges where the strains on the crust are at maximum.

Zulu is continuously losing air and water into space at a high rate because of its water geysers and its low gravity. The air and water molecules that have enough kinetic energy to escape from Zulu's gravity into space, do not, however, have enough kinetic energy to escape from the much stronger gravity field of the giant planet Gargantua. Most of the air and water molecules stay in a torus centered at Zulu's orbit, although some drift inward toward the giant planet, and some drift outward to be swept up by the moon Zuni. As Zulu moves through the torus of air and water in its tidally locked orientation, its gravity field pulls in air and water molecules from the torus, where they fall on the "leading" pole of the moon, creating a continuously replenished moist high pressure area, the source of most storms on Zulu.

Illumination:

The major source of illumination on Zulu is from the star Barnard. Barnard, however, not only has a weak luminosity of 0.05% that of the Sun, but it has an angular diameter of only 0.25° in the skies of Zulu, which is half the diameter of the Sun in the skies of Earth. Gargantua is so large and so close to Zulu that it covers 35° in the sky over Zulu. As a result, a substantial amount of illumination comes from the planet in addition to the light from Barnard. On Zulu, at "full moon," when Barnard is over the outer pole, the light from Gargantua is nearly 4% of the light from Barnard. For comparison, the light flux from the Earth's Moon is only one-millionth that of the Sun, because the Moon has a low albedo and covers only a half-degree in the sky, while Gargantua has a high albedo and covers 35° in the sky.

The illumination from Gargantua is most noticeable at a site on the inner pole of Zulu, where there is always light, either from Barnard or from Gargantua. A site on the outer pole of Zulu, however, never seeing Gargantua anyway, is only illuminated by the light from Barnard, and so therefore has a normal day-night cycle (although 14.8 hours long instead of 24 hours long).

Eclipses:

Zulu experiences an eclipse of Barnard by Gargantua once every rotation. The total eclipse time is 1.4 hours, which is 10% of the Zulu "day" of 14.8 hours, or 20% of the daylight hours. The eclipses are most noticeable at an observation site on the "inner" pole of the moon that always faces Gargantua. Here, the eclipse occurs at high noon. If the observation site is on the "leading" pole of the moon—the pole that always faces the direction of the motion along the orbit—then Gargantua hangs perpetually on the sunrise side of the horizon, cut in half by the horizon. Barnard rises from behind Gargantua, causing a late sunrise. For a site on the "trailing" pole, there is an early sunset as Barnard sets behind Gargantua hanging perpetually halfway down the sunset horizon. For sites on the "outer" pole of Zulu, always facing away from Gargantua, the eclipse occurs at local midnight, way off on the other side of Zulu, so nothing really noticeable happens. For observation sites near the north or south poles, Gargantua hangs halfway down the horizon toward the inner pole. Depending upon whether it is summer or winter, Barnard will either be constantly above the horizon, eclipsed once a day by Gargantua, or Barnard will be constantly below the horizon and the only illumination will come from the half-circle of Gargantua hanging on the horizon, going through moonlike phases once a Zulu "day" of 14.8 hours.

SECTION 3
ALIEN BIOLOGY

Prepared by:
Cinnamon Byrd—Ichthyology
Katrina Kauffmann—Biology
Deirdre O'Connor—Zoology
Nels Larson—Botany and Genetics

To date, the Barnard Star Expedition has uncovered four major intelligent life-forms in the Barnard star system. One on the Roche lobe of the double-planet Rocheworld, one on the Eau lobe of Rocheworld, and two (technically one) on Zulu. This Phase III report will concentrate on the alien biology of Zulu. Since the aliens found on the Eau lobe of Rocheworld, commonly known as the "flouwen," assisted the human crew in the exploration of Zulu, a brief background summary of flouwen biology is included. Those interested in the aliens found on the Roche lobe of Rocheworld, commonly known as the "gummies," should read the biology section of the Phase II report.

Parenthetically, it is interesting to note that *none* of the four intelligent life-forms found to date in the Barnard system would have been discovered using radio searches for extraterrestrial intelligence. Either the life-form had not yet evolved sufficient intelligence to develop radio, or the life-form was highly intelligent, but lived in an environment that precluded the development of electromagnetic technology. In order to meet and communicate with these intelligent, and sometimes valuable, new friends of the human race, it was necessary for humans to physically cross the interstellar void in spacecraft, rather than just staying at home on Earth, waiting for a message to be sent.

Flouwen Biology

The flouwen are formless, eyeless, flowing blobs of jelly weighing many tons, that were found by the humans swimming in the ocean on the Eau lobe of Rocheworld. Like whales or dolphins, the flouwen group into social "pods," and normally use sound to "see." Although the flouwen have no eyes, they are sensitive to light, and can use light to "look" at things with their bodies, although poorly. The primary way in which they visualize objects is by their sonar, which gives them a three-dimensional image of not only the surface, but the interior of an object. This sense can be used well only underwater. Their sonar can be used in air, but the signal is highly attenuated in the transition between their bodies and the air, and again on the return from air to their bodies. Also, the speed of sound in air is one-fifth that of the speed of sound in water, so objects in air seem to be further away than they really are, since the signal takes five times as long to make the round trip.

The flouwen IQ is many times that of humans, but their only developed sciences are mathematics and biology. All the cells in a flouwen are identical, and large, about the size of a small ant. Like an ant colony, a small portion of a flouwen can function like a full-sized flouwen, except for decreased physical and mental capabilities. Thus, a human-sized portion of flouwen, weighing only a tenth of a ton (100 kilograms or 220 pounds), can bud off from the multi-ton main flouwen body, get into a specially-built "drysuit," and ride in human space vehicles in order to take part in joint expeditions with the humans. This segment of flouwen still has an IQ several times that of a human. More about the biology of the flouwen can be found in the Phase I and Phase II reports published previously.

Zulu Biology

There are two dominant life-forms on Zulu. For a long time it was thought that the two life-forms were two different species. It later turned out that the two distinctly different looking life-forms were just different "stages" or "sexes" of the same species. The common names given to the two forms are the icerugs and the coelasharks (see-la-sharks).

Icerugs:

The icerugs are large blue-green ruglike creatures that

live on and in the thick ice covering the Gargantuan
moon, Zulu. Like the flouwen, most of their multi-ton
body consists of undifferentiated cells. In the icerugs,
these cells are spread out in a thin layer on the surface of
the ice and on the walls of tunnels the icerugs have exca-
vated in the ice lying under their bodies. Although most
of the mass of an icerug body is invested in its plantlike
"leaf canopy" and "root" system made of undifferentiated
cells, there is a small specialized "node" portion made of
differentiated cells that are the head, feet, arms, and eye
of the icerug. The spherical "head" portion of the node,
about the size of a large beach ball, is held up off the
ground by a thick pedestal "foot" about a half-meter high.
The pedestal seems to be made out of the same blue-
green undifferentiated cells that make up the canopy and
root system.

At the bottom of the spherical head, just where it
meets the pedestal, there are four stubby tentacles, also
made out of blue-green undifferentiated cells. These can
be extended in length at will, and are used for pointing,
writing, and manipulating objects. Extending from the
top of the head is a large single eyeball on a flexible stalk.
With the pedestal and the eye-stalk at full vertical extension, an icerug node is slightly taller than a human.

The single eye of the icerug is very large and owllike,
almost ten centimeters (four inches) across. The large
size is probably needed for optimum light collection in
the weak light from Barnard as well as for seeing down in
the dark tunnels. The lens and iris are completely round
and the eye does not seem to have a preferred orientation
with respect to gravity, since the eye rotates as it scans
around on its stalk to look in different directions.

In order to see at night and in the underground
tunnels, the spherical head portion emits blue biolumi-

nescent light to illuminate the surroundings. The light emission from the head is controlled so that light is emitted only from a the portion of the sphere facing in the direction that the eye is looking. The illuminated portion of the head becomes concave prior to emitting light, so as to shield the eye above from the light-emitting portion.

Since the icerug normally breathes through its extended body, the spherical head of the icerug has no nose. It does have a small mouth with sharp teeth for grinding up occasional bites of meat and seaweed to supplement the minerals it gets from its roots, and the energy it gets from photosynthesis.

The total area of the portion of an icerug body spread out on the surface of the ice is typically 4000 square meters (about one acre or 40% of a hectare). It is calculated that approximately twelve kilowatts of sunlight falls on a typical icerug body during a clear day, more than enough to sustain the central "node" of the body.

Since the icerug head does not breathe, the icerugs don't have lungs and vocal cords. They can, however, talk with other nodes, humans, and flouwen by means of sound waves generated by vibrating portions of their surfaces. Because of the large surface area of the spherical head, the typical "voice" of an icerug is a deep rumbling bass.

The node moves by the "gliding" motion of the pedestal across the thin canopy of its body that is covering the ice. The motion of the node does not occur by a "walking" or "crawling" movement of the pedestal, but is more like that of a cork being carried along by a white-capped wave or a beach ball being passed along in a crowded stadium. The portion of the canopy ahead of the desired direction of motion gathers together, rises up, and assumes support of the node, while the material previously in the pedestal flows back down into the canopy. The surface skin, instead of being a membrane, as in human bodies, is more like a liquid, as in flouwen bodies.

Using this mode of travel, the node can move rapidly (faster than a human can run) above its canopy spread out on the surface of the ice and also inside those tunnels that are lined with its own "root" skin. The node can also venture into areas and tunnels where the icerug body cells are not already present, but this involves the physical transfer of body cells into the clear area and, as a result, the progress of the node is much slower.

Coelasharks

The second major alien type on Zulu is the coelashark (see-la-shark). These creatures live underwater near the volcanic vents that surround each major geyser. A coelashark is a large semi-intelligent fish with sharklike teeth and temperament, four stubby legs ending in fins like a coelacanth, and four stubby tentacles coming out from under its chest area. They are highly territorial animals that attempt to gain and maintain control of the major volcanic vents as their food source.

Coelasharks eat anything, including each other. Primarily, however, they concentrate on eating the abundant plant and animal life that live around the volcanic vents. These plants and animals can not only survive, but thrive, in water that comes out of the vents hotter than boiling because the water is under pressure. The water is too hot for the coelasharks, so the plants and animals grow undisturbed until the vent weakens or the animal attempts to leave, at which time the coelashark controlling the vent moves in. The coelasharks are not very intelligent, although they show more intelligence than Earth sharks, since they can carry on simple conversations with each other and the flouwen.

Zula

After further research by the humans and the flouwen, aided by the icerugs, it was determined that the icerugs and coelasharks are different forms of the same species. This fact was unknown even to the intelligent icerugs, who had regarded the coelasharks merely as a food animal, not as a sex partner.

The icerugs and coelasharks are different forms of the same species. The common name given by the humans to this joint species is "Zula" (singular "Zulum"). The Zula reproduce primarily by sexual union of two different sexes, but they have an alternate form of reproduction that takes over when sexual union is not possible. The coelasharks are one of the sexes, but their sex is neither male nor female in the mammal sense of the words. Like salmon swimming up a stream to spawn and die, the coelasharks swim up the geyser to spawn and die. The coelasharks carry single-celled wormlike gametes in cystlike sacs embedded in their cheeks. Each worm contains one-half the genes of the zygote cells of the coelashark parent. The icerugs search out the ejected coelasharks to obtain and eat the cysts. The wormlike gametes are released into the icerug stomach and are fertilized there, by a method still unknown, to form functional zygotes of coelasharks. The embryo coelasharks are then ejected through the icerug gut back into the ocean to compete with each other and complete the sexual part of the cycle. Bouts of watery "diarrhea" in the icerug assist in the rapid and safe passage of the miniature coelasharks through the icerug gut.

If, however, a coelashark falls on bare ice, and is not eaten by an icerug, then the monoploid gametes in the mouth cysts live off the body of their dead coelashark parent and replicate rapidly without growing or differentiating, each forming a slime-moldlike colony of like cells. The colonies compete with each other until just one colony survives. The surviving colony grows into a large rug of undifferentiated monoploid cells, starts photosynthesis, differentiates and develops a node and an eye, and becomes a new icerug child.

How the Zula species, with its two distinctly different sexual forms growing in extremely different environments, managed to evolve to its present state from a simpler form is still a major unanswered question. Earth biologists, after much study, finally determined the evolutionary path of the much more complicated four-stage (winged, egg, larva, and pupa) cycle of the butterfly species, so it is expected that follow-on expeditions will, in time, be able to determine the evolutionary path for the Zula species also.

CASTING

The initial crew of the Barnard Star Expedition consisted of twenty people when it left the solar system. One of the crew, Dr. William Wang, during the long process of curing the rest of the crew from an infectious type of cancer, died from the same cancer while en route to Barnard. Although the crew spent forty calendar years traveling from the solar system to Barnard, their aging rate during the long journey was slowed by a factor of four through the use of the drug No-Die. As a result, upon arrival at Barnard, the effective biological age of the crew had only increased ten years over their age at the start of the mission. The crew then spent two years decelerating and three years surveying the Barnard planetary system and the double-planet Rocheworld. The ages given below are their effective biological ages when they landed on Zulu.

LANDING PARTY

The landing party for the surface exploration of Zulu consisted of ten crew members:

Colonel George G. Gudunov—Second-in-Command of Barnard Star Expedition, commander of the landing party. Height: 185 cm (6'1"). Weight: 100 kg (220 lbs). Biological Age: 66 years. George is the oldest person on the mission. He obtained an Air Force ROTC commission from the University of Maryland and was first in his class in flight school. His first assignment was with the Space Command Laser Forts project. When a twenty-three-year-old Captain, he suggested testing the laser fort system by using it to send interstellar probes to the nearest star systems. When a number of space laser forts suffered catastrophic failure under this two day test, he was commended by Congress for exposing the problems, but the military brass never forgave him. They shunted him off to be a permanent Flight Instructor, and he was promoted as slowly as they could legally do it without raising the ire of Congress. When the positive reports from the Barnard probe came in twenty-four years later, he had just made Lieutenant Colonel. Despite his age, he was promoted to Colonel and allowed to go on the Expedition.

Deirdre O'Connor—Biologist and Levibotany specialist. Height: 168 cm (5'6"). Weight: 60 kg (132 lb). Biological Age: 44 years. Glacier green eyes, and abundant red-brown curls carelessly stuffed into a bun contained by her Christmas imp. She emigrated to the Greater United States after her ecstatically-happy marriage ended with the accidental death of her husband. Quiet and self-sufficient, she is inwardly passionate about the mission and its discoveries. Her animal companion, "Foxx," is a woosel, a formerly unknown marsupial which Deirdre discovered in the Amazon Basin. When the last known female was killed with six rice-grain-sized young still hanging from teats in its pouch, Deirdre managed to deep-freeze them, get them to safety, and construct an artificial teat to nourish the embryos. All six survived, and one of the brood's grandchildren joined her for this interstellar flight. It was kept as a frozen embryo for the forty years of "No-Die" Deirdre endured, and revived to share the experiences of its friend.

Shirley Everett—Chief engineer and pilot. Height: 190 cm (6'3"). Weight: 85 kg (185 lbs). Biological Age: 48 years. Shirley is the epitome of a tall, strong, tanned, blue-eyed, blond-haired "California Surfer Girl." At USC, she obtained a B.S. in electrical engineering with minors in nuclear engineering and mechanical engineering. She played on both women's and men's basketball teams in college, and was top scorer in women's collegiate basketball. She became the third woman to play on a men's professional basketball team, but gave up her basketball career to return to USC to get an Engineering Doctorate. After learning to fly, she went to work for the company that designed and built the aerospace planes used on the Expedition. With her eidetic memory, Shirley knows everything about the spacecraft they fly, except details of the computer software programs, where David Greystoke takes over. She can fix anything, not with the proverbial hairpin—she is too well trained and equipped for that—but could if she had to.

Cinnamon Byrd—Levichthyhusbandry specialist, medic, and pilot. Height: 172 cm (5'8"). Weight: 53 kg (117 lb). Biological Age: 43 years. Tall and skinny, Cinnamon wears her long straight black hair in two low braids to cover her large ears. Cinnamon was born in Alaska to an Eskimo woman and her outback doctor husband, altruistic scion of a prominent East Coast family. By 16, Cinnamon had became both a pilot and an emergency medical technician in order to help her father during emergencies. Distressed with the pollution fouling the beauty and ocean life of her home state, she studied oceanic fish-farming (ichthyhusbandry) courses at the University of Alaska. Through the International Space University, she did graduate work in levichthyhusbandry at Goddard Station, where she met Nels Larson and proved to be invaluable to him. She was brought along on the Expedition largely at Nels' request, although it helped that she aced the GNASA piloting tests, and qualified as a backup pilot for both the rocket landers and the aerospace planes.

Richard Redwing—Planetary geoscientist. Height: 195 cm (6'4"). Weight: 110 kg (225 lbs). Biological Age: 49 years. Richard is a very large, very strong outdoorsman of American Indian heritage. He was a college champion weight lifter and won a gold medal in the Olympics. He earned his B.S. in geophysics and started work for a mining company in the Alps. He also worked as a part-time mountain-climbing guide who distinguished himself in a mountain rescue which cost him his two little toes. He grew tired of the lack of mental challenge and returned to school to get his Ph.D. in planetary physics and geophysics. He did his post-doctoral field training on the Moon and Mars, participated in the Ceres and Vesta expeditions, and was part of Callisto field crew when he was accepted for the Barnard Star Expedition.

Sam Houston—Planetary geoscientist. Height: 200 cm (6'7"). Weight: 80 kg (176 lbs). Biological Age: 60 years. Sam is very tall and very thin, with pale face and skin, long bones with knobby joints, gray-blue eyes, and long graying hair. Oil, discovered on his father's barren Texas ranch, changed Sam's life. The tough, hard-working, but good-natured youngster became fascinated by the black stuff which bought him an undreamed-of education, and that led him naturally into geology. He does not have a doctorate, but instead has years of experience in the field. On Earth, he has worked on all the continents, both poles, and the continental shelves of five of the seven seas. After making a preliminary geological map of the backside of the Moon, he spent two years on Mars with the first Mars colony. His experience made him the lead geologist on the "Big-Four" asteroid mapping expedition. His experiences on Ceres, Vesta, Pallas, and Juno, followed by two moons of Jupiter—Ganymede and Callisto—made him an obvious choice for the Barnard Star Expedition.

Arielle Trudeau—Aerodynamicist and pilot. Height: 165 cm (5'5"). Weight: 50 kg (110 lbs). Biological Age: 50 years. Arielle is thin, delicate, beautiful, shy, and fair-skinned, with short, curly light-brown hair and deep-brown eyes. She was born and raised in Quebec, Canada before the secession of Quebec from Canada. She emigrated to the United States and became an American citizen after the absorption of the rest of the Canadian provinces into the Greater United States of America. Her father taught her how to fly at an early age and she has hundreds of hours experience in a glider. She obtained a Ph.D. in aerodynamics at CalTech and entered the space program as a non-pilot mission specialist. On her first flight into space, there was an explosion that killed both Super-Shuttle pilots. Single-handed, encumbered by a spacesuit, she brought the crippled Super-Shuttle safely down in the smoothest landing ever recorded on the shuttle program. Arielle was given special dispensation to take Super-Shuttle pilot training after public acclaim, and later became one of the best shuttle pilots. She was training for lunar pilot status when the Barnard Star Expedition let her travel to the stars.

David Greystoke—Electronics and computer engineer. Height: 158 cm (5'2"). Weight: 50 kg (110 lbs). Biological Age: 50 years. David is a short, thin, red-haired, quiet young man. He has perfect pitch and perfect color sense. An undergraduate at the prestigious liberal arts college at Grinnell, Iowa, he went on to Carnegie-Mellon University for a Ph.D. in robotics and computer programming, with a minor in music. He wrote most of the programs used on the computers operating the various vehicles. David's hobby is creating computer generated animated art-music forms and laser light shows.

Katrina Kauffmann—Nurse and biochemist. Height: 150 cm (4'11"). Weight: 45 kg (99 lbs). Biological Age: 55 years. Katrina is a small, compact scientist who keeps her glossy brown hair cut into a severely efficient cap, but the huge blue eyes, with their long sooty lashes, reveal a compassion almost sentimental. After earning her R. N. degree in Germany, she discovered that working with illness upset her. Acquaintance with a biochemist even shorter than herself sparked an interest in the worlds to be explored on a microscope slide, and she eagerly headed for the University of Frankfurt a.M. where she received a Ph.D. in Biochemistry. She came to the Greater United States on a post-doctoral fellowship and stayed until she was picked for the mission. The strangely beautiful poetry Katrina writes is sometimes found tucked into a bit of colorful needlework which she has carelessly left behind. When working, she remains totally absorbed for hours, and her analyses are precise, objective, and complete.

Captain Thomas St. Thomas—Astrodynamicist and pilot. Height: 188 cm (6'2"). Weight: 85 kg (187 lbs). Biological Age: 48 years. Slender and good-looking, Thomas is a credit to his large Jamaican family. After graduation from the U.S. Air Force Academy, he became a Rhodes scholar, and obtained his Ph.D. in astrodynamics at Oxford in England. On return, he went into Air Force pilot training and became a heavy-lift rocket pilot. He had over five years of experience raising and lowering the heavy, cumbersome rockets in Earth's gravity before joining the Barnard Star Expedition. His real passion, however, is photography, and his strikingly artistic photographs of the exotic locales visited by the crew are major contributions to the expedition reports.

Sailcraft Crew

The backup crew up in space, on the lightsail spacecraft *Prometheus*, consists of:

Major General Virginia "Jinjur" Jones—Commander of the Barnard Star Expedition. Height: 158.5 cm (5'2"). Weight: 61 kg (135 lbs). Biological Age: 57 years. Jinjur is short and solid with dark-black skin and a no-nonsense black pixie Afro haircut. She graduated high in her class at the U.S. Naval Academy and chose the Marines. During her first tour of duty with the Marine Recruit Training Command, she distinguished herself in the Greater San Diego tourist riots. She rose to become commander of a Space Marine fleet of lightweight solar sailcraft that kept the spacelanes swept of debris, inspected foreign spacecraft for compliance with the Space Treaty, and resupplied and protected the Laser

Forts. Jinjur's nickname (bestowed on her by her Space Marines) was taken from the name of the spicy female general that conquered the Emerald City in one of the lesser-known Oz books.

Carmen Cortez—Communications engineer. Height: 165 cm (5'5"). Weight: 80 kg (176 lbs). Biological Age: 43 years. Carmen is a chunky, very feminine Spanish señorita, with black, nearly-afro, curly hair. She always wears makeup and a tightly tailored uniform. She went to the University of Guadalajara, and became president of the College Radio Amateur Club. She was in charge of the generator-powered base station during a radio transmitter hunt, when the 9.1 magnitude earthquake struck Salamanca, Mexico, killing her father. For 48 hours she ran the only operational emergency communication services in West Central Mexico. She obtained her B.S. in Engineering from the University of Guadalajara, then a Doctorate of Electrical Engineering *magna cum laude* from the University of California, San Diego. She applied for the Barnard Star Expedition upon graduation and was placed on the back-up list. She was in training on Titan for the Alpha Centauri Expedition when she was activated for the mission at the last minute in order to replace a primary crew member who had to resign and return to Earth for health reasons.

Caroline Tanaka—Fiber-optics engineer and astronomer. Height: 165 cm (5'5"). Weight: 60 kg (132 lb). Biological Age: 48 years. Caroline has long dark-brown hair, brown eyes, and light-brown skin from a mixed Hawaiian heritage. Although moderately good-looking, she is an intense, hard-working engineer who pays no attention to her looks. Caroline did all the design, fabrication (with the help of the Christmas Bush), installation, and check-out of a laser communicator that was left behind for use by the flouwen on Rocheworld after the humans had departed. The flouwen use the laser to communicate with the Expedition crew on the lightcraft *Prometheus*, as well as human scientists back in the solar system.

Captain Anthony "Tony" Roma—Lightsail and aerospaceplane pilot. Height: 168 cm (5'6"). Weight: 70 kg (155 lb). Biological Age: 45 years. Tony is small and very handsome, with a dark complexion, dark eyes, dark wavy hair, and a neat mustache. He was a cadet in the first class at the Space Force Academy and went directly from aircraft pilot school into lightsail pilot training. When picked for the mission, he was on assignment as a pilot in General Virginia Jones's Space Marines Interceptor Fleet, where he invented a number of new lightsail maneuvers.

John Kennedy—Engineer and nurse. Height: 183 cm (6'0"). Weight: 80 kg (176 lb). Biological Age: 47 years. John bears a striking resemblance to his distant relative. He tried the premed curriculum at USC, but gave it up in his sophomore year and went on to get a Ph.D in electromechanical engineering. He didn't feel satisfied working solely on machines and went back to get his R.N. His strange mix of talents just fit a slot on the Expedition. John's lungs were seriously injured when his suit failed in the ammonia-filled waters of Rocheworld. He is still in the process of recovering.

Nels Larson — Leviponics specialist. Height: 178 cm (5'10"). Weight: 75 kg (165 lb). Biological Age: 48 years. Nels has very muscular arms, a barrel torso, and a large handsome head with a strong jaw, light-blue eyes, and long yellow-white hair that he combs straight back. When Nels was born with flipper-like feet in place of legs, his parents quit their jobs on Earth and moved to Goddard

Station where Nels grew up. He took college courses by video and apprenticed in levibotany and levihusbandry at the Leviponics Research Facility on Goddard. He initiated the famous Larson chicken breast tissue culture ("Chicken Little" to most astronauts) and many new strains of algae with various exotic flavors. Nels's primary duties were on *Prometheus*, where, with its near free-fall environment, legs are more of a handicap than a help. Recently, Nels was instructed by the flouwen on a method for regeneration of limbs in advanced species. Using himself as a guinea pig, Nels built a limb regeneration tank and grew himself a new pair of legs.

Elizabeth "Red" Vengeance—Asteroidologist and pilot. Height: 178 cm (5'10"). Weight: 70 kg (154 lbs). Biological Age: 53 years. Red is tall and thin, with an aristocratic nose, a short, straight cap of red hair, green eyes, and the typical redhead complexion with freckles resulting from an Irish heritage. She has over 150 hours of credits in mining and mineralogy from the University of Arizona but no degree. Elizabeth was one of the first independent prospectors in the asteroid belt. She struck it rich, became a billionaire, and then realized that there were more interesting things to do than loafing for the rest of her life. Her extensive space experience as an asteroid prospector and heavy-lift asteroid-tug operator got her onto the Barnard Star Expedition.

Linda Regan—Solar astrophysicist. Height: 155 cm (5'1"). Weight: 55 kg (121 lb). Biological Age: 46 years. Linda is a short, stocky, bouncy "cheerleader" type, with sparkling green eyes, curly brown hair, and lots of energy. She took physics at USC, went on to get a Ph.D. in astronomy at CalTech, and earned her way to a position at the Solar Observatory around Mercury, then onto the Barnard Star Expedition.

Reiki LeRoux—Computer programmer and anthropologist. Height 163 cm (5'4"). Weight: 53 kg (117 lb). Biological Age: 44 years. Reiki is the daughter of a Japanese woman of good family, who met and fell in love with a US Navy aircraft carrier pilot stationed in Japan. His family were oil-rich Louisiana Cajuns. The couple married, but he was killed in a training crash before Reiki was born. Reiki spent her childhood in Japan among a large family, who loved her, but found her alien appearance constantly unsettling. Her skin is almost apricot, her black hair is curly, and her dark eyes are round. With money no problem, she was sent early to a boarding school in Scotland, where she pursued a wide variety of studies and excelled in them all. She specialized in computer programming and anthropology at Glasgow University, graduating with honors. Her natural talents in cooperation have been augmented by years of experience with an amazing variety of people. She has developed a passion for etiquette, which the others find entertaining. She is a quiet person, very good at her work, which is designing user-friendly computer interfaces, and keeps a detailed diary in the slim electronic journal which goes with her everywhere.

ABOUT THE AUTHORS

Dr. Robert L. Forward writes science fiction novels and short stories, as well as science fact books and magazine articles. Through his scientific consulting company, Forward Unlimited, he also engages in contracted research on advanced space propulsion and exotic physical phenomena. Dr. Forward obtained his Ph.D. in Gravitational Physics from the University of Maryland. For his thesis he constructed and operated the world's first bar antenna for the detection of gravitational radiation. The antenna is now at the Smithsonian museum.

For 31 years, from 1956 until 1987, when he left in order to spend more time writing, Dr. Forward worked at the Hughes Aircraft Company Corporate Research Laboratories in Malibu, California, in positions of increasing responsibility, culminating with the position of Senior Scientist on the staff to the Director of the Laboratories. During that time he constructed and operated the world's first laser gravitational radiation detector, invented the rotating gravitational mass sensor, published over 65 technical publications, and was awarded 18 patents.

From 1983 to the present, Dr. Forward has had a series of contracts from the U.S. Air Force and NASA to explore the forefront of physics and engineering in order to find breakthrough concepts in space power and propulsion. He has published journal papers and contract reports on antiproton annihilation propulsion, laser beam and microwave beam interstellar propulsion, negative matter propulsion, space tethers, space warps, and a method for extracting electrical energy from vacuum fluctuations, and was awarded a patent for a Statite: a sunlight-levitated direct-broadcast solar-sail spacecraft that does not orbit the earth, but "hovers" over the North Pole.

In addition to his professional publications, Dr. Forward has written over 80 popular science articles for publications such as the Encyclopaedia Britannica Yearbook, *Omni*, *New Scientist*, *Aerospace America*, *Science Digest*, *Science 80*, *Analog*, and *Galaxy*. His most recent science fact books are *Future Magic* and *Mirror Matter: Pioneering Antimatter Physics* (with Joel Davis). *Future Magic* will shortly be replaced by the Baen Book, *Indistinguishable From Magic*, which contains updated science fact chapters from *Future Magic*, along with short fiction by Dr. Forward. His science fiction novels are *Dragon's Egg* and its sequel *Starquake*, *Martian Rainbow*, *Timemaster*, *Camelot 30K*, and *Rocheworld*. He is presently in the process of writing four sequels to *Rocheworld* with members of his family. The first sequel, *Return to Rocheworld*, was written with his daughter, Julie Forward Fuller, while *Marooned On Eden*, and this sequel, *Ocean Under the Ice*, were written with his wife, Martha Dodson Forward. He is presently working on the last sequel,

Rescued From Paradise, with his daughter Julie Forward Fuller. The novels are of the "hard" science fiction category, where the science is as accurate as possible.

Dr. Forward is a Fellow of the British Interplanetary Society and former editor of the Interstellar Studies issues of its journal, Associate Fellow of the American Institute of Aeronautics and Astronautics, and a member of the American Physical Society, Sigma Xi, Sigma Pi Sigma, National Space Society, the Science Fiction Writers of America, and the Author's Guild.

Martha Dodson Forward obtained a Bachelor of Arts degree in English from the University of South Carolina in 1956 and took graduate courses at UCLA. Her primary literary output consists of letters to a wide circle of family and friends, some of whom save them assiduously with the fond and foolish hope of becoming wealthy from their publication after her demise.

PRAISE FOR
LOIS MCMASTER BUJOLD

What the critics say:

The Warrior's Apprentice: "Now here's a fun romp through the spaceways—not so much a space opera as space ballet.... it has all the 'right stuff.' A lot of thought and thoughtfulness stand behind the all-too-human characters. Enjoy this one, and look forward to the next."   —Dean Lambe, *SF Reviews*

"The pace is breathless, the characterization thoughtful and emotionally powerful, and the author's narrative technique and command of language compelling. Highly recommended."   —*Booklist*

Brothers in Arms: "... she gives it a geniune depth of character, while reveling in the wild turnings of her tale. ... Bujold is as audacious as her favorite hero, and as brilliantly (if sneakily) successful."   —*Locus*

"Miles Vorkosigan is such a great character that I'll read anything Lois wants to write about him. ... a book to re-read on cold rainy days." —Robert Coulson, *Comics Buyer's Guide*

Borders of Infinity: "Bujold's series hero Miles Vorkosigan may be a lord by birth and an admiral by rank, but a bone disease that has left him hobbled and in frequent pain has sensitized him to the suffering of outcasts in his very hierarchical era.... Playing off Miles's reserve and cleverness, Bujold draws outrageous and outlandish foils to color her high-minded adventures."   —*Publishers Weekly*

Falling Free: "In *Falling Free* Lois McMaster Bujold has written her fourth straight superb novel. ... How to break down a talent like Bujold's into analyzable components? Best not to try. Best to say 'Read, or you will be missing something extraordinary.' " —Roland Green, *Chicago Sun-Times*

The Vor Game: "The chronicles of Miles Vorkosigan are far too witty to be literary junk food, but they rouse the kind of craving that makes popcorn magically vanish during a double feature."   —Faren Miller, *Locus*

MORE PRAISE FOR
LOIS MCMASTER BUJOLD

What the readers say:

"My copy of *Shards of Honor* is falling apart I've reread it so often.... I'll read whatever you write. You've certainly proved yourself a grand storyteller."
—Liesl Kolbe, Colorado Springs, CO

"I experience the stories of Miles Vorkosigan as almost viscerally uplifting.... But certainly, even the weightiest theme would have less impact than a cinder on snow were it not for a rousing good story, and good storytelling with it. This is the second thing I want to thank you for.... I suppose if you boiled down all I've said to its simplest expression, it would be that I immensely enjoy and admire your work. I submit that, as literature, your work raises the overall level of the science fiction genre, and spiritually, your work cannot avoid positively influencing all who read it."
—Glen Stonebraker, Gaithersburg, MD

" 'The Mountains of Mourning' [in *Borders of Infinity*] was one of the best-crafted, and simply best, works I'd ever read. When I finished it, I immediately turned back to the beginning and read it again, and I can't remember the last time I did that." —Betsy Bizot, Lisle, IL

"I can only hope that you will continue to write, so that I can continue to read (and of course buy) your books, for they make me laugh and cry and think ... rare indeed." —Steven Knott, Major, USAF

What do you say?

Send me these books!

Shards of Honor 72087-2 $4.99 _____
The Warrior's Apprentice 72066-X $4.50 _____
Ethan of Athos 65604-X $5.99 _____
Falling Free 65398-9 $4.99 _____
Brothers in Arms 69799-4 $5.99 _____
Borders of Infinity 69841-9 $4.99 _____
The Vor Game 72014-7 $4.99 _____
Barrayar 72083-X $4.99 _____
The Spirit Ring (hardcover) 72142-9 $17.00 _____
The Spirit Ring (paperback) 72188-7 $5.99 _____
Mirror Dance (hardcover) 72210-7 $21.00 _____

Lois McMaster Bujold:
Only from Baen Books

If these books are not available at your local bookstore, just check your choices above, fill out this coupon and send a check or money order for the cover price to Baen Books, Dept. BA, P.O. Box 1403, Riverdale, NY 10471.

NAME: _____

ADDRESS: _____

I have enclosed a check or money order in the amount of $ _____.

S.M. STIRLING
and
THE DOMINATION OF THE DRAKA

In 1782 the Loyalists fled the American Revolution to settle in a new land: South Africa, Drake's Land. They found a new home, and built a new nation: The Domination of the Draka, an empire of cruelty and beauty, a warrior people, possessed by a wolfish will to power. This is alternate history at its best.

"A tour de force."   —David Drake

"It's an exciting, evocative, thought-provoking—but of course horrifying—read."
       —Poul Anderson

MARCHING THROUGH GEORGIA
Six generations of his family had made war for the Domination of the Draka. Eric von Shrakenberg wanted to make peace—but to succeed he would have to be a better killer than any of them.

UNDER THE YOKE
In *Marching Through Georgia* we saw the Draka's "good" side, as they fought and beat that more obvious horror, the Nazis. Now, with a conquered Europe supine beneath them, we see them as they truly are; for conquest is only the *beginning* of their plans ... All races are created equal—as slaves of the Draka.

THE STONE DOGS
The cold war between the Alliance of North America and the Domination is heating up. The Alliance, using its superiority in computer technologies, is preparing a master stroke of electronic warfare. But the Draka, supreme in the ruthless manipulation of life's genetic code, have a secret weapon of their own. . . .

POUL ANDERSON

Poul Anderson is one of the most honored authors of our time. He has won seven Hugo Awards, three Nebula Awards, and the Gandalf Award for Achievement in Fantasy, among others. His most popular series include the Polesotechnic League/Terran Empire tales and the Time Patrol series. Here are fine books by Poul Anderson available through Baen Books:

THE GAME OF EMPIRE

A *new* novel in Anderson's Polesotechnic League/Terran Empire series! Diana Crowfeather, daughter of Dominic Flandry, proves well capable of following in his adventurous footsteps.

FIRE TIME

Once every thousand years the Deathstar orbits close enough to burn the surface of the planet Ishtar. This is known as the Fire Time, and it is then that the barbarians flee the scorched lands, bringing havoc to the civilized South.

AFTER DOOMSDAY

Earth has been destroyed, and the handful of surviving humans must discover which of three alien races is guilty before it's too late.

THE BROKEN SWORD

It is a time when Christos is new to the land, and the Elder Gods and the Elven Folk still hold sway. In 11th-century Scandinavia Christianity is beginning to replace the old religion, but the Old Gods still have power, and men are still oppressed by the folk of the Faerie. "Pure gold!"—Anthony Boucher.

THE DEVIL'S GAME

Seven people gather on a remote island, each competing for a share in a tax-free fortune. The "contest" is ostensibly sponsored by an eccentric billionaire—but the rich man is in league with an alien masquerading as a demon . . . or is it the other way around?

THE ENEMY STARS

Includes for the first time the sequel to "The Enemy Stars"; "The Ways of Love." Fast-paced adventure science fiction from a master.

SEVEN CONQUESTS

Seven brilliant tales examine the many ways human beings—most dangerous and violent of all species—react under the stress of conflict and high technology.

STRANGERS FROM EARTH

Classic Anderson: A stranded alien spends his life masquerading as a human, hoping to contact his own world. He succeeds, but the result is a bigger problem than before . . . What if our reality is a fiction? Nothing more than a book written by a very powerful Author? Two philosophers stumble on the truth and try to puzzle out the Ending . . .

ROBERT A. HEINLEIN

"Heinlein knows more about blending provocative scientific thinking with strong human stories than any dozen other contemporary science fiction writers." —*Chicago Sun-Times*

"Robert A. Heinlein wears imagination as though it were his private suit of clothes. What makes his work so rich is that he combines his lively, creative sense with an approach that is at once literate, informed, and exciting."

—*New York Times*

Eight of Robert A. Heinlein's best-loved titles are now available in superbly packaged new Baen editions. And don't miss Heinlein's nonfiction blueprint for changing the government, written at the height of his powers: *Take Back Your Government!* Collect them all by sending in the order form below: